BEHIND DARKNESS DUET BOOK TWO

INSIDE THE Wicked

CHLOE C. PEÑARANDA

LUMARIAS PRESS

Published by Lumarias Press
www.lumariaspress.com

First Edition published May 2024

Cover design © 2024 Lumarias Press
Interior Art © 2024 @lepra.art, @kaylerinarts, @nicolillies
Edited by Bryony Leah
www.bryonyleah.com

Identifiers
ISBN: 978-1-915534-18-7 (eBook)
ISBN: 978-1-915534-17-0 (paperback)
ISBN: 978-1-915534-16-3 (hardback)

www.ccpenaranda.com

This book contains the following subject matter:
Violence, death, murder, gun violence, mention of self harm (chapter 3), death
of a child, on-page sexual assault (chapter 25), deep grief, suicidal ideation,
themes of human trafficking, explicit sexual scenes, PTSD, captivity, mentions
of underage sexual assault and grooming.

Playlist

Criminal
Britney Spears
Hurts Like Hell
Tomme Profitt, Fleurie
You've Created A Monster
Bohnes
Play With Fire
Sam Tinnesz, Yacht Money
Vigilante Shit
Taylor Swift
all the good girls go to hell
Billie Eilish
Darkside
Neoni
Him & I
G-Eazy, Halsey
Heathens
Twenty One Pilots
You Don't Own Me
SAYGRACE, G-Easy

Dedication

For you.
This is your sign to enter your villain era, welcome to the
wicked.

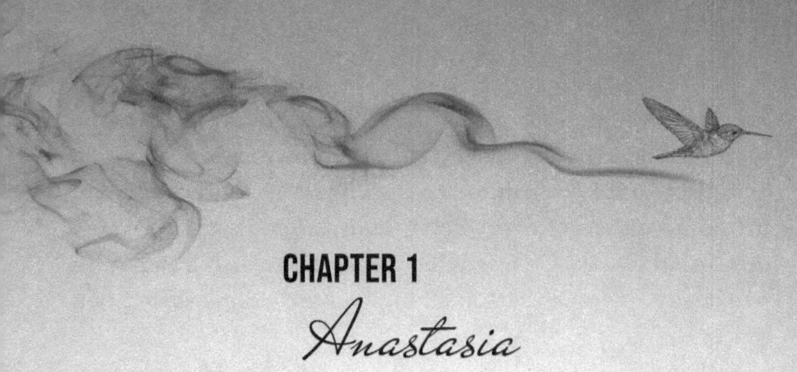

CHAPTER 1

Anastasia

Ninety-three days have passed without Rhett. I wear the scars of each one on my heart, wondering if the days will ever pass without cutting.

I sit across from Alistair Lanshall in his musty old office. The man who took everything from me. He looks at me from his tall seat by the fireplace as if I'm his weapon in the making, not knowing my sharpening edge will take his blood when it's time. I have the patience to get it right. If I were to cut off the head of the network by killing Alistair, it would only grow another.

He never took my red serpent earrings from me. More than three months with Alistair Lanshall and he never once questioned them. It's my secret triumph, the only color I wear now. And the King of the Vipers remains oblivious to the serpent in his den. At the end of the war, it doesn't matter that those around me have fangs primed with venom, only who has the cunning to strike first.

"You've been excelling, Anastasia," Alistair praises, lighting a cigar.

He sits in the wingback armchair opposite me as we both

lose ourselves to the fire blazing in the hearth of his elaborate office. It's nearly summer, but it's as if this mansion refuses to hold heat, and I often think it's the lingering death clinging to the dark corners of every room that causes its chill. I know this space all too well as Alistair has taken my training on personally—apparently something he hasn't done since Rhett Kaiser.

I thought over time the loss of him might be easier to face. Yet time is cruel, taunting. The present can be distracted, but the future will always be without Rhett, and every time I remember that fact my heart breaks with a new crack. Grief never silences; it's ever-present. A slow kind of death until we get to join the lost. My heart became cold to everyone and my mind is focused on my task: to learn everything I can about Alistair Lanshall and ruin him in the wreckage I plan to make of his empire.

My hand runs down Shadow's fur as I say, "I'll be graduating soon, then I'll have more time."

He allowed me to continue my PHD and live my own life for show. My station and access are invaluable to him now my father is President, residing in the White House.

I got my own apartment despite my father's protests. After everything that happened with the Forbes, his security detail around me became insufferable, but it didn't take long for Alistair to kill off the agents assigned to me and have his own resume their identities. Their deaths will forever linger on my conscience.

I tried to find out if Alistair could be tricking me. If Rhett could still be alive and somehow being kept from me. Every day where I turn up nothing darkens my despair. Every week dissolves more of my denial. Every month sinks me deeper and deeper into my depression.

He isn't coming back.

"Excellent. It's time to see you work for everything you've

been training toward. I need you to start earning back what I've spent on you."

He doesn't just mean money. Alistair values his time and effort, and in exchange I will perform for him. My only condition was that I wouldn't sell my body to these monsters, and to my relief, he wholeheartedly agreed. He's a possessive man even if he doesn't have eyes for me that way. He doesn't like people touching what's his.

I've learned how to use a gun properly, precisely. I still have a lot of training to go, but I can lift, aim, and shoot without a single tremble of fear now. He's taught me how to be a master manipulator and seductress—something he's told me many times I'm born for, what with how quickly I've adopted the patterns of the women in the clubs he's taken me to for the sole purpose of witnessing them at work.

Every day I'm not in university or with my parents for events, I'm here, with him. My best friend Riley is often concerned for me, but I told her I got a job working at some higher law firm that will go toward extra credits, and that I need the distraction.

Both my parents and Riley notice the change in me. They walk on glass around me as if they're waiting for me to get over my grief. I won't. And I'm playing a very dangerous game with Alistair Lanshall that I'm not certain I'll walk away from.

I'm doing it all for Rhett.

"Good. It's been getting rather dull around here," I say.

Alistair smiles sinfully, tipping his head back to observe me silently. He'll occasionally get affectionate and touch me, but to my relief, it's always the touch of someone admiring their prized work rather than the product of lust. I never would have stayed if that was his goal with me.

"Darkness has most certainly become you, and it has been

utterly breathtaking to watch the potential I saw in you come out to play."

Alistair thinks he made me, but that's only his delusional arrogance.

"I want to take you with me on a job tomorrow," he says. It's not a request.

"I have dinner with my parents."

"I'm sure you can reschedule."

I have done so many times that I'm beginning to feel guilty. They hardly see me now. But if my plans involved something public, Alistair would let me attend. He wants my reputation in the press to be stellar, and I often wonder if it's for his own twisted satisfaction. He'll spend far too long marveling over the papers with me, my image poised and proper. I've been painted as America's broken-hearted sweet-heart, and only he knows my darkness—the darkness he thinks he planted and harvested. He thinks I'm a puppet under his hand that the world is oblivious to.

"I have class in an hour." I sigh, pushing myself up. "I'll be here tomorrow."

"Time is precious. Graduation can't come soon enough with this nonsense draining so much of it."

I don't respond, leaving his dark and ominous study. Though I've never been attached to my postgrad English liter-ature degree, it has opened doors of future potential, but I can't deny I somewhat agree with Alistair now.

Alistair's manor is huge and impressive in its architecture. Tucked away in deep woodland on the edge of Washington, D.C., it's not his main residence, but he's taken a more perma-nent residency here while I finish my postgrad year.

My black boots clack across the marble and Shadow follows at my heel. Together, we're a stroke of darkness. I don't spare a glance at any of the men stationed around this manor I often spend more time in during the week than I do in my own apartment. They avoid my eye anyway, and I relish in the power of being Alistair's protégée, his most prized possession, as it keeps every one of them at my command.

Alistair has made me use that authority several times before. He'll stand by with wicked glee as I order them around like dogs. I ask them to fetch and they scramble at my request. I ask them to kneel and they hit the ground with heads bowed. It's twisted of me to find satisfaction in it, but these people are all sick criminals, and I would gladly set fire to this manor and watch them burn within it.

Some might think I'm throwing my life away for nothing. That I've blackened my soul over one lost love. It wasn't just losing Rhett that left me with nothing to lose—it was all that loss represented. *How* he was taken from me. The realization that this corruption will continue to spread like poison, and I have the chance now to push a blade between the eyes of the snake, once and for all.

I put on black sunglasses and step out into the sunny morning. The door to the black SUV is opened for me, and I slip into the back seat, letting the world drift by as my body-guard, Tony, drives me. To his credit, he tries to be friendly. I can't reciprocate. It doesn't matter who is placed by my side— they only ever remind me every single moment that they aren't Rhett.

He will never be here.

I've become numb to the routine of my university days, trying to engage with people as little as possible. Riley remains persistent, and there's a small part of my heart left for her, grateful she didn't give up on me when sometimes I can't help distancing myself from everyone.

As I push my salad around at the quaint cafe we've come to for lunch break, my mind wanders every now and then while Riley talks on.

"I'm not going to be around much longer," she says.

The quiet sorrow in her voice catches my attention, and I frown. Riley's look is pitiful, like I'm the sad puppy she has to leave behind for vacation.

Then I realize . . .

"You got the placement at Keithlington?" I ask with the most enthusiasm I've felt in a while.

She smiles like she doesn't want to gloat in my sad company, and that sinks me. I've been an awful friend. "I did," she says, straightening in excitement. Then her shoulders fall a fraction as she takes a sip of her tea. "Though I wasn't the only one."

"Nolan Flynn? I thought they were only taking one student."

"That's what the placement said. I guess they changed their minds, and now I have a whole year of internship stuck with that insufferable idiot."

My smile feels forgotten and foreign, but I endure the sensation for her. "I'm so proud of you, Ry. You're going to kill it, and they'll have no choice but to offer you a full-time job there once it's over."

Her eyes fall to her tea as uncertainty clouds her face. "Since there was only supposed to be one intern, they've said they'll only offer one full-time placement at the end. It's like I'll never be free of the torment and competition of Nolan fucking Flynn." She huffs, sinking back in her chair.

A laugh lingers on my lips, but like anything bright, it loses the fight to become whole.

"That's it!" she says with a sudden rise in volume. Her hands hit the table lightly, rattling our cups. "We're going out tonight."

My mouth opens to protest, but her rising hand stops me.

"I won't take no for an answer. I know where you live, and I'm picking you up at eight."

"I'll only bring the night down," I grumble.

"I'm making it my mission that you have fun. You're *allowed* to have fun, Ana."

I appreciate my friend for trying—I know I would do the same for her. So I smile, though it holds no real enthusiasm. Riley seems to know it with her pitying look.

"And I demand you add some color to your style. You only ever wear black now, and I'm surprised your red hair hasn't followed the trend."

I'm in mourning.

I don't tell her this. She won't understand, and I don't expect her to.

"I should get to class," I say, slinging my bag over my shoulder.

Riley isn't in this module of classical studies. I've fallen behind in class since everything happened, so this catch-up module is a result of that.

Tony lingers a table away, and he stands as I do.

"Eight o'clock!" Riley sings at my back.

In the theater hall I take a space near the back with no one around me. My peace doesn't last long before Adam Sullevan occupies the seat next to me. I wish he wouldn't. Despite making amends with him, and despite him being the only person who knows what I truly get up to with my time, I don't want any company.

"I wanted to check how you're doing," he says quietly, cautiously. Like he knows about the serpent I am.

"Fine."

"Ana—"

"Do you need something, Adam?"

"I need to know you're not being forced to do shit you don't want to," he hisses low.

The lights dim for the lecturer's presentation.

"I'm still there by my own will," I drawl. "You can quit your concern."

"It's been months. How long do you plan to keep this up?"

"As long as it takes."

"To do what?"

I turn my head toward him, and he winces at my cold eyes. "I made sure he spared your life once. I won't be able to do it again if you keep prodding. Leave me alone, Adam. Forget my existence if you must. You don't want to keep sniffing around business that could get you killed."

"And who looks out for you, huh?"

"I do."

"You don't have to do it alone."

He truly believes he can help. I pity his lack of self-preservation. Hypocritical, maybe.

"Yes, I do."

Adam gives up with a shake of his head as he turns back to the projector screen.

"I heard you're going out to the Night Palace tonight," he says.

It's the first time I've known where Riley plans to take me.

"Is there something happening there tonight?" I inquire.

"Some rich kid's birthday, I think. Not the most elaborate venue, but a lot of students will be there."

I can hardly suppress my groan. Then again, it could work to my advantage that Riley will have others to keep her company while I inevitably pretend to drink too much and have to leave. I can't get even close to drunk tonight. I don't want to know what punishment Alistair will have in store for me if I show up hungover tomorrow.

"I want to help you," Adam says softly. I hate the gentleness.

"You can't," I snap. "I don't need saving. Stop looking at me like some sort of damsel in distress."

"You're letting him change you."

"You're wrong. This has always been me. It's just a shock because no one wants to believe it."

"Kaiser wouldn't want to see you this way."

I'm close to erupting, and this is not the place to break. My voice turns venomous. "None of you knew him. You don't get to throw his *wants* at me. He's not fucking here."

Alistair was right—classes are a waste of my damn time, and so I gather my things and leave the hall. To my irritation, Adam follows me.

"Listen, I'm trying. We're all fucking trying, yet you won't let anyone in."

"Then take the fucking hint."

Adam's hand lands on my shoulder, intending to push me against the wall, but I move on instinct. Months of intense, often brutal, training have me grabbing his wrist and twisting his arm back, which he hisses at. Then I force his front against the wall instead.

"Shit," he says through a breath. "What the hell has he been training you to do?"

"Do I need to put you on your ass to make it more obvious?"

No one knows that some days I spend eight hours straight in Alistair's underground training room at the secluded mansion fighting men twice my size until I can outwit them in combat, though they always outmatch me in strength. Sometimes I've been so exerted beyond my limits that Alistair has carried me to a room and I've stayed the night at his manor, only to wake at dawn and do it all again.

"Nope. Point taken."

I release him with a shove, heading to the parking lot.

"Are you going to his place now?"

"No. I have a party to get ready for, remember?"

"Ahh, right. I'll see you there, A."

I don't answer as Tony opens the door for me to slip inside. Maybe I've become a coldhearted bitch to those around me, but if they'd seen inside the wicked and lost what I have, they'd be broken too. And it's either let the pieces cut inside or aim them at the enemy.

CHAPTER 2

Rhett

The small nail I dug out from a crevice in the wall weeks ago scores the stone. It's the only way I can keep track of how much time has passed, and it's the third one I've found. The previous two ended up in one guy's eye and another guy's jugular. I kept this one though. I need something to keep track of the days.

I finish the two curves, the familiar scrape of the metal across stone always delivering a new kernel of despair. Another day without my little bird. I trace my carving, then my hand drops as I tip my head back and stare up at the wall covered in them.

Ninety-three little birds scatter the concrete, and I sit here like the disturbance that sent them flying.

I'm not surprised it's been so long. I don't expect Xoid to find me when Alistair would have been meticulous in where he decided to keep me. He had a long fucking time to plan.

He's trying to break me, condition me. My skin has been carved, burned, and drowned. My mind has been tested for pain and endurance, but I know this is only the beginning of his plans for me.

Of everything that could hurt me, the real torture is watching Ana. I've not seen a hint of color on her in these long, agonizing months. Seeing her onscreen every day, whether in that wretched office or at training, makes me forget so much time has passed even though I can see her changing before my very eyes. I can see the slow spread of darkness in her heart, and I hope she keeps the strength not to let it go cold. The darkness can be wild and passionate, but ice will only ever be numb and unforgiving.

All that keeps my heart warm is the thought of getting back to her. The hope that she'll forgive me for leaving her all this time and that we'll be able to work through it.

Fuck, I love her so painfully it's all that's keeping me alive.

The black screen floods with color, and I shift, facing it. Ana is in Alistair's office. She's become so at ease there, and whether it's through masterful composure or genuine familiarity, I can hardly bear it.

I believe she's smarter than to fall for whatever Alistair offers. My only conclusion, seeing her so dedicated to him—training, practicing, conditioning—is because she's preparing. Ana wants revenge, and my little bird has somehow figured out how to grab my uncle's interest. It's no easy feat. Being the president's daughter wouldn't have had him personally taking her under his wing.

No—she's harboring a plan right under his.

It terrifies me. One wrong move, one slight slipup, and it won't matter who she is. Alistair is not merciful.

Before all this, I wanted to keep her away from me to prevent what I'm watching unfold. Now I see that we need each other for balance. It's never been clearer that Anastasia Kinsley was made for me and I for her.

I think he's making me watch to get me to concede. But I know him. Saying I'll be his weapon, as he's always wanted, won't reunite us. He'll make me prove my loyalty, and that would mean giving up Xoid. Not just disbanding but turning on them all. Perhaps even killing them.

I will never.

The familiar sound of steel scraping stone signals company. I don't move at all from the mattress on the floor, knee bent and head tipped back. The intrusion breaks my tormenting thoughts.

"You're advancing today," Micah sings. I've fantasized many ways of killing him. I'm not sure what I'll settle on, but ripping the head off his shoulders has been a recurring thought. "Lanshall thinks it's about time we push your *cooperation*."

I don't respond or even look at the sick bastard.

"What I wouldn't give to fuck her," Micah says, admiring the screen. "I think I will. After all my work here, it'll be my prize from Alistair. You'll be so broken you'll be helpless to watch it too. My cock is hard just thinking about it."

My fists clamp tight, and I'm seconds from lunging. There are brutes just outside the door, but I think I could get at least one good punch in to knock him out before they tackled me.

Killing him isn't enough. I'm going to make him suffer for ever even thinking of Ana.

She stands, and I'm relieved to see Shadow still by her side often. When she leaves the office the screen goes black again.

"Let's go, Everett," Micah orders. He uses my birth name to make me feel small, back in the body of the boy who escaped this place once before, but I never give him the satisfaction.

When I don't move, it only takes seconds for the familiar shuffling to advance toward me. The two guys haul me up, and I let them. My reactions only feed their desire to cause pain and suffering. So I give them nothing at all.

One pushes me to walk, and I grit my teeth, heading down the hallway that's become too familiar now. We don't turn toward the room Micah uses for electrocution and water torture, nor do we make the turn toward his chosen room to draw blood.

I don't remember the feeling before aching bones and weak muscle. Between the torture and the shit sleeping setup of a thin spring mattress on the floor, the pain is constant, all over my body. I push through it to exercise in my stone prison daily anyway. I would go mad with the solitude otherwise.

To keep me from breaking, all I picture is a future I'm not confident I'll ever see. It starts with Ana wearing my ring. She would make the most breathtaking bride. I feel her smile, all bright teeth and light in her eyes, as she meets me down the aisle. I think about how, out of all the wicked bastards in hell, it's a miracle I got there, holding the most perfect, resilient, courageous woman in the world.

Most of all, I think about how she chose me back, and how after all this, I hope that hasn't changed, no matter how selfish it makes me to want her.

Finally, after what feels like an endless trek with my heavy steps, we get to a door that grinds open. Inside I turn tight with anger at the sight of a teen, maybe seventeen years old, strapped to a chair. His mouth is gagged with a tight strip of fabric, but he's not blindfolded. When he sees us, his wide, bloodshot brown eyes fill with pure terror.

"This is Jack," Micah says, passing me.

The boy's breathing picks up, and a noise of fear escapes him when Micah claps a hand to his shoulder, smiling with cruel amusement at his distress.

I've seen this before—captives. Both as a teen myself, still chained to Alistair, and from my work in Xoid. The only difference is . . . Alistair's captives more often than not leave in a body bag.

"Please," the boy manages in a distorted muffle.

"I don't know what he's pleading for—do you?" Micah asks me.

He's the type of corrupted soul who finds sick pleasure in this work. Innocent people's fear is a drug to him.

Micah's eyes fall bored at my lack of response. "Poor Jack here is merely collateral damage. His father owes us a lot of money and has had several opportunities to pay. Hate to tell ya, kid, but it seems your old man cares more about himself than his family."

He reaches behind himself, pulling out a gun. After circling the kid he comes back to me, and to my surprise, I stare down at the gun he holds out to me as if it's a grenade.

"You're going to kill him."

My blood runs cold. Of all the things they could do to me, this is the fucking worst. I can't, *won't*, kill an innocent kid.

When I don't take the gun, Micah's patience snaps. The two guys grab my arms to prevent me from attempting to block the strike of the barrel across my jaw. Warmth runs down my cheek with the explosion of pain. I blink back my vision, as I've done many times, and straighten when they let me go.

"Don't make this difficult, Everett. Think of this like a promotion. Prove yourself in this role, and you can be reunited with . . . what is it you call her? Ahh, right, the little bird."

Fury rattles in my bones, but I suffer through it. There's no use exhausting myself to entertain his cheap attempts at getting me to lose my shit. I'll store everything to make my time with him as long and excruciating as possible when I finally get my chance.

"Take the gun," he says, more of a serious command now.

I do. It's a revolver, and the weight of it immediately tells me it's not fully loaded. That would have been fucking idiotic of them—I'd have been out of here in minutes. I hope it's empty. That this is just a test. But there could also be one bullet. Just one, to end Jack's life, and no others to take out those highly deserving of a bullet through their skulls.

It's a gamble. How am I to live with myself if I kill this boy before he becomes a man? He's someone's son, perhaps a brother. Maybe he has a girlfriend who loves him. Yet he's here for someone else's crime, and it's so fucking tragic and despicable I can hardly contain my outrage.

"I had a feeling you'd need more motivation," Micah drawls. "It makes this more fun for me."

There's a screen behind the kid, and it turns on.

Ana sits with her friend Riley in a cafe. I know this isn't what they want me to see, and my eyes scan the rest of the room rapidly. It's fairly quiet, round tables, mostly couples. Then I see him. A man pretending to read a newspaper, wearing a baseball cap pulled low on his forehead. He reaches to his side, and I know what he's there for. Seeing the slight flicker of a gun licks a cold trail down my spine.

"Will it be a bullet in his head or hers?" Micah taunts.

The kid cries, struggling against his bonds, and muffled pleas spill past his gag.

I have to take a moment to blink. Breathe. Fucking *think*. My chest pounds as I try to calculate what to do.

The chamber could be empty. It could have one or even two bullets and I wouldn't be able to tell the difference in weight. Still, I pass it from one hand to the other, trying to determine if it's empty.

"Ticktock, Lanshall," Micah says.

I want to aim it for his fucking eye. Would they risk giving me even one bullet for this? If I kill Micah, I think I can take out the men behind me, but my confidence starts to falter when I think of needing to free the kid from tight bonds. That won't be easy with bare hands. By then, the place would have heard the gunshot and come swarming.

SHIT.

If I aim this gun at Micah and it's empty, the kid and I will be in deep fucking shit, to his sadistic satisfaction.

It's a gamble. A choice of instinct.

I watch the man onscreen click off the safety of his gun, hidden by the newspaper from where he's tucked in a quiet corner, but in perfect view of the surveillance feed.

I lose it.

My breaths heave as I point the gun at Jack's head.

He's a good-looking kid. Short brown hair and deep brown eyes. I picture him as a smart type. Books, not sports. He has a bright future ahead of him and he should be heading for it, not staring down the barrel of a gun that could turn his prospects to sand in the wind.

"Five seconds," Micah warns.

Jack turns frantic, and I click off the safety.

If there's one bullet . . .

I could kill Micah at least.

I don't think Jack is getting out of this even if I do, but I won't be the one to take his life.

I could kill Micah.

My whole body is stone to keep me from shaking with the absolute fury of being in this sick, twisted position.

My finger presses a fraction on the trigger.

I could kill Micah.

It's that thought that makes my choice sure. The barrel points unwavering on Jack's forehead . . .

And I pull the trigger.

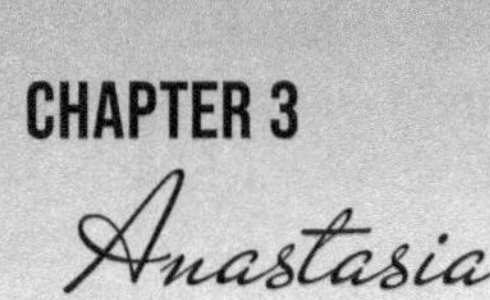

CHAPTER 3

Anastasia

I don't like being idle even for a moment. Silence is the key to unlock the vaults I seal my grief behind. I'm ready too early, and the fifteen minutes I have to wait for Riley make my skin itch. I don't like to spend longer than necessary in this penthouse where I can't stop conjuring images of Rhett. Cooking in the untouched white and black marble kitchen that occupies the side of the room. Watching movies on the cinema TV with the strip fire lit beneath it, entangled on the deep black sofa.

He's never set foot in here, and still, it feels vacant without him.

I'm lying on the floor, against the cold white marble. It's not a place you'd expect to find a person, and for a strange, still moment I pretend I don't exist. Should someone walk into my apartment now, I would merely be a ghost.

I think about Riley and how excited she is to be going to Keithlington next month—her dream internship. I think of Adam and how he still holds hope to rekindle things with Henry someday—the love that got away. I think of my parents

and how my father is thriving as the new president, ambitious and inspiring.

Then I think of how I'm lying here, my existence forgotten even if just for a pause of time, and how I hope no one will ever ask me what I want in the present or the future when I'm stuck in the past. I will always be there, in this endless tragedy, waiting for someone. Time passing without him is empty hope.

Maybe that's all I'll ever be. *Empty.*

At least through the agony I believe in one thing with aching certainty: there are soulmates in this world, and Rhett was mine. It's clear to me in the way I can't accept he's gone even three months later. What we had between us was more than what most people discover in a lifetime together.

I hiss at the sting of my hand and curse. My moment of pretend is over. I can't risk getting blood on my outfit for tonight. Though I suppose no one would know. I could bleed and bleed under this black dress and no one would see my pain camouflaged against the stark material. They wouldn't know I was dying right in front of them if they couldn't see it.

But that's how life is, I suppose. Silent. Suffering. And a complete fucking tragedy.

Heading to the sink, I run the broken skin of my thumb under the water. I bleed onto the porcelain, remembering all the times I did so out of choice. My thigh has three scars now. Each one I gave myself when I conquered something.

The first fight I won.

The first time I finally hit dead center on the shooting-range targets.

Then when I beat five players in a chess tournament. They weren't world champions, but I was proud of myself.

Alistair isn't all about brute strength and killing. His most prized assets are strategists, analysts, the most cunning minds that can cut out competition or problems before you ever knew they were coming.

He didn't demand those cuts of me, but I know he did from Rhett for his triumphs. I don't care what anyone thinks; I did it to know what it felt like for him.

My intercom buzzes and I startle, turning off the water.

I really don't want to go out tonight, but if I pretend not to be in, or perhaps asleep, Riley will flirt with the concierge until she gets a key pass up here, and I fear her wrath more than some of the brutes I've faced in a sparring ring.

Meeting Riley in the foyer, I try for her sake to match her smile at least. She's beaming, practically hopping, before I reach her and we link arms to head out.

"We're going to have the best night! Graduation is only weeks away, and you will mourn these missed opportunities."

I doubt that, but I don't say it.

"Do you even know whose birthday it is?"

She waves me off as we get into the Uber. "Doesn't matter. We're going to have fun and forget *all* of life's hardships for the night."

Riley means well, but I can't deny the thought irks me. Losing Rhett isn't a hardship. It's part of me now, and I wish people would accept that.

At the club the bass of the music can already be heard, and I want to call back the Uber that took off. I don't have to look to know Tony is somewhere nearby. Alistair's vipers are always circling. He'll likely be the only one to follow me in, but there will be others of Alistair's men keeping watch over his prize jewel from outside.

It's dark, with strobe lights making me flinch so often I already want to leave. I need a drink—maybe I'll risk two— just to take the edge off me so I can survive at least an hour.

Those intentions are great until I'm accepting a third

vodka lemonade, and I think I might have had one—two?—shots of tequila.

Fuck it.

I'll order a greasy breakfast in the morning to go with my Advil before I meet with Alistair. It'll be worth it for the numbness that starts to take over me.

In the past, I would be buzzing with excitement and trying to pull some hot guy by now with the liquid confidence of alcohol. Now, as I dance mindlessly with Riley, every pair of hands that touches me makes me want to vomit. It feels like betrayal to Rhett, and when I can't take it anymore I try to leave the dance floor.

I'm stopped by a firm hook around my waist, which flares my anger this time. I spin in his hold, about to do something that will likely get me kicked out of this place, but I don't fucking care.

"Whoa, wait, please—Ana," the guy says as if he's anticipating my fist before I've even raised it fully. "We're being watched by more than just your guard dog over there. Dance with me and trust you don't even have the right parts for me to be interested in you that way."

He keeps an intimate hold on me I want to rip free from, but I listen. The fact he knows about Alistair's watchdog spikes my adrenaline and sobers me a little. I examine him closer while trying to blend in with the partygoers. He's the same height as me in heels, and he has a slim but muscular build. He's handsome, with dark brown tousled hair, brown eyes, and a kind face. When I see the tattoo of a serpent's head poking out from his dark T-shirt collar, my eyes snap to his.

"You're from Xoid?"

"My name is Rixon Bennett, but only a few know my full name."

"Rix," I whisper.

He nods.

My eyes widen, and I shake my head with the wave of dizziness that passes. His arm tightens as if he anticipates it. I know his name. Rhett spoke of him often as his best hacker and the one he was most regularly in contact with. The fact Rix told me his full name is a serious token of trust considering his work.

I don't know where to begin. What to ask. My heart is racing. This feels like gaining a piece of Rhett back—something I never thought I would get again. His network found me.

They could have found me far sooner.

Now I'm clashing with anger and upset. Too many emotions turn my stomach.

"Come. I don't think your spy will want to follow, and I'm praying I'll keep my balls after this." Rix's lips press to mine suddenly—only once, but it's long and needy, and it shocks me still. Then he takes my hand, and I can do nothing but let him lead me toward the restroom.

It's so crowded the women barely notice Rix, who leads me into a stall and locks the door.

"Sorry," he mutters, running a nervous hand through his disheveled hair. "Had to make it somewhat believable we'd come in here to fuck. Buys us a little time."

We lean against the walls on opposite sides of the stall, but his proximity is unnerving.

"What took you so long?" The demand is the first thing to come out of me. *Three months, and only now someone from Rhett's network is seeking me out?*

Rix hooks a brow and folds his arms. "Were you expecting us sooner?"

Yes, I want to say. I've thought about them often. But I've taken the hand of their greatest enemy, the person who took Rhett from them too, and I guess I assumed Xoid despised me for the betrayal.

"Why now?" I amend.

Rix looks me over as if he's wondering if his next words will pull a detonator on me. "I didn't want to come to you until I was pretty damn sure . . ." He stalls, taking a deep breath, and the music pounding in the background starts to match my growing headache.

"Sure of what?" I dare to let the slither of hope surface. It's already pricking my eyes.

Three months. Ninety-three torturous days. What else would take them so long to come to me?

They want to be sure . . .

"Rhett is alive," he says.

My eyes blur, and I have to sit on the toilet when I'm slammed by the three words I've clung to all this time. Three words that are worth the agony of not falling through the deep cracks in my world since he left.

Rhett is alive.

"How do you know?" I ask. My hope is dangerous, it's taunting, but I want to fight the demons that mock me for it.

"It's taken a long damn time. Xoid has been a wreck without him. Everyone is lost and no one knows what to do. Who to turn to. Me and a few others have been focusing all our efforts all this time on trying to find him. He's Rhett fucking Kaiser—there's no way he's going down in a car accident when I've seen the guy take a bullet to the chest and live."

My brow furrows. I knew there was a reason I couldn't fully let him go. I couldn't accept he was truly gone.

Because he's been out there, waiting for us.

Me.

"Oh god," I whisper. What has he been going through all this time?

"Hey, none of that," Rix says in reprimand as if he's a

mind reader. "We don't fixate on anything but now. Getting him back."

"I've tried," I say, and I curse the crack in my voice.

Rix's expression falls for a second, understanding.

"I couldn't truly believe he was dead either. I've been with Alistair this whole time thinking he would slip up and I would know for sure my hope wasn't pathetic bullshit. I've been through countless files every small chance I get. I've tried eavesdropping on his meetings. I've tried compliance, as if he'll finally admit he's been holding him, and I've found *nothing*. I failed him."

"You did no such thing. You have an in at the place none of us have ever been able to infiltrate. You gained Alistair's trust. Rhett would be furious to know where you've been, because he's protective as shit, but he'd also be so damn proud of you."

A dry sob escapes me. I miss him so fucking much, and it's a pain that grows every day.

"What did you find?" I ask.

"A lead. It took all this time for one of our guys to gain enough trust to be accepted into Alistair's network. We lost three just by trying. Any slight slipup or suspicion and they don't take chances."

"They found him?"

"Mention of him. We still don't know his location, but we have confirmation Rhett is being kept somewhere alive."

"Your guy on the inside—is he safe now?"

Rix tenses at the topic. His fists flex. "He's my little brother, Jeremy. He was never supposed to even *attempt* it, but he went behind our backs, the little shit. He has no choice but to keep it up now until we can get him the fuck out."

My stomach tightens. I know a little about Jeremy too, and my nerves sharpen for the audacious teen.

"I want in," I say.

"I was hoping you'd say that."

I smile, and for the first time in what seems like an eternity, I feel alive. Rhett is out there, and all my time with his uncle won't have been for nothing. I'm stronger, smarter, and I have more knowledge of this underworld that's shaking on the brink of war.

"I have an in with Jacob Forthson too," I admit.

Rix's eyes snap to me with shock. "Holy shit. How are you pulling that off?"

"He wants me to take down Alistair. I want to take them both down."

Rix looks me over as if I've turned into a new person. "Well, damn, Red. It's one thing to hear admiration about you, but I'm considering switching teams right now just for a chance."

I huff a laugh and stand. "What do you need me to do?"

"We still have some pretty damn hard networks to get through before we can get a trace on his location. Don't do anything yet. If Alistair finds out we know, he'll only move him, and I don't want to imagine what he'll do to you if he finds you in places you shouldn't be. Hang tight for now."

He can't be serious. There's no damn way I'm *hanging tight* with the confirmation Rhett is out there. Pushing my guilt aside at how long it took to get the confirmation, now I'm more determined than ever. No matter what it takes.

"Can you take me to Xoid? Rhett once spoke of a den."

"Can you shake your guard dogs? If they find our place . . . it'll be detrimental."

That racks me with turmoil, but I have to do this.

"I'll find a way."

Rix purses his lips and folds his arms. "Fine. We're trusting you, Red. Because Rhett sure as hell did."

Pride blooms in my chest. "Have you heard from Allie?"

"Shit, I thought you knew. We haven't been able to find her

since she was taken the same day Rhett disappeared. I discovered who she really is, but her family seem to be under the impression she's taken a five-month leave, so there's no missing persons report on their part."

"Shit," I say, shaking my head.

"Yeah. If Rhett were here, it wouldn't just be my balls I'd be worried about."

"No trace of her?" I ask.

The shake of his head is a blow to my gut.

"She's been harder to trace than Rhett. At least we know he's in Alistair's network somewhere. The guy just has a fuck-ton of real estate and other shady locations. I don't even think we've found half of them. But with Allie, there's been no talk of her anywhere, and I fear . . . *Shit*, I don't want to say this, but . . . I fear she could have been sold to someone. The trace on the sapphire earrings turned up cold—literally. We found the body of the man who bought her, some filthy-rich lawyer who must have had a thing for her and caught wind of the sale. There's absolutely no insight as to where she vanished to."

My mind reels with the news, which doesn't help my headache. I shouldn't have had the extra drinks. While I'm not too drunk, I want to be sober as hell right now to start figuring out how we're going to find both of them.

"We need to focus on one at a time," I say, much as it raises acid in my throat to target all focus on Rhett.

"Agreed. If there's anyone who'll find Allie, it'll be him anyway. I don't know how he does what he does sometimes."

My hand rubs my chest at the racing of my heart. The thought of having Rhett with us surges me alive with the need to storm from here now and raise hell to find him.

He's alive.

My euphoria is too much. A delirious laugh escapes me and my vision blurs.

"Ana!" I jerk at the loud, deep shout of my name over the music and the chatter of the ladies' room.

"Shit." I unlock the door and slip out, coming face-to-face with a scary-looking Adam Sullevan.

"Christ, A. I thought something happened to you," he says, irritable, and I wonder how long he's been searching for me.

His brown eyes slip over my shoulder, then his expression relaxes in realization.

"It's not what it looks like," I say.

It's clear from Adam's raised brow of suspicion he doesn't believe me, but he's not about to shame me for whatever happened with the guy following me out the stall.

Rix says, a note of bitterness in his tone, "You, on the other hand, have the right parts to interest me, but I've heard a lot about you, Sullevan."

"Who the fuck are you?"

I don't need to suffocate in the male ego that's about to grow between them.

"Can we get out of here before we end up spreading gossip of a threesome?" I hiss.

"Now, that would make for some interesting news," Rix comments.

"Again, who the fuck are you?" Adam bites out.

"Not someone you wanna piss off, buddy."

"Buddy?" Adam flares.

"I'm sure you punch like a kid too, so go ahead." Rix indicates with his chin to Adam's clenched fist.

Women are giving us dirty looks, and I want to be out of here.

"I'll explain later," I tell Adam. Then I turn to Rix. "When will I see you again?"

He drags his smirk from Adam as if he's found a new source of entertainment. "Here." Rix pulls out a phone. "Don't bring yours when you come. Don't even take any of your cars if there's even a slight chance that shithead could have a tracker on them. This will tell you where to go and when."

I nod, understanding the gravity of the situation.

"Soon?" I ask desperately.

Rix nods with a soft smile before he casts one last look at Adam. "Consider very carefully who you can really trust."

He's leaving before I have the chance to say anything.

"He's a prick," Adam grumbles. "Want to tell me what this is all about? Does he work for Alistair?"

I'm blinking after the ghost of Rix and resisting the urge to go after him, to not let him out of my sight at all, because what if this was all some crazed, alcohol-induced hallucination?

I say out loud for the first time. "Rhett is alive."

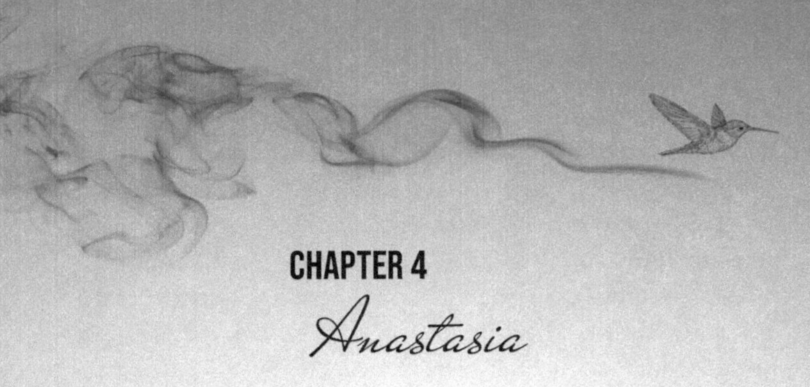

CHAPTER 4

Anastasia

I'm not taken to Alistair's manor for the *job* he wants me to see. Or participate in. My nerves grow in the back of the car while Tony drives. I've watched several men die by Alistair's hand or at his orchestration, but something about this is important enough for him to want me there.

We circle down into an underground garage, where the car stops and I spy another next to us. When Tony opens my door I get out and walk around our black SUV to slide into the small awaiting limo. Across from me is Alistair Lanshall; beside me is a stunning woman.

For a moment, though, it's just me and him. I stare into his blue eyes with more hatred than I've ever felt before. He's been holding Rhett hostage somewhere all this time. I think a part of me knew—a small, hopeful part that never let Rhett truly die and held onto the belief he was coming home.

I'm filled with more determination than ever to find him, and we will collapse Alistair's empire. Together.

I keep my expression as cold and indifferent as ever as I drag my attention to his companion in the car with us.

She has long, straight jet-black hair, and her deep green

eyes regard me with icy indifference. It's like she knows every detail about me and has already made up her mind about how she feels. It's not friendly—that much is clear.

"I'd like you to meet Kenna Radley. She's my best spy and assassin." Alistair introduces her.

My eyes rove over her again. I never would have guessed her line of work. She's dressed in a small black dress with heels I would surely break my neck in. Her bust is pushed up to draw attention, and she wears an array of purple jewels and diamonds around her neck, as well as in her earrings and bracelets. Her makeup is impeccable, with winged eyeliner that gives her piecing irises a feline, seductive edge, and that's where her power lies—in a look that could make a man beg at her feet and not know what for. Everything about her screams wealth, but also authority.

"Where are we going?" I ask.

"You two are going on a job for me," Alistair says, crossing his ankle over his knee and reaching for a short glass of whiskey. This car is fancier than some bars I've been in.

"I might be underdressed," I say, admittedly intimidated by Kenna now I know what she's capable of. Her beauty is merely a mask.

"Yes, you are," Alistair says in such a way that I know he planned for this. "Before you go, I wanted to tell you myself what will happen."

"We're not here?"

"No. The club I need you to get inside is . . . *off-limits* to me."

"I didn't think such a place existed."

He gives a boastful smile. "Few do. However, the owner of this establishment is very particular about who he lets in. His name is Silas Balenheizer, the son of a *very* powerful cartel leader in Miami. Word is he's thinking of moving to the D.C area, which is already overcrowded."

I don't give away any hint of recognition at the name, but my heart speeds up and my hands go clammy at the mention. Matthew Forbes was Damien Balenheizer's true son, and I'm overcome with nausea that another son of his who grew up by his side could be far fucking worse.

"Does Jacob know he's in the city?" I ask, trying to remain neutral in my interest.

"I can't be certain, but this is why we have to move in tonight and gain his interest first before Forthson gets the same idea."

"What makes you confident he'll yield leadership to you?"

"I'd like to propose it to him as more of a . . . partnership of sorts. If he joins with me, it'll give him a false sense of authority, while I have the respect and loyalty here that he does not."

"And if he chooses Jacob?"

"He won't," he says, far too lax in his confidence. My skin prickles in anticipation. "I'm confident Damien will be interested in an alliance between his eldest son and the First Daughter of the United States."

I straighten in my seat and ice douses me.

He can't mean . . .

He wouldn't . . .

"You promised I wouldn't be sold for my body." My composure is crumbling. My hand reaches for the door, but the lock clicks down as I do and ice spears my gut. "Let me out." Images of Matthew slam into me. I think I'm going to be sick. I can't face another son of Damien.

"Let me explain, Anastasia."

"It seems pretty fucking clear what you want," I hiss. "And I'm not *yours*."

"I thought you understood what you signed up for when I came for you. This doesn't have to be a resistance."

"You're not giving me a choice."

"Your choice is this: you go into that club tonight and

begin to charm Silas. You won't win him over in a day—it will take weeks, perhaps months—but eventually, he'll fall for you. In truth, your happiness does mean something to me, and I hope you might fall for him too. After you're married, Damien will become my ally. It's the most amicable way."

Married.

My throat tightens as though he's wrapped his hand around it.

"You want to sell me."

"Only if you choose to see it that way."

He's a sick, twisted bastard. I'm not surprised, but at the same time, I could never have seen this coming. Did he know about Silas's possible move here all those months ago? And I was right there, desperate and vulnerable enough, naïve enough, to take his hand and think *I* was the only one with a hidden motive.

It takes everything in me to keep my composure. "What if he doesn't fall for me?" I ask bitterly.

"I don't operate by what-ifs. You get the job done, or I'll find another use for you that won't be so kind."

My teeth grind.

He says, bored now, "Off you go. Kenna will see to it you're appropriately dressed for his venue."

Our doors are opened then, and I linger one last look of simmering hatred on Alistair Lanshall.

I follow Kenna, flanked by two security. We slip into an elevator, and she towers over me in those heels while I wear flat boots. We don't speak, and I find her silence tense, as if she could snap at me at any moment.

We get to a penthouse hotel room. *A bit much to spend on a changing room.*

"I don't know why Alistair thinks someone who barely speaks can pull this off," Kenna says. Her voice is silky and seductive. I don't think I've ever admired another woman for her voice before. Kenna plants her hand on my shoulder, forcing me to sit in front of a vanity.

I scowl through the reflection. "You haven't spoken either," I counter.

"We are not even close to the same. My job requires silence, stillness. Yours, as the president's daughter, and what you naively signed up for with Alistair, requires the opposite. I don't know why he's allowed you to waste all your time fighting when that will never be your role."

"You've been watching me?" I blanch at the thought. *For how long?* Best spy indeed, as I don't recall seeing even a glimpse of her at Alistair's manor.

Kenna doesn't answer. She folds her arms as two women approach me. One fusses over what to do with my hair; another lays out a box of makeup products. I internally groan as I sit there like a doll for them to dress.

When my hair is freshly curled, my lips a bright red, and my eyes more seductive than I've ever seen them, I sigh and stand, led over to the outfit on the bed.

"I'm not wearing that," I say immediately.

The short slip dress is a deep silk red with a waterfall neckline.

"It matches your hair. What's wrong with it?" Kenna says, irritated.

I can't wear color. The thought makes me sick.

"Don't you have a black dress?" I ask.

"No. Now hurry up—the car is here."

Unless they forcibly dress me, I won't put it on. I may know Rhett's alive, but until we're together and out of this nightmare, I can't pretend like I'm fine.

Kenna's look slices me with ire, but she sighs and reaches for the zip of her dress. My mouth opens to protest, but she's already shimmying out of it.

"We're about the same size," she says, holding it out to me.

In her lacy black underwear, I can't help but appreciate her physique. She's beautiful in every imperfection she wears. I notice various lighter scores of raised skin all over her and wonder what each scar is from.

"Thanks," I mutter.

I'm surprised by her offer, but I assume it's not through kindness or consideration of my feelings that she's offering me her dress, but rather that her impatience with me is running dangerously thin.

Kenna takes off her purple jewelry too. While the red dress looks stunning on her, she definitely knows purple and black suit her best.

"Men fuck with their eyes the instant they land on you. Men like Silas are possessive and will decide if you're worth the pursuit in seconds. The red dress would have been a natural magnet on you. I hope you've been working on your seduction as much as your lame left hook."

I barely get the final piece of diamond jewelry on before she's marching from the room, and I scramble to follow.

"My left hook isn't *lame*," I say, jogging after her, but the ridiculous heels I'm wearing make it more of a hobble.

"Your round kick is often humorous to watch too," she adds.

My mouth parts at her jesting, and I realize she must have been watching me many times, maybe every time, to have such opinions on my fighting.

"Why hasn't he asked you to train me? All I've been tried against are men."

"Because you'd never face someone like me, nor need the kind of skill I have, in the real world. He doesn't want you for an assassin. He merely indulges your fire to let you release all that rage, and so you won't be defenseless if you come under attack. You don't need the finesse and precision knowledge."

She presses the garage button in the elevator, and I'm

starting to be awed by her. Though she still scares the shit out of me.

"I want to learn," I argue.

She slips her green eyes to me, and I wonder if she's recalculating the opinions she's only gathered about me from afar. I don't think she finds anything admirable in me though.

"You may think you're part of this underworld, that you know what goes on, but you've only caught a glimpse. Protect your innocence, Anastasia. It's not always ignorance. It's peace you can't ever get back if you allow every part of it to be taken."

I don't expect her words. They feel like a warning. Wisdom about something she's already lost. Perhaps she wishes there had been someone to help *her*. I don't push for details about her life—we're barely more than strangers, and I'm quite sure she hates me.

"Just Ana," I say.

It's a small token of amity. Even if her vine has thorns, it may be the only thing I can grapple for the composure to face Silas.

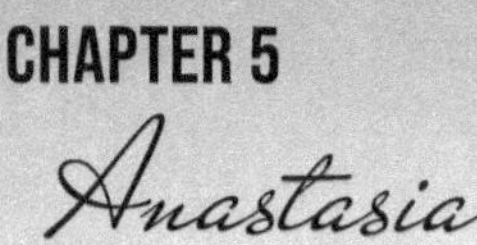

CHAPTER 5

Anastasia

We get to the club called Lumina Lounge. It's a spectacle even from afar. The entire front is made of frosted glass, with each panel lit up in a hypnotizing gradient. It isn't a place where just anyone can decide they'd like to go to for the night. Apparently, you need a VIP pass that requires a fingerprint scan to enter, and they're given by invitation only.

Alistair sent my request weeks ago, leaving his name out entirely and making sure it couldn't be traced back to him. It seems to have taken that long to get the approval, and now I recall the time he made me press my thumbprint to a document he claimed was for his own keeping.

I can feel the bass of the music before we even get out of the car, and my nerves start to rattle. This is what Alistair wanted me for. Not to fight or smuggle or participate in his blood money. I'm a power pawn, used only for my status, to gain for him prettily.

I resent it.

"Arrogance is everything to people like Silas," Kenna says. "Don't fuck this up."

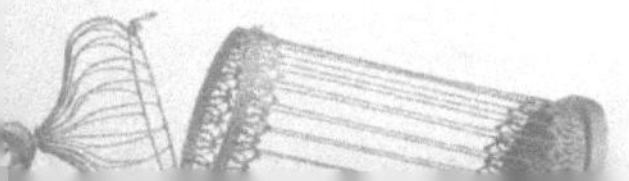

"Great confidence boost," I mutter.

I'm trying to focus on my breathing so I won't turn into a sweating, flustering mess. Silas is just another arrogant man with far too much money. I've dealt with his kind before.

"You'll be going in first. I'll have eyes on you, and I'll be in the car when it's over."

My head snaps to her with my spike of adrenaline. "You won't be with me?"

She shakes her head and my confidence wilts.

"Alistair doesn't want to risk diverting his attention."

"What will you be doing?"

"What I do best, just like you. If we're lucky."

I hope that doesn't mean killing inside. Spying? I don't know how she's going to manage it in a bustling establishment.

"Go—we can't linger. Everything you do and say will be analyzed."

I nod, but I'm so awash with dizziness now it's time to perform that the cool summer air does nothing to help me breathe when I step out of the car.

The doors are guarded by two giant men. They don't speak, and that's an intimidation in itself. I don't give away my anxiety as one reaches into his coat and produces a finger scanner. I place my thumb on it, and after a second, it beeps and the man takes it back, reading what appears on the other side. Then they each take a handle, and I wonder what the fuck kind of movie I've stepped into with the ominous reception.

"Have a good evening, Miss Kinsley. Silas himself eagerly awaits you."

I don't smile at them, though it feels wrong. *Arrogance is everything.* I have to play like I'm above everyone, perhaps even Silas. I'm riddled with nerves with every step closer to the source of the music as my jacket is taken, my purse searched, and I step through a body scanner, which I assume is to detect concealed weapons or recording equipment.

This is a man who doesn't take chances, and I doubt has ever given a second.

I'm escorted into the main room, which comes alive in an impressive hall. There's a front stage at the far end and several smaller platforms with poles where women dance. It's elegant and it gives off an air of prestige. As I continue to follow, I try to gauge the dancers who appear lost in their own world, oblivious to the eyes that drink them in. But they're also aware of the attention, as if it's what moves their bodies to the music with confidence. Their wears are sparkling and beautiful, some in short bodysuits and others in two-piece outfits. It isn't the type of place sleazy men reach to grope and holler or toss and tuck bills; these patrons are awed and are in here to admire the performances.

Circular tables litter the ground level, and there's a long bar at one side of the hall. Above, there are booths like in a theater, but in particular, one observation area spans the whole left side, and I'm led toward the stairs up to it.

I try to calm my racing pulse by listening to the music. It's not pop or rock like I would expect to find in most clubs; there's an element of jazz in the song playing, and I admire the saxophone all the way up the black-carpeted spiral stairs.

At the top I try not to balk at the dominant male ratio. I count at least a dozen men and only four women. There's a smaller personal bar up here, a pool table, and several sets of sofas and armchairs facing each other for groups.

It doesn't take me long to guess which of the wealthy men is Silas Balenheizer. I watch one of his tattooed hands bring a cigarette to his mouth, and he takes a long drag. I've only ever experimented with smoking if I'm drunk, but I've never seen someone make it look *seductive*. The way he watches the smoke he blows out toward the ceiling, it's as if all the thoughts he had on the inhale scatter in the air before him on the exhale, and he's oblivious to the liveliness of the night around him.

He screams power and danger, with dark hair that gives off a sheen and a few strands that flick over his forehead. Tattoos crawl up his neck, and I wonder from the few undone buttons of his black shirt if his whole chest is covered. His arms too, since so many pictures decorate his skin from his hands to where his black shirt sleeves are rolled up to his elbows. His face has an impeccable sculpture, with his angular, clean-shaven jaw. I find his eyes a deep brown as he watches the venue below and a moving light catches on them.

When they slip to me, I realize my assessment of him has taken over my thoughts, and now I'm standing right beside the sofa that hosts the two men opposite him. He gives little away in that seconds-long stare he lingers on me, but the skin around his eyes flexes in recognition.

"I never thought I'd be hosting America's First Daughter in my club," he says in a deep voice of ash and smoke.

"I had to see for myself why people boast their membership," I say.

Silas merely looks at those seated opposite him, and they stand, leaving the whole sofa vacant. I understand the way he can talk without words when his gaze falls back on me and I'm compelled to take their place.

He leans forward, tapping the ash off his cigarette. "And what do you see, Miss Kinsley?"

I wonder if I'm already failing since Silas seems so unimpressed by my presence. What's another beautiful heiress to him?

"I see a man trying prove he's not just his father's son."

"Is that so?"

I notice the lights dim below, and the music tapers off. The front stage is dark as a silhouette walks on. There are three poles, but no one joins her.

"When we're born into a name that tries to define us, I think it's inevitable we search for fulfillment in something we created ourselves," I say, but I'm not looking at him—I'm attracted to this performance.

I realize why when the spotlight hits her, and I don't react as I see Kenna posed on the stage. She's changed into black tights with embellished high-waisted black shorts and a full-black diamond crop top, but she's wearing the same platform heels.

When I remember who I'm sitting with, I snap my sight away from her, but Silas is watching her too, forearms leaning on his thighs.

"Why are you really here, Anastasia?" he asks, but his words are as vacant as I felt a moment ago as he seems to lose himself to Kenna's dance.

"Rebellion, boredom . . . Do I really need a reason?" I pick up the cigarette he set down, taking a long inhale. I'm not used to it, and it without any alcohol I decide it's foul-tasting and not something I want to try again.

Silas says, to seemingly no one, "Miss Kinsley will have a French martini."

He stands, heading over to the balcony and leaning his forearms on the rail. *Shit.* I'm failing already, and Kenna's refusal to be with me so as *not* to distract him is only back-firing with her alternative plan. He's fully engrossed, and as I stand, following him to watch, I can see why.

So she's an assassin, a spy, and a masterful dancer.

Even I'm entranced by the way she moves.

Silas sees these women dancing likely every night—he's got a taste for it—and I try to soothe my faltering confidence by believing he would have been drawn to watch any of his main performers.

But Kenna . . . she's got a form and elegance that stands out. I feel the answer nagging in my mind, but I can't catch it. The dance is seductive, like modern burlesque, but there's something different about the way Kenna performs it. The point of her toes, the arch of her back, the full split of her legs.

Then it hits me, so obvious now.

She's a ballet dancer. Or at least she was once. For enough years that her skill will always be imbedded in the way she moves.

"Time is money, Anastasia, and I do hope you haven't come to waste mine," Silas says absentmindedly.

I'm pulled from my trance too. "Do you require all your guests to offer you something?"

"Like you said, we're all searching for our purpose. I don't come here every night to merely smoke and drink and watch the pretty dancers."

I look around the venue again, seeing every polished individual as a business transaction. *Is he trafficking women through this setup like Jacob?* The thought turns me nauseous. I don't know what I'll do if I discover that to be true.

The French martini is brought to me, while Silas is handed a short glass of an amber liquor that could be whiskey or scotch. I take a sip, hoping it'll help calm me.

"How did you know I'd want this drink?" I ask.

"You seem like a sweet girl, with just the right hint of bitterness."

I hook a brow. "What do you base your assumptions on?"

"I make it my business to know every person who comes through these doors."

That enlightenment coils in my stomach and I find myself scrambling through my past, which is boringly innocent for the most part, as if some skeleton I've forgotten I'm hiding will unveil itself to Silas Balenheizer.

"I'm sorry for your loss. Rhett Kaiser, wasn't it?"

Fuck. He has no reason to look deeper into Rhett. He isn't here.

My silence must last too long as he forces his fixed gaze from Kenna to me.

"I came here to forget about it."

Silas smiles, but it's not the kind of smile that curls fully on his mouth. It dances in his eyes like he's playing a game I don't know I'm part of.

When the song finishes and the room floods with applause, Silas leans in to whisper something to a man by his other side, who sets off. He finally gives me his full attention, leaning sideways on the balcony, facing me. His dark eyes trail over me from head to toe, and I try not to stiffen with the blatant assessment.

"What do *you* see, Silas?"

He's finding entertainment in me, but I have a feeling it's not in what I'm trying to achieve.

"I see a woman trying so hard to hide a broken heart under a steel guise. You could fuck any man you desired, that's not why you're here. So tell me: Lanshall or Forthson?"

My heart tumbles out of my fucking ass.

I don't know how to respond, and Silas goes back to sitting, leaving me there like a dear in fucking headlights, but I keep my expression cool as I join him again.

"Neither," I say. "And both."

That sparks his intrigue.

"And which does Kenna Radley belong to?"

I don't react, but my mind is spinning. It was futile from the beginning to believe someone like Silas Balenheizer wouldn't be one step ahead. Or perhaps Alistair knew it was a possibility and still expects me to convince him to *fall* for me.

When I don't answer, Silas reclines in his smugness.

"Neither." Kenna's tone is cold as it creeps up behind me. She's escorted by the man Silas spoke to after her dance.

"And both?" Silas adds.

"No."

The way he looks at her is how I'd picture someone appreciating fine art. He savors her—it's clear in every lingering impression of his eyes over her body.

Kenna drags her flat look from him to pin me with the accusation I meet sheepishly.

"I didn't say anything," I defend.

"I'm going to wager Lanshall," Silas says. "I heard he acquired a rather high-profile alliance. Though I'll admit, it was quite the surprise to conclude it was the president's daughter." He lights another cigarette, and again I study how it seems to untangle his thoughts. "Sit, Miss Radley," he invites.

She doesn't, and that only earns the most genuinely thrilled smile I've seen on him.

Silas goes on. "After the death of Everett Lanshall, his uncle recruits his sad, lost girlfriend. But what reason does she have to walk into the underworld now? To be used for this? To gain my alliance, but how—?" He pauses and his head cants, eyes on me as he seems to conclude it too easily. He gives a short, deep chuckle. "I'm more interested in your friend, Anastasia. No offense."

I'm taken aback but admittedly relieved.

"None taken," I say.

"Speak for yourself," Kenna cuts in, low and cold. "We're not friends. And I'm not interested in *you*, rich boy."

His eyes spark on her as he takes a drag of his cigarette. "Money isn't an insult, sweetheart." He blows out the smoke and sets it down. "But I will fuck the word 'boy' out of you."

"A woman has never told you no before, have they?"

"Oh, they have. It's just never stopped me."

I tense, and Kenna's eyes heat and narrow on Silas.

"You ever touch me, it'll be the last thing you feel at all."

Silas grins, and I wonder what's the truth and what he's saying just to provoke Kenna from the wild thrill in his stare. "When I touch you, you'll be begging me not to stop. And no other man ever will touch you again, or their hands will arrive in a pretty package on your doorstep. I don't share."

Kenna seems to have a venomous response lingering at the tip of her tongue, but she thinks better than to provoke him. We need him.

This night has gone to complete shit and I haven't even finished my first martini. Thinking of it, I lift it from the table and finish it off in three gulps.

Silas says, "This is the most fun and intrigue I've had in years. And something tells me we're just getting started."

CHAPTER 6

Rhett

The meals I get are barely fit for a dog. Tonight is particularly foul, with mold growing on the bread and the beans dried up as if they were meant to be served days ago. I don't even attempt to eat it though I've been without food for two days now.

It's another attempt to keep me too weak to fight back even if the opportunity presents itself. They underestimate my will to stay alive and get my little bird back. If there was a moment I believed I could get out, I would push through the pain of broken bones to do it.

I never learned the fate of the boy, Jack. My instinct was right, and the gun fired empty on every spin of the revolver. Micah is deranged, but he's no fool. Had there been one bullet in the chamber, he knows I would have used it on him even though it wouldn't have granted me my way out. The *click* of the trigger was still enough to make the kid piss his pants, and Micah's maniacal laughter at the sick show haunts me still.

I'm halfway to sleep when the sound of the door opening grates across my skin.

"I thought it was about time I come by myself, nephew."

It's been three months, and only now does Alistair fucking Lanshall pay a visit. His voice will never fail to tense my body in a reaction so specific to his presence. It's like holding a double-ended knife. I want to let go of more than six years of brutal conditioning to submit to his voice, but I keep holding onto the blade, resisting, even if the will to take his life with the other end bleeds me dry.

"This is no way to greet your uncle. I taught you better."

My back is still to him and I'm staring with such hatred into the stone wall. I listen to him walk in further, even picturing the sleek black polish of his shoes clacking slowly across the ground, the same fucking brand as twelve years ago.

One minute I'm focusing all my efforts on containing my impulsive anger, and the next I'm barely registering the shuffle of feet before I'm doused in ice water. It's not just freezing; it fucking pierces my skin with a thousand deep needles that send my system into shock.

I don't feel the broad, vicious brute of a man haul me up and slam me to the wall. I do feel the nasty punch he strikes across my face before I'm dropped, barely catching myself on my knees.

My mind travels elsewhere. It finds a light in all this darkness, the only thing guiding me through this hell. If I didn't have Ana or the peace of the memories we made, I don't think I'd have any will left to truly get out of this.

"You're wasting your time," I rasp, coming to, though I wish I weren't when the awareness amplifies the beating pain of my jaw and head, along with the violent tremors I try to suppress. I watch the droplets of water fall from my hair to the ground.

"Look at me when you speak," he orders, as cool and calm as ever.

If I don't do as he wants, his guy will keep hitting. It takes everything in me not to lunge for Alistair's throat when I look up.

It torments me to see him and to feel such loathing in my being. I was only ten when my parents died, but he looks so much like my dad, who would have been horrified at what his brother became.

Alistair doesn't look at me like a son; he assesses me like he would a case of rifles. Am I too damaged, too worn, too impractical now?

"Your network . . . Xoid, is it? I'll admit it's an impressive setup, even if juvenile."

"Many of your operations were stopped by it."

"Yes, I've been keeping track of how much you owe me. I'm sure I'll see it all back once I weed out everything you've planted."

The threat to Xoid turns my blood molten. He's trying to get under my skin, and I can't allow that. He will feed on my anger and my protection of the people at Xoid.

Someone pulls up a chair, and Alistair retrieves a cigar before he sits. He lights it and leans back as if he's lounging in the fucking sun.

"Did you know Forthson tried to get to you first?" he says casually, blowing out smoke that chokes the air. "He tried to get your little high-profile confidant too. Though it seems Alyra DeVerre is missing entirely now."

My stomach sinks. *Shit.* Was Rix not able to trace her kidnappers? My jaw clenches so tight my teeth might break, because if she's been missing all this time I've been captive . . .

I have more determination than ever to get the fuck out of here.

"I find it all rather amusing, don't you? Forthson thinks we're equals in this underworld, but he's nothing more than a child born with a dark heart and the kind of wealth that creates boredom. He'll never know what it means to start from the fucking ground."

"Why are you telling me this? I have no care for your petty feud."

Alistair smiles. The kind that delights in my question, for it opens the door for him to share his delusional brilliance. "I have one way I plan to win over Forthson, but should that fail, I always like to have a backup."

"I have no connection to Jacob Forthson. In fact, I want him dead, second to you."

"See? We do have a common goal, nephew."

"We have nothing in common."

"He has a younger brother, only twelve. Did you know that? He's kept him a secret from me for so long, but he slipped up recently, and I found him."

I have a really bad fucking feeling about where this is going.

"Going after his brother won't gain you shit." I know I'm wrong, but this kid's only crime is being blood-related to an evil being, and he doesn't deserve to be a target for his brother's crimes.

"My reports say they're *very* close. That Forthson is highly protective of him, which must be true if he's hidden him all this time."

"What's your point?"

"I want you to extract him and kill him."

An incredulous, breathy laugh accompanies the shake of my head. "You put a weapon in my hands, you know I'll aim them at your guys."

"Not when it's her life at stake."

"You son of a bitch."

He takes an arrogant drag of his cigar as he stands, and I contemplate how I could end his life with the chair. It's dragged out again before I can think of a sure, efficient way.

"I will have both of you or neither of you," Alistair says as he leaves. "The choice is yours."

I ponder his words in silence, pacing the room. The habit reminds me of Ana. I've often wondered how she didn't turn herself nauseous with the back and forth, but now I get it. As if I'm a human metronome, it unwinds my restless thoughts.

Alistair wouldn't have spent these past three months with Ana if he was prepared to kill her because of my noncompliance. It's a gamble, but I can't help but think she's too valuable to him.

Having to choose between my morality and the thing I love the most in this fucking world might be what breaks me once and for all.

CHAPTER 7

Anastasia

I sit in a rooftop restaurant, the midday sun streaking through the window as I sip my tea. It'd be beautiful, peaceful, if it weren't for my company, which leaves little to be desired about being here.

"You seem . . . distracted today, darling," Jacob says across from me.

This venue is exclusive, private. Alistair's men can't follow me in here, and I always arrive a half hour after Jacob and leave first so he's never spotted. Alistair agreed to let me have an hour here alone when I begged after a month with him, telling him I needed the moment of complete unsurveilled freedom before I lost my mind.

"I've given you intel on several of Alistair's movements," I say.

A smile shadow's Jacob's mouth. He's dressed in an impeccable casual light suit, the top buttons of his shirt undone. It's almost frighting how innocent and charming he looks when he harbors so much evil.

"You have," he drawls, taking a sip of his coffee.

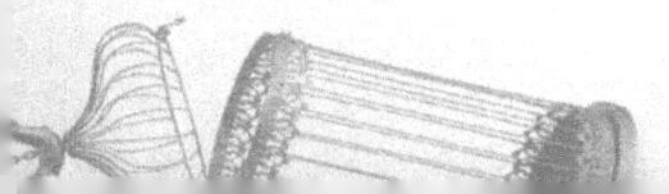

He knows I'm about to ask for something. My adrenaline threatens my composure as I reconsider despite lying awake all night reeling over what to do with Rix's information.

"I need something in return before I can take down Alistair for good."

His dark brow hooks with intrigue. "What can I do for you?"

"Find Rhett Kaiser."

Both his brows shoot up then as he sets his cup down. Jacob leans back in his chair skeptically.

"Where did you hear that he's even alive after all this time?"

"That doesn't matter. Can you do it?"

"If you're asking if I know every possible location my enemy owns, then yes. You could say it's a particular hobby of mine to store meticulous intel so our networks don't cross territories."

Hope sparks in my chest. "We've tried many of his estates and locations, but we can't have them all."

"Ahh, and by 'we,' you mean Kaiser's adorable vigilante group effort."

The mockery and belittlement of Xoid makes my teeth clench. "Can you find him or not?" I grind out.

"Perhaps." He shrugs as if it means little to him as he looks out over the city. "But you forget he owes me a lot of money, darling. It's brave of you to tell me he's out there. What's stopping me from finding him myself and having my vengeance?"

"Me," I say. Confidence squares my shoulders as I grab his attention.

"I have you," he counters.

"Do you know Silas Belenheizer is in town?"

"Of course. I'm guessing Lanshall is making a move now if he's told you."

"He wants to use me to gain full allegiance with Damien."

A muscle in his jaw shifts. I'd like to think I've become observant of his tells after all our meetings. He's calculating as he always likes to figure things out for himself.

"Marriage," he concludes.

My lips press together, and Jacob smiles at his own brilliance. "If you find Rhett, I'll follow Alistair's plan, but it'll be you I'll tell Silas and Damien I want to ally with."

Jacob chuckles. "I'm not a fool, Anastasia. If I find Kaiser and you and the savior crew somehow manage to get him out with your lives, Kaiser will never let you go. I would have to kill him."

"He'll let me go if I say that's what I want."

"Again, I don't know what you take me for, but I don't believe that for a second. Then I would have to kill you too for the lie, and what a pretty waste that would be."

"What if I can get Damian and Silas to ally with you without the marriage?"

"That would be your ideal situation, which often makes it the hardest to achieve."

"Would we have a deal?"

Jacob's eyes flare with intrigue. "If you can arrange for Silas Balenheizer to meet with me and convince me of an alliance, I'll get you Rhett Kaiser's precise location."

It's a dangerous game I'm playing, but Rhett is worth it. I feel triumph in my strides toward getting him back, and I can only hope it won't take much time. I don't know how I'm going to pull it off with Silas. Truthfully, it's the most frightening prospect I've faced so far, but I *have* to make this work.

I turn cold suddenly at the thought of Silas telling Alistair about my proposal with Jacob. It would all be over. Alistair might even reveal Rhett to me just to make me watch as he puts a bullet in his head for the betrayal.

"Backing out already?" Jacob muses as if he can hear my every haunting thought.

I take a deep breath to compose myself and have a drink of my tea to make sure I can speak. "No. I'm just planning out my strategy."

Jacob knows it's a lie, but he doesn't call it out. "You think you're ready to play in the lion's den?"

"I'm already here, and I'm not the prey this time."

Not the little bird. She belonged to Rhett and always will.

Jacob smiles, and it's all intrigue and desire. "Don't rush, darling. It makes for reckless decisions, and I won't be able to save you if your master finds out about your double agency. It may take a bit of time to locate Kaiser."

"You claim to be better than Alistair, yet he can find a person in days."

"Don't provoke me, Anastasia. It won't work. I'll find Kaiser tomorrow just to lay his body at your feet and prove a point."

Jacob is evil incarnate in the prettiest form. He's younger than Alistair, which gives him an added air of innocence, as if someone with less than thirty years on this earth can't possibly be so corrupted by it. That's because he wasn't. Jacob was born this way, with a silver spoon in his mouth and nothing to blame but sinister taste.

What I've come to learn about Jacob Forthson is that he likes nothing more than a tango of fire.

I stand, leaning my hands on the table as I say, "If I can get Silas to agree to an alliance with you and you don't have Rhett's location by then, I'll make sure he knows you're a man of hollow promise."

As I move to walk away, Jacob catches my wrist. His smile shows bright teeth, and he stares up at me with a spark in his eye. "What if I have another offer?" he says, tracing that hand up my forearm.

I don't give him the satisfaction of balking, but my cold eyes pin him.

"Abandon this pitiful Lanshall family feud. Forget Silas and be with me instead. We could bow empires and move mountains together. I would give up D.C. and a very powerful prospective partnership with Balenheizer for you."

I discover that Jacob has everything a person could ever want; he can gain anything. Control everything. But he's never had *love*. I wonder for a moment what his version of the word translates to in a person, in actions, but it doesn't matter. For all his heinous crimes, I condemn him to always be wondering about the one thing he'll never truly feel.

"You could have bought me yourself at your gala," I say.

"There's no satisfaction in that. I want you to *want* me."

"You look at me and you see a sparkling ruby. As soon as it's in your possession, you'll realize red isn't your preferred color after all."

"What if I said it is my favorite color?"

"I'd say there aren't enough rubies in the world to make you feel the power you do when you *win*. Giving up this alliance to have me is a forfeit to your enemy."

Jacob lifts my hand to his mouth, planting a chaste kiss there. "I think you know me too well in too little time, Anastasia. It's what makes you so tempting that I'd contemplate giving it all up."

I smile. "It's only to my benefit to know you, Jacob. Double agent, remember?"

As I try to pull away again his grip tightens, shooting adrenaline through me.

"I remember," he says with an edge of warning. "As I hope you won't forget that if I get one hint of suspicion, one reason to believe you've betrayed me, that you've been telling Lanshall about me, I'll make you watch as I kill every person you hold dear. I'll start at the beginning—your parents, Liam Forbes, Riley O'Neil, Adam Sullevan, Rhett Kaiser—"

"You've made your point," I snap.

His stare is made of steel now, nothing of finesse and elegance. This is the monster that lurks within.

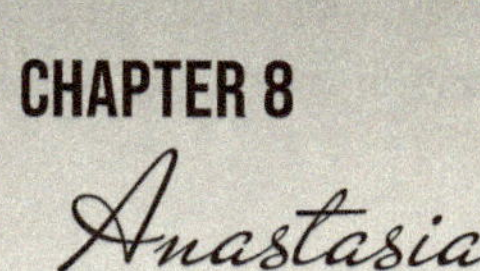

CHAPTER 8

Anastasia

I don't attend my graduation. Riley makes her best attempt to persuade me, and I think I might for her sake, but I can't go through with it. I can't watch as my parents and Riley sit in such close proximity to the man I loathe more than I thought myself capable of. Alistair wouldn't miss it if I went.

Though I can't get out of the *celebratory* dinner my parents insist on. It's strange, being in the White House. It will never feel like home, and when I come here it doesn't feel like I'm visiting my parents' home. So it's as good as fine dining out at any fancy restaurant in the city.

Better, in fact. The staff around the banquet hall are here only to serve us. We don't have to stare awkwardly at a menu and then wait for food. We're waited upon like royalty, and though I'm used to a certain degree of this from our old home, it's intimidating as hell.

I'm already eager to leave when we're served our starter of the smallest and fanciest rendition of what I believe to be a Caesar salad.

"Have you thought about what you plan to do with your

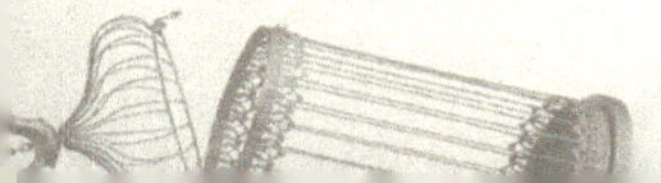

time now? What field you might pursue with your degree?" Dad asks.

The diploma has barely grazed my fingers before the wrecking ball of a question comes swinging. I expected it, but it doesn't make me prepared with an answer that will satisfy the President of the United States.

I hate that I've grown bitter and resentful, but after every-thing, my father has never apologized for how he condemned Rhett as a criminal despite the hurt I carry. I don't care that our secret is out—that I clearly loved him to be hurting this much. It doesn't change his harsh judgment of Rhett. I've disappointed him. In my father's eyes, I'm mourning a monster and I should move on with my life, focus on my prospects.

"I'm not sure," I say. It's pitiful, but it's the truth to them at least.

I'm sure he would disown me as a daughter completely if he knew where I really spend my time. If he finds out I've picked up what Rhett started, and that I won't stop until Alis-tair Lanshall is torn to pieces from the inside out.

"You can't lock yourself away in that apartment forever," he says with a hint of sourness that makes me sink internally.

I feel like I lost a father months ago too, and what kills me is that I don't know if the daughter he wants is ever coming back.

"You'll figure it out, honey," Mom says, always trying to add amity to the tense room. "Teaching was strongly on your mind, remember? And you raised funds that are still waiting to go toward opening that school you always wanted."

I partially smile because this is a fond memory, a dream I wish I could hold . . . but everything hopeful turns to sand in my hands, and I wish I could pass it to someone else.

"Yeah," I say, pushing my salad around my plate. "Maybe someday."

If I survive the trenches of the underworld with Rhett by my side, perhaps I can dare to dream again.

"You're still taking part in the Young Musicians performance, aren't you? We've all been looking forward to it," Mom says.

I agreed to play my violin in the live show here at the White House that will be broadcast on TV. My parents wouldn't stop asking even when my initial response was no. It's a huge step up in overcoming my nerves from the Christmas party last year. I caved eventually, if only because I couldn't suffer another look of disappointment from my father. I don't think he would have pushed, and maybe his anger is because my mom is saddened by my distance.

"Yes," I say tightly.

I can plaster on a smile for the cameras, get one song over with, then leave the party before I suffocate in the company of people so oblivious to the dark world I'm holding hands with. I don't want to dine and drink and laugh as though the world is turning and nothing else matters but our wealth.

"Wonderful!" Mom exclaims.

It's a deceptive kind of cheer. She doesn't fully believe I'll show, but I've sworn that commitment to myself no matter what. I feel guilt for the pain I seem to be causing her—this small agreement is a Band-Aid on a relationship I hope can be salvaged.

I just need Rhett back, and for all that has wronged us to be taken down. Then, in the peace we deserve and have bled for, maybe we can rebuild and become far stronger together than when we met as two separate wandering souls.

After dinner I have to release all the pent-up tension.

I train my focus on the aim of the gun between my hands

and shoot five rounds. I'm getting better at target practice, just not good enough yet. I can aim for the chest and they'll all hit the area, but I want more. A precision that will ensure my aim is absolute enough to make five shots look like one.

They're getting closer.

"Decent," Kenna says when I take off the ear defenders.

I'm at a range on the outskirts of Washington D.C., needing away from Alistair's manor even though he has a small setup for shooting there. I don't deign to ask how Kenna found me, nor how long she was watching before she made herself known.

"I'm going to assume you call everything less than your skill 'decent,'" I mutter.

"Probably," she says, folding her arm and looking out over the paper figure set up at the far end. "It takes practice—*a lot* of practice."

I watch as she pulls her own gun from a holster under her leather jacket. She checks the clip, and I listen to a series of quick clicks as she handles the weapon like a seasoned expert. Kenna takes a beautifully lethal stance, and I admire her form. Then she shoots, eight times in quick succession, before changing the round as if she could do so in her sleep and firing another full round.

I'm so busy gawking at her poise and unflinching confidence that I don't watch where the bullets go. She fits her gun away and turns to me, no smugness, no hint of any emotion.

Then I look at her paper target.

The first round all hit dead center of the target's forehead; the second made an eerie smiling face on the chest, with two holes for eyes, six curving in a mouth.

Holy shit.

"How long have you been with Alistair?" It's the first question to come to mind at her masterful skill level since she doesn't appear much older than me.

Kenna folds her arms, leaning against the side of the shooting booth. She wears a low black tank top under her leather jacket, tucked into tight black jean pants and modest, wide-heeled ankle boots.

"I ended up with Alistair when I was fifteen," she says. "I'm twenty-eight."

She's the same age as Rhett, who got away from Alistair when he was sixteen, and I realize with wide eyes . . .

"You knew him."

Her jaw tightens. It makes me want to press, to know if they were friends, but my mention of it doesn't thaw the ice in her green eyes.

"I came here because we need to talk about what to do about Silas," she says, matter-of-fact.

It's often like she doesn't know how to socialize, only to give and take orders, and that tightens my chest for her even though we're not friends.

"It seems pretty clear. Your attempt to *not* earn his attention seems to have attracted it more so."

"He's likely seen hundreds of dancers on that stage. He's not really interested in me—he's only finding a thrill in figuring out who we are and who we work for. You need to do a better job of convincing him you're not hung up on your dead ex."

Those last words pierce me, aimed with precision and no apology, like her bullets.

I take a second to breathe and remember they're not true.

Rhett is alive.

Rhett is alive.

Rhett is alive.

My mood plummets. Impatience starts to grow reckless roots through me, and the phone Rix gave me becomes a dead weight in my pocket. I often want to throw it out of frustration. It's been more than a week of silence.

"Once you make him believe you're all in for him, he'll focus his attention on you," Kenna says.

"Or we could let him indulge in his fixation on you. It would still give Alistair the alliance."

"It won't," she snaps. "I'm no one, Ana. Absolutely no one. There's not a chance Damien Balenheizer would ally with Alistair because his son chose someone like me."

For some reason, I pity Kenna as much as I admire her.

"Did you know him?" I ask again, barely a whisper since Kenna keeps herself in the middle of a minefield, ready to detonate anything that could break her defense.

"I knew Everett Lanshall," she says, so icy I shiver at it. Kenna pushes herself upright, looking me dead in the eyes. "He was a fucking coward, and he deserved the inevitable fate he got."

I decide I don't like her.

I might even hate her in the heat of the anger that rushes to the surface all at once.

My fists tremble at my sides, and her eyes dip to them.

"Are you going to bottle that rage or try me?"

I'll admit I'm fucking tempted, but I also know how futile and embarrassing it would be for me. She might see me as a fool, but I'm not about to prove I am one.

"You're all alone in this world, and you deserve to be," I say just as coldly.

Her chuckle is dark. "I'm alone because I choose to be."

"How long did you train in ballet?"

The question throws her off, and I feel like I've won something.

"I haven't."

I huff a bitter laugh. "Right. God forbid anyone observe you have a talent that requires passion of your own sweat and blood, not draining it from others."

"Keep your sights on yourself," she says, stepping closer

to me, and the space between us hums like a warning. "Right now, that means figuring out how to get Silas to fall for you and carry out this plan, or you won't want to face what Alistair might do if you fail. Don't tell him anything but what he wants to hear. And get the job done."

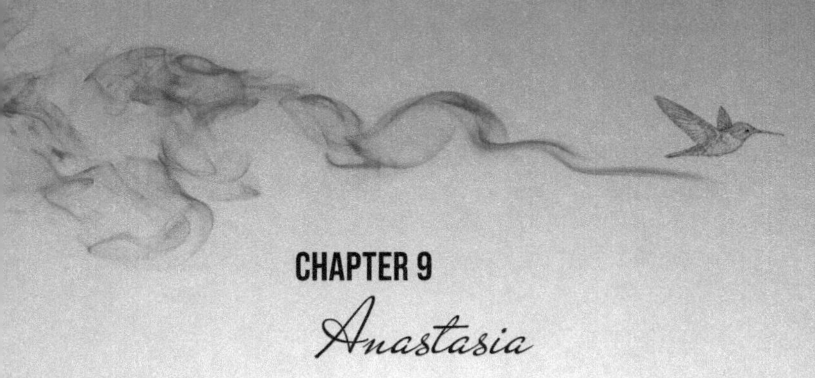

CHAPTER 9

Anastasia

It's midnight and I'm curled up on the deep black sofa in my apartment. The TV plays *Grey's Anatomy*, but after five seasons of outlandish scenarios and every couple failing, it's become mere background noise in my attempt to busy my restless thoughts.

A six-beat tone jerks me from my numb state, and I scramble to untangle myself from the two blankets I've buried myself in. Shadow leaps off the sofa, alert eyes tracking me.

It's the phone Rix gave me.

Heart beating in my throat, I snatch it from the coffee table, and there's one notification from an app I don't recognize. I tap into it and read the text:

Leave the apartment on my signal.

I shoot up and rush to stuff my feet into boots and sling on a black jacket. I pull up the hood of Rhett's sweater that's starting to look old and tired, but I don't care.

At the door I wait, hardly able to be still in my racing anticipation. Shadow sits by my heel. He never said I couldn't bring him.

The first message disappears, and I stare at the dark gray

background, chewing my thumb and waiting for another to appear.

When it does, I feel as if my heart will burst from my chest.

Hall is clear. Take the elevator to the garage floor. Don't get out until I say.

I don't miss a beat. My blood soars as I make my way hurriedly down the hall. I glance up as I reach the elevator, clicking the button too many times as if it will bring it twenty-two floors up to the top level faster.

Rix must have cut the camera, and he's probably only cutting one at a time so the missing time will be a near unde-tectable few seconds in each feed. Tony recently switched with the night guard posted outside my door after checking I was safe inside. I wonder how Rix made him wander away long enough for me to slip out.

The chime of the elevator is music to my ears, and I slip in, heading down. It's like a chase, as if there's someone after me this very second, and if Alistair discovers me missing, the consequences don't bear thinking about. He's a controlling, possessive man, so finding out one of his own has eluded him would be as good as any betrayal.

The doors open, and my heart thrums in the silence.

Then the message comes.

Now.

As I leave the elevator another instruction comes.

Left exit. Walk down 5th Avenue.

Merging into the trickling pedestrian traffic, I clip on Shad-ow's leash, more for other people's peace of mind than as a necessity. I march fast.

Another message chimes.

Slow down before someone stops you out of suspicion.

Scowling at the device as the message fades away, I try my best to slow. Be calm. But between the giddiness of hearing from Rix and the potential I could be caught by Alistair's spies, a wrecking ball swings loose in my mind.

A black car with reg XDL will approach you. Get in.

Suddenly I'm awash with doubt. Nerves. What if it wasn't Rix at the club? In my desperation I believed him, but now, reservations I should have had back then freeze me. The car approaches, and I can't move. I stare at it like a fool.

The window rolls down, and the driver—Rix—leans over the passenger seat. "Less than forty seconds until those street cameras come back on, Red," he hisses.

That snaps me to move. *Shit.* I have no other choice.

I open the back door for Shadow and then slip in the front, staring straight ahead as Rix speeds off.

"I don't bite," Rix says at my stiffness and refusal to look at him. "Well, depends who you ask, actually."

I want to relax at his humor, but my thoughts are scrambled. Shadow would bite if I commanded it. He's my security right now, lying in the back seat.

"You don't speak anymore?"

"How do I know you are who you say you are?" I rush out.

I slide him a look then. He doesn't appear offended by my doubt.

He reaches into his side compartment and then holds a card out to me between two fingers. I recognize it. As I take it, the logo of Xoid surfaces the painful memory of when Rhett showed me.

Welcome the lost, pity the found.

"I guess I am lost now," I mutter.

"Which is why, thanks to your excellent connections, you're getting a fast-track to Xoid HQ. Not many get to come here, by the way. We have many other setups in many states, but the Den is where it all began."

I flip over the card to find his initials are on it: "RB."

Beneath it is a six-digit code like the one Rhett had.

"What does the code mean?"

"When someone calls it, it connects to the phone of whoever they're trying to reach. Not a call though—instead it's like a temporary virus to them while our phones completely copy their data. We know who called, where they live, and so much more that we can usually guess why they contacted us. And then we can decide if we'll answer, and they won't know until we show up. Or don't."

I find that fascinating.

My unease doesn't fully settle from being given the piece of card; it lingers for the twenty-minute drive. When he cuts the engine, I stare out at the pitch-black deserted building beyond chain-link fencing with new anxiety.

"Afraid of the dark?" Rix asks.

I jump at his voice, not hearing him step out. He leans in his open door.

Unbuckling, I know I've reached a whole new level of reckless judgment to have gotten in a car with a stranger and let him lead me to somewhere far away from civilization in the middle of the night.

Oh well. Too late to find my sanity now.

I get out, clutching Shadow's leash tightly as I follow Rix through the dark. He has a flashlight, but we don't go through the chain-link fence.

"Where are we?" I whisper.

"It's an ex-army camp."

"Isn't it . . . trespassing? Illegal?"

"Highly."

I gawk at his back, but he doesn't elaborate to ease my new fear.

He goes through an open metal side door into a building long forgotten. It's creepy as fuck, and I feel like I've just stepped into a haunted bunker. I'm waiting for Michael Myers to appear around the next corner with a chainsaw to rattle the eerie silence.

"Never judge a place by the exterior," Rix mutters.

We step into a huge elevator, the newest-looking thing I've seen so far, and Rix presses his thumb to a scanner before typing a code into the keypad.

"Did you have to bring the wolf?" Rix asks as we start heading down.

"I may be a desperate fool to follow you in the middle of the night, but I'm not *that* naïve. He's the best source of protection I have."

"Fair point. I only say because . . . well, don't let him eat Frodo and Sam, will you? I mean, between you and me, I wouldn't cry about it, but I'd never hear the end of it from Jeremy when he gets back."

"Who are—?"

The doors slide open, and I'm taken away, thoughts stolen, at what expands before us. I step out, trying to take it all in.

It's a massive tin-looking construction, a hall with so many screens and computers, desks, and chairs seating countless people. Surveillance feeds, data, websites . . . I follow Rix mindlessly down the middle, trying to take it all in. For some reason, I imagined the "Den" consisted of Rix holed up in an apartment alone, surrounded by empty pizza boxes and soda cans. I giggle at that image now.

"What's so funny?" Rix asks, walking backward. He smiles too, and I'm overcome with how much hope he gives me.

This place.

It's real.

I'm in Xoid. And we're going to get Rhett back.

I stop walking, and people start noticing our intrusion of their workspace. It's so casual, but at the same time I can read the laser focus of everyone here. Feel the family they've found in each other, but also the gravity of *how*.

"Listen up, guys," Rix says, clapping his hands together.

I shift with the attention of the room as he silences their idle chatter.

"This is Anastasia Kinsley, Kaiser's girl." He crosses over to me, slinging an arm around my shoulders. "Which means she's *our* girl."

"'Bout time, Kinsley!" a guy shouts out. His grin is so warm and welcoming, and others begin greeting me.

I'm so overjoyed that all my reservations fade away at once. Looking over everyone, I've never felt such pride swelling in me. For all these people; for Rhett, who built this; for me, as I hope to do him proud.

A door at the far end opens, and I don't expect the elderly woman who comes out. Just then, yapping echoes through the hall, and I stiffen. Shadow growls, and then I see them: two tiny Chihuahuas come speeding toward us as if the old woman set them off as fireworks.

"Frodo and Sam?" I guess.

"Part of the 'Xoidship.'" Rix sighs, reciting his brother, I assume, with a grin.

For a second I hold my breath in case Shadow reacts badly to their obnoxious barking, but he merely watches them, tail wagging, as they snap around him like piranhas out of water, as if he couldn't swallow them in one mouthful. You have to admire little-dog confidence.

They start to calm when Shadow doesn't react, but the moment he takes a step forward in intrigue, the Chihuahua sirens are off again.

"That's it," Rix says, scooping them up, and that silences them immediately. "We don't have time for dog showdowns right now."

He carries them while nudging me forward. "There's someone I think you'd like to meet."

We head toward the elderly woman, who waits expectantly, leaning on a daisy-scattered pink cane.

"About time indeed," she says warmly when we reach her. "I've been waiting to meet you, Ana."

She heads back inside the room, which is like a small studio apartment. The scent immediately hits me: the comfort, safety, and love that any elderly person's home embodies. It's decorated with pastel florals over the sage-green couch and the table linen. She heads over to the kitchen area, which isn't so much for cooking, but it has a stove where an old kettle whistles.

"Let me get that," Rix says, putting the two dogs down, and they must feel the same sense of calm in here as they don't immediately go for Shadow. Instead their paws tap across the hard ground, over the carpeted rug, and into a small house I don't think Shadow would even fit his head into.

"Ana, this is our Oma." He introduces us, pouring boiling water into three cups.

"A pleasure to meet you," I say. *Was that awkward?* I wring my hands, unsure why I feel like getting this woman's approval is important.

"Sit, sit." She ushers me over to the four-seater dining table.

Rix brings over the tea, joining us. He begins dropping in more sugar cubes than I think anyone can take, and he adds a helping of milk.

"You live here?" I ask timidly.

"Since the beginning," she answers cheerfully.

"I don't mean to pry . . . but why?"

"Oma is a retired trauma therapist. Well, should be retired." Rix casts her a playful pointed look. "She refuses to be fired and live out her days in complete relaxation above ground, spoiled by us."

I add one cube of sugar and watch it dissolve with the swirl of my spoon.

Oma says, "I still have a mind and ears and knowledge. I'll retire when I'm dead. My grandson likes to fuss."

It makes sense. Though I wonder with a heavy heart if Rix and Jeremy still have parents.

"Oma raised us." Rix answers the question that must be written on my face. "Then she happened to find out about Xoid when Rhett and I met up and began setting it up and she decided her soap operas weren't keeping her entertained enough."

"You've never been good with secrets," she says.

Rix adds milk to her tea, no sugar. She takes a sip.

"So you help the people working here . . . or the victims they save?" I ask.

Rix answers for her. "Sometimes both. Though mostly our people. They've been through some dark shit—"

"Language, boy," Oma scolds.

I bite my lip at his sheepish look.

"Sorry. Dark *stuff*, and when they choose to join us, they know what they're signing up for. For many, getting to help others out of similar situations and shut down bad guys helps them heal, but everyone needs help. Oma is an absolute credit."

I'm completely awed by her selflessness. She waves off his praise as if what she does isn't all that much. But it's lifesaving.

"I can't imagine what Rhett's going through," I whisper. What kind of torture is Alistair inflicting on him? My panic starts to rise fast, terrified of the awful conjurings of my mind.

"We'll be here for him," Rix says. "You'll be here. I've known Rhett far longer than I've been in Xoid. We met because of Alistair, ironically enough. My dad was a drug dealer, far lower in the chain than Alistair. He was basically his footstool. Rhett frequented our house for a while to drop off new street drugs. We were twelve."

Despair fills my chest for the young boys who were exposed to far more than any child should be.

Rix continues. "I guess what I'm trying to say is, I've known every dark shade of Rhett Kaiser. He's the most resilient fucker—shit, sorry Oma—*man* I've ever known. He lives to get things done, push through hardships, and pull others out with him. He lives to save people. But he's never lived for himself. He's never let anyone save *him*. Until you."

I'm so sick of crying, but I can't help it when his words make my heart too big for my chest. It's painful. "I miss him," I whisper. "So much."

"Me too, dear," Oma says, reaching a hand over mine on the table.

We sit with Oma for a half hour before heading back into the main room.

"If you ever need to talk, dear," Oma says warmly.

"Thank you," I say.

I thought I'd feel out of place when I finally got to come here, but I feel at home. I feel so warm and welcome, and this is leaps closer to Rhett. No one looks at me like the president's daughter who doesn't possibly belong here. They don't watch me with distain for my wealth or status, and I'm so relieved that I wish I knew how to show it.

"It's been more than a week since I saw you," I say as we wander around and Rix tries to explain what happens at some of the stations.

"Sorry. We got caught up in stopping a possible trafficking target. It took longer than I thought. Rhett would be livid if we let all of Xoid's work slip to save him."

I think so too, but it doesn't make it easier to want to fight Rhett on his selflessness when he isn't even here.

"I took the liberty of making these," he says, swiping up a card-size, deep red metal wallet.

I take the offering, and there's a lever on the side, which I pull down. It opens, and I pluck out a card.

"A.K.," and below it, a six-digit number.

"It connects to the phone I gave you. Welcome to the Xoidship."

I'm speechless. It's a token of belonging that makes me feel so warm and *powerful.*

"Thank you," I say, but it doesn't feel enough for how easily he's accepted me.

Rix merely smiles, perching on the desk that is so neatly organized. Four black pencils sit in a formal line next to a straight notepad. A small black globe. A coaster with the Xoid logo. A wireless phone-charger pad. I figure this is Rix's station, but I don't expect the controlled tidiness that has me wondering if he'd combust if I shifted a pencil out of line. Definitely not an empty pizza box and soda can kinda guy.

"This is where I hack surveillance feeds, communications, and the like," he explains about the half-dozen screens around him. Some are split, with many feeds on one, and I become overwhelmed with one glance at what they're keeping track of daily.

Rhett is out there somewhere.

As the feeds occasionally change, I can't help but think he could be in the vicinity of somewhere I'm looking directly at. He doesn't know we're looking for him. Perhaps he's given up hope, believing we all think the car wreck killed him and no one is coming.

The thought leaves me hardly able to breathe, imagining his loneliness and neglect.

Then something sparks to my mind with a skip of my pulse. I ask, "Can you hack into a live performance feed?"

Rix slips a curious eye my way. "Very possible. Though I don't think we've tried before."

"What about something broadcast from the White House?"

"What are you thinking, Red?"

I bite my lip. My idea sounds highly risky, but it makes me giddy as hell. "I'm thinking it's about time Rhett Kaiser knows Xoid is active, and that we're coming for *him* this time."

CHAPTER 10

Rhett

I realize now why they tried to starve me. Sitting across from me at a long mahogany table is Alistair, dining pretentiously on his steak. I have the same meal in front of me, and though I want to fight taking anything from him, I have to remind myself it's just sustenance and it can give me invaluable strength back.

So I eat with him.

Alistair's mouth tugs a little as he chews, and I tighten my grip on the serrated steak knife against throwing it at him. I'm surprised he gave me one at all, but he knows me so well it's getting under my skin. Two guys stand in such close proximity that I believe they'd stop me before the knife could effectively launch. I won't risk inflicting the error on my little bird.

"Why are you doing this?" I grind out after too long in insufferable silence.

Alistair looks up, sets down his cutlery, and wipes his mouth before reaching for his wineglass. "We used to dine like this a lot. Don't you remember, nephew?"

"Don't call me that."

"You can't bleed out your heritage."

I don't deny that, but the way he uses the family term is like a brand. He owned me once, and now he's caught me to reclaim me. I've been suffering in torment about it. How all this time I was a damned fool to think I could catch *him*.

I've spent years reciting what I'd say to him. What I'd do. Now I have him right in front of me, I'm drawing blanks at his mercy, except for one thing.

"My parents died in a car accident," I say.

Alistair leans back in his stupidly expensive chair. "That is the truth."

My teeth grind because I don't want to say it. I want him to fucking admit it.

"I've always thought it was coincidence. How you claim to know how perfect of a son I'd have been for you. Your twisted perception tried to make me believe my parents didn't understand someone like me."

"Because they didn't," he says, his tone taking a harsh edge. "They coddled you and reprimanded you."

"That's what parents fucking do."

"No. They would have smothered you, and your dark side would have landed you in places that would try to *fix* you. Don't you see? I *saved* you."

"You took everything from me!"

The plates and glasses around me shatter with the rage that has me swiping my hand across the table. Men shift toward me, but Alistair raises a hand, and they don't touch me.

"Look in the mirror, Everett. You know we're not so different."

"You killed them."

"Yes."

I've waited eighteen years to hear that confirmation. One single word with the weight of the world attached to it. Now I have it, that crushing force sinks me back into the chair.

I want to fight the defeat threatening my resilience. It's not like I didn't already know in my heart the truth, but I guess this suffering is proof I've clung to denial all this time.

It's not that I'm shocked or that I believed it above Alistair. This is the sort of heinous crime he'll stoop to, killing his own brother and wife. It's that I wish it wasn't true for how despicably my life was shredded by one calculated, evil person my parents *trusted*.

My eyes are dead when they lift to Alistair. I didn't think I could hate him more, nor wish his death in their stead more powerfully, but I do. It's the type of loathing that tunes out humanity completely. Cancels out the whole fucking world.

I don't really judge movement or feel what I'm doing; I see blood and know my hand holds the knife plunged into the neck of one guy. Then I jab someone else with my elbow, my fist cracks against someone's jaw, and the rest is just blind violence.

Until I can't make another move, because something strikes hard against my temple, blackening my vision enough that I can't catch my fall. When the pain returns, I guess my adrenaline-fueled rage is starting to wear off.

I come to in slow blinks that bring a round of agony pounding in my head.

Somehow I'm sitting against the wall, and I manage to lift my head. Alistair crouches down as I peel my eyes open.

"You are remarkable, Everett. You just need to allow me to guide your potential."

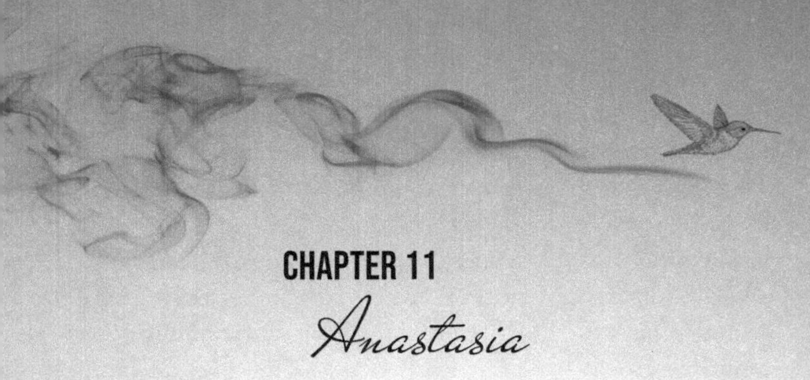

CHAPTER 11

Anastasia

I sit opposite Silas Balenheizer for the second time, thinking it doesn't matter how prepared I come, he'll always make me feel like he can see under my skin. When he looks at me, his dark eyes are all intrigue and business. Frequently, though, his attention is on Kenna, who doesn't hide her reluctance to be here as she tries to stay out of our conversation, leaning on the back of the sofa behind me.

"I find your back as enthralling as your front, if your intention is not to distract me," Silas says to her. His ankle is crossed over his knee and his elbow is propped on the arm of the chair.

I swivel my head enough to peer up at her side profile. She's watching the venue below us. She doesn't give him a flicker of a reaction, but I've come to notice he enjoys that about her.

His eyes are back on me as he drawls, "So when do I hear the proposal?"

My hands start to clam up, and I reach for my martini. "I'm not interested in a man with wandering eyes," I play along.

"As you shouldn't be. You're a stunning, intelligent woman, Anastasia. You deserve no less than a man who will boast his riches not in material things, but in having you by his side."

I believe his words aren't just pretty and hollow. Unexpectedly, I think I might be finding a trickle of respect for him. Though I can't forget I have a lot to learn about him. I don't doubt his cruelty could switch as fast as the likes of Jacob Forthson. Both he and Alistair fear and respect Silas's family name, and I remember the evil his half-brother committed and had planned for me too.

"Then won't you entertain the idea of us?" I ask.

Silas lights a cigarette, and I think it's disappointment in the furrowing of his brow. "Before I decide, I want to know, what does Alistair Lanshall have over America's most eligible bachelorette to make her such a bargaining chip to my father?"

"Nothing. I came to him."

His head tilts as he takes a drag of his cigarette and contemplates each of my words as if he's dissecting the layers of each one. "Some kind of guilty conscience for what happened to Rhett Kaiser?"

"Something like that."

He smiles like he's caught me in a lie, and my skin flushes. His company is exhausting with the intensity of it. Rhett is masterful at reading people, but so is Silas. The only difference is, Silas finds great pleasure in playing with his findings in the moment and watching his prey squirm.

His gaze flicks to Kenna again, and it's as if he switches to a different layer of the same personality each time. "Sweetheart, as glorious as those heels make your legs look, and as much as I look forward to the day I'll fuck you with just them on, you must want to rest those feet. Sit," he says.

It's the most seriousness I've heard in his commands to

her. Usually, he speaks them as flirtations he knows she'll brush over her cold shoulder. This is his concern, and I have to admit, her resilience in those platform heels is impressive.

It earns sharp daggers from her. If it wasn't for the implication she'll sleep with him, I think she would have ignored him like she's been doing all night. Then she does something I don't expect. She smiles sweetly, and I'm chilled by it.

"You're right. I am in need of a seat."

I'm tense as I watch her walk across the space toward a second set of sofas. The man reclining on one has been watching us, and I think most, if not all, of the men here are the same as last time. I'm taken aback, stiffness turning to absolute stone, when she doesn't hesitate to sink one knee into the mahogany Cheshire couch and sling her other leg over his lap.

I think the air could be cut with a knife, and I can't even bring myself to see Silas's reaction. I'm too dumbstruck by her boldness as she takes his face and kisses him. Her tight dress rises to the top of her hips.

It only lasts a beat—until his hands brace on her thighs. That's the moment Silas stands and I'm drawn back to watch him. His expression is absolutely frightening. Livid. I've been waiting to see why people cower at the name "Balenheizer," and Kenna has provoked front-row fucking seats.

His dark eyes don't leave Kenna and the man. I can practically see, *feel*, the meter of unhinged calm climbing in Silas with each second. He wordlessly holds out his hand, which someone places a gun into. Another hands him a magazine, and he loads, pulls back the slide, and clicks off the safety, keeping his simmering sights on the duo. I only know they've pulled apart from the man's protests, which turn more desperate and apologetic the closer he's dragged this way.

I don't know what to do. I sit there too stunned to intervene, and it's not my place to anyway.

Silas takes another inhale of his cigarette before setting it down and accepting a silencer, which he screws on next. He does everything with his eyes glued to this man as his number-one enemy.

Holy shit, is he going to execute him for what Kenna did?

As he's dragged over to the pool table and held down against it, I snap an incredulous look to Kenna. She merely stands with her arms crossed at the end of my couch, looking pissed off as hell.

"Everyone here remembers what I said the other night," Silas practically sings.

"I-I didn't, man. I don't know what you're talking about!" the man protests.

Honestly, neither do I.

"You haven't touched me," Kenna argues. "And you never will. This is stupid."

His smile to her isn't friendly. "I said when I touch you, I'll send any wandering hands to your doorstep from then on. Until then, this will suffice as a warning."

The man's hand is forced to splay out over the pool table by the guy holding him down, face contorted against the deep green velvet. Silas aims the gun, but he drinks in Kenna's heated stare as he pulls the trigger.

The man is prevented from crying out at the shot through his palm by a towel stuffed into his mouth before he's dragged away again, down the stairs.

I think I'm watching a movie until my spectator adrenaline starts to wear down. I glance over the balcony, but no one is looking up. Perhaps they didn't hear over the music that never stops, and if someone happened to catch a glimpse, I guess it's confirmation this is normal occurrence here.

"Well, shit," Silas says, examining the tear in the velvet and the fresh blood still soaking into it. "Now this needs replacing."

Silas hands off his gun, runs a lazy hand through his hair, and picks up his cigarette. He takes a drag and then offers it to Kenna nonchalantly.

"You make it so easy to waste your men and money," she says, dropping her arms and turning away.

"Keep testing me, little viper. It turns me on."

She casts one last glare at him as she descends the stairs.

Silas watches her with hunger in his eyes, tracking her with a devilish smile before she dips out of view. Then he remembers I exist. He extends the cigarette to me instead, but I reach for my drink.

"Another martini would be better," I say, still in a daze over that extreme reaction.

His eyes speak the order to someone through his cloud of smoke as he wanders over to the balcony. I join him, finding Kenna sitting alone at the bar.

"Magnificent, isn't she?"

"Indeed."

There's a lot to admire at a glance about Kenna. Her beauty, maybe even the challenge of her icy exterior.

I say, "You don't really know her."

"Not nearly as much as I'd like to, but I know enough. I believe everyone has a certain magnetism about them. The most expensive wine doesn't always suit the taste of the one wealthy enough to sample it."

"I hope you're not calling her cheap wine."

He chuckles smoothly. "She's absolutely priceless."

"How can you tell without getting to know her?"

Silas looks at me. "How did you tell?"

"It was a while before I realized . . ." I stop myself with the lump forming in my throat, thinking of the day I knew I'd fallen for Rhett completely.

Then I get what he means. That Christmas Day was when I

submitted to the full force of it, but looking back, I'd been falling for Rhett since we met.

"Obsession is a quick root in us all. Some just enjoy embracing the madness of it."

"I hate to state the obvious, but I don't think she feels the same."

His smile borders on fond as he finds her again. "She's crafted tough armor around herself. All she needs is to realize I'm not going to replace it, but reinforce it."

I don't know if I should be alarmed for Kenna, or perhaps I'm insane for thinking her *safe* in his terrifying sights. *No. No way.* This is Silas fucking Balenheizer, and I'm falling into some kind of twisted hypnotism to be so at ease around him. I just watched him blast a bullet through a man's hand for touching a woman he's interested in. *I* am the mad one for not sprinting the fuck out of here.

"Jacob Forthson and Alistair Lanshall speak proudly of women that way too," I say, testing lethal waters. "Then they buy and sell them like jewelry."

"I hope you're not suggesting what I think you are," he says, a deceptively playful warning.

"That this place could be trafficking just like Jacob's charity auctions? I would never."

He cuts me with a look, and I'm more than mildly relieved to see his smile rather than the flash of darkness he wears before he retrieves a gun. "Those kinds of men are the most vile of the underworld. I don't associate. I quite like our dance, Anastasia, but I'm in the mood to be *kind*. You can stop wasting your breath trying to convince me to side with Lanshall or Forthson. However, I do hope you'll still visit me with your friend."

I don't reiterate that Kenna is not a friend. And should this mission fail, I doubt he'll ever see her again.

My heart is racing. I shouldn't trust what he says,

shouldn't believe he could be above trafficking all together, but I'm running out of options.

"Your father is notorious. Your mere name has both of them willing to draw as much blood as it takes to ally with you. How am I to believe you're not just as heinous as them?"

"Because I am. You just watched me shoot a hole through a man's hand for touching what is mine, and I'll warn you, that was *highly* merciful of me. But I don't want to frighten my little viper too much too soon."

"I don't think you could frighten her," I mutter.

"Oh?"

"She's Alistair's most trusted spy and assassin. I haven't seen all she's capable of, but the glimpse I've had is enough to see why."

Silas's eyes flex as he stares at her, shifting his weight. "Fascinating." Then he eyes me with a note of suspicion. "Why are you telling me this? I don't think your master would appreciate the intel."

"He doesn't own me."

"You're turning out to be more intriguing than I anticipated, Miss Kinsley. It's not often I'm surprised."

I have no choice but to trust my instinct, but I try to tread carefully since this could all blow up in my face at any moment.

"I knew your brother," I say.

"I have two."

"Your half-brother."

From Silas's dark shift as he straightens from the rail, I can tell he knows about Matthew.

"Well then, I think we'd best have a seat for this."

I take my martini slowly this time as I've stepped onto a minefield with my exposure, and I can't be certain what will end the risky game I'm playing. If I lose Silas, it's all over.

"You'd better not be fooling me, Anastasia. I will warn

you, I don't react kindly to lies or betrayal, no matter how pretty they are."

"I knew him as Matthew Forbes," I say.

Silas finishes his cigarette, and it's the first I've seen him light another straight away. "That son of a bitch." I've noticed he runs a hand through his hair when he's mildly or very stressed. The chain-smoking suggests the latter.

"Did you know him?"

Silas looks at me as if it's a joke, but when he sees I'm serious, he huffs out a laugh with the shake of his head.

"I don't know what he told you under his new name, but he's Matt Balenheizer. He lived with us part-time, spending the rest with his mother. He's only a year older than me. You could say we were close."

So Silas is thirty years old. I'm eager to dive deeper into the trove of the infamous Silas Balenheizer as it begins to crack open.

"He said his father tried to kill him," I say.

"You keep talking of him in the past-tense."

"He's dead."

Silas isn't surprised, but he's curious. "When?"

"Just last winter, he . . . he tried to buy me. He'd previously held my friend in captivity for five years, and I never knew. All because she looked like *me*." I swallow over the marble of guilt that forms in my throat.

Silas leans forward, his expression turning frightening and serious.

I go on. "I watched him die. Jacob orchestrated the sale of me and knew he would never be able to pay what he owed. He shot him in the head. Then he planted the idea of an alliance in my mind if I wanted to take down Alistair Lanshall."

It spills out of me before I can stop it. I don't know why. It's reckless, but Silas has this bewitchment about him that pulls it from me before I know what I've done. My pulse is racing. He could take all of this to Alistair tonight, or perhaps he knows exactly what he's doing and is waiting to gather all his evidence before he feeds me to the hounds.

Fuck. What have I done?

"I should go," I say.

I find it easy to keep my cards to my chest and be patient, smart, with Alistair and Jacob. But with Silas, I've exposed too much too fast. Opened a door of vulnerability for him to exploit.

"Don't leave," Silas says as I stand. It's the softest tone I've heard from him. He pushes up from the sofa, coming closer. "Trust is a series of coin flips. Let me show you my side of this one."

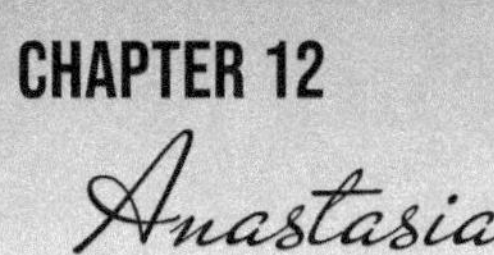

CHAPTER 12

Anastasia

I'm rolling a dart between my fingers next to Silas as he takes his turn. My aim with a gun is getting better, but I have little coordination with this game. To Silas, however, it's clearly a pastime. I'm glad for the movement though, rather than just sitting and observing the crowd of Lumina Lounge. It helps me process what we speak of.

"So Matthew was taken away by his mother when he was ten, not cast out," I repeat.

"Perhaps his mother lied to him about the why. You'll have to decide what you believe. My truth is just that. Damien hasn't earned his name on hollow gossip. He only has one rule: no harming women or children. He's a very powerful man. Matt's mother was obsessed with my dad even when she found out he had a mistress. Out of respect for her, he kept the marriage and provided for them in another home, but he moved my mother into his own house to have me, then eventually my two brothers, a year apart. When I was nine, Damien finally divorced Matt's mother to marry mine. Matt's mother turned crazy, obsessive, and for my mother's safety he cut all ties, but for our

sake, as we'd grown to know Matt as a brother, he requested joint custody. She told him no, she'd met someone else, and he figured it wasn't worth the battle. We later learned she'd met this *someone else* years ago; they already had a son together."

I throw my dart, which hits the outer ring, crooked. "He said Damien tried to have them killed."

"Like I said, his mother likely spun that story in her own delusion. I have no doubt he was firm and clear with her. Maybe he did threaten her if she threatened my mother in any way. People interpret things how they want to hear them sometimes."

Silas went to retrieve the six darts we'd thrown, stalking back with them.

"Do you think he could have turned out differently . . .? Do think all of that with his mother, who his father is too, made him the monster he became?"

"Honestly? No. I don't believe rape, battery of women, and seeing flesh with a price tag can be blamed on nurture or blood relations. I don't believe there are any *what-ifs* to a person's circumstances for that. There are criminals like me—and I've warned you before, I'm among the most wicked of them—but then there's pure evil. Nothing more than sick, vile pleasure. If Matt were alive, now I know all he's done, I would kill him myself."

He says it so cold and confidently. He despises what Matthew did even though he doesn't know me or Nina, or if there were others. This is his side of trust. And it's time to flip a new coin. Each one feels dangerous, but Silas might be my only hope to get to Rhett.

I can't help the glance I spare behind us. Kenna sits nearby, on a stool by the private bar now, leaning with her elbows on it as her crossed leg swings and she idly watches the crowd, lost in thought.

Silas hands me three darts, voicing his observation quietly. "You don't trust her?"

"I barely know her. I've never truly been in Alistair's service, but she has, for more than thirteen years. She's his best spy. It's her job to tell him information he wants."

"She's never smiled—not truly."

"Your point?"

"Do you know *how* she came to be in Lanshall's service?"

"No." I shift my eyes to him then as a muscle in his jaw flexes as he watches her.

He asks tightly, "How do women usually end up in his service?"

I frown. "He deals in trafficking, but I don't know any other women there recruited against their will."

"You know one of his locations. One of dozens, Ana."

"She— No, she can't be there against her will. I'm pretty sure she'd assassinate him tomorrow if that was her wish."

Silas sets down his darts, and I shiver at the change in him this topic has evoked. I watch him. It's as if he's dissecting every possible prospect and scenario regarding Kenna Radley and Alistair Lanshall.

"How do you know she's just an assassin and a spy?" he asks. His dark eyes lock on me, and I feel the threat in them. He studies me as if he's waiting for the slightest reaction that will give him reason to make me his enemy and shatter the small dose of trust we've built.

"I . . . I don't. I've only been there just over three months, and the first time I even seen Kenna was for this task."

Something I said relaxes an inch of him, but his mind is still storming.

"Wouldn't it be highly possible she was sold to him young, trained by him, and now used by him? For all we know, she has nowhere to go, and perhaps there are more *skills* of hers he's exploited as his *best*."

I realize what he means. Why this is getting to him so much that I'm beginning to fear he might march out of here and confront Alistair for the sure answer himself. He thinks Kenna is sleeping with Alistair, perhaps against her will. If not by force, then by manipulation.

Now I have the idea in my head, it's racing my thoughts too. She's so cold, distant. Kenna wears steel around her mind, heart, and soul. What if that's the only way she copes with things I can't begin to imagine?

"Oh god," I whisper.

"Don't say that. I'm already one loose thread away from doing something very reckless."

"You can't do anything—please."

"Give me one good reason why I shouldn't pay our friend Lanshall a visit right now to discuss this alliance that will begin and end with a bullet in his eye?"

My heart pounds; my skin slicks. He can't. *He can't.*

"Rhett Kaiser is alive," I blurt.

I'm panting shallowly now, braced on a razor's edge of anticipation. That shocks him enough to snap his eyes from Kenna to me.

"He's alive, and I need your help to get him back."

Silas's eyes flex. "So you've had an agenda for me this whole time, and it started with Alistair Lanshall?" he says darkly.

"No. I didn't know I'd be meeting you, but I think that has always been Alistair's idea with me. He staged Rhett's death and thinks all this time I've believed it. Honestly, I had no real help or proof until recently."

"Let me guess—Xoid?"

"You know of it?"

"Of course I do. I actually might say I admire their work."

It's a small trickle of relief amid the tension to explain what I can while Silas balances all our fates in his hands.

"They have a guy who made it into Alistair's network to confirm Rhett is being held somewhere. Then Alistair told me about you—his plan for *us*—and I had to come up with something. Truthfully, I didn't have high hopes after what I'd been through with Matthew and what I'd heard about your father. I thought you would be just like them, and that I would have no hope here. But you're not like them. At least, I really still hope you aren't."

I can hardly breathe, and he must notice. Silas takes me by the elbow over to the sofas, a little farther away from Kenna. Someone brings me a glass of ice water.

"You're not what I expected," Silas says.

I huff a laugh because Rhett told me that before, and I still don't know what it means.

"What did you think I could do for you?" he asks.

After the ice water numbs the pain in my throat, I try to pick up from where I tapered off in panic. "Jacob knows I'm with Alistair. I've been feeding him information to keep him satisfied. Alistair doesn't know about my meetings with him, or I'm sure I wouldn't be sitting here. Before you, I planned to tell Alistair something about Jacob and have him believe it was intel I gained for him through the skills he taught me. I wanted to get it right and watch them tear each other apart before I stepped in and finished the job. If Rhett were truly gone, all I wanted was to avenge him. Then, when I knew he was alive, I asked Jacob to find him, and in exchange I would get you to meet with him instead under Alistair's radar."

I laugh at myself, because this must sound like child's play to him. A woman in over her head in a den of vipers. It's too late to stop the confession now.

"I hoped to ally with you. As me, not for either of them. I wanted you to help me by meeting with both of them of your own interest, as a ruse to keep them content and busy. Then help me get Rhett back."

Silas takes a long, deliberate breath when I finish. Then he takes out a cigarette, even offers me one, but I decline, and he leans back, folding his ankle over his knee and hooking his elbow over the back of the sofa.

My knee starts a nervous bounce as I watch him. It shakes the water in my glass, and I'm starting to get too cold, so I place it down and rub my arms.

Silas doesn't speak. He's thinking deeply over every detail I've so brazenly spilled and deciding if I'm worth his efforts to save. He's taken three drags of his cigarette, watching the smoke as usual. Sometimes he blows it out carefully, deliberately.

Then he chuckles, as if he's gotten to a part in my story in his mind that amuses him.

"I've given you several sides of my coins," I say. Maybe it's pitiful, but I'm crumbling here.

"Indeed, you have. I'm bathing in my riches right now," he answers with a smile.

"Please."

"Don't beg, Ana. You've come this far without it, and I much prefer the woman who stormed in here with the confidence of this rather . . . interesting plan. I could be exactly like Matt. I could be far worse. What might you do then?"

"I would have still tried."

"So what's in it for me?"

"You want to relocate to D.C. You have this club, but you'll want to expand. I want to take down Alistair and Jacob, and once I do, their empires will be waiting, full of power, influence, and money, for someone to step in."

"I have no interest in the trafficking business."

"Come on, Silas. You may be a criminal, but you're a businessman. I've seen the meticulous control you have in here, how they fear you, but they respect you more. You'd know exactly how to keep what you want out of the wreckage we make of their networks. Kill off the pure evil and pluck at the bones that are left that will still hold astronomical roots of wealth throughout several states. You'll have done something your father never attempted. People won't hear the name Balenheizer and think Damien first—they'll think of Silas, the man who single-handedly took D.C. all for himself."

"Single-handedly?"

"The president's daughter can't very well take any of the credit."

Silas leans in, his eyes dancing with fiery delight. "Well, well, Miss Kinsley. You had me worried there for a second, but you are one incredible woman."

"All I want is Rhett back. Him, Xoid, they won't want any credit either. Truthfully, you'll still be operating other kinds of shit they take down daily, but we'll help for this goal of stopping the trafficking . . . It would be worth it."

"I wouldn't want them to stop. A little threat keeps the fire burning."

My anxiety can't be settled yet. Even if this is his agreement, he could decide at any moment it's too much, too difficult, and abandon me. But for now, it's the best chance I have.

"He must mean a lot to you," Silas says, taking a drink. "Rhett Kaiser."

"He's everything to me."

Silas doesn't fully look back at Kenna, but in the shift of his eyes to his shoulder, I know where his thoughts have gone. Perhaps he's wondering what it would feel like to have someone regard him that way.

"One day at a time," Silas says—the best sort of alliance agreement I'm going to get for now. "In the meantime, I have a condition."

My stomach knots, and he tries to suppress his amusement, so I know it's going to be something I won't like.

"I want to know everything about Kenna Radley."

"Don't you have the means to get that yourself?"

"The moment she stepped inside Lanshall's home she became untraceable, unless I want to risk a lot of shit, and then we would not have a prospective alliance. But what I want to know is if she's there by her will."

"I have just as much chance of getting close to her to find that out as you do."

Silas shrugs. "You have more opportunities. That is my condition. Get me that answer—and it had better be the truth —and you have yourself a deal, Anastasia."

I inwardly groan. *Talk about impossible.*

"And a note for encouragement. If you can trust her enough and get her in on this, you have my word I won't back down. You'll have Kaiser, and I won't stop until their empires are ashes."

CHAPTER 13

Anastasia

The room hosting the live performances in the White House is packed full. I stand behind a curtain, and for once I'm not nervous about the crowd. I'm pacing and struggling to get my thoughts in order, but it's all to do with Silas and Xoid and Alistair and Rhett. Playing my violin in front of people is the least of my problems right now.

"You okay?" Adam asks. He must have talked his way back here to where only the performers are supposed to be.

"Fine." My answer is short, but not for lack of wanting him here.

I'll be the last to perform as requested, and I'm bubbling with adrenaline knowing it's soon as a beautiful singer entertains the crowd.

"You're making *me* dizzy," Adam says, taking my arms to stop my pacing.

"You know how I get for these kinds of things," I say.

"I know. Deep breaths, okay? I'll be right here." I appreciate his comfort. Among everything that was broken in me, Adam and Riley have remained the only things that aren't sharp and cutting.

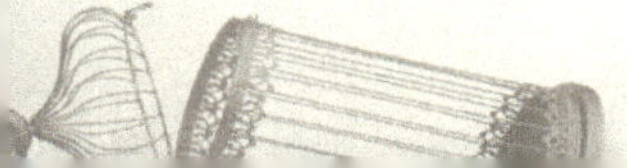

Riley left for New York a week ago, and I miss her here, though she swore she was tuning in to watch and would call right after.

"Distract me with something else," I say, watching the beautiful singer onstage.

"Henry and I are finished."

That steals my attention, and I whip around to him. "What happened? You were only just rekindling."

I'm sad for him. Adam seemed so taken by Henry. I never met him, but he sounded kind and charming.

Adam shrugs, but it does little to brush off his dejection. "He met someone else. It seems pretty serious, or at least it could become so, whereas I come with the caveat of, 'Please be patient, because I'm still locked in the closet and don't know if I'll ever get out.'"

My face falls. "You deserve someone who can be patient for you."

"Yeah, maybe."

He speaks like he's already given up hope. I can't bear the thought of him settling for someone just because he doesn't believe anyone will understand his life and why he's not ready for people to know about his bisexuality.

"Have you been getting into any more trouble?" he asks. "What was the deal with that asshole in the bathroom at the club who claims to know Rhett's alive?"

"He's, uh, Rhett's friend. His name is Rix," I say.

While Adam knows Rhett's credentials as Secret Service were fraudulent, I haven't gotten around to telling him the whole story yet.

"Be careful, Ana. You're vulnerable to exploitation when it comes to him," he says.

"I know that," I snap. "I'm not naïve. You don't know what I do."

"Then tell me, please. I've been trying to make up for last

year, and I'm being patient as fuck, but you still don't trust me."

I sigh deeply. "It's not that. It's just . . . it's dangerous shit I'd rather no one else was involved in."

He gives me a pleading look. "I *want* to be involved. If it were me, you'd want in too."

I purse my lips at that, remembering how it was with me and Rhett. I wouldn't have accepted his refusal to keep me out of his affairs once I knew about it.

"Fine. It starts with this," I say.

A round of applause breaks out as the singer finishes and begins to walk offstage.

"With what?"

"Just watch."

The host announces me after a short speech and a brief interlude. I take a deep breath, thinking of Rhett, his confidence in me.

Then I walk on with a bright smile and my chin held high.

"It's a pleasure to perform for you all tonight," I say. I can make out most of the rows of seats, especially my parents sitting at the front. Even my dad is smiling with a warmth I've missed dearly.

I'm doing this for them. And for Rhett.

Wherever he is, I hope he sees this broadcast. Alistair might be making him watch me if only to make him suffer, to make him think I've moved on and I'm happily living my life without him.

When my accompanying pianist begins, I lift the violin to my chin, and I play.

For a few minutes I forget the crowd and pretend it's Christmas Eve again. I've chosen to play the same song as that night, and Rhett will know it's for him. Even though he's alive, grief still holds a tight fist in my chest, and it won't release until I see him for myself. Hold him for real. Our future together balances on a fragile thread, and I try to wrap more promise and determination around it as I play this song.

I feel the cold and the snowfall. I feel Rhett's eyes on me. Then, as I finish, I expect to find him pulling me into him, and instead the hall of strangers and the buzz of applause shatters the dream.

I don't move, glancing over the crowd, who are pleased and clapping and joyful. I watch them all as their attention is stolen by the screens around featuring the feed of my performance. I look too as the image of me on this stage flickers with an interference. I bow as it changes from me to a black screen.

Then the animation plays—a serpent that weaves its way across, loops around, and crosses over itself, forming the infinity symbol. Xoid.

Then I smile at the addition, at the little bird that flies over and stops at the serpent's head.

The little bird *can* survive in the pit of serpents.

The crowd is restless, confused, and scared as the image keeps flickering from me to the mysterious advert. Security dart around the place as if the interference is the warning of a live threat. One comes for me while others escort my parents out. I reach Adam, who puts his arm around me as we're instructed by security on where to go, and my adrenaline races with triumph.

Adam leans in, speaking quietly. "Shit, did you have something to do with that?"

I'm giddy as fuck inside, but I try to keep it from my face to appear as shocked as those around me. "You sure you want to know?" I ask, giving him one last chance to back out.

He blows out a breath. "At least it'll be a party in hell."

Adam is the one pacing now, in the room the two of us were dumped in while security clear the house and try to figure out what happened. I explain what I can to him about Alistair and Jacob and Xoid. I leave out a lot about Silas for now.

"How do we know he'll see it? Shit, all this time . . . Who knows what he's been going through? Fuck, sorry, I know you're probably thinking that too. But has Forthson not found him yet? And fuck, it's all over if either of them get even a slight tip-off about your secrets."

"Adam—"

"And this Balenheizer guy sounds real slippery. But Xoid, now that's impressive. Kaiser always seemed intimidating as fuck, but a whole underground network of illegal crime-fighters?!"

"If you would just—"

"I mean, I *have* to see the setup. You can take me, right? Trusted advisor of Kaiser's girlfriend and all. This is some wild movie shit. I'm still not certain you're not just pulling my leg here—I wouldn't be surprised after the dick I was to you last year—"

"Adam!"

He stops his rambling then as I massage the tension he's building in my head.

"Don't make me regret telling you. If you can't handle it—"

"Of course I can," he says. "It may be twisted of me to find excitement in this, but it's been so dull lately with postgrad shit over and nothing to do but stare into the face of my father's disappointment."

"I know the feeling," I mumble.

He gives me a look of understanding as he throws himself into the armchair. "I bet they compare disappointment scores over presidential whiskey."

I'm leaning against the windowsill, surveying the guests leaving and security still being excessive.

After all that was exposed by the anonymous tip-off I knew was from Jacob early this year, Gregory Forbes was put behind bars. Adam's father, Rolf Sullevan, stepped in as vice president. The nation called it the most amicable partnership in American history given they'd run as competitors in the presidential election.

"What do you plan to do when we manage to find steady ground in a sane life?" I ask.

Adam groans. "Not you too. Do you have a plan?"

I huff a laugh. "Not exactly. The tragic woes of rich kids."

"Do you think it'll ever feel like we earned it? That we can decide on a career and belong in it for what we offer, not for who we are?"

"I think it depends how much we lean into our name, I suppose. Use it for gain."

"It's a gain without trying."

I understand what he means. I've often wondered the same, and it's why the dream of opening a school felt *right* to me. My name could be used for good, for someone else. I don't tell Adam about it. It feels too fragile right now.

"There's a woman in Xoid—she's absolutely brilliant. She comes from a *very* high-profile family, like us in a way, but she helps Xoid with her talent and connections for nothing in return." My chest constricts as I think of Allie.

"Yeah? Can I meet her?"

"She's missing," I whisper.

Adam's look turns grave. He's starting to see the gravity of what we're up against. It makes him think. "Have you still not heard from Liam?"

"No," I say with a heavy heart.

I've read the last text message he sent me just before Rhett's accident many times: *Meet me at Twilight.*

He's been missing for more than three months since, and no one has been able to find him. I've been tormented that I didn't see the text to go to him, not even knowing where he wanted to meet me. There's a warrant out for his arrest now, and for that I'm glad he's not here. Maybe they'll find him innocent of his father's crimes, but I'm too afraid there's something that will land him in prison to rot with Gregory. I wouldn't be able to live with that. I believe he's in hiding. I just wish he would have told me, trusted me, before he left.

"So," Adam says, pushing up and wandering over to me. He looks at my earring and his mouth curls. "When do I get my serpent?"

CHAPTER 14

Rhett

Ana is performing tonight, and Alistair is making me watch. She's an absolute spectacle without having to do a thing. Her full-length black dress exposes one glorious leg with every movement, and I'm hypnotized the moment she comes on screen.

I stand from my lax position on the mattress, compelled to her as if she's within reach. Her red hair is curled and braided away from her face to show off her perfect sculpture. Those hazel eyes bore right into the camera that closes in on her, and it's as if I could just reach out . . . just touch her once . . .

The static hum of the TV against my fingers is a worse lashing than the leather that scored my flesh last week.

She begins to play, and I'm slammed, utterly broken, to hear the song she played on Christmas Eve last year. Is it a coincidence? No—it can't be. She could have chosen any song. In my misery I choose to grapple with the small dose of warmth that she's playing this song for us. For me. Even if she's moving on, she hasn't forgotten.

I know this is why she never wears color anymore. At first

I thought that a coincidence too, but now I'm certain it's deliberate. She believes I'm dead, and she's still mourning.

Oh, little bird, don't cage yourself for me.

She was so free and light, and I never should have infiltrated her life and let her care for me so much that it's affecting her even after this much time.

When her song finishes she looks around, so sad and lost, only for a second before she fixes on a mask for the crowd. I'm torn to fucking shreds.

The TV starts glitching, and I assume they're about to cut the feed, leave me here in silence and solitude as my mental torture. I start to turn away, but a flicker in the corner catches my attention. It skips my pulse.

What the fuck?

A serpent head snakes across the screen. I've seen this animation before. I blink hard several times, believing wholeheartedly this is some delusion I'm conjuring in my delirium.

He's truly breaking me. I'm losing it.

I watch as the serpent crosses into the infinity symbol. Xoid's symbol.

The picture is still changing between this and Ana. This and Ana. When she smiles, it's as if my whole world erupts, and I know it's not a trick. Not an illusion.

What I haven't seen before is the addition of a little bird that stops at the serpent's head.

What are you up to, Anastasia?

Have Xoid found her? But why the message, unless they know . . .

They know I'm alive. Or at least they believe it enough to hope I'll see this. I stumble back as the screen turns fully black, and nothing comes back on.

I brace my hands on the back wall, replaying her performance. The sign. Every small flicker. I'm shaking with dread and terror and euphoria. I don't want Ana involved any more than she already is. If Alistair finds out she had anything to do with that display . . . I can't fathom what he'll do to her, and I want to explode with the rage in me.

It's been too long. They've won for too long, and I have to get the fuck out of here. There may be little of me left by the time I do, but I want to lay those last pieces of me at Ana's feet, or use them to destroy every last evil who ever set their sights on my little bird.

The door groaning open doesn't evoke anything in me anymore. I don't anticipate what they'll try to do to me. I just become hollow and brace for the worst.

"My favorite time of the week," Micah sings chillingly.

I've met his kind before—the truly sick in the head kind —but this is the longest I've had to tolerate one at their mercy.

I'm led down the same path as the last, so I know what's coming. After Alistair's visit, I know he's pivoting on what he's conditioning me for. Trying to break me for.

Sure enough, when we enter the same room Jack was in last, there's another kid in his place. The same age, around seventeen, and my fear is that they'll keep getting younger. Forthson's brother is only twelve.

Of course, Alistair has many in his service that would carry out the task of assassinating a child. *Sadistic, evil fucks.* But he wants it to be me. He knows it's the worst thing he could make me do.

Micah wanders over to me, dark eyes sparking with amusement. He holds the same revolver.

"I know each time I give you this you're going to wonder if there's a bullet inside. If you knew, I'm certain you would try aim for me, and that makes this so thrilling. You can take the chance. Let me warn you though. If you pull that trigger on me and it's empty, the missing bullet will end up in Ana. We won't kill her, of course—that would be such a waste. But I wonder how many shots she can take to that perfect body of hers."

I've been forced into a twisted version of Russian fucking roulette.

If there's a bullet and I choose wrong, aim for the kid, I'll kill an innocent. I've done a lot of heinous things in my life, but this would be irredeemable. I wouldn't know how to live with myself.

If there isn't a bullet and I choose wrong, aim for Micah, he'll hurt Ana.

He places the gun in my hand, and it feels exactly like the last time. I need to shoot the full round before he'll let me go, and it's near impossible to tell the added weight of a single bullet.

The kid is blond this time. With blue eyes. It's almost like looking in a damn mirror, and I can't allow myself to feel this personally. I have to turn my heart to ice and my mind to steel. Each time I face this, the chances of a bullet being loaded are higher.

"His name is—"

I lift and pull the trigger before I can hear the name. I round off again. And again. And again. Each time the click pounds in my chest and slicks my skin. I'm braced for the impact to change. Again. Again. And . . .

The final round *clicks*.

My next breath shudders out of me, and I throw the fucking gun at the wall as the kid cries hysterically, muffled by his gag. He pisses his pants too, and I can't blame him. I don't know if they'll meet death anyway beyond my test here.

This is the most cruel and villainous form of torture Alistair could have forced upon me, and I can hardly clamp my fists tight enough to stifle my tremors of fury.

"Your dedication is impressive," Micah comments.

I have to fucking hit something, and before I can care

about what the repercussions will be, I've spun around. The guy behind me is near double my build, but he goes down at the impact of my fist on his face. I don't register anything else but my feral blind attack on this man. I land punch after punch, and he's too bloodied and disoriented to fight back. They let me take my rage out on him as no one comes to haul me off. I'm certain they'll let me kill him, and in the heat of this release I'm not certain I won't when this guy works for Alistair and I know no mercy for that fact. Until a spark of defiance in my mind reminds me this is what Lanshall wants. The blood, rage, and savagery. The killer. The monster. The person who will do the worst for him.

Pushing up, my breaths heave out of me, and I don't recognize myself right now. I want to claw myself free from my own mind and body, but it's the one place I can never escape.

My eyes catch on the gun.

There would be one way.

One bullet.

The thought creeps up from the depths of my mind like a dark old friend. The next time I hold a gun with the chance of a bullet inside, there won't just be two choices. There'll be three.

Micah, the kid . . . or me.

CHAPTER 15
Anastasia

"That was insane! Completely epic!" Rix gushes.

He's still talking about the stunt we pulled off by intercepting the live feed to broadcast Xoid's logo. Everyone in the Den is buzzing with the excitement of it, and though my thoughts are distracted by Lanshall and Silas, I'm uplifted by the spirits in here considering the grimness they experience daily.

"How the fuck do you hack into such a thing?" Adam asks from beside me.

Rix still isn't best pleased I've brought him with me, and the reminder Adam is here drops his eager expression.

"Not something you'd understand," Rix says.

"No one would understand unless they're shown," I argue, meeting his look with a partial plea to *try* to be receptive to Adam.

"Are you sure we can trust him?" Rix grumbles, folding his arms as he leans against the desk.

"Hello? Right here," Adam says as bitterly.

"I'm trying to forget that," Rix counters without looking at him.

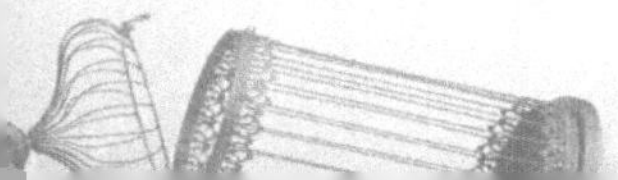

"You're an ass," Adam shoots.

"Never would have pegged you as the type to think of a guy's ass, pun wholly intended," Rix says, casting a devilish look at him now.

Adam shifts and turns away, trying to disguise the pink creeping up his neck. "Whatever," he mutters.

I've never seen Adam so at a loss, conceding so easily. I pin Rix with a warning look. "I trust him, and he's got more to offer than you're willing to see. No one would have believed me capable of anything if it wasn't for Rhett."

Rix looks back at the many surveillance feeds in front of us. "Fine, pretty boy," he says, dragging out a chair. "Let's see what you've got."

Adam lifts a brow at the offering, as if the chair is one of those altered to catapult him through the roof. He sits after holding daggers of warning on Rix, who delights in watching his unease. Then Rix leans over him, tapping the keys for a few seconds, which switches the feeds.

"What am I looking at?" Adam asks.

"I've been tracking my idiot younger brother," Rix says. On another screen, a map appears, and there are three red lines. "We know he's staying here. These other three locations are as far as we can track him before he disappears, so we've assumed he's been granted access to three of Lanshall's secret setups. But mostly, he goes here."

Another screen pulls up an establishment in a more rural part of D.C.

"Foxglove Country Club? My dad frequents there," Adam says.

Rix gives him a curious look. "Access here is *highly* restricted and by personal invite only."

"It's just a golf and equestrian resort . . ." Adam says, puzzled. Then his face relaxes as he leans back with a note of dread. "*Please* tell me it's just a golf and equestrian resort."

"By all official registrations, yes."

"Why do I get the feeling there's a 'but'?"

"Well, it's not like any of us are going to get an invite," Rix says, straightening. "Perhaps you can be useful after all, pretty boy."

"Can you not call me that?"

"Since you asked so nicely, I'll use it more often."

Perhaps bringing Adam in on this was a bad idea if I'll have to suffer their bickering.

"Do you think you can go with your father next time?" I ask him.

"I don't see why he wouldn't agree. He's always complaining we don't spend enough time together."

"Golf and horses not your thing?" Rix asks. I wait for the teasing remark to follow, but he actually seems curious about Adam for once.

"Too pretentious—where my father likes to go anyway. I went to another club with him once."

"So if he doesn't let you go with him . . ." I trail off.

"Guess we'll have our answer that the club is a cover-up," Rix says.

I really fucking hope Rolf Sullevan doesn't turn out to harbor some dark, vindictive secrets like Gregory Forbes.

I shake my head, pacing away with the weight of the possibility. It would break Adam if his father was involved in anything as heinous as trafficking. And I don't think I could handle the heartbreak either.

"I know my father," Adam defends at everyone's unspoken fear. "If there is a cover-up, he won't know anything about it."

"Let's hope so," is all Rix says.

The eruption of yaps as little fur bullets dart for Shadow pulls away everyone's attention. Oma comes out. A woman hugs her, and when they part, Oma is staring right at us.

"Now, who is this handsome young man you've neglected to bring to me?" Her cane taps the ground in sync with her shuffling footsteps.

"This is Adam Sullevan. Adam, this is Oma," I introduce.

"Ahh," she says, instantly recognizing the name. Her blue eyes shift to Rix for a beat. "Now it makes sense."

"Pleasure to meet you," Adam says politely.

"So posh and proper, you people are. Come here, boy. We greet with love in here."

Adam stands, giving Rix a once-over and muttering, "Never would have guessed."

Then he looks to me for help, but I shrug. He goes over to her, and I bite my lip at the awkward way he leans down to Oma's awaiting arms and she hugs him tightly with a content smile.

"So tall and strong," she says, approving of his embrace.

"Well, Oma, we have work to do," Rix says, grabbing his jacket.

"We do?" I say.

"Not you. I'm looking forward to meeting the Vice President of the United States."

"What?" Adam snaps. "No way in hell."

"You want in? This is it. Tell me now, before I waste my damned time."

Even I'm confused. "Why do you want to meet Rolf?"

"My little brother is out there. This is a place he frequents by Alistair's demand. If Adam is getting a way in, I'm damn well going in too."

"If it's as confidential as you say, it's going to be a challenge to get a plus-one invite for his *son*, never mind a plus-*two* for a guy he's never met," Adam argues.

"Best convince him how much you trust me. Lucky for us, I happen to have a particular knowledge of golf, and I'm a spectacular actor to pull off our years-long friendship you neglected to tell him about. As it so happens, I've just arrived back in town, and look at us, joined at the hip, inseparable. It's like I never left." Rix plays out the vague rundown of their story off the top of his head, and I'm impressed. It could work, and I don't doubt his ability to pull it off.

Adam, on the other hand . . . I'm concerned for his ability to act and lie to his father.

"That is *not* going to work," Adam grumbles. "And I don't want you in my house."

"Are we doing this or not?" Rix says, bored.

Seeing it as an ultimatum—this plan or leave—Adam simmers in his reluctant acceptance.

"What should I be doing?" I ask as we head out.

"As I hear, you have your hands perfectly full. We'll keep you updated. You keep us in the know about the shit with Lanshall and Balenheizer. Anything goes to shit on either end —" Rix pauses, pressing his thumb to the scanner in the elevator. "Well, make sure nothing goes to shit. There isn't really a plan B for either of us."

CHAPTER 16
Anastasia

Kenna is untraceable. Impossible. The only way I can get a moment with her is if she comes out of her shadowed seclusion to seek me out. I don't like the lack of control. The waiting. I've tried to ask around the manor for her, but all I receive are bored shrugs, scared glances when they hear her name, or grunts that mean "piss off, little girl." I hate most of the brute statues roaming around here.

I'm about to try the gym when Alistair calls my name from inside his study. I need to pass it to get to the stairs. I shiver at the slow, enticing way he speaks it, as if he's a snake charmer and I'm the cobra charmed to obey him.

When I slip inside it's an effort to keep my mouth from dropping open. I find Kenna at least. She's perched on Alistair's desk, and his hand is on her leg absentmindedly while he looks over a piece of paper. He sets it down when I enter, and those deep blue eyes never fail to cut through me.

My anxiety explodes like an ant's nest across my skin. I consider Kenna's presence, their closeness, why he's called me in here with her.

Has Kenna told him something? Is she a far more cunning

spy than I thought and did she hear all my confessions to Silas in Lumina?

"I'm losing patience, dear," Alistair says, taking off the small rectangular glasses he uses for reading. "By now I expected to have some hint that you're moving forward and that you've arranged a meeting with Silas, even though I'd much rather have had one already."

I observe his hand on Kenna. It seems relaxing for him, but not for her. She gives away nothing at all as her hands prop her up from behind and she keeps her back to me, staring off at the fire. It doesn't feel like enough to make any firm assumptions.

"He's a powerful and highly cautious man—it was always going to take time to win him over," I say.

"And are you?"

"I think so."

Alistair sighs—the kind bearing disappointment. "I don't like uncertainty in those who work for me, Ana. Are you close to achieving my job or not?"

"Yes," I amend.

I feel like a solider in front of him. He's strict and emotionless.

"Then I expect to hear from Silas Balenhaizer by week's end."

The "or else" is implied, and my confidence shrinks at the countdown he's placed on me. *Shit. Fuck. Shit.*

I have Silas willing to comply and meet with Alistair if I can find out about Kenna's desire to be here—and right now, she seems pretty damn comfortable. Was he hoping she was here against her will? Will he decide the alliance with me is off if she's happy working for Alistair?

Shit. I don't want to imagine she's been here all this time against her will, but I also fear I've lost my only hope with

Silas, and in turn failed for Alistair in this job, if she isn't. *SHIT.*

"Then we should go to Lumina tonight," I say, speaking partially to Kenna.

She doesn't look at me, and Alistair answers for her, running a hand up her calf, and only then does her leg stop swinging. Her shoulders lock a near undetectable fraction.

"My Kenna has another job tonight. I think by now you're capable on your own. She only accompanied you thus far to ensure your safety."

So much SHIT.

All the strings of my plan are fraying in my fingertips, and I'm grappling with my composure in the hope I can salvage it.

"How can you be sure I'm safe in there now?"

"If you're doing your job right, you will be. Tell me, has he fucked you yet?"

My mouth drops open, and I think my dignity falls out of it. "No."

Another of those long, disapproving stares. "Kenna tells me he's very keen. I hope you're not holding out on him. A man like Silas won't hold out long before someone else comes along."

I'm surprised Kenna would report anything positive. Silas and I have barely touched. He certainly hasn't made any moves to suggest he's interested in me that way, and he point-blank, no guessing needed, shot a guy through the hand to declare his interest in Kenna.

Perhaps that's why she told Alistair the lie. She's not interested in Silas. Maybe she's already taken by Alistair. My stomach plummets as I remember how old she was when she first came here. Did he wait? Or does he indulge in the same villainy he spreads, like the monsters he feeds in his work?

I think I'm going to be sick.

"I'd better go get ready," I say.

Alistair nods, dismissing me. I flash one last look at Kenna, but she's as good as stone, an unfeeling, immobile statue, and that disturbs me. So much I almost stay and try to insist again that I need her with me. But as Alistair looks at me, wondering why I'm still standing here, his dismissal turns to a warning, and I scurry out.

I rush to my room with a new urgency. Kenna doesn't like me—she said Rhett deserved to die for leaving—but still, I can't bear the thoughts that are wracking my mind right now. I need answers. I never expected to want to know the truth as much as Silas, but now each hour I don't know her story feels heavier. So I dress quickly, and I head to Lumina Lounge.

When Silas looks up after his next pool shot, he doesn't smile, but his eyes give away that he's pleased to see me. Or at least I can pretend like it's for me for a second before he straightens, surveying behind me, then plucks the cigarette from his mouth, casting the smoke over the balcony as he peers out in search of a particular stunning, prickly, black-haired woman.

The question bounces back to me in another glance, and I swear, it's unnerving how much he speaks with his expressions alone.

"She's not here, so you can save yourself searching the dark corners of the roof next," I say.

His displeasure isn't subtle as he passes off his pool cue, slipping that hand into his pocket as he stalks over. "Your company is divine, Anastasia, but I might find myself growing bored quickly."

I don't take it as an insult. Silas deals in thrills and madness, and he knows what I want. If Kenna won't come back and she's truly loyal to Alistair, I'm going to have to work harder to keep his interest.

"Alistair wants a meeting by the end of the week," I say.

Silas sits, always in the same place. "I like you, Ana. I admire your confidence and will to do what it takes to get your boyfriend back. But it is not my problem. I've considered what you proposed, what I could gain out of all of this, and you're right—it would be legendary. But it is also putting everything on the line for a chance. An alliance with an inexperienced princess, for all intents and purposes, and her band of vigilantes. I'm happy with my lot."

"You're content," I counter, growing panicked and angry.

"I have everything I need."

"You'll always want more. Always be in the shadow of your father."

"You have no idea how I feel when it comes to that. Perhaps I don't mind at all."

My teeth clench. I can't fucking lose this.

"So you'd do it all for a woman you don't know. Who doesn't *want* you."

"Careful."

"That's what you are, all you'll ever be—*careful*."

Silas stands, towering over me, and yeah, I'll admit, I'm fucking terrified. But I can't back down now.

He approaches me, and I can't move. I square my shoulders as if through bravery, tracking his eyes, but really, I'm rooted with the thought that one upturned palm could have someone placing a gun into it. I don't think he's above killing me with the right motivation.

"It's been an honor hosting you, Miss Kinsley. Now I advise you to leave, as your membership seems to have expired."

Silas all but banishes me from his club with a slow drag of his cigarette, blowing out the smoke into the air above me. Then he turns, stubbing it out in the black ashtray before heading over to the pool table again.

"That's it then? You just give up?"

His dark eyes cut into me, and it's the first time I've felt the tension of the whole room thicken, with a few of his men even shifting on their feet. I guess people don't tend to get to leave this place if they dare defy his clear dismissal.

"I don't give up, because I never enter into things I can't win," he says, so low and cold.

"What about Kenna?"

"If her relationship with Lanshall is genuine, I won't pursue someone who's taken."

"I can't find that out without you," I say.

Irritation flexes his eyes. "Speak clearly, Ana, before you find out how little patience I have."

"I-I don't know if her loyalty is true. But she's been there since she was only fifteen. I've not seen her in all the three months I've been there, yet today she was sitting on his desk while he—"

I falter at his white-knuckle grip on the back of the sofa.

"They might be intimate, but I don't know how long for. I don't know how she ended up there, but it can't be good, can it? It can't be innocent or coincidence. What if she was sold to him? Even if she believes she's loyal to him, she's been groomed since she was just a fucking child."

Silas closes his eyes and his head bows, almost shakes. I'm sure he's millimeters of pressure away from ripping the couch. His men are restless, either ready to sprint at any command or bolt from Silas's trembling explosion.

He straightens, and his walk to the pool table is chillingly calm. He takes a sip of his drink, then it goes crashing into the wall.

"I know you have a plan, someone you want back, Ana, but I don't know if I can wait that long when I have the means to storm in there and take her, kicking and screaming, and Alistair wouldn't dare face me to get her back."

"Please," I say gently, approaching the storm everyone is braced to bolt from. "We can have everything we want and more if we just work together. I've been three agonizing months without Rhett, believing he was dead. I can hardly look at myself in the mirror since I took the hand of the vile monster who tortured and captured the only man I've ever loved. I did it for Rhett. I had to be sure he was gone for good, and if he was, that I had the patience to get this right. To hurt Alistair worse than he hurt me."

My breath comes harder. My throat is so bone-dry it's painful to squeeze any words out, but I can't stop.

"Now I know he's been alive all this time, and I can't fathom what Alistair has been doing to him. If I knew where he was, I'd be tempted to rage there right now and get him back too. But it would never fix the fact that the monster who caused his pain is still out there. As long as he gets to keep going, he wins. Maybe Kenna doesn't want to be saved because she doesn't know she needs to be. She doesn't believe anyone is coming after her after all this time. If you take her, the man who broke her still has his empire."

"Then I'll burn it to the fucking ground for her," he snaps.

"I'm begging you," I say. "Do this with me. For both of them. We can save them and have our revenge on Lanshall in ways that'd make him beg for death. To watch as you take it all."

"I told you not to fucking beg."

Silas paces, occasionally fixing his frightening, calculating stare on me as he does. Deliberating my fate. Rhett's fate. He could abandon me completely and still get what he wants. Focus his efforts only on getting Kenna out, even if she doesn't want to leave.

And I would understand. Love is crazy. It makes people do wild things they never would have thought themselves capable of in the name of someone else. But while most harbor their obsession, whether root or full bloom, Silas wears his for the world to see.

I find myself wanting to be as bold and reckless in my love for Rhett. To make the world know nothing could get in the way of him being mine.

"All right, Kinsley. We'll try this your way."

My relief strains to burst, but it's held in the painful bubble of my chest as he lights another cigarette and approaches me with eyes primed to strike.

"I'm sure learning what Kaiser did was frightening to you. Then you dove deeper and discovered Lanshall and Forthson are terrifying. You've reached the very bottom now, princess, where everything above is like fucking paradise."

CHAPTER 17

Anastasia

I never thought I'd be able to say I sat with Silas Balenheizer across from Alistair Lanshall in the office only the most trusted of his people have ever been in.

What I don't expect is for Kenna to be sitting with Alistair on the long sofa opposite ours. At least, her body's here, but it's as if she left her mind behind. She's dressed in a stunning, modest purple dinner dress, leg crossed toward Alistair. I wonder if he's asked her to be here to make himself seem like a man of honor and respect despite what he does to other women.

Alistair has been charming Silas, but I know it's only simmering the rage he came in here with. I'm trying to play my part, as wrong as it feels. I smile fondly at Silas, turning into him, and occasionally brush the hair at his nape while his hand lies on my thigh. We're the perfect show of an enamored couple.

"She made a convincing case to see you," Silas says. He smokes a cigar this time, gifted by Alistair. I decide I hate the scent of those far more than cigarettes.

"Anastasia is in every way America's Darling," Alistair appraises.

"Don't feel the need to flatter me," I say. It's an effort not to stiffen every time I meet eyes with Silas. "We're just looking forward to growing our empires together, aren't we?"

He hears my hidden meaning, giving a wicked curve of his mouth.

"As long as I have you," he says.

Kenna has barely looked at us. Alistair lays a hand on her thigh like our affection inspires him. When it climbs a fraction higher, my fingers thread and tighten in the back of Silas's hair. My pulse skips, but it's as if I can feel him humming with an impulse to tear Alistair's hand from her body this second. Literally.

A muscle in his jaw works, and he gives me a pained smile, patting my thigh. His signal that his bloodlust is tamed for now.

"Why don't you ladies give us a moment to discuss serious matters?" Silas says.

He's only saying this because he wants me to follow Kenna. I'm not looking forward to this confrontation. Getting any information from a spy who's trained for a decade is impossible.

Kenna doesn't miss a beat, heading out without a glance at us, and I stand too, trying not to balk under Alistair's scrutiny as I leave.

Letting Kenna out of my sight for a second is enough for her to vanish. I don't even hear the resounding click of her heels, and I was only seconds behind her.

I'm skipping around this ridiculously big, stupid forest home like a new guest about to wet her pants with no directions to the bathroom. I can't miss this chance again. Silas is so close to dropping me in his plan, and I can't. Lose. Him.

My heart tumbles out of my ass with the relief of spotting

her outside an open set of balcony doors. I approach tentatively, as if she's a raven that could fly away, as she's perched on the thin railing, shoes off, swinging her legs. She blows out a cloud of smoke from her cigarette, and I almost feel bad to disrupt her seemingly rare moment of peace. It's as if no one is watching.

"I know you're there," she says, bored.

I step out. I don't know how she has the confidence to balance there. The drop is *far* down into a ravine, with this side of the house on the edge of a small cliff.

"You didn't tell me you were involved with Alistair like that," I say carefully.

"It's none of your business."

"Is that why you brush off Silas?"

She huffs a laugh with bitter notes and shakes her head in mock amusement. "Silas is nothing more than an arrogant ass who thinks he's owed what he sees. He's just like the rest of them."

"You said you were only fifteen when you came here . . . Did he—?"

"Did he wait until I was at least of an age to consent, even if still illegal, before he fucked me?"

I wince. Inside my stomach turns to liquid at the thought. But I'm getting the sense Kenna would be repelled by my pity.

"He could help, you know," I say delicately.

Kenna doesn't snap. Doesn't outrage. It's worse . . . because she shows nothing at all. She merely takes another long inhale of her cigarette and closes her eyes on the exhale.

"I'm not in need of saving. Not like you."

"How old were you?"

"Leave me the fuck alone."

"Rhett is alive," I whisper.

I don't think she hears me. My heart is pounding so hard in my ears I hardly hear it myself, and my head whips around at my reckless words, terrified one of Alistair's men is close enough. We're alone, and in my distraction I turn back and gasp as Kenna spins her legs around, hops off the railing, and steps into me in the space of a breath. At the same time she reaches to her thigh, plucking a small dagger out from a concealed sheath.

"You far surpass my expectations of how much of a pining fool you are," she hisses, her minty, smoky breath fanning my face.

"Alistair never told you," I say.

She doesn't believe me. "Because it's not true. He's been waiting to kill that son of a bitch for years. He's fucking *gone*."

I'm hyper-aware of the lethal blade at my throat.

"He's not. Alistair has been holding him somewhere."

Kenna laughs, haughty and sinister.

"You desperate idiot," she mutters.

"You don't have to defend him anymore. We're going to find Rhett, and we can keep you safe."

"We?"

I don't confirm my alliance with Silas. How this meeting is just a ruse, and the intent is to recruit her, not Alistair.

"We came for you," I say, barely a whisper when it might be the stone that trips the explosives she's crafted around herself.

But Kenna blinks as if she hears four words of another language instead. As though they're both utterly indigestible, but still, she's said them to herself a hundred times. Maybe in a dozen variations. Her press against me slackens.

"You're going to get yourself killed," she says, voice devoid of any emotion, and I stare at the ghost of her. Wherever she's gone, it's familiar to her. Cold and detached, but her only safety.

Her blade scratches under my chin as she steps away, eyes

unblinking as she says, "Absolutely everything is legal to him. He didn't wait."

My heart shatters as she confirms the worst of what I feared for her.

"He didn't wait. Rhett knew about it, and he left me here anyway."

CHAPTER 18
Anastasia

I'm silent, numb, in my shock. There aren't words to console her with what she confessed to me—not a single one that wouldn't sound like an insult to what she's been though. The childhood innocence she lost. Words for something like this are a Band-Aid to a broken bone. A cup of water to a house fire.

That's what I want to do, as I stare up at this hauntingly beautiful but wretchedly tarnished manor. I want to burn it to the ground, and I would listen to Alistair scream as he went down in flames as if it were fucking music.

I don't recognize myself with these dark, horrific thoughts. But he would deserve it. He deserves far worse.

"You ever speak a word of this to anyone, I'm not above killing you myself. I don't care who you are. I have little to lose, Ana. Don't test me," Kenna says.

The flash of vulnerability is gone, and I believe her.

"He's going to pay," I say with renewed resolution. "We're going to make him pay—"

"There is no *we*," she hisses, glancing around as if Alistair could be around the corner. "I only told you that because I

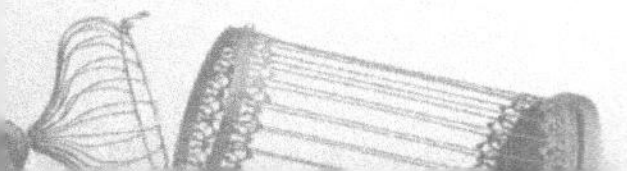

don't *care* about Rhett. If he is still alive, it's bad fucking news to me."

"You don't mean that."

For a second I think hurt, maybe even betrayal, crosses her eyes.

"You're just like him. Fucking perfect for each other, and if you don't stop, you'll end up another tragic martyr for him like Sarah Carter."

I'm slammed by that. "You knew about his fiancée?"

She doesn't respond, but she knows she's slipped up. Alistair could have told her, but she's his best spy . . .

"Have you been watching him all this time?" I ask.

"I have better things to do with my time."

I can't tell if she's lying when her poker face is so masterful.

"Kenna." I say her name gently, but she reacts to that tone like I've pricked her skin. "Come back to Lumina Lounge with me tomorrow."

"I'm tired of that place."

"You wound me, sweetheart." Silas's velvety voice joins us outside. I'm relieved Alistair isn't following behind him. He stops daringly close to a scowling Kenna. "How might Lumina be more accommodating to your tastes?"

"With you not being there, for starters."

"Would that make you dance again?"

"No."

"Why not? I've never seen a creature so free from life's burdens as you were when you danced for me."

"It wasn't for you."

"Not personally. We'll fix that soon enough. I'm a very patient man. But in my club, everything is for me."

"Well, I'm not coming back. Whatever you two are up to, I want no part in it."

"Work for me," he says before she can step around him.

Kenna huffs, a sour sound. Their arms near brush, but he doesn't touch her, as if he's savoring it, waiting, though I don't know what for. Only that if this is his infatuation with her now, I don't think she'd ever escape him if he touched her. It's as if he's aware of that possessive hold that would take over him. *Her.* They're like magnets, and it's fascinating to watch their resistance toward a pull so strong that when one finally dares that fraction closer, they'll snap together, and it will either be cataclysmic or euphoric.

"You're all the same. Work for me, bend for me, kneel for me."

"Let me rephrase," he says, low and entrancingly seductive. "Work with me, bend with me, and I'll kneel for *you.*"

"You want to use me against him."

"I want to use you in ways you could only imagine, Kenna." Her name rolls off his tongue as though he'd been savoring the taste of it in his mouth all this time. Now he delivers it coated in desire, so she'll know it's a fine wine he'll keep coming back for.

"Go to hell," she says.

"We're living in hell, sweetheart. I'm just waiting for you to decide if you're going to stay in the part that burns or let me show you how to craft fire into a palace."

She shakes her head, and my gut plummets. If Silas can't convince her either, I have no hope. He won't be patient enough to help me without her.

"I think I'll just watch from my front-row seat. Watch you all fight fire with fire, and I'll walk over the ashes when it's over and feel absolutely *nothing.*"

Silas's jaw works. His arm twitches like he's straining not to grab her by the wrist as she walks by him. "You already feel nothing," he says quietly, not turning around, and they stand with their backs to each other. "When you're ready to give in to your want to feel *something,* I'll be waiting for you."

She doesn't answer, but her pause for thought before she walks away is a small flicker of hope she might change her mind.

Silas wanders over to the balcony railing, leaning his forearms on it. "For what it's worth, it was never going to be easy," he says.

"Where's Alistair?" I ask, joining him and being mindful of the potential eavesdroppers.

"Likely boasting of my interest in his pitiful network. He thinks I don't see what this alliance would mean—that he plans to grow in power with *my* name and yet remain at the top of it all." He shakes his head, amused. "I'll admit, I'm impressed he's made such roots and maintained such an established network all this time. I don't know what his followers see in him."

"Fear, I guess."

"A trainer of cowering dogs is nothing to an alpha of wolves who follow out of respect *and* fear. Balance makes all the difference."

The silence stretches between us for a moment, and my heart weighs so heavy. I want Rhett back so much, so desperately, I think I'm losing my mind some days. I still have Jacob, who said he would find Rhett's location.

"Did you meet with Forthson?" I whisper.

"I did. Honestly, it's hard to tell them apart."

I'm meeting with Jacob by week's end, and inside me erupts the hope he's found Rhett in exchange, like he bargained. Xoid may not hold Silas Balenheizer's power to get him out, nor the alliance to tear down Lanshall and Forthson, but we're something. We're resilient and determined, and I believe in us.

"If she doesn't come, do what you have to," I say.

Silas turns his head to me.

"Forget about what I said. Forget my begs. Just do what you have to do for her."

I head back inside and hold my chin high against everything wanting to sink me to the ground. This is just one lost opportunity, and I can't be selfish for it. Not this time. Come hell or high water, I still have hope. I will get Rhett back even if I have to tear through the city myself.

CHAPTER 19

Rhett

*M*icah, the kid, or me. Micah, the kid, or me. Micah, the kid, or me. Micah, the kid, or me. Micah, the kid, or me.

"You have ten more seconds, Everett, before I choose for you."

Micah, the kid, or me. Micah, the kid, or me. Micah, the kid, or me.

Evil, innocent, or damaged.

Risk, condemnation, or cowardice.

Micah, the kid, or me.

It's the third time I've stood holding this revolver. The kid is around fifteen now. I'm trying to lean on odds, instincts, the fucking impossible, to deduce if this could be the time he's placed a bullet in the chamber.

I'm so sorry, Ana.

I want the life we painted together during that first date I refused to believe in the tucked-away Italian restaurant. It was the first day of the beginning of our lives, and we fucking deserve to see life through together.

"Fine—"

I lift the barrel toward Micah, and I *shoot*.

Again.

Again.

Again.

Each *click* is agony and flashes of Ana.

Again.

Agony.

Again.

Ana.

The tension in me pours out when I'm left still standing, facing off with Micah, and I drop the gun, bracing on my knees with violent trembles.

"Well, that was stupid," Micah says.

I snap, lunging for him, but I'm dragged back before I can even get close. One strike to my temple, and I black out.

CHAPTER 20

Anastasia

The atmosphere of Lumina has never felt so dark, so cloudy. Silas doesn't speak; neither do I. We just sit, waiting.

Kenna doesn't come.

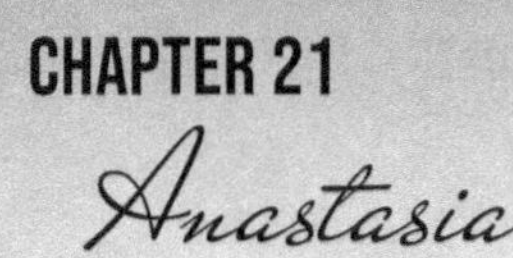

CHAPTER 21
Anastasia

My skin feels like it's rippling with shallow flame. I haven't been able to eat much for days, and I'm so tired, getting so weak, and it's only my adrenaline pushing me forward.

I sit in the rooftop restaurant with Jacob, losing my confidence. I can feel it slipping from my grasp like the cold water I'm drinking. My stomach can't handle anything else when I'm consciously trying not to excuse myself to the bathroom to throw up.

"You don't look well, darling," Jacob says. I believe his concern, but only because he'd lose interest in sickly things.

"Just a bit of flu," I lie.

He's not fully convinced, but he doesn't push.

"Perhaps this will lift your spirits," he says, pushing an envelope toward me.

I'm already lightheaded, and my vision sways with the sudden burst of hope I'm afraid to feel. "Did you find him?" I whisper.

"I did."

I don't really feel the chair beneath me anymore. I don't

hear the low chatter of the other diners. I swallow hard against the vomit that rises in me, because I can't quite believe it. I stare and stare at every crease of that white envelope as if Rhett will be inside.

He *is* inside. And outside. My eyes cast over the city. He's *right. There.*

I dare to reach for it, but Jacob's hand stops me. "First I need you to sign this," he says, sliding another document to me.

"What is it?"

"Do you want Kaiser's location or not?"

The only part visible is the signature area, already signed by him on one side. I understand the gravity of putting my name on a document like this, but he won't yield to me, and I want Rhett too desperately to risk him taking back the intel on where he is if I argue.

Jacob offers me an expensive fountain pen, and I scrawl fast, trying to pretend I don't feel the condemnation in doing so. I watch the ink dry with a thundering heart and set the pen down.

"You've done well, Anastasia. You've earned this."

I fight the sting in my nose. Force back the tears pooling in my eyes. All my exhaustion bears down at once, and I have to take a moment. He takes his document back and hands it to one of his men. I take the envelope with Rhett inside, and my fingers clench as if Jacob will try to snatch it back.

I have to move fast. Now. I have to get this information to Rix so we can begin our plan, which has to happen before Silas breaks.

If he moves first and takes Kenna from Alistair, everything will be exposed. He'll know I betrayed him and that there was never anything between me and Silas. Jacob will hear about how I played them both. Alistair will move Rhett, maybe even kill him, in his rage. I don't know what he'll do to me.

It's become a race.

"I must get going," Jacob says.

I always leave first, but I can't. I think if I stand I'll collapse before I reach the door, and I curse myself for the neglect of my body and the stress that's been eating me alive.

"I think I'll get something to eat," I say. It's not a lie. I need to try holding something down to get my strength back.

Jacob stands, buttoning his suit jacket. "I'll be seeing you soon, my love."

The term of endearment crawls over my skin. I hope to not see him anytime soon, but I smile.

When he leaves, I inhale a new clear breath. A tear escapes, a crack in my bottle, but I swipe it away.

I spend the next hour forcing down a chicken salad. I've already sent a picture of the location to Rix, who has it pinned, guys already being assigned to scope it out first in case it's a trap.

We're coming for you, Rhett.

Now I'm riddled with terror over how we'll find him. How many pieces Alistair will have made of him. But I'm ready to love each one for as long as it takes to put him back together.

The food helps, and I take a long breath of determination as the sun starts to set. I head out and slip into the car Tony drives. I keep a tight grip on my phone from Xoid, antsy for an update. The street speeds by like my thoughts, a blurred, rushing mess. My knee bounces, and I taste the blood in my mouth from biting my thumb raw.

It's when the car slows to turn at a junction that my awareness starts to trickle back. I stop biting. He's supposed to take me home, but I recognize the route to the secluded manor.

"Why are you taking me there?" I ask.

"Alistair's instruction, ma'am."

Now I'm concluding the worst. That Kenna has told him

everything. Silas has kidnapped her and I'm to blame. He's found out I know Rhett's alive.

The effort I put into eating and holding down the salad is about to be wasted when we pull up at the hauntingly familiar house. I hope to one day stand before it in ashes instead.

I head straight to Alistair's office, knocking before entering. Kenna is here, and that brings on a new hot flush. I swallow down the sickness threatening to show them both my measly dinner.

She's not dead. Not kidnapped.

It's twisted to have hoped for the latter, if only because I wanted to believe my intuition was right and Silas was a lesser, if far more powerful, evil than Alistair.

Alistair sits in his tall chair by the fire. Kenna stands by his desk and regards me with no emotion at all. I'm used to it, but I still wish she would yield something.

"Sit, Anastasia," Alistair orders. It sends chills down my spine.

Hot and cold, I can't regulate myself. I've spent so much time pushing through everything I should have felt in these three months, and now it's all punishing me, reversing the resilience I've built in myself. The fear of him; the dread of what he could do. I've not faced any punishment before, and I think that's about to change.

Be brave, little bird.

I breathe. I calm. I sit.

I'm offered a glass of water, which I take eagerly, but I sip it carefully.

"I'm rather tired today," I say. "Why am I here?"

"It's been a week, and you've not been back to Lumina."

Alistair doesn't even look at me. He smokes a cigar and watches the fire, because this isn't an interrogation; he holds all the answers.

"I didn't realize I had a schedule to be there."

"Silas won't answer my request for another meeting."

"He's a very busy man."

"Ana." He drawls my name, and when his blue eyes do shift to me, they're testing. "Tell me why I've been told Silas has also met with Forthson."

My blood runs cold. *Shit.*

Shit. Shit. Shit.

I don't lift my eyes to Kenna to figure out if she betrayed me. It would give away that I even thought it, and that's as good as proof. Kenna has no warmth toward me, certainly no allegiance. If Alistair was breathing down her neck, I can't blame her for giving something up.

"I guess he wants to be sure the competition is worth dropping for this."

"You see, I'm not convinced you're doing your job as well as you displayed here with him. Unless something happened . . .?"

"No," I say quickly.

"Then I expect you to go back to his club, and if I don't hear from him by tomorrow, I'll suspect you're lying to me."

"Silas doesn't take well to being pressured."

"Then you'd better not make it seem so."

He wants me to go there tonight.

"Will Kenna be coming with me?"

It's the first time she meets my eye, but there's nothing friendly in it. The opposite, in fact. She looks like she's itching to hold a knife to my throat again.

"No."

I shiver at Alistair's tone. He can't know about Silas's interest in her, can he?

"Shame. The dominant male ego in that place gets suffocating." I hope it's enough to ease his growing suspicion as I stand, appearing bored.

I head out of his office, but Alistair speaks at my back. "What a disappointment it will be to have to punish you for failing your first job."

My steps slow, but I don't stop. I'm barely present as I change into high-waisted black tailored shorts, a black tank top, and over-the-knee boots. Everything feels like it's crumbling around me. All I've tried to hold together to see through this madness that I stepped into for Rhett.

I can't fall apart now.

Outside Lumina, I can already anticipate what's going to happen. Silas doesn't dwell on things that didn't work out for him; he's likely moved on, forgotten about both Kenna and me if he's discovered she's content with Alistair.

I texted Rix on the way here, telling him not to panic, but if something happened to me for a while and he didn't hear from me, he couldn't lose focus as we're so close to finding Rhett. Perhaps they'll find him without me—then, when my nightmare is over, we'll find each other, and perhaps our broken pieces will fit just perfectly for us to mend each other together.

I get out of the car, numb as I approach the familiar security out front. They pull out the scanner as usual, and I count each second it takes for them to read the screen.

"Apologies, Miss Kinsley. Silas won't be seeing you tonight."

I'm not surprised by his announcement. I anticipated it. Silas said he revoked my membership, and we have no common goal anymore.

"Can you ask him again?" I say anyway.

One of them speaks into a small, concealed device, and we wait. I assume he hears the response through his earpiece as he tells me the same thing. Silas won't come. Won't allow me inside to see him.

I'm angry now. He's a fucking *coward*. A pretentious, arrogant asshole like the rest of them.

"Then you can tell him this for me . . ." I say coldly, hoping he can hear me through whatever they're wearing. "Taking her now may be another powerful man doing something against her will, but leaving her shouldn't be an option. Tell him if he didn't just see a possession like everyone else, it would be worth the patience and the challenge. But I guess he's just like them."

I storm away, tears hot behind my eyes, but I force them to stay put. Taking a route around the club, I try to avoid Tony. I can't go back—I fear Alistair now more than ever, even though I knew this day could come. He wants to punish me, and I don't know what it'll entail. I hurry down the sidewalk, typing to Rix. If they can reach me first, perhaps I can hide. They'll have a safe house or something to make me disappear until we get Rhett back.

I need him right now.

I thought I could do this, be strong and brave and resilient, but I'm just one fucking person. One person who hasn't stopped grieving and has pushed past her reserves of adrenaline and anger to see this through.

My pace is brisk, but Rix isn't responding. My frantic messages disappear one by one, and I try not to break down in my fear, feeling like it's too late anyway.

My instinct was right about that at least.

A hand covers my mouth, smothering my scream. My vision blurs as I inhale a sharp scent that lures my conscious to sleep, but they tie a blindfold over my eyes anyway. Two people, I think as I'm drifting. One picks me up while the other makes quick work of tying my hands and the blindfold.

It's over in seconds.

That's the pity of being the little bird. Freedom is high and endless, but all it takes is one swoop too low to become trapped between the palms of cruel hands once again.

CHAPTER 22

Rhett

I'm directly across the table from the kid, trying to disassociate from the terrified, blubbering mess of him. He pleads with me, and it's soul-tarnishing.

I'm not holding a gun yet, and the fact I'm seated this time tells me Micah has a different plan.

"I've decided you can join the game for your little stunt last time."

He spins a revolver on the table, then he produces another.

"One has a bullet. The other is entirely empty. Take your pick, Kaiser."

This sadistic motherfucker.

My hand reaches for one, my eyes on him like a hawk. He smiles to throw me off, and I reach for the other. His head cants, eyes turning wild. He's truly the most vile creature on the planet.

It's a fifty-fifty guess. I try hovering my hand over each again to get a read on him. Then again. All his face speaks is pure sardonic pleasure, and I think he'll delight in this no matter the outcome.

Out of all I've faced, nothing has worn me down as easily

and rapidly as this. The fourth time I've been forced before an innocent young boy and made to balance his long life in my palm with the power to crush it.

I pick up my choice after my fourth attempt at figuring out which one might have the bullet. The screen in front of me turns on, and instinctively, I shoot to my feet. A firm hand stops me, slamming me back down.

Is Ana here?

The room is sparse like where they're keeping me, but her bed has a frame. She has a desk too. Ana lies still on the mattress, and I assume she's unconscious. I start to pick apart what's different enough to shatter my hope she's in the same four walls as me. The ceiling is lower and the lights are different. Her walls aren't raw concrete, they're soundproofed, and I despair for her to wake up in the maddening kind of silence I know too well.

"What the fuck have you done to her?" I snarl.

I was weak and exhausted, but now I'm wide-awake, teeming with rage.

"Nothing . . . yet. I might decide to exact your punishment on her in other ways for trying to shoot me."

I'm detonating from the inside with no way out.

Micah adds, "Alistair is disappointed with her, and he feels she's better off here for your *motivation*."

"You're going to wish you were never born."

"No need for lullabies while we do this."

Micah picks up the other gun. "Here's how it goes. You take that gun to the head, and I take this one to little Ryan here. We each take shots. Easy, right? One of you lives, one of you dies. Best get a good last look of the little bird. Truthfully? I'm hoping the bullet is in yours so I can take her. I bet she fucks real good—"

My impulse to aim my gun at Micah wins. I fire the whole round. And they're all fucking empty.

Micah's manic laughter chills my sweat-slicked skin. He shivers in delight like a real fucked-up piece of shit. "I was hoping you would do that. Now we know this one is loaded."

The gun in his hand is slipped across the table to me. My teeth grit so hard they might break.

On the screen the door to Ana's room opens, and a man enters. I haven't felt this helplessly, violently ill since the day I watched Sarah get shot. Ana is so vulnerable I want to yell and yell and hope she'll hear me through some fucking mental plane of existence and wake up.

He points a gun at her sleeping form.

"You have ten seconds," Micha sings.

I pick up the gun, unable to contain my tremors. I look away from the screen to *breathe, focus, breathe*. I have no choice. My will to protect Ana trumps everything—my morals, my safety, my well-being. She will always come first no matter what I have to sacrifice.

"Five." Micah teases the countdown. "And don't look away."

I lift the gun, staring the terror-stricken kid in the eyes, and it's a mild relief that he closes his tightly. Fucking brave kid. It takes far more bravery to find acceptance than to plead a powerless case.

I make it quick, firing all rounds faster than I ever have before, braced with a blackening soul and a mind for the *click* to turn into the condemning blast of a bullet.

It never does.

The boy peels his eyes open, meeting mine, wide and terrified, but as his tears fall there's a flicker of *hope* in them. I don't know if it's a blessing he feels even a little relief he might make it out after all, because the next second Micah produces another gun, aiming it at his temple.

"Huh, I actually thought you'd aim for me again."

He pulls the trigger.

I look away as the boy's head goes limp. I'm so mind-numbingly cold.

"I may have fired the real bullet, but your willingness killed him first."

I killed him.

I killed him.

I killed him.

I don't deserve to look at Ana, but I have to know she's safe. The only light in this hell is that she's alone again. So still and peaceful.

The gun is in my hand one second, then flying across the short space to crack off Micah's skull the next. He doesn't expect it, and I lunge for him, slamming him to the wall. I get one good punch across his jaw before I'm pulled off by two guys. One lands a punch to my gut, the other across my face, until I'm spitting blood on the floor like Micah, but it was fucking worth it.

"You're going to pay for that," Micah snarls, peeling himself up.

I don't care. About anything anymore. Ana will find a way out. Xoid will keep her safe even if I never get back to her. It's a pitiful, weak thought. I think about how she would scold me for it, and I laugh. I haven't heard the sound from myself in months, and though it's delirious and strange, I laugh some more.

They're about to unleash their anger on me, and I brace myself for it, but the impact slamming into me doesn't come from anyone in the room. It comes from the room *itself*. Stone, debris, and clouds of smoke. I come to fairly quickly—at least I think I do. I push a slab of rock off my legs, and I groan, getting to my hands and knees.

Someone steps over the small mounds of crumbled wall, and I look up. I don't know who the fuck I'm staring at, but he plucks the cigarette from his mouth with a tattooed hand, strolling in here like he's arrived fashionably late to a summer fucking barbecue.

"Apologies for the dramatic entrance. I have a thing for explosives—gets the chaos going," he says, so lax and amused, but not with the kind of sadism Micah possesses.

"Who the fuck are you?" I wheeze, getting to my feet.

"My name is Silas Balenheizer."

My blood runs cold. I don't realize we're not alone until he holds out a hand and someone places a gun in it. To my shock, he extends it to me.

"I guess you could say a little bird sent me."

The impact of the blast was nothing compared to what slams into me at this.

Oh Ana, what the hell have you been up to?

I don't have time to consider the impossibly of how Ana managed to get a Balenheizer on her side. "Where the fuck did he go?" I snarl, looking around, but Micah's body isn't in the debris.

"Who?" Silas asks, taking another drag of his cigarette.

Ignoring him, I stumble over the debris and check down the halls. *That damned rat.*

"Infiltrating this place was like walking into a child's playground. But I imagine there will be backup soon, and I don't like wasting unnecessary resources," Silas says.

I store Micah's name high on my list of people to find and kill. He might even have earned himself a spot above Forthson.

Silas has guys around us, but some of Lanshall's are still around. We duck behind walls when shots are fired at us. I don't wait around for anyone else to get the job done—I have three fucking months' worth of pent-up rage to unleash, and so I take my chances after a quick look to determine there are three motherfuckers at the end of the hall.

Ducking out, I time my maneuver perfectly to hit one guy

between the eyes when he tries to get a gauge on my position. The other two are on my side of the wall, a better angle for Silas and his guys, but I step out brazenly, darting across to the wall as they fire at me. I keep moving so they can't get an aim, advancing before they can scramble an accurate shot, until they're swallowing my bullets instead.

"Glad to see you're not all talk, Kaiser," Silas says. He finishes his cigarette and flicks it onto one of the bodies. Their clothes catch flame, and he walks past them without a care in the world. "There's more where that bomb came from, so we'd better get far and fast."

CHAPTER 23

Anastasia

I groan, waking as if I partied far too hard last night. *Did I drink too much at Lumina?*

No . . . I never got inside.

I lick my bone-dry lips and try to gather some moisture in my mouth, which feels like sandpaper. Whatever they used to knock me out was powerful shit. My panic is there, it's just that my body has all the motivation of a rock to move, so I can't lunge up and start pounding on the metal door.

Metal.

Where the fuck am I?

The walls are cushioned in what I think is soundproof foam.

Oh god. Why would that be necessary? I start to force myself out of my comatose state with the adrenaline coursing stronger each minute.

I'm on a small bed. In the room there's a desk with some paper and pencils on it. *Considerate of them to leave me weapons.* I train my eyes on the plastic cup of water and bite my lip at the ache of my dormant muscles when I'm too eager to reach

it. I gulp down the liquid greedily, some of it trickling down my chin.

Alistair must have been waiting, perhaps knowing I wouldn't get into Lumina, and now he knows it was all a lie. This is my punishment. Solitude. Silence. For failing in his task.

My lip wobbles as I think of Rhett in my loneliness. How many times was he subjected to this absolute nothingness? With the soundproofing, it's like I've only just discovered the true meaning of *silence*. It's not a pleasant or even fascinating discovery. I've only been awake for a few minutes and I'm frightened by it, how nothing has even a little echo and I'm scared to try my voice. Only if they opened the door would I feel like I was actually part of the world still, not a foreign object floating in space.

I sit back on the bed and hug my knees to my chest.

Don't cry, little bird.

Don't cry. Don't cry. Don't cry.

I have to keep my mind strong, or this place could break me. I don't know how long Alistair intends to lock me in here. The door has a slot for food and a small hatch above it. Other than that, I have no contact.

I find a camera in the corner of the room and my skin crawls. I want to hide, but there's nowhere to do so. I'm fully exposed for them to watch me like a lab rat and observe what the slow madness might do to me.

Then I remember my parents. They expect me every Sunday for dinner.

My small flicker of hope winks out. I have no doubt Alistair will have my phone, and with all the times I've made excuses before, one text is all it would take for them not to be concerned.

Adam and Rix may know what's happened, but there's nothing they can do. They'll just have to wait until I'm released. Two weeks maximum, I think. At least, I would like to believe my father still cares enough that he'll insist on a wellness check if I skip out of more than two dinners in a row.

Though I still turn cold and scared at the thought of spending fourteen days in here.

I don't know what to do. I thought Alistair would see me awake and come to talk and tell me all he knows, gloat about my punishment. I would at least find out how long I've been out and how many days he plans to keep me here.

No one comes.

Maybe it's the silence already driving me mad and I'm counting the minutes as hours. My chest constricts. Shit, has he restricted the air in here too? My eyes flutter, and I lean against the wall for balance.

I'm going to die in here.

I shake my head, not understanding why I can't calm the fuck down.

"Breathe, Ana," I tell myself in a hushed, eerie whisper. It's as if the words don't really leave my lips—there's nothing for the sound to rebound off.

This is a sick, twisted method of torture.

My anxiety is rising rapidly. Blood soaring. Forehead slicking. Chronic pacing.

I realize what's happening, and that only makes it worse.

It's happened to me once before—a panic attack so vicious they say the symptoms are like a heart attack.

I can't let it happen here. Not fucking here.

My body isn't hearing me though.

I just want Rhett. I think of how he would hold me, how he would know what to do. I think of the time he caught me in the maze, and how I might have spiraled to this state then had he not been there. I can't explain how he reaches my mind like no one else can. How his touch soothes any ache, even those deep and hidden to everyone. Not to him. No part of me has ever been hidden to him, and I *need* him now.

I . . . shatter.

Sinking to my knees, I break into a violent cry.

I want to tear out the thing pounding like a caged beast in my chest, because it's causing me so much pain I think I might stop breathing to kill it instead.

Make it stop.

Make it stop.

My consciousness starts to slip, and I let it. I don't want this pain anymore.

"Ana."

I think someone says my name, but I don't want to listen. It's not Rhett. I want them to let me go.

Instead strong arms encircle me. They don't stop my rocking; they move with me.

"Just breathe," they say, so calm, and younger than I expected. "Shit, I don't know what I'm doing. Uh, what color is grass, Ana?"

What did he ask? I can't focus. I can't *breathe.*

"Shit. Okay. Uhh—" His arms tighten, and the pressure helps. I think his mouth leans to my ear with his next quiet words. "What color are Rhett's eyes?"

Rhett's eyes.

"Blue," I wheeze.

"Good. Yes. Keep going."

"They're like . . . a clear ocean blue . . ." I say.

I close my eyes and think of only his irises.

Breathe, little bird.

"Sometimes they look darker in the night," I whisper. *God,* I miss how my heart skips and my stomach flutters every time he looks at me. How they make me feel like I'm the only person in the world.

I'm so exhausted I don't even care about the stranger's

arms around me. At least it's someone. The door is cracked open, and seeing there's space beyond this terrible cage begins to calm me.

"Good. This is good, I think."

He sounds kind of panicked, and that makes me curious. I wouldn't expect any of Alistair's men to have consideration for me. In fact, I bet most of them would enjoy seeing me this way after I walked around their halls as Alistair's precious prized pet.

It makes me wonder if we're in his manor. No—why would they blindfold and drug me to get me here? They don't want me to be able to identify this place. Another curious thing.

It's what reels me back to feeling like myself again. The prickling heat over my skin starts to subside. The cloudiness in my mind starts to dissipate. I'm about to ease out of the stranger's arms, but they tighten on me as I do.

He leans his mouth to my ear again, and I lock still.

"I hoped we'd meet under far better circumstances," he whispers.

We're still rocking. We have our backs to the camera.

"Who are you?" I dare to ask.

"My name is Jeremy."

I breathe a shallow gasp. *This isn't real.*

"Jeremy," I repeat, like this an illusion I've conjured in my panicked delirium.

"Have you been to Xoid HQ yet?" he asks. "How are Frodo and Sam? Just say they're missing me so I can feel like someone will be happy to see me when I get out of this."

My eyes flood. Jeremy is holding me. Rix's little brother. I'm both so, so relieved and absolutely terrified he's here.

"Yes, I have. Rix is so worried about you," I whisper.

"He's always like that. I was the only one who could do this. Alistair has a particular interest in young ones. Sick bastard likes to think he's *crafting* us. He believes I'm sixteen."

I don't know what he looks like yet, but my gut twists with the thought of how many other young people end up in the wrong hands. The *lost* . . . Had they just wandered a different path, perhaps Xoid could have found them first.

"Where are we?" I dread his answer.

"Some stupidly pretentious country club. You're great to hug, by the way."

I'm trying to calculate with that information.

"Have you seen Rix or Adam?"

"Sullevan? Why the hell would they be together? Rix hates that guy after hearing all about his possible involvement in chopping your hair, the ass he was to you regardless. I think we'd need to keep a chaperone with them."

"You thought Adam was responsible for my attack?"

"Rhett did. There was pretty strong evidence in our investigations. Anyway, besides the point."

"Rix and Adam traced your location to a country club Adam's dad frequents. Last I saw them a few weeks ago, they were trying to get Rolf to take them along to see why you'd be here."

"Well, shit," Jeremy mutters. "No, haven't seen 'em. Though I'm mostly down here or watching what . . . goes on. This is basically a pick-up point."

My stomach plummets at the sinister meaning.

"Is Rhett here?"

"No. Sorry, Red. But I got the confirmation he's somewhere, because they've been boasting about him up topside. They call him the White Knight. Like, what is this—some lame-ass budget DC comic in the making? Anyway, they say he's deadly. That he'll kill anyone, no questions, no limits."

I'm going to be sick.

"Rhett would never."

"Of course not. It has to be against his will, and there are only two things he'd cave to save: Xoid or you. And we'd know if there was a threat to us."

"Oh my god," I say. All this time . . . has Alistair been threatening him with killing me?

"Don't panic—please. That scared the shit out of me. I thought you might die in my arms."

A deeper, more vicious new voice rattles me.

"What the fuck is taking so long? Let the bitch suffer."

Jeremy's arms tighten a fraction. Then he releases me.

"We were told to make sure she lives, and that wouldn't have been the damned case if we'd left her for a moment longer," Jeremy snaps back.

I tense, turning to find a man twice his size in every way. Certainly far older, and as ugly as he sounds. Then I look up at Jeremy as he stands, and I'm close to falling apart. He shouldn't be here. He's too young and joyous, with curly brown hair and boyish brown eyes. He easily passes for a more mature-looking sixteen-year-old.

"Looks fine to me," the man grunts.

I cower back on the bed, too tired to even glower at that asshole. He isn't worth the effort. I can't even shift my expression from Jeremy with the man and the camera watching. I have to pretend I'm just as cold to his company as the rest of them.

So I look away, lying down and giving them my back. The more I sleep, the less I'll have to endure the coming days, or weeks, in this solitude of hell.

CHAPTER 24
Rhett

Riding in the back of a car across from Silas Balenheizer is something I hoped to never do in my life. I have so many questions, but I don't trust this guy for the answers.

"Where's Ana?" I demand.

Silas takes an assessing breath. "It was either save her or you. Alistair already had plans to hold her, and had I taken her in for safety, he likely would have moved you, or killed you, out of fear I'd allied with Ana to come for you."

"You should have chosen her," I snap.

Silas's eyes flex, and I'm aware how dangerous his family name is.

"Alistair won't kill her. It would be a tragic waste, and he's not stupid. After he learns of this, he probably plans to sell her so you'll have a hard time getting her back and she'll be in tiny, broken pieces by the time you do."

"Stop the fucking car."

"We haven't gotten to know each other yet."

I reach for the door, but it's locked. I'm locked in a moving box with him while Ana's time is ticking fast.

"What do you want?" I snarl.

"As I told your little bird, who was so willing with me, trust is a coin flip. Show me inside your house, and I'll tell you where she is."

I understand what he means, but there's no fucking way I'm giving up the location of any part of Xoid to him.

"I'll find her myself," I say, controlling the anger I have nowhere to unleash.

"Disappointing. I'm rather curious of your operation."

"You don't let a rat loose in a snake pit."

"Because it would outsmart them all."

"You've wasted your time if that's all you want. I'm taking you nowhere near Xoid."

"Your girl trusted me."

"She wouldn't for this, and you know it."

Silas shrugs. "Suit yourself." He taps on the glass behind him, and the car stops. "Good luck, Kaiser. And tell Ana I expect to see her soon."

I get out without another thought, and Silas's car doesn't linger. I have no clue where I am. All I need is a phone. My body is aching all over, but adrenaline is a numbing drug to it. My dignity plummets with every disgruntled look as I ask to use a cell phone.

My last resort leads me into a small store. Usually, my finesse for theft is impeccable, but I'm desperate, jittery, and annoyed as fuck. I still have the gun Silas gave me, and I despise what I have to do.

At the counter the worker is reading a newspaper. The store is quiet, with only a couple deciding on snacks at the back.

"Don't make a fucking sound," I say quietly, but with enough threat.

The man looks up as I lay my hand holding the gun on the

counter. Contrary to my warning, he launches up in fright, swearing and knocking into the back display.

Well, fuck me.

"I need a phone and sim *now*," I growl.

"H-holy shit. Okay, all right, hold on."

The couple at the back try to scurry out, but I point the gun at them. I can't have the police scrambling in here before I get what I need and get far away.

"Just sit the fuck down, and if I see a phone, I swear to god, I'm not in the mood to be nice right now," I warn.

I have no intention of firing the gun. They could take their chances and run out and I wouldn't stop them. I must look as unhinged as I feel right now, as they cower into themselves in the corner.

"They make and model o-okay for you, man? I-I think I might have a better—"

"Put the sim in and start it up," I order.

His chubby, dirty fingers fumble with the packaging and I grow antsier by the second. He does what I ask, and as soon as the screen lights up, I snatch it from him.

"Thanks," I say, not wasting a second to open the dial. "I'll try remember to get someone to swing by with the cash for it."

"No-no problem," he mutters in a state of shock.

I leave and tuck the gun out of sight under my T-shirt.

I know many people's six-digit Xoid code, but I dial Rix's. It only rings once before static hums down the line.

"It's me. Get a tracker on this thing right fucking now."

The line cuts off. It isn't designed for two-way conversation in case someone slips up or hacks us back.

I keep walking, cutting down alleys and keeping out of sight. I'm aware I'm supposed to be dead, that there's a chance from all the press last year with Ana that someone might recognize me. The shop was a risk, but I had no choice.

It takes ten minutes too fucking long before a black car comes down the underpass I'm waiting in.

"Dude, you're alive!" Rix calls out the window.

I slip into the passenger seat, and he takes off.

"Aw shit, is it good to see you, man! We've been a wreck without you. I know you don't like sappy, but everyone is going to lose their minds having you back, so be prepared for the waterworks. I'm even holding back myself."

My eyes flick up to the rearview, and I spin in my seat. "Sullevan?" I snarl.

Rix says, "Fuck. Shit. Yeah, a lot of explaining to do there, but keep a lid on that rage to hear it, will you?"

My lethal glare cuts from Adam in the back seat to Rix. "Tell me he hasn't been there," I say, low and deadly.

"Hey, it was *not* me who brought him to the Den, all right? You can save that pissed-off-ness for Ana."

Adam grumbles, "I never did buy into your innocent transfer grad student facade, Kaiser."

I have to close my eyes to collect my sanity. *Ana.* She's all that matters right now.

"Alistair has her locked somewhere?"

"We know. I've been trying to get a trace, but her phone from us goes cold at a venue that was a setup. They knew we'd come for her and planted it there. We lost two guys," he informs me with the terrible weight of sorrow. It never gets easier no matter how many we lose, nor how well they all know the risks.

"How'd you escape?" Adam asks me.

The mere sound of his voice is a trigger to my volatility.

"Silas," I answer. "Ana has sure been fucking busy."

I'm torn with pride and madness and incredulity. From the moment I met her, I knew she was one to be underestimated by many, but this is a whole new level of unpredictability.

"Incredible, right? She managed to convince Silas fucking

Balenheizer to collude with her right under the nose of Forthson *and* Lanshall. She's damn brilliant."

Yeah, she is.

We get to the Den, and I'm slammed with the impact of this being one of the very few places I've ever considered a home. The elevator doors open, and it's the first time in what feels like days that time finally slows as I take in the place.

People speak, some start clapping, until the whole room is alive with it, and I wish they wouldn't applaud me. Not with the new stain I harbor and the failure I am for getting caught only to rot away for three months. There's nothing to celebrate.

Rix makes sure no one approaches as I head to his desk. We need to get to work on finding Ana.

"First, man, you need those wounds seen to. You'll be of no use if you catch an infection," Rix says.

Yapping erupts, and I internally groan.

"In here, young man," Oma croaks from across the room.

"Go. We're on it," Rix encourages.

I don't know if I can sit still for even a moment long enough to get patched up. I head to Oma, but I have no intention of speaking to her right now when her sessions can go on for hours. I only lean down to kiss her head.

"Long time no see, Oma," I say.

"Come inside, my boy. You need to stop for just a moment."

"I can't. Soon, I promise."

I head back to Rix. His eyes reprimand me, but he says nothing. I sit in a chair as Coraline approaches, an ex-army doctor.

"You're going to have to take off your shirt," she says gently.

I look at her, all beautiful glowing brown skin and kind

brown eyes. She's an absolute credit to everyone here for her selfless work in patching us up.

I'm afraid to even look in the mirror to discover the mess left of my skin, but I pull my T-shirt off, and don't look at anyone, for their reactions might give off the same effect.

"Holy shit—*omph.*" Rix cuts Adam off with a jab to his chest.

I'm still seething that he's here, of all places, as if his mere presence wasn't enough. He's horrified by the bruises and scars over me, and I can't blame him. He's likely never sustained more than a nasty paper cut.

"Silas said he's likely going to sell her," I say through my teeth. I hiss at the alcohol as it's poured over my bicep.

Rix runs a hand down his face. "I'm sure he'll have a list lined up, no auction necessary."

"Then she'll be at the country club?" Adam says.

I snap my gaze to him, and he balks.

"Or not. What do I know? But you said it was pick-up point, no?" he directs to Rix.

Rix doesn't answer right away, blinking at Adam. "You're quick, Sullevan, I'll give you that."

"What country club?" I ask.

"We visited twice," Rix explains. "Foxglove. We believe most of the members are completely oblivious, but now and then new guys show up just with day passes, and you need a private invite. Adam managed to create a distraction long enough for me to follow one of these *new* guys as he left. He didn't go through the main doors on his way out—he went out a back way that leads down to a basement, and he left with a woman. You know how it is—by the time they get to that point, most are so broken down into compliance that she seemed to leave willingly, but I've seen this shit before. It has to be a collection cover-up venue in broad fucking daylight."

"We're going tonight," I say.

Coraline says, "I would *highly* advise against that. You're one hit away from shattered ribs and internal bleeding. If you don't want to risk a hospital visit—"

"Thank you, Coraline," I cut her off.

She sighs her disappointment, knowing I'll disregard her warning. I lay my hand on hers in thanks.

"Tonight," I repeat to Rix.

CHAPTER 25

Anastasia

I think days have passed, though it might be weeks. Time is peculiar in this place. It mocks and torments, and the only way to get through this is to pretend time doesn't exist.

I've been trying to write a letter, and it's distracting me from the lonely hours. It's like I can pretend there's someone here; that I'm talking to someone.

Rhett, I don't know how we got here—

No—too grim.

To Rhett Kaiser—

I scratch that out in a messy scribble instead of using the eraser. *Stupidly formal.*

Rhett motherfucking Kaiser, you'd better stay the fuck alive, because I haven't been searching for you just for all this to be for nothing—

I sigh, snap the pencil, and reach for a new one. I only have one whole left. By the end I'm sure there won't be any, and that seems fitting.

At least it gives me something to do. I want to get this right, though I don't know what exactly I'm writing this letter for. It's not that I've given up hope. I stare at the blank page

each time with the opposite of lost hope swelling in my chest. I didn't get the chance to tell him how much he means to me before we were torn apart, and now I have all this stillness to decide how to do it. Maybe it's silly and wasted time. Maybe it should come in the moment, from the heart.

But this might be my only moment, and he's always in my heart.

Dear Alistair, see you in fucking hell.

I tear off that sentence and decide not to shred it. I slide it to the top of the table, and my hatred grows at seeing his name.

I engross myself in words, scribbles, paper, and this last 2B pencil.

My next train of thought is to write words desperately, my hand aching to keep up. So when the tip breaks mid-sentence I know I've been here far too long with words, scribbles, and this last damned pencil, because I lose it.

The chair knocks back as I stand, furious with this stupid fucking pencil for failing me. I break it, let it go, and stand around the four pencils I've made into eight. I stuff my half-finished letter into my pocket. I'm still wearing exactly what I wore in Lumina. There's a *bucket* where I've been forced to relieve myself, and I've cried several times, as silently as I could, at the fact I have no privacy.

This is inhumane. So deplorable.

I turn and glare up at the camera, imagining Alistair enjoying my spiral to madness, waiting for me to beg for forgiveness, plead for his company, promise to do better . . . I'm fucking livid.

Dragging the chair over, I stand on it. My hands wrap around the neck of the camera, and I step off with gritted teeth. It's more robust on the wall than I anticipate, so I let go.

I stand, grab, and *jump* off this time. Something snaps. *One more time.*

Stand, grab, jump.

It snaps from the wall, and I heave breaths of exertion.

"Show fucking over," I say, tossing it to the side.

Part of me is crawling with nerves over what Alistair might do in response to my act of rebellion. A larger part doesn't care. He's a damn coward to not have faced me at all since locking me in here.

It doesn't take long for someone to come. I wonder if they're worried I'll do something to myself, and I can't deny I've thought of it.

I'm so, so tired. My heart is in pieces, and it's easy to want it all to stop in the moments of weakness. The pain won't be over if I manage to get Rhett back. In fact, I think it could get worse, and what if we don't know how to make the new sharp edges made of us fit together anymore? I can't bear the thought.

And so some days . . . just for a moment . . . I want to give up.

You're not allowed to give up, little bird.

I hardly react when the metal door groans against the stone. I have a flicker of hope it'll be Jeremy, but it's not. I haven't seen him again since the first time I woke, and I don't know how many days have passed since then.

Instead it's a man I've never seen before, but I can tell by the way he smiles, feline and hungry, he's seen me. He has a wicked black eye and a split lip that makes him all the more menacing.

"I've been most looking forward to seeing you at last, Miss Kinsley," he says.

"Can't say the same."

"You might soon."

I highly doubt that, but I say nothing more.

He stalks in, and only then does fear trickle over me. What crumbles my composure is his glance down at the broken camera, and then I realize with cold horror what I've done.

No one is watching.

No one would know if he—

I cry out at his sudden lunge for me, managing to slip from his loose grip. Grabbing the chair is my first instinct. I swing it, but he manages to wrap a hand around the leg, pulling it from me. Then it almost feels over.

He can't win.

He can't win.

The man barrels into me, so we knock into the desk. He's too tall. Stronger and far more feral than me. I fight with all my months of training, as hard as I can. I remember everything Rhett taught me in self-defense last year, but it's as if it was all a game, and when faced with a threat as vicious and unrelenting as this, I never stood a chance.

I block his first attempt to slap me and manage to jab his throat. He chokes, and I spin, but I only get one step away before he circles my waist and his hand slams the door shut that I was *so* close to escaping through. His hand grips my hair, but I don't get out a yelp before he slams my head against the metal door.

I become boneless to the sweep of darkness.

I'm overpowered when he straddles me on the floor, and an animalistic growl vibrates close to my neck as he pins my wrists by my head.

I fight to stay awake. *Keep fighting, little bird.*

His hand grips my jaw tightly, and tears well in my eyes at the bruising hold. His disgusting breath fans across my cheek.

"My name is Micah," he says, so low and hungry. "I want you to cry it out when I fuck you."

No. NO.

I strain against him with everything I have, but he's

managed to reach a hand down to undo the buttons of my shorts, pulling the fly down too.

I'm crying now.

I'm too hot. Heavy.

I'm drowning and suffocating.

When I come to enough, I feel his hand dipping down past the waistline of my shorts. His guttural moans tighten painfully in my stomach, and for a moment I want to disconnect. To let my mind drift far away from this nightmare until it's over.

He can't win.

He can't win.

Don't give up, little bird.

My hand flexes, arm stretching out, as he can't hold me and finger-fuck me at the same time. His fingers slip out of me to reach for his jeans button.

Then I feel it. Absolute rage and disgust gripped in my fist in the shape of a broken 2B pencil.

I don't contemplate. I don't hesitate.

With a scream, I plunge it into his neck.

He chokes, immediately clutching the eraser tip only just peeking through his fingers as they flood crimson. So much blood pours out of him, onto me, and I push him off. Rolling away, I gag at the sticky crimson. My chest heaves with breaths of such volatile fury that my whole body shakes with it as I stand, fastening my shorts.

"My name," I say, needing to pause because my throat is so tight, caught between the need to break down in uncontrollable sobs or stab him again and again to leave him there like a fucking pencil holder. "My name is Anastasia Kaiser. Remember it, and this face, because I'm coming for you worse in hell, you vile piece of shit."

He can't respond. His mouth flounders and he coughs

blood. Terror starts to creep over me, my adrenaline dwindling. Those wide, cold brown eyes will always haunt me.

Don't let him win.

I heave the door open and slip out, trying to hold myself together, but the realization of what just happened turns me cold. Vacant.

Blinking consciously, I try to reorient myself to figure out how to get out of here. The sound of voices turns me into a deer in headlights. They're advancing fast, and I'm disoriented, trying to look around for a place to hide. I spy a cleaning cart and duck behind it, clamping a hand around my mouth, close to releasing the emotions straining in my chest.

The men don't pass me—they continue straight. I jump back up and keep walking, trying to focus my hearing. The ceiling is low, with long bar lights. The stone walls have no decor. It's like an underground stone maze, and I could be trapped, never to find a way out.

I'm trying not to let my thoughts rouse a panic that will make sure I never get out of here.

Breathe. Breathe.

Rhett's eyes are blue.

A beautiful ocean kind of blue.

I turn another corner, then another.

Soon I'm jogging, tormented I'm tracing the same halls over and over and this place is mocking me. I blink hard when my sight starts to blur, and now I'm running. Recklessly. All I need is air—it's too thin down here.

I'm going to suffocate.

I turn the next corner, and my steps shuffle to a stop. Every nerve in my body freezes still.

Rhett's eyes are blue.

A perfect ocean shade.

And they're right in front of me.

Down a few meters of hall.

He looks so worn and tired. Beaten and bruised. But his eyes still light up at seeing me.

I wonder if I'm still in the nightmare, still pinned to cold floor, and I've successfully managed to take my mind to a better place to survive it.

Until he speaks . . .

"Ana."

One word. My name. And it's enough to shatter everything I am.

"Rhett," I barely say. It feels too good, too hopeful.

"Oh, Ana."

He moves toward me, and then I can't stop. I run, because if this is a dream, it's better than the hell I've been living anyway.

We collide, fracturing and becoming whole at the same time as my legs wrap his waist, my arms clamp his neck, and . . . this is *real*.

I break into an inconsolable mess of tears and sobs, wondering what we'll be when we manage to make it out. Not just out of here, but all of it. It doesn't matter as long as we're together. We'll fix our broken pieces one by one and know that we'll be one soul, one heart, one mind.

"I've got you, little bird."

I sob at that. I didn't think I'd ever hear it again.

"How?" I croak.

His fingers brush tangled strands of my hair when I pull back enough. Then they continue down, and a frightening look flexes his eyes. I follow. I don't remember when Micah tore the front of my shirt. I'm not fully exposed, but the damage is enough to be obviously intentional. And the blood . . . I want to peel my skin off to be rid of his blood on me.

My hand wipes at my chest as if it might make some of the blood disappear.

Rhett takes my wrists, snapping me from my ghostly trance. "Are you wounded, Ana? Is this blood yours?"

I shake my head, which feels hollow. "Not this, but I . . ." I reach to the side of my head with the throbbing that returns at his question.

"Who the fuck did this to you?" he asks in a slow, deadly calm.

"He didn't— I mean, he almost, or he-he could have, but I—"

It's as if his hands are on me again now, and I try step out of Rhett's hold. It's too firm and warm.

"Shh, baby. I'm right here," he soothes, stroking a hand down my hair. I wish I could keep it together, but I'm falling apart where we stand.

He leans down, and I let him carry me because I think I might not make it out otherwise.

"I want to go home with you," I whisper.

"We're going home, baby."

I nod, fighting more tears, because we're still in the devil's basement, and I don't know how Rhett is here. I don't care about anything but his heart beating under my palm as I slip it over his chest.

This is real.

My senses feel sure, but I'm so tired that logically I'm struggling to believe it's really Rhett. Right here. Then I break a little more . . . because I was supposed to come for him.

He was the one who was lost and held captive for months, and I didn't come for him.

"I'm sorry," I say. "I'm so, so sorry."

Voices echo ahead, and my terror spikes. I grip Rhett's shirt, but he doesn't try to hide us. My head turns only enough to catch a glimpse of Rix jogging toward us and my whole body caves in relief. Two other guys stand by a stairwell.

"Where's Jeremy?" I ask.

"He's not here. We're not sure where he is yet," Rhett says, pained.

"He was here. I-I met him."

"You did?" Rix presses when he reaches us. "Where? When? *Shit.* We must have missed him."

"A few days . . . it could have a been a week. I-I'm sorry, I don't remember."

"We need to get the fuck out of here—now," Rhett orders.

It's as if he never left. The way he sounds. How focused and authoritative he can become. But I know by now adrenaline is a powerful, deceptive drug. Sometimes it even feels like a superpower to get us through the worst.

Right now, I'm soaring in Rhett's arms. I press myself to him as tightly as I can. As soon we're out of here, when survival mode and the high of finding each other dwindles, divulging the dark and bloody details of what we've been through will begin our fight to *live.*

"This way!" Rix hisses.

I squint at the light flooding toward us around the next bend. A way out. It feels too good to be true, and I lift my head enough to peer back over Rhett's shoulder.

When I see the absolute horror of a gun pointing at Rhett's back I grip his shoulder with a gasp. He reads my reaction right as a shot fires, and I scream, flinching into him.

My feet meet the ground, and I'm pushed behind him as Rhett pulls out his own gun.

"Get her out of here!" Rhett calls to those behind me.

There are two men shooting, and we barely have cover in a small dip in the wall. I don't know who tries to take my arm, but I'm glued to Rhett.

My hand falls down his back, and I still at the second gun I feel in his waistband.

I can't think logically in this moment as I pull it free.

Like I said, adrenaline is a powerful, stupid drug.

Ducking so Rhett and the others are their prime visible focus, I take a deep breath and peek out to spot one guy dipping around the bend. I wait for his next attempt to shoot, then I fire once. Twice. Three times.

One of them hits him as he cries out, and Rhett twists out of cover fully to take out the other assailant. I can't quite believe I hit him. Unlike Rhett's fatal bullet in his target, mine only wounded my guy's knee, and he army-crawls around the bend. My gun in still aimed, my arms still outstretched.

Rhett's hands cover mine, taking the gun from me. He pulls me back to standing, and I snap my wide eyes from the body to his face.

I don't know what to do about the disturbance that crosses Rhett's face. Is he horrified by what I've become? He met a woman who had never held a gun before. One who never would have been able to pull the trigger no matter the wickedness it was pointed at. What if he can't accept that all that has changed?

Rix drapes a jacket over my shoulders and Rhett helps me into it, zipping up the front. I'm glad it hides the blood.

Wordlessly, he takes my hand and our fingers entwine. I grip him for dear life as he leads us out the door. A car speeds up to us, and there's chatter, commotion, but I barely register it. I climb inside the back when Rhett yanks it open, and to my relief, he slips in with me. Rix is driving. Someone I don't know is in the passenger seat talking to him.

"Come here," Rhett says softly.

I'm reminded all over again that Rhett is right there. The high of the escape is cooling my body, and I've turned so cold I'm afraid to even look sideways at him.

"Ana."

His hand touches my thigh, and my trembling fingers reach for it.

Then everything I've packed against a straining dam finally breaks.

I bite my lip hard as I shuffle over and end up sitting on his lap, feet on the seats. All he does is hold me, and my sobs are painful as I try to suppress what I can.

"We obviously can't take you to your parents, though they should hear from you," Rix says. "I was thinking we'd go to the Den in the meantime."

"I want to go home," I say.

Rix looks at me through the rearview mirror. "Alistair knows your apartment."

"You got your apartment," Rhett says, more to himself, and my heart cleaves at the distance in his tone. It's the first cry of agony in my chest for the things he's missed. I know he'll blame himself for not being here, but I'm ready to show him how much he always was. That I've kept him so close to me every day since we were torn apart.

"I got it for us," I whisper.

His hand cups my cheek resting against his chest, and he presses his lips to my head. I clutch him tighter. This still feels like a dream riddled with corners of terror.

"Take us there," Rhett says. "I want to see our home."

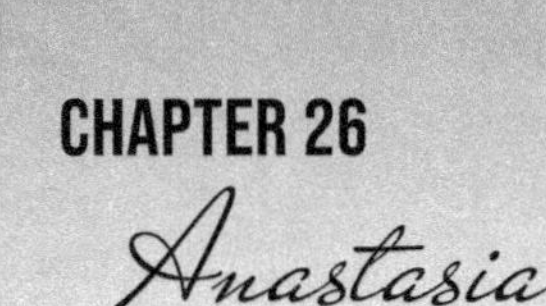

The apartment is searched by Rix and the other man before they leave us. The moment Rhett and I are alone, I don't know what to do. How to feel.

I drop the keys onto the kitchen island and watch Rhett float around the place. There wasn't a day I didn't imagine him here, and it's hard to believe he isn't just in my imagination right now.

I've pictured the day we would be reunited a hundred times, yet nothing comes close to the reality. I expected the heaviness, but it doesn't make facing it any easier.

"We can change anything," I whisper, because I worry he's going to shut me out any second.

How will I tell him I've been with Alistair all this time? That it's how I know how to use a gun. Will he forgive me for taking the hand of his evil uncle, colluding with Jacob Forthson, and trying to gain the help of Silas Balenheizer? Everyone Rhett despises.

Rhett runs a hand along the couch as his blue eyes shift to me. "You said you got this place for *us*," he says, equally as

quiet. "Yet you saw the car wreck. He said you believed I was dead."

"I couldn't," I say, taking tentative steps toward him. "You promised you wouldn't leave me, and I believed you. I couldn't accept you were gone, and I-I did things. Some terrible things, because I had to *try* to find you. I don't know what it makes me now, if you'll even still see me the same or what . . ." I trail off. My throat becomes too tight.

"Ana—"

I shake my head. "You don't have to say anything. Not until you hear all I've done—" My words are cut off by the whimper that escapes me when Rhett takes my face in his hands.

"I know," he says, searching me with those blue eyes I've missed so painfully. "He made me watch you often. I know you were with him, and I think I know why. But when you're ready, I'll hear it all from you."

I'm slammed by shock.

He was watching me all this time? I don't know how to feel about it. Relief that he knows. Anger at Alistair, as I'm sure it was some twisted tactic to torment Rhett. Sadness. Such terrible sadness, because I know it would have worked, and once again I was a weapon used against him.

"I'm so sorry," I choke out.

"You said that before, and I don't want to hear it again. Please. I can't bear it."

"I just wanted to be strong enough. Brave enough. I wanted to find *you*, yet somehow you still found me first."

His thumb sweeps the tear falling down my face. "No. You found me, little bird. Only, I'm still reeling at how, because out of everything I think I'm pretty damn good at figuring out, I can't for the life of me work out how the fuck you managed to ally with Silas Balenheizer."

My next breath shudders in disbelief. "He got you out?"

He only nods. "You are everything, Ana. You're the most strong, brave, and brilliant person I've ever known. And I fucking missed you every second of every damn day."

His lips angle to meet mine, and waves of longing and relief crash into me in a sob that escapes between our desperate kiss. We have so much to talk about. It's a long road to healing and mending and finishing what we started. We're inside the wicked now, and the only way to kill the kings of the underworld is together.

I lift myself up into Rhett's arms, and he sets me on the kitchen island.

"This place is perfect," he says, trailing his lips down my neck. "But it's not safe for us to stay here."

"Where will we go?"

"The safest place for you would be to stay with your parents for a while."

My hand tightens in his hair, forcing him to look up at me. I can hardly stand the bruises and cuts over his perfect face. My fingers lightly reach for a scab on his temple.

"Don't say that." I'm angry, riddled with anxiety, because I feared he'd push me away.

"It's true."

"But not what you want."

"No." He squeezes my thighs. With a palm flattened on my lower back, he presses me tighter to him. "I don't ever want you out of my sight again."

My eyes flutter with the relief. "Good." I kiss him, only once, as a promise. "I'm not going anywhere you're not going."

"I wish you wouldn't say that, but more so, it's selfish of me to be damn relieved to hear it."

My legs tighten, and it's as if we can never be close enough. I don't want any fraction of distance from him.

"Where's the bathroom?" he asks, lifting me off the counter.

I direct him into the en suite, and he lets me turn on the large walk-in shower.

Rhett looks me over, pain slicing his eyes once again. I must look an absolute sorry state. Smudged makeup, tangled hair, ripped clothing. Bloodstained. I can't bear to look in the mirror when I fear I'll picture Micah.

Neither of us move for a painstaking minute.

I take in his appearance too. His clothing is new. His hands are bandaged. I wonder how long he was out of his hell before he managed to find me in mine.

Rhett steps closer, and I let him unzip the jacket, peeling it from my shoulders. His fingers reach for the button of my shorts, but I panic. My breathing spikes as I lay my hands over his to stop him.

It's Rhett.

I want to let him undress me, but it feels like a pretense with what's torturing me inside.

He lets go without a word, and I can't look up. The pain in his eyes would only break my spirit more. Instead Rhett takes off his black T-shirt, and I find distraction in the new marks all over him. My chest aches at every fresh bruise and new scar. I reach up, hesitating in case he doesn't want me to touch him. When he doesn't move, I melt at the feeling of his skin under my palms. There are so many new marks I don't know where to begin.

"What did he do to you?" I whisper.

"I don't care about any of the physical," he says, detached from emotion.

It cleaves me when, with that, I realize there's something he cares about. Something that isn't physical to him, which Alistair tortured him with.

I look up as if I'll find the answer floating to the surface of the ocean in his eyes, but he's guarding that part. I lean forward and press my lips to his chest. I can wait as long as it takes for him to open up to me.

"I'm right here. You can tell me anything, and I'll always be right here," I say.

"Let's start with a shower," he says, tipping my chin. He tries a smile, but it's anchored by a burden.

I want to wash more than anything. To scrub and scrub and hope to be rid of the impression of Micah's vile hands on me. But I don't want Rhett to see it. I fiddle with the hem of my untucked blouse, trying to quell the shame in me while I pace the same two steps.

It was not my fault.

It was not my fault.

If I hadn't broken the camera, he wouldn't have had the opportunity to attempt the assault.

It was not my fault.

I take off my ruined top. In my hands I stare at it, wondering how I can't remember the moment he tore it. I toss it aside. Reaching for the buttons of my shorts, I undo them one by one, with trembling fingers, because what I do remember is his hands doing this. His hand slipping past the hem of my underwear. His fingers moving against me, curving inside me.

I can't do it.

My hands cover my face.

"I'll wait right outside," Rhett says gently.

I want to ask him to stay. It chokes in my throat, and when I let him leave I release my pain. I trained so hard. I didn't want to be helpless. Yet I feel like I've let myself down.

When I step into the shower I lather my body with soap. I wash my hair and hiss at the wound from Micah slamming me to the door. The reminder breaks me, and I cry, sinking down in the shower to release some of the pressure building in me while the water muffles the sound. I don't stay down for long when my anxiety that Rhett could leave climbs through my grief. I scrub my skin raw quickly and wash my face.

Stepping out, my stomach flutters at the folded pajamas Rhett must have found in the bedroom, along with a fresh towel slung on the heated rail.

I dry and change quickly, giving my hair a quick towel-dry too before I emerge into the bedroom. He's not here, and I immediately head into the open kitchen/living area. My heart stops speeding when I find him by the fridge.

"You were quick," he says, closing it after finding two bottles of water.

"I missed you." It tumbles out of me. I mean it far more than just during my stupid ten-minute shower.

I don't want to cry anymore, but I can't fucking stop. I'm so, so exhausted, but I'm glad for it. This kind of tiredness is all for him. I don't want to miss a second, a flicker, anything, now he's back with me.

"You left so quickly, so sudden," I croak. "I don't think I can survive it again."

When he's close enough I wrap my arms around him, listening to his heartbeat.

"I'm not going anywhere without you, baby." He presses a cold bottle to my hands when I let him go. "I'm so fucking sorry, Ana. Everything you've been through is because of me. Of everything that's happened to me, that is my greatest punishment."

"I'm sorry too, but not for that. Everything that's happened to me . . . I would *choose* to go through it again if it brought me back to you in the end."

Rhett kisses my forehead with a sigh. "I have a lot to say about that, but all that matters is you right now. Are you hungry?"

I think I should be, but my emotions are crashing too much to let me feel it. "Maybe a little," I say.

"Good. I ordered Italian."

For the first time since he left, a short, breathy laugh escapes me. My fingers clench the new T-shirt he put on. "We have a lot to talk about," I say, meeting his troubled eyes.

He's shielding a lot from me right now, as if I'm the more damaged one when he was held captive and tortured for months.

"Not tonight," he says, taking my hand and leading me over to the sofa.

He picks up one of the thick throws and makes me sit with it while he wanders over to the strip fireplace. He's clearly encountered one before as he knows exactly how to light it.

Rhett comes back to me and lifts a bottle from the table, tipping two Advil into his palm and offering them to me. They're a relief to my throbbing head, and I throw them back, taking a drink of water. After I do, Rhett examines my head.

"It doesn't look like it needs stitches," he says, his voice hushed as if speaking any louder will shake it with anger.

"You look worse than me." I observe each cut and bruise on him.

"Nothing on me hurts more than seeing a wound on you."

When he sits on the sofa, we maneuver like magnets until we're both lying in a comfortable entanglement.

He murmurs over our peaceful silence, "I missed you, Ana. For 126 days. You're right here in my arms and I still miss you."

My brow pinches and my eyes close peacefully, sinking into him further. "It's not over," I say.

"Not even close."

"Tomorrow. We'll face it tomorrow, together."

CHAPTER 27
Anastasia

We're woken by loud pounding at my door. I lunge up from the couch we fell asleep on, as does Rhett. Somehow there's already a gun in his hands, and I can barely breathe through my heart beating in my throat.

"Go to the bedroom and lock yourself in the bathroom," Rhett orders in a hushed whisper.

He pulls out a phone, but I can't do as he asks.

Then a voice calls through.

"Anastasia, if you don't open in the next minute, I'm coming in."

It's my dad.

"Shit." Rhett can't be seen here. "You have to hide," I hiss, pushing him, though it's futile with him being the rock he is.

"It could be a trap," he protests.

"Ana!" Dad shouts through.

"He's the fucking president, and he'll be with a shit-ton of security—go!"

I manage to push him into the bedroom and point in all seriousness to the closet for him to hide before I rush back out.

I hear keys since my dad was adamant to hold a spare set, but I get to the door, hauling it open and setting my flustered, bewildered look on him.

"What time is it?" I demand.

"Past midday," he says, matching my disapproval.

Well, shit. I'd hoped I could be angry at him for the early intrusion, but . . . did we really sleep that late?

He doesn't wait to be invited in, and that irks me. I don't want him here even though it's been weeks since I saw him. He doesn't know the hell I've been through, and I don't want him to. But Rhett knows, and right now he's forced to hide when I'm certain my dad would have him arrested on the spot.

It's something I never considered, and now I'm slammed unexpectedly with the notion, my heart cries. Our relationship was a secret before, but at least we could be seen together. Now, I don't know if we'll ever get that again.

"Your mother is worried sick," Dad rants as he wanders into the living area. Two security follow him in and begin checking the area to clear it for safety. One heads toward the bedroom, and my skin slicks with panic.

"Don't!" I yell. It's abrupt, but it works, and they look to my father at the outburst. I scramble to come up with something. "By all means, be scandalized by whatever I've left lying around my own fucking bedroom."

It's enough insinuation of a lingering sex toy or stray underwear that they second-guess themselves in scoping it out. To my immense relief, Dad gives them a nod and they back away.

He cuts me with a look of warning, however. Then his gaze falls behind me and his face relaxes. I spin, realizing there's no talking myself out of the obvious two bottles of water and the two plates of leftover Italian food.

"If there's someone in your bedroom, they have to—"

"There's not," I say, snapping back around. "It was a hookup, and he left this morning. Is that what you want to know?"

His frown smooths out and he sighs deeply, rubbing the back of his neck. "I'm glad you're moving on, Ana. But I hope you're taking the precautions we talked about."

Meaning: He hopes I'm getting my one-night stands to sign an NDA.

I grind my teeth. "Did you need something?" I bite out.

"You've missed two dinners in a row and haven't even bothered to pick up the phone. A few text messages were not what we agreed on in letting you live here alone."

"You can't *let* me do anything. I'm not a child."

"Then stop acting like one!"

My eyes prick. I'm so torn because I can't even blame his perception of me. To him, to my mom, it's exactly what I must seem. The agony inside of me wants to be held in his strong arms, which always felt like the safest place in the world. Now that place is Rhett. And my father will never know how I was held captive and assaulted, nearly raped. It's the first time the term even slithers into my mind, and I want to shower all over again with the shame that coats me.

It was not my fault.

It was not my fault.

Would Dad blame me for it? After all, I willingly took Alistair's hand. I knew the kind of man he was, and those who worked for him, and I put myself within reach of those vile men.

It was not. My. Fault.

"I'm sorry," I say, but it's cold and forced. He knows it.

I'm met with a familiar look—one that can't seem to settle on anger or disappointment. To me the blade is the same.

"Will you come this Sunday? The Van der Laizes are coming and would love to see you."

I doubt they'll care, but I nod.

"Good."

He takes a step, hesitates, and ultimately decides our tension is too thick to give in to an embrace. Dad leaves without another word, and I shiver at the ice he left behind.

I don't realize I haven't moved, still staring at the door and the ghost of him, until Rhett's arms snake around me. I melt into him—the only sure, warm, and safe thing I know right now.

"What are we going to do?" I whisper against his chest.

"One day at a time," he says, kissing my head. "We'll figure it out."

"He'll never see you as anything but a criminal."

"I am nothing but a criminal."

I pull my head back to peer up with a frown, but the sight of his small smile is such a relief.

"I killed someone," I say. It's the first time I truly understand the tarnish on my soul. I don't think Micah could have survived the half-pencil in his neck. "So I guess I'm one too."

A muscle in Rhett's jaw shifts, and he searches my eyes, likely looking for the sign I'm going to break down because of what I did.

"Do you need to talk to someone, Ana?"

He only uses my name when he's worried.

"I'm talking to you."

"To someone who isn't to blame for what happened to you and what you were forced to do."

"No one forced me. I went with Alistair by choice. I knew what I was doing, as do I now. The only thing I need is you."

His eyes close as if this hurts him to hear. He can't back away now.

Rhett's arms drop from me, and he turns away.

"Don't leave me," I say. It slips out in a panic. "Don't come to some bullshit conclusion that I'd be better off without you after all this."

He shakes his head. "You don't know what I've done."

"I don't care."

"You should," he snaps. I flinch, and his face turns desolate. "You should," he repeats in a gentler tone, as if my reaction is all the proof he needs.

"What did he do to you?" I ask again, carefully.

I'm only wearing short pajamas, and suddenly I'm too cold, rubbing my arms.

Rhett wordlessly reaches for the throw on the couch and comes close enough to drape it over me. When he tries to step away again, I grasp the front of his shirt.

"You don't get to push me away now. I went through fucking hell to find you, and you were captive there, waiting for me. Don't say you weren't. That you didn't want to get back to me."

"I watched you train, and you were fucking exquisite in doing so. I watched you learn chess with your brilliant mind at work. I watched you pick up a gun and learn to shoot without fear. I watched you in his office, and that was what tormented me the most. Because every time you sat in that chair, I could only see myself. I knew you didn't want to be there, but you felt like you had to be. I watched you every day."

I'm trying to figure out why. *Why* would Alistair have made him watch? He always has a motive.

"What did he make you do?" I ask carefully.

"I can't," he says, and I ache at his pain. "I need a while longer to have you look at me like nothing's changed."

"Nothing has changed. Not my feelings for you."

"Stop. Please."

I can see him struggling against shutting me out. I can be patient for him, but I can't stand there being any walls between us.

"Then just kiss me. Kiss me like you want to fight for us no matter what we've done or might have to do. Because I'm going to fight for you, Rhett Kaiser. Even if you try to get rid of me, I'll fight *you* if I have to."

"So damn stubborn," he mutters, then his lips crash with mine, and every burden is lost in the heat of what burns between us.

More than ever before, I feel the threads of us entwining. If he left, neither of us would survive it.

Rhett pulls me to him, and I moan into his mouth when his hand trails up my spine under my tank top. "We can't work," he says, but he doesn't stop his assault. "I can't ever be seen with you, and you deserve someone you can be open and honest with."

We end up by the couch, and his arm hooks around me to lower us.

"I deserve you," I say, becoming breathless at the press of his body over mine, sinking us into the couch.

But something strikes alarm in my mind. It comes sudden and terrifying. It tangles this beautiful desire for Rhett with something dark and ugly, and my breath turns labored not through want, but panic.

"Stop," I rasp, laying a hand on his chest.

Rhett eases off me immediately, sitting beside me, and I push myself up, clutching the blanket to my chest. I scrunch my eyes shut, trying to dispel the wicked thoughts of Micah's body caging me in instead.

"What happened to you in that room?" Rhett asks.

I can't look at him. His voice is chillingly calm, trying to be gentle and patient, but it's like he's simmering to erupt and kill someone.

"I think I need a while longer too," I confess.

I think he's going to leave with the stretch of silence. How can two damaged people ever hope to mend each other? What if there isn't enough glue and tape and we're both fucked anyway?

"Can I hold you?" he asks softly.

My lip wobbles, and I nod, shuffling over until I'm lying across his lap.

I say, "I don't care if you're my secret forever and my parents have to believe I've become celibate."

Rhett gives a soft chuckle. "You're prepared enough, at least."

I'm confused for a few seconds, then heat crawls up my skin as I push off him. His devious look as he tries to appear innocent widens my eyes a fraction more.

He says, "In my defense, I was looking for your pajamas."

I shift until I'm straddling him. "Everyone knows the top nightstand drawer is off-limits."

"On the contrary, I think I'll be visiting that particular drawer very soon."

My desire doesn't just come back—it rushes between my legs, and my knees tighten around him subconsciously. Rhett's hand slips over my bare thighs slowly, watching for my every flicker of reaction before his palms curve over my ass.

"To join or watch me?" I say with an edge of seduction.

"Both." He squeezes my ass. "When you're ready."

I want to say I am. My body certainly agrees. But I'm afraid I could ruin it all if the thoughts of Micah come back. I just need a little time. It's still so raw and fresh in my mind, and I *hope* all I need is a few more days, maybe weeks. I can't let that bastard break off that piece of me and win by keeping it. I'm determined to get it back.

"Soon," I say, kissing him. "Very soon."

"We'll have all the time in the world."

"Promise?"

He stalls, rethinking his words. "I can't. Tomorrow is a promise to no one. But until my last day, I'm wholly yours."

CHAPTER 28
Rhett

I knew we shouldn't have risked more than a day in Ana's apartment, never mind three. The small dose of happiness she gained from us being here, getting to show me the space she picked for us—I wanted to give her that for as long as possible.

I'm awoken by the buzz of my phone, and I snatch it up immediately. Ana stirs as I read the text I fucking feared.

Alistair's men have come.

"We need to go, baby," I whisper, pulling back the covers for her and getting changed swiftly.

Ana pushes herself up, rubbing her tired eyes. They slowly turn frightened as she registers my urgency. *Fuck*, I would give anything to never have to see that specific look of horror on her beautiful face again. She knows what's wrong.

I'm dressed and helping her. She doesn't protest, sitting on the bed and pulling on my black hoodie as I slip the fluffy socks she likes onto her feet and fetch her boots.

"Are they here?" she barely whispers.

"Nearly. You're safe with me. On my life, Anastasia."

I don't use her full name a lot, but I need her to know how much I fucking mean it. I would take bullets for her.

She nods, standing and getting her coat while I reach into the dresser drawer and pull out two guns. I slide one into the back of my jeans and approach Ana.

"Only take it if it'll make you feel safer, but I fully intend to make sure you don't have to use it."

Her eyes contemplate the gun I'm holding out. Only for a few seconds before her hand reaches for it. "I'm getting good at my aim," she says quietly.

"I know," I say, kissing her hand and taking it.

I fit my earpiece in and have Rix ready to direct us with eyes on the cameras.

"They're just pulling into the garage," Rix says.

"Cut the hallway and elevator," I reply.

"All clear."

We leave, jogging down the hall.

"Shit, stop. Take the stairs," Rix says.

Pivoting, we push through the door to the stairwell.

"Fuck! Stop and stay fucking silent."

Pulling Ana to me, I press a finger to my lips. Her brow furrows, trying to read my eyes for any signal. I hear the commotion then. They have to be coming up from both the stairwell and the elevator, knowing I could be tipped off.

"Your only way is up, man." I hear the panic in his voice, and it's not fucking helping.

Ana lives in the penthouse. Our only other exit is the rooftop, and then we're cornered. I don't know this building, but I'm praying to fucking God and Satan—whoever will grant us the mercy of a damn fire escape outside.

Emerging onto the roof, we race across it, and—*thank fuck* —I spy the escape down on the side of the building.

"Motherfuckers," Rix says.

I stop, taking a pause for sanity before I lose it. "They're climbing the fire escape too?" I confirm with Rix.

"They're halfway up. You'll have to try to hide."

They'll reach the top and scour every inch.

"How many?" I ask.

"Six outside, eight inside."

I can't risk Ana getting hurt while I take out that many. Especially if those inside hear the gunshots and race up to help.

"The building . . ." I contemplate the insanity of my thoughts. "It has wraparound ledges?"

"You're not seriously thinking . . ." Rix trails off too.

We don't have another option.

I pull Ana along, my adrenaline the driving force drowning everything out.

Back inside, we're silent as we fall down a level. It's the closest drop to the first ledge.

"Rhett, what are we doing?" Ana asks.

I can't answer because I know she'll panic. She might fight against me doing this, and I'm going to prolong that as much as I can. The window slides up, and I slip one leg through.

"Trust me." I pull her to me, but she resists. "I won't let you fall."

The voices are growing louder up the echoing stairwell. My jaw tightens.

"Please, baby," I coax.

She's not good with heights. I understand the safety and prestige of a penthouse apartment, but right now, it's the worst location.

Ana clutches me for dear life as she slips one leg through, straddling the windowsill with me. My toes barely touch the ledge, which is only the width of my foot.

"I'm scared." She shudders.

"I'm right here, baby. Be brave for me, okay?"

Ana nods, but her full focus is on the task. I hold her tightly as she maneuvers her other leg through and then lowers until her toes reach the ledge, but her fingers don't let go of the sill.

"I can't," she breathes in a panic.

"Yes, you can, little bird. Let go and shuffle along."

It takes a few seconds that pound in my chest as we're so close to being caught. When she's across enough for me to fit through, I slide out, dragging the window down with me, until it's only a slither open. Hopefully undetectable to Alistair's brainless henchmen.

The wall has barely any kind of purchase, and our balance is everything in this desperate, reckless plan.

"If we died this way, that would be really disappointing," Ana breathes.

Our fronts are pressed to the wall, and I risk slipping one arm around her for further support.

"They could make our story poetic," I say. "Modern-day Romeo and Juliet."

"You know Romeo and Juliet?"

"You made me learn about that Shakespeare guy for your debate, remember?"

"I didn't make you read his plays."

"I didn't. There's a movie, but it was deliriously dull. In fact, I'm still angry at their stupidity."

Ana chuckles softly. "Don't make me laugh—my balance isn't great as it is."

"I missed it," I say. "Your laugh."

She doesn't answer for a few beats.

"What would you have done?" she asks.

I'm so proud of her for the calm she's maintaining despite our ludicrous, life-threatening situation.

"When?"

"If you were Romeo and I was Juliet. What would you have done if you found me and thought I was dead?"

"I'd yell at you for the stupidity."

"I faked it for you!"

I grin until my thoughts turn serious.

"You have so much to give, Anastasia Kinsley. That doesn't die with me, and I demand you stay alive."

"Pushy."

"It's my job I'm informally taking back. How else would I get you to follow me out of a twenty-eight-story window?"

"Your bodyguarding methods are very unorthodox."

"In more ways than one."

"In better ways than others."

"Are we thinking about that top drawer again?"

Ana giggles, breathy and a little delirious given our precarious situation, but it's a sound that calms me and reminds me there's still goodness in this hellscape.

"You two are fucking adorable," Rix coos in my ear.

I didn't forget he was there—I just don't care.

"They're on the ledge?" another voice in the background says.

"Who is with you?" I demand. There's never anyone around him when he's working with me.

"Uh . . . probably not the best time for you to hear that answer."

Ana shivers, and I try to shuffle tighter to her.

"It's probably Adam," she says. Then her eyes flick up as mine snap down. "Shit, I forgot you don't know yet."

"Oh, I know already," I grumble.

"It's a long story." She winces.

Rix says, "Okay, we're going to get the all-clear soon. Hang tight a few minutes more."

"Not like we have a choice," I say.

"This was the most insane idea," Ana says. She hasn't

moved a single inch from standing straight, palms splayed and cheek pressed to the wall.

"Not too late to choose the White House for refuge."

"I've been through arguably more threatening things," she says. "Silas could have been exactly like Matthew, and I walked right in."

I don't need to be reminded of that right now. I haven't decided if I trust Silas or not. I'm leaning more toward absolutely no way in seven hells. But he got me out more swiftly than I've ever seen before considering the secure and highly guarded location. He'd strolled in as if he damn well owned the place and I have no doubt Alistair Lanshall is losing his shit over it.

"You have a whole lot of explaining to do, little bird."

"All clear," Rix says.

Thank fuck.

I shuffle along, taking Ana with me, back under the window. It's going to be a tricky balance to get it open. I strain with my feet against the wall, push the window up, and manage to haul myself over. I don't miss a beat, leaning out to grab Ana around her forearms.

"You need to hold onto me back, and I'll pull you up," I say as calmly as I can.

I know Rix has eyes on the place, but I can't let go of my racing adrenaline that he could miss someone before I get Ana back onto solid ground.

"Don't let me fall," she says, voice laced with fear.

"Never. Look at me."

Those stunning hazel eyes turn up, and I promise my soul to her in them.

"I've got you."

Ana gasps, reaching up. It wobbles her back a fraction, and she whimpers, but I have her.

"Use your feet to climb if you can," I instruct. She does so, and from there it's a few effortless seconds before I'm pulling her through the window into my arms.

Our heartbeats slam together as I hold her tight, leaning back against the side wall.

"I can't believe we just did that," she pants.

Honestly, me too. Of all the wild and crazy scenarios I've found myself in over the years, this definitely shot to top of the list for spur-of-the-moment insanity.

She laughs, and I know it's the high of adrenaline and the absolute fuckery of our lives right now, but I join her.

"You two had better get your asses down to the garage before you lose any more of your minds. We're just about to pull up," Rix says.

I take out the earpiece to have a moment alone with her after all that.

"You're incredible," I say, tucking her bed-tousled, windswept, deep red hair behind her ear. Not a thing has changed, and no matter what, she's still the most perfect thing I've ever seen.

"All I did was follow," she says.

I take her hand as we make our way down the stairs and untuck my gun as a precaution.

"You shouldn't put so much trust in a criminal," I muse.

"Bodyguard criminals are an exception."

I catch a glimpse of the gun Ana's holding too, and I can't decide what I feel to see her so ready to fire with me. Escape with me. Run with me. Guilt, so much guilt, wraps around me, but only because I'm so damn *proud* and relieved she's still here. I haven't quite processed all she did to try to find me, because I'm sure owing her my life isn't enough anymore, and I'm still trying to figure out how to give this woman everything she deserves and so much fucking more.

We pause in the doorway into the garage, and I lean out, gun raised, to check the area. It's silent until a car comes down. We change our plates often, and the windows are tinted black, so I don't immediately trust it's Rix.

The back door opens, and my finger bears down a fraction more on the safety until a large black dog comes bounding out.

"Hey, boy!" Ana gushes when Shadow sniffs her out instantly.

I relax, watching her kneel and nuzzle into the dog.

"Let's go!" Rix hollers.

It's then I look up and see Adam Sullevan getting out the back and slipping into the front.

"You have seconds to give me one good reason why my hands shouldn't wrap around his throat from the back seat," I say darkly, pulling Ana toward the SUV.

"You're not the only one with a ruse," she says. "I mean, his is simply the asshole ruse, and I guess it was kind of genuine, but he apologized and has actually been a good friend since, well, you died."

I cast her an unamused look as she slips into the car giving me an innocent smile.

"Too soon?"

I'm worried about her. I'm terrifyingly, obsessively worried about her. At least it keeps my mind off my own shit. I think she's deflecting her trauma, and I can't figure out the right way to mend us together until I know every piece of the story from *her* since the day I left. I want to believe it's just time I need to give, but after three months away from her, time has become too precious to me.

"I'm glad you're alive for Ana's sake, Kaiser, but I'm not apologizing to you," Adam says as Rix takes off.

"Good, because I'd shove it back down your fucking throat, Sullevan."

He huffs a laugh, but his smile falls to fear the instant he looks back and catches my glare. Ana scoots over to the middle seat, and her hand on my thigh calms the beast wanting to reach for Adam. I was too lost in my drive to find Ana the first time I saw him, and now I have her, I have the headspace to loathe the fact he's here.

"Be nice," Ana says, tipping her head back and trying her best pleading eyes.

"This is my nice."

I'll admit, that look could get me to kneel on hot coals for her, but I haven't forgotten a single word or look Adam gave Ana over the semester to pin him high on my list of people to give hell to.

"I missed your graduation," I mutter absentmindedly at the thought of college.

"So did I," she says nonchalantly.

That disturbs me, but I don't let it show. Her smile is tinted with sadness, but she merely inches closer, tucking her arm around mine and leaning her head on my shoulder. It's fucking bliss. After all the torment, I feared something would be amiss, different, when I got to her again. I'm going to find out what the fuck happened to her in that time of seclusion, and I'm going to burn every one of Alistair's evil lairs to the fucking ground.

CHAPTER 29
Rhett

"**Y**ou didn't tell me you succeeded in getting Balenheizer on your side." Rix complains to Ana from his surveillance table in the Den.

She says, "*I didn't know he was on my side. I'm surprised he came. The last I saw of him, he all but said he wouldn't get involved unless Kenna was a part of it.*"

My eyes slide from the feeds to her. "Who?"

Ana looks at me, and her face relaxes as she realizes something. "Kenna Radley. She said she knew you from when you were with Alistair."

I've never understood what people mean when they say their world stops spinning. Until right now. My world stops and fucking reverses at a speed I find dizzying. I have to walk away to think.

Kenna Radley.

It has to be a coincidence.

"Who was she to you?" Ana asks carefully as she approaches.

"She was . . . a friend, I guess. In the most tragic sense."

That's not her real name.

I doubt Ana knows that.

"What does she look like?" I ask, dread rising from the pit of my stomach. I'm a fucking coward for hoping her description won't match, because I tried years ago to find her, and I was led to believe she was dead.

"Long, straight black hair, green eyes, tall, unfairly stunning—"

"Fuck," I mutter.

I pinch the bridge of my nose and lean a hand on the table. A quake of rage begins in my damn kneecaps and shakes through my whole body until I can't contain it. Whatever is on the table in front of me scatters through the hall, but I barely register the commotion I've caused.

"Dude! You know how I feel about my shit!" Rix cries.

How many times can Alistair fucking Lanshall win before I kill him?

I'm pacing like a caged beast. It's been twelve goddamn years, and he's had her all this time. Because I was looking for another name—one that led me to a house fire, where I found what I thought was her body. The news broadcast her death. Her cowardly, sick father, who sold her to pay off his debt to Lanshall, appeared onscreen *mourning* her. I almost went to kill him that night, aged only seventeen, but I didn't have the confidence or skills to get away with it back then, and I had a bigger plan to get back at him and Lanshall for everything they did.

I need to break something. Hit something. I march to the desk again, sights targeting Rix's black globe, but he anticipates it, snatching it in a protective grip. I'm intercepted by Ana's small, gentle hands flattening on my abdomen anyway.

"Rhett Kaiser." The wavering aged voice of Oma cuts across the space as it goes silent.

My breathing is harsh, but I start coming around. Seeing Ana's face pinched in concern, I slip an absentminded hand over her cheek as if I can take it all away. Scanning the room, more than two dozen people here are giving me similar looks, and it grates on me. Then I find Oma leaning on her cane in the doorway of her small dwelling.

I don't want to set foot in there. The woman has a fucking superpower that makes people talk about everything they've buried, no matter how deep. I don't want to talk. I don't have *time* to talk.

I need to fucking *act*.

When I begin shaking my head her cane taps the ground. "Don't give me that, young man. You're not setting foot out of here until you've set foot in here."

"You can't piss off Oma, man," Rix mutters.

"She's kinda as frighting as you are," Adam adds.

"Go," Ana says softly. "For me—please?"

My jaw tightens. I can't right now. Allie is still missing. I've learned Kenna is alive. Jeremy is in Alistair's network too. And right now, Lanshall and Forthson will have prime targets on my little bird for all she brilliantly pulled off.

"It's not me who should be in there," I say.

Ana swallows and averts her gaze.

"Will you speak to her, if not me? Please?"

"I want to be here with you."

"You are. I'm right here."

"Okay," she whispers.

I take her over to Oma, and it's not without sharp eyes of warning from her that she accepts Ana in my place.

"Thank you," I say, giving Oma a short embrace.

She's an absolute treasure to our network, helping people heal their trauma and learn to live with all the shit they've been through and continue to see in our work.

Ana doesn't look back as she walks shyly into the room. I heard she was here before, but now she knows she's here to talk about herself and not just for a visit. I want to be with her, but I can't. I don't take my eyes off her as the door closes, and it tears me apart to see her so small and frightened.

I tear myself away to storm back to Rix.

"You can only go so long keeping yourself together with rage and vengeance," Rix says tentatively.

"I don't need a lecture," I say, folding my arms and pondering the surveillance footage to think.

"You owe it to Ana to get yourself better too," Adam says.

He's the last voice I want to hear right now, and I can't help the lethal stare I target on him.

"You shouldn't fucking be here," I snap.

Rix says, while typing at some code, "He's actually proved quite useful. We wouldn't have gotten inside the country club without him. His father's a member, clear of the bullshit though. We don't have another Gregory Forbes on our hands, thank fuck."

I'm wondering who the fuck was daring enough to risk touching her. I can barely think about it without feeling like I might combust into a damn inferno. I want to rip the guy's hands off and feed them to him. I'm having the most intense and downright savage thoughts I've ever had, and I don't know how to manage them except to keep myself busy.

"I want absolutely every resource on Allie right now," I tell Rix. "Comb through every inch of the DeVerres."

"Yes, boss," Rix says, swinging around in his swivel chair. "I'm keeping an eye on my little shithead of a brother too."

There are three people I need to get back, and it'll take careful patience, because I'll be damned if I lose any one of them.

"He's not been back to the country club?" I ask.

"No. It's got me worried as shit. I haven't seen him in any feed for a week."

Alistair is difficult to find. I know he took up bold residency in his manor in D.C. while he had Ana, but I assume he'll be leaving there soon knowing I'm on the loose and coming for him.

"DeVerre?" Adam backtracks. "As in, the most renowned law firm in the States?"

I'm trying to forget his presence when his voice buzzes like a mosquito I want to swat.

"Crazy, right? I couldn't believe it. I knew she was rich as fuck, but I didn't think she was basically Kardashian levels of fame," Rix says.

"Her family are just buying a five-month leave? She's barely even taken two weeks off in six years," I say irritably.

"They say they spoke to her directly—full phone call, not just a text—and that they've heard from her every few weeks from Kauai, apparently. We have an inside guy in the firm feeding us their updates on her."

It's such bullshit, and I can only think they don't want to cause a scandal by assuming she's run off-grid like her brother did four years ago. They've never been the most loving or caring family, and I feel for Allie and her loneliness.

"Liam Forbes—where the fuck is he?" I demand.

"Should we be looking into him?" Rix asks.

"He's been missing since the shit with his father," Adam informs us. "I would guess he's hiding from law enforcement, which makes him look guilty as fuck."

His father was exposed around the same time Allie was taken. It's not a damn coincidence, and my fist slams the desk.

"Dude, I swear you're gonna owe me a whole new setup in a minute," Rix says.

I can't decide if it's relief or dread I should feel when my conclusion seems so glaringly obvious. "Liam has Allie," I say.

Adam and Rix snap their heads to me. I don't know how long that motherfucker has been working with Rix, but it's unnerving to witness their synchronization since the moment we got here.

"How can you be sure?" Rix quizzes with a hooked brow.

"I can't be certain he has her, but I'm rarely wrong. I believe he's still in love with her from a long while back. Perhaps he found out about the hit in time to get to her. I just don't know if he's a twisted fuck like his half-brother and he kidnapped her, or if he could actually have saved her a whole shitload of trauma."

"Glad to have you back, man. I knew you'd find her as quickly as Sherlock."

"He hasn't found her," Adam counters.

I take a few steps toward him, which wisely has him dropping his comfortable stance. "I don't know why she's forgiven you. I don't fucking care. But you're in *my* network now, and there's no taking that back. So when I say jump, you fucking jump. Got it?"

Adam concedes with a look, turning to the screens again. "I don't know what you got her to see in you," he grumbles.

Neither do I, but I've decided not to question the one absolute blessing in my life.

I cast my eyes to Oma's door. I don't know how long they'll be in there, but I'm not leaving even for a piss.

"So the question is, where would Liam have taken her?" Rix ponders, leaning back in his chair.

Ana's the only person who might have even a slight lead on that. I pull over another chair, but I doubt I'll manage to stay still for long.

"Let try to work out where Jeremy is for now," I say.

It's past midnight, and most of the people here have left or gone to sleep. A lot of them live here. There are several rooms with bunks, and they find peace and safety in being together.

Rix and Adam are still here, but the three of us are barely hanging on after a full day of scouring screens trying to figure shit out. We're not much closer to finding Jeremy. I owe my life to the kid, as stupid and reckless as he was for going behind Rix's back to get an in with Lanshall.

I rub my eyes, but when the familiar creak echoes across the room, suddenly I'm wide-awake. Oma peeks out and beckons me over, and I don't hesitate. Her face is pulled in with sadness as she steps aside.

"She's very passionate and strong. She cares about you deeply."

Ana is asleep on the floral sofa. The two Chihuahuas Jeremy stole last year are curled into her.

"I shouldn't have let that happen," I say. She's so breath-taking when she sleeps. So free from burden.

"You think you've disrupted and destroyed her life, and while what you do is dangerous, that's not true. In fact, I think you saved each other at just the right time."

I walk in gently, not wanting to wake her. "Did she tell you what happened?"

"She told me everything. In time, she'll want to *show* you everything. It's how she communicates with you. Have patience, son."

"I will."

"But Rhett, you can't begin to help her until you help yourself."

I lift Ana into my arms, and she's the weight of bliss. I breathe in her scent of honey and vanilla and know I'm exactly where I belong.

"Thank you, Oma."

"You know where to find me when you're ready."

I don't answer. Heading out with Ana is the only thing on my mind right now. Taking her somewhere safe.

"You should go home," I say to Rix, who's still combing through feeds, not wanting to miss a moment Jeremy might appear.

"I'm good. I'll let you know if I find anything."

Adam doesn't look like he's leaving either as he picks up a slice of cold pizza from hours ago. I might not like him, but Rix seems to ease off in his company, and I'm glad he's not alone.

I take one of the new Jeeps, and Ana moans sleepily when I put her in the passenger seat.

"Where are we going?" she mumbles, barely peeling open her eyes as I reach over to clip in her seat belt.

"Home," I say, kissing her softly.

I can't get enough. I want to lock her away with me for all the months we missed together, but I know that's not an option.

"We can't go back to the apartment. I don't fancy any more building ledge hideouts," she says as I slip in the driver's seat.

I nearly smile at her humor. Always our light. Always our balance.

"We have a few homes. They'll have to do until we get you the one with the porch."

"And a pond."

"Anything you want, baby."

I take her hand as I drive, and for a moment it feels like we're back four months ago, when everything felt good and right.

"How are you feeling?" I ask, not really expecting a deep answer.

"Fine."

"'Fine' is what people say to hide the truth. Don't hide from me. I can't bear it."

"It's all I have right now, because I won't be *good* until we are. Me and you, and then us."

She's right. I know it won't be easy, and we still have a lot to deal with before we can even focus on ourselves.

"Me and you, and then us," I repeat as a promise we will have that, no matter how dark my soul has to become to get us there.

CHAPTER 30
Anastasia

Rhett pulls up outside what looks like a road full of abandoned warehouses. I don't question anything as he gets out. He always manages to make it around to my side before I've finished unclipping my seat belt.

He's got his gun out, eyes tracking the entire deserted area, and his earpiece is in. A creeping sense of unease skitters across my skin as I get out the car and his arm encircles me. The outside is ominous, but we don't linger. Rhett leads me inside, and we ascend a spiral staircase to the top before he pulls out keys.

"This is where you live?" I ask in a hushed tone since everything echoes in here.

"In D.C., yes."

So he has more homes than one.

Inside I'm taken aback at the stark contrast of open beauty and homely warmth. It's like an industrial-style loft converted into a large open-plan apartment. There's a black and dark wood kitchen with an island in the back left corner, and the living area opposite it is like nothing I've seen before. It's as if the sofa is double-sided. One side faces a rustic fireplace and a cubby stacked with wood; the other faces a projector screen spanning the wall, and in front of it is a rug and a coffee table. Even the bathroom is semi-open, with an elegant double shower, a deep freestanding bathtub, and the toilet in a lockable cubicle. On the other side is an impressive setup of a desk, a chair, and so many screens, like back in the Den. Then, finally, I take in the large four-poster bed with black linens.

I'm craning my neck and gawking at the space made of original wood and brick, with slanted wood beams on the ceiling, but the place has a modern touch.

"I think I like your place better," I say, wandering in deeper.

"I imagine your father had a lot of sway in yours."

Rhett drops his keys onto the island and shuffles out of his jacket. I watch him head over to the fireplace to light it. It's not electric like the one in the penthouse, and I'm in awe of something so simple as Rhett sparking real flame onto the wood he piles in.

There's something different about him in here. This is his safe place. No doubt highly guarded by more cameras than I can count, and he's so relaxed, like we've stepped into a world where evil can't touch us.

I take off my jacket, looking for somewhere to hang it. I feel like a careful tourist, not warning to disturb his peace in here.

"This place is yours too now—you know that, right?"

"Do you promise?" I say. It comes out in a bubble of panic that bursts. After everything I confessed to Oma today, what exhausted me the most was thinking this could end. "You said you can't promise tomorrow, but promise you won't want to leave me. No matter what's to come."

More bubbles grow in me when he paces away. My brow furrows. I'm bracing for a rejection, or at least an uncertain brush off, and I'll just have to understand.

"I've thought about it," he confesses, and it slices me inside. "I thought about everything in all those months, because I didn't know how I was going to live with what I'd done. But the worst part is that it wouldn't matter if I left you. I could leave here today and never see you again, but even if ten years went by, I would still do it all again if someone took you. I would always choose to condemn my soul, no matter how wicked, to save you, because I can never stop loving you. I will do whatever it takes to make sure your heart only expires after it's full of everything you ever desired from this life."

"You love me," I breathe. It's a knife in my chest but an immense pressure relieved at the same time.

He turns back, and I've never seen him look so desperate and desolate. "I fucking *live* for you, Anastasia Kinsley. I want to marry you and build that damn house with the porch. I want to love you until we're six feet under, and I'll find you in the next hell. What I feel for you isn't something anything in life prepares you for. You're in my fucking *bones*, my every thought. If such a thing as a soul exists, you're half of mine— there's no other explanation. So leaving only lets him win. I'm going to love you in every day, every fucking second. I've caught you, little bird, and I'm never letting you fly away, because I'm going with you."

My lip wobbles, and I hug myself. "I live for you too, Rhett Kaiser. I think the last four reckless, insane, terrible months have made that pretty damn clear. And yes."

"Yes?"

"Anastasia Kaiser sounds better anyway, so I guess my answer is yes, I'll marry you."

Rhett breathes a short, disbelieving laugh with the shake of his head. He crosses over to me, and I lean into him when he's close enough.

"Your father would have me assassinated to hear that," he says, but it doesn't stop him from taking my face in his hands.

"Probably," I whisper.

"Anastasia Kaiser," he repeats like he's tasting it on his tongue. There's a flare of desire in his blue eyes that search mine. "That sounds sexy as hell."

He kisses me hard, promising.

"I love you," I say. Then it's as if a strain in me is finally relieved. I'm free. "When you were gone it was all I could think about. How I never got to tell you I love you. That you mean everything to me, and nothing can change that. I don't want this to ever end."

Rhett's eyes close, and he leans his forehead on mine. "We never end. In this life and the next. I found you first, and you found me back. We're inevitable. I love you, Anastasia. With everything I am, I love you."

Something changes in our kiss. The air. The way we move. It's declaring and binding that this is absolute. I lift myself up into his arms, and he moves.

"Fire or movie?" he murmurs against my lips.

"Fire," I say breathlessly. "Definitely."

He lies me down, hovering over me, and I try to stay with him. Here. I try to keep hold of what's burning so perfectly between us, but when his body presses to mine and his hand slips down my side, I'm right back there in my stone cell.

"Wait," I pant.

Rhett stops, pulling back. I don't know what to say, but he doesn't need anything. He tucks my hair behind my ear and settles down beside me instead on the deep plush sofa. I turn so we're face-to-face.

For a long stretch of silence, we share chaste kisses and soft touches until my heart calms again.

"Rhett?"

"Yes, baby?"

"This is going to sound very *un*sexy, but Oma is under the impression I'd do better to act rather than talk," I say tentatively.

"You can act and talk whatever you want with me."

"I want you to put your hand down my pants."

Rhett almost breaks a smile, but as quickly as a snuffed-out candle it falls to dark, barely suppressed anger.

"Is that what he did to you?"

"Please," I say, pressing closer and kissing him. "No talking."

Rhett's thumb strokes my cheek. Then his hand makes a slow trail down my body. Over my chin, across my neck. He pauses on my breast, and my brow pulls together with the parting of my lips when he squeezes then pinches my nipple. Rhett captures my moan, deepening our kiss. His touch travels lower, skimming my bare skin where my top has raised. He gets to the button of my black jeans, and that's when the slither of panic starts to weave through my lust.

I reach my hands up his chest, kissing him harder, as if it will drown out the fear. He pulls down my zipper, and his fingers brush under the waistline of my underwear.

"Tell me if you need me to stop," he says, voice laced with pain.

My hands clutch his black T-shirt as if my life depends on it as he half-hovers over me, but I don't want to stop.

"Keep going," I whisper.

My heart is thundering, but I want this. I want him more than anything, and that bastard doesn't get to take Rhett from me for another moment.

I moan when his fingers slip over my core.

"I change my mind," I rasp.

His hand begins to pull out, but mine lashes around his wrist to keep him down there.

"Not about that." I scramble. "Talk—please. Say anything."

Rhett pushes up a little more to lean over me, searching my face. "We don't have to go too fast. If you tell me you want this, I'll take over, but one word and I'll stop."

"This is what I want."

He nods, then he takes control.

One of his legs slips between mine, and he turns more demanding and heated, determined to make me forget everything but him.

"You're going to be my wife, Anastasia," he says huskily, blowing my name like sand across my chest.

"Yes," I breathe.

"It's just you and me. I will never hurt you."

Rhett pulls my top over my head, and I slip out of it. I reach for the clasp of my bra as he hooks his fingers to pull down my jeans and underwear. There's something erotic about having him over me fully clothed while I lie here completely bare to him.

"You are so fucking perfect," he growls.

I arch into his assault when his mouth sucks on my nipple while his hand gives the other attention. Unashamedly, my hips lift, desperate for friction with his thigh between my legs.

"You're mine," he says, lips trailing up my neck.

"I'm yours."

"My Ana. My little bird. My wife."

Yes. Yes. Yes.

Every word inspires surges of pleasure between my thighs, and I'm desperate for him to relieve the ache.

"Please do something," I beg.

Rhett smiles against my skin. "I am. I'm making sure you never remember a single hand upon you that wasn't mine. I'm promising you that any hand that does will have it torn from their damn body before I kill them. You've always known who I am, what I'm capable of. I don't have limits when it comes to protecting you. So now, I'm going to take my time to worship every inch of what's mine. If that's okay with you, Mrs. Kaiser."

I'm becoming so wet for him. It's not normal how much he can turn me on with his words alone. Finally, his fingers slide over my pussy again, and I moan louder this time. He curves one finger into me, swearing thickly at the easy glide, then adds another on his second pass.

There's still a note of panic in my chest at the feeling, and as if he can sense it, Rhett kisses me once.

"Eyes on me, little bird. Don't take them off me, or I'll stop."

I hold onto his blue eyes, and it wipes away all other thought.

It's Rhett's hands on me. Rhett's body over mine.

I love him. I love him. I love him.

His mouth carries on down my chest, and his teeth nip each of my nipples, sending sparks straight to my clit. Two fingers work me slowly, until I'm whimpering for *more*.

"When I watched you train, all I could think about was how I wanted to be on the receiving end of the heat and passion it inspires in you. And how it would have ended with you spread out on your back for me."

Sex with Rhett after training would be explosive—still high from the endorphins and already stretched and sweat-slicked.

"I thought about you touching me often," I confess. "The top drawer could never come close."

His eyes flick up from my navel with fiery desire. "We need a top drawer here. I'm most curious about what we could do together on you."

Rhett kisses my hip bone and my hips lift. He's setting my

skin on fire, inch by inch, and I need his mouth between my legs like I need air.

"I've craved the taste of you and been deprived for too long," he growls.

I throw my head back with a cry when he sucks my clit. My legs fall open for him and his fingers slip out of me, arms hooking around my thighs to devour me without mercy. It's all he focuses on, and pleasure tightens over my skin. His mouth sucks, then his tongue lashes over me. When he spears his tongue into me I lose it. My hands tighten in his hair, and while I want to ask him to fuck me with the emptiness I feel, I'm also so close from this assault alone.

"Watch me," he says thickly, the vibrations tingling over my clit.

I manage to prop myself up on one elbow while my other hand threads though his silver locks, and *oh my god*, the sight is so damn sinful and erotic I come, crying out his name.

My thighs shake and I fall back down, sent into a state of otherworldly bliss as he turns more ravenous, groaning against me to stretch out my orgasm so it feels endless. His grip on my thighs tightens as my body spasms. I'm unraveling from the inside out, but he doesn't stop.

Tears gather in the corners of my eyes as he combines bliss and torture. It's unexplainable how I want him to keep going, to do more, and to stop because my clit turns so hypersensitive.

"Again," he says.

I'm a panting mess, but I don't tell him no. Even though each stroke of his tongue jolts through me, I don't want it to end yet.

I think he's going to pause and undress, that this next time he'll make me come on his cock, but his position only shifts to slip two fingers back into me.

"Rhett." I say his name in a whimper, clawing into the couch.

"So tight," he mutters. He's gentle, treating my pussy with such care to prepare me for his next round of assault. "I've missed you so fucking much."

"Me too," I rasp. I forget everything but what he's doing to me.

Rhett's fingers pull out, and when they next push in, my back arches at the change of fullness.

"Oh god." The fullness is addicting, and it surfaces the small anxiety that I don't think he'll fit three fingers.

He works them slowly, and my body abides his every wish, because the stretch lessens as I take what he wants to give me.

"Such a good girl," he says.

My head tips up to watch, and Rhett marvels between my legs, watching his fingers disappear into me. They don't quite make it to his knuckles, and I don't think they will when I'm so full.

"One more for me, baby," he says, kissing the inside of my thigh.

He switches back to two fingers, hooking them, which hits a spot inside me that my body starts begging for, again and again. His mouth joins, and my pleasure starts to accelerate. He picks up pace, reaching his other hand over my ribs and massaging my breast.

"Right there," I say, sprinting right to the edge before he pushes me off with a pinch of my nipple. "Yes, yes—*shit.*"

This one doesn't last as long as the first, but I'm a trembling, euphoric mess all the same. He's so tender in the way he helps me come down. Slowing his pace, trailing tender kisses across my skin. His fingers slip out of me, and I moan at the coolness of the puddle he's made of me.

Rhett climbs back up my body, and I don't think I can take

anymore, but I want to give him what he gave me. I reach for his belt, but Rhett takes my hands, interlocking our fingers by my head as he captures my mouth.

"This was just about you," he murmurs against my lips. "Bath or shower?"

"Will you join me?"

"Just to wash and relax, yes."

"Bath then."

"Good choice." He kisses me once more and then eases away. Rhett covers me with a blanket before heading to run the water.

I curl up on the sofa and watch him for a moment. "Who is Kenna to you?" I ask carefully. I haven't forgotten how bitter she was when speaking about Rhett.

He runs a hand through his hair with a sigh. "We were fifteen when we met. I only knew her for a year before I left. She was sold to Alistair by her father, who was in debt to him. I knew her by another name. For the first time, Alistair took *personal* interest in her."

My stomach clenches, knowing what that means in more ways than one.

"You left her behind? At least, she believes you did."

His eyes fill with misery. "I thought she was dead. I came back for her, but . . ." He shakes his head. "We promised we'd make it out together, that we'd adopt new names and he wouldn't find us. I would be Rhett Kaiser . . . and she would be Kenna Radley. I didn't think she would have taken that name anyway, and that fucking tears me apart. I should have looked again. Investigated more. Instead I accepted Alistair's perfect setup as he must have known I would come for her."

"It's not your fault."

Rhett doesn't accept that, but he doesn't answer. Instead he folds out of his shirt and checks the water temperature.

"How was she?" he asks quietly.

"She's . . ." I don't know what to say. There's no point in lying. "She reminded me a lot of you. When we first met, at least. She's guarded and cold, but she carries herself like nothing could hurt her when she's the one person in room the whose pain no one could begin to fathom."

That drops his gaze, and I head over to him, keeping the blanket around myself. My hand cups his cheek.

"You couldn't have known she was still there."

"I could have. I could have tried harder, and I didn't. I was so scared, and you know . . . when I thought I'd found her, it killed a piece of me, but also . . . there was a part of me that was relieved, because she wouldn't have to suffer anymore."

"I'm so sorry," I say. It's not enough to even touch what he's going through, but all I can do is be there for him.

"Want to tell me how you made an ally out of Silas Balenheizer?" he asks, hooking a brow at me.

"I don't know if I'd call him that. Last I spoke to him, I believed he abandoned the idea because Kenna won't turn on Alistair."

"She's been by his side for thirteen years. Even if there's a part of her that still wants out, it's not going to be easy to make her feel like she can trust anyone. Especially after what I did."

"Let us keep trying with her."

"Us?" he says darkly, drawing me to him with an arm around me. "I don't like the thought of you and Silas being an *us* for anything."

"I can handle him."

"It seems so, but I still don't like it."

I run a hand up his chest with a tilting smile. "Are you jealous?"

"Wildly."

Rhett slants his lips over mine, and I take the opportunity

to undo his belt this time, slipping my hand over his hard cock. He groans into my mouth.

"You're killing me."

"Then let me."

He shakes his head, pushing the blanket off my shoulders. "Right now, what I want more is just you, me, and this bath. Nothing more."

"I called it from the start," I muse, dipping into the hot water. "Underneath the dark, stern exterior that often repels company, you're a hopeless romantic, Rhett Kaiser."

"Only for you, little bird," he says, stripping off his black jeans. "Only for you."

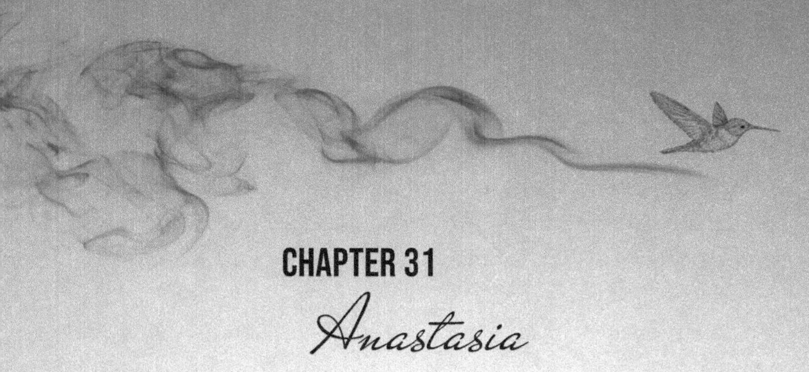

CHAPTER 31
Anastasia

I'm halfway through dinner with my parents in the White House, hardly able to keep my sights off the clock on the mantle. All I want is for it to be over so I can get back to Rhett.

Adam sits beside me. Across from us, Aurora Van der Laize dines with us while her parents chat with mine and Adam's. We're not friends, but her family is close to mine, and we've dined together or attended the same parties often enough that maybe people expect us to be.

She's strange though not in an off-putting way. I just can't figure out what is about her that makes me uneasy. It's like her smile is an alluring mask. She has electric blue highlights through her long, curled dark hair, which she wears in a high ponytail, but I've seen those highlights in purple, silver, and neon pink. She has heterochromia, with one eye dark brown and one a mossy green. Adam tried flirting with her once, but even he agreed there was something that made his hair stand on end in her presence.

"Can you stop that?" Adam mutters to me.

"What?"

Aurora says, "The incessant bouncing of your knee. It's shaking the table."

She doesn't speak much, but I've often noted the different personalities she adopts. As if she knows how to craft her entire being to be what someone wants.

"Sorry," I say.

Adam eyes Aurora, who goes back to acting as if we're that last people she'd give her attention to. "You haven't stopped checking the time. What are you getting up to after this?" He leans in to whisper to me.

I can't risk talking about it here. Even though our parents are loudly engrossed in conversation, I don't trust Aurora can't hear. She might not know the specifics of anything, but she knows about Rhett from the tabloids and likely my father.

"Not here," I whisper back.

"No fun," Aurora whines, lifting her wineglass.

She's my age of twenty-four, but she never went to college. I don't know much about her other than the times my father would say he was glad I had the ambition to get a higher education when the Van der Laizes were at their wit's end with Aurora. She got kicked out of three high schools before they sent her away to boarding school for her final two years.

I find her unpredictable and unnervingly observant. When we were younger, I used to admire her confidence and rebellious streak, but now I'm cautious about it.

We finish up dinner, and our parents all migrate to a lounge room, where they'll drink, likely smoke, and keep talking for hours.

I plan to slip out undetected.

Adam and I are heading into the main foyer when Aurora's voice stops us.

"You look like two people on a mission."

We stop, exchanging a look, and I've plastered on a kind smile by the time we turn to her.

"I don't care for the extravagance of this place," I say casually.

She doesn't usually take any interest in us. Like I said, she's too observant, and the last I saw her, I wasn't part of the underworld. I was just Anastasia Kinsley, the hopeful president's daughter, and an absolute hollow existence.

"Agreed. Can I come with you?" she asks.

I look to Adam for help. His brow curves, and he flounders as much as I do.

"We're just going home," he says.

"Are you two a thing again?"

She's so bold, brazen, in the way she speaks and moves. Aurora slides a hand over the round table in the center of the foyer and then hoists herself onto it. It's against all etiquette and decorum, but while the staff around shift like they should scold her, no one does with the tilted eyes and daring smile she casts over them like a spell.

I decide she reminds me of Silas, wearing her madness on her sleeve, but her composure is enough to pass it off as confidence—or arrogance, depending on your perception.

"No, we're not," Adam answers.

"Because you're all hung up on that dead boyfriend still, right? I wish our parents wouldn't keep repeating the same boring bullshit," she says, canting her head at me.

My jaw tightens at that.

Aurora sighs, swinging her legs. "Ana, the tragically heartbroken and cold kid. Adam, the reserved and uninspired kid. Me, the unhinged and troublesome kid. We're all lost causes—may as well live up to the hell we seem to give them."

Adam says, "They say I'm reserved and uninspired?"

Aurora hops off the table, giving him a playful smile. "Unlike them, I know closet doors when I see them," she says.

That turns Adam sour and me defensive.

She stops shoulder to shoulder with me. "And it takes one

with a secret to see another is hiding one too," she says, personal to me. Then she sighs, seeming bored of our company already. "I have something better planned for tonight anyway."

Adam and I watch her as she leaves, her black heels clicking off the marble, ponytail swaying as she descends the front steps.

"What's her deal?" Adam comments.

"I don't think we want to know," I say.

Both of us shake off the presence of her that lingers like a ghost.

"Want to tell me what *your* deal is then?"

"Rhett and I are going to see Silas tonight," I tell him after a careful scan around.

Adam's brow pulls together. "What are you hoping for with that?"

"He saved Rhett. I have to believe he's still open to an alliance."

"If Kenna is involved."

"After we take down Alistair, we'll get her out. It's the longer way, but Silas will benefit more than anyone if he can maintain the patience."

"I don't like this."

"None of us do. We're not in the clear yet—not even close. There's no telling how any of this shitshow will go."

"Rix is out of his mind with worry with Jeremy still missing."

Adam looks out of the doors as if his mind is drifting to be there with Rix now.

"Is that where you're heading?" I guess at his thoughts.

"Yeah. I might not have his skills, but I've bounced a few ideas around that I don't think are completely hopeless."

My chest warms as I watch his firm expression looking at nothing in particular.

"You're anything but hopeless." I nudge him. "What happened to still hopeful Henry?"

His head snaps to me. "Why do you ask? It's not like it's this or him. Or that I'm finding interest elsewhere. I just like hanging out somewhere and—"

"Relax," I chuckle. "I just mean no one will hold it against you if you take some time for yourself. I know you were hoping to travel and see him more."

Adam's shoulders visibly lose tension. "Right. Well, he seems pretty serious with that other guy anyway."

"Damn, that sucks."

"Yeah, I guess."

He's acting strange, but I can't really blame him when this is all new to him. It's still new to me, and the shit we've found ourselves wrapped in would send our parents to an early grave.

"What are you and Kaiser going to do? You know, if we all manage to come out of this with our lives."

It's a question I don't want to face. That time has to come, and I'm determined we *will* be triumphant. But even when we succeed against Lanshall and Forthson, the fact Rhett and I can never be seen together shatters my heart.

"I don't know," I admit.

Adam's face falls in understanding. "I mean, if you want help with faking your death too . . . epic lengths for love, if you ask me."

I chuckle, and we head out. My dad has a car waiting for me outside the White House gates, but I know somehow Rhett will have found a way to take their place. Giddiness erupts in me as I slip into the passenger seat and I'm met with his stunning face.

"Hi," I say.

"Hi," he echoes, then he leans in to kiss me.

"None of that with the kids in the back," Rix grumbles.

Rhett's mouth twitches with a near smile as he drives off. I'm longing to see a full one. A bright, rare smile feels like distant treasure, but I'll wait for it.

We drop Adam and Rix off at the Den as night falls, and then we head to Lumina.

"Are you sure about this?" Rhett asks as we get close to pulling up.

"I haven't been sure about anything when it comes to playing in the devil's playground," I say.

Rhett takes my hand. "I'm torn to say this, but welcome to my world, little bird."

Outside Lumina, I don't think Rhett's ever held my hand so tightly before.

"I'm not waiting outside if he decides to only see you," Rhett says, handing off the keys to the valet.

I don't mention that's a high possibility. Silas is very particular about who he lets in. He might have saved Rhett for my sake, and to gain Lanshall and Forthson assets at the end of all this, but he knows Rhett is also the leader of a notorious network.

When we get to security, we both press our fingers to the scanners.

"Silas will only be seeing Miss Kinsley tonight," one says.

Rhett's hand flexes in mine, but I sigh dramatically.

"Pity," I say, turning to Rhett. His eyes ask what I'm up to as I reach up his chest. "I'm not here as Miss Kinsley. I'm here as Mrs. Kaiser, and Silas will see us both or not at all."

I might have officially lost my damn mind as I reach under Rhett's formal coat, pulling his gun from his concealed holster, and aim it at the security guy's head.

Rhett slips a tense arm around me as the other guy arms himself, pointing his gun at my head.

"We don't have time to play, Silas," I say. I'm confident he's listening in.

"This wasn't part of the plan," Rhett says in my ear.

"Plans always go to shit anyway."

"You continue to surprise me, princess," Silas says with a smile in his voice.

He emerges from behind the security guards. They try to block him, but he makes them yield. The moment he's in view, I shift my aim to him. Silas pulls out a cigarette, lighting it with a hint of a devil's curve on his mouth.

"I wanted to see what happens when you try to separate the Kaisers. I'm not disappointed." His gaze roves over Rhett as he blows out smoke, slipping a hand into his pocket. "You look more patched up than when I found you at least."

It's then I notice Silas is the first guy I've met to match Rhett's tall height.

"I was under the impression you weren't interested anymore when I came here and you declined to see me," I say. I'm indebted to him for getting Rhett out, but I can't smother my note of resentment that I might have avoided being taken that night if he'd let me in.

"Come—we have much to talk about," Silas says, heading back inside.

Security look pissed as hell when we hold our aims for a few seconds longer in challenge. I smile sweetly, lowering my gun, and the one I aimed it at holds out his hand for it with a disgruntled expression.

I hand it over and pat Rhett's chest. "See? Job done."

He shakes his head, with a huff somewhere between amusement and incredulity. Our fingers link as we follow Silas in.

"I can't tell if I'm proud of you or concerned for you."

"It's your role as my boyfriend to be proud, and your job as my bodyguard to be concerned."

Rhett presses a kiss to my temple as we walk, and the music grows louder.

"When do I get the upgrade to husband for real?"

"When my left hand feels a diamond heavier."

He chuckles, and it's the most genuine sound of happiness he's made since I got him back. He squeezes my waist. "That's a fair bargain."

We wind up the spiral stairs to Silas's personal level of the club and find him already reclining in his usual spot on the sofa, facing us. He finishes the last drag of his cigarette and leans toward the ashtray on the table as he flicks his gaze up.

Silas tips his head, and one of his men lean in to hear his request. As Rhett and I sit on the sofa opposite him, everyone on the level starts to leave.

I cross my legs, angling toward Rhett, who claims me with a hand over my thigh. As the men leave I cast a look over the balcony, and I'm stunned to see a glass panel rising from the ground. It's one-way tinted glass. No one below is able to see us, but we can still see them. I shift with a note of caution at why it's necessary, until the glass screen drowns out a lot of the music, leaving only a distant beat.

The bartender comes over with a tray, setting down three glasses, then he's the last to leave.

We're alone with Silas, save for one guy lingering at the back wall. I wager he's Silas's right-hand man.

"We didn't expect such exclusive treatment," I say light-heartedly.

With the screen and the emptiness, this space feels more like an elaborate office.

"With what we have to discuss, I won't take any chances with anyone leaking information. I don't like mess in the midst of a well-crafted plan."

My eyes flick to the guy in the shadows across the room.

Silas says, "That's Julio. He doesn't have a tongue to speak, but even then, he's been my guy for a decade. I don't say this lightly—I trust him."

I'm curious about how he lost his tongue, but it's not appropriate to ask.

"Now, you have this one night to convince me to trust *you*, Kaiser. And if you don't, my saving you from Lanshall will become a worse fate than if you were still there."

CHAPTER 32
Rhett

We're sitting at the complete mercy of the most notorious family in the underworld. I knew the gun I had would be taken if we made it inside, and my cock is still semi-hard from how sexy Ana's stunt was with it. It terrifies me to see her confidence in all this, but I'm also overwhelmed with awe for her.

I don't have my earpiece in as we were scanned and checked before we could follow Silas in, and I expected that too. I'm placing a whole lot of faith in Ana alone that we'll emerge from here with a powerful alliance, not a bigger target on our backs.

It's just me, her, and Silas Balenheizer.

"You know, when you hear of the president's daughter falling for an infamous criminal, so much so that she puts her own life on the line and steps out of her topside life to save him, the obvious question is, what the fuck does this guy have to offer her?" Silas reaches for the dry martini, sliding it across the table with eyes on Ana. "But I get it. I didn't until right now. Apart, no one would guess you two were a match. But together, it's undeniable you're far more than that."

Everything Silas does and says has a motive. I don't take the appraisal as a mere compliment, nor do I give a fuck about his thoughts or feelings regarding me and Ana.

"Your driving motivation for this is Kenna Radley. Why?" I ask.

It's dangerous to assert myself like this with Silas, but from my assessment of him so far, the only way he communicates is with fire on fire.

"Motivation? No. Make no mistake, Kaiser. I don't entertain such radical ideas as overthrowing two very powerful cartel lines on a whim because of a beautiful woman seemingly tied to one of them. I'll admit, I find her fascinating, alluring. I would have been thrilled for her to have joined us, and you would have found me in better spirits. But this is between us. A highly risky business deal if we find everything aligns between us."

"She's not tied to him out of want. She'll make it seem like she is because it would expose her chains to admit she had no other choice," I say. "As part of the deal, we get her out. Kicking and screaming, if need be."

Silas reaches for one of the two glasses of scotch, pushing it across to me. "We're off to a mutual start, it seems," he says, picking up the other and taking a drink.

I reach for Ana's martini, passing it to her. I don't pick up the other scotch.

Silas notices, canting his head a fraction as if he's reassessing his first instinct about me. His presence holds true to what I've heard about the Balenheizers from whispers. He's a masterful observer of people and a manipulator. He can make a person doubt everything they are as if he can see the truths buried behind their eyes.

"I got the drink right—you just won't take it," he decides, more to himself.

"I don't drink."

"You're not a recovering alcoholic, so what happened while you were under the influence that you think you could have prevented if you weren't?"

Ana's hand caresses my arm as if she can sense my stiffness.

"We're not here to talk about me."

"On the contrary, I like to know exactly who I'm getting into business with before we go any further."

"It goes both ways," Ana says. "There's a reason you took such immediate interest in Kenna and not me. It could be that she reminds you of someone, or perhaps you have some savior complex because you think you failed someone in your past."

My hand flexes on her thigh in warning, and my senses spike at the dark shift in Silas's eyes.

"You're right. And also very dangerously wrong."

"My fiancée was killed the night I proposed four years ago," I confess. "We had been drinking. I'll never be relieved of the torment of wondering if I could have stood a chance at fighting them off if I were sober."

Silas latches onto my story to my relief. "Then you went on to found Xoid?"

"Yes. I wanted to hunt down Alistair Lanshall and tear his empire apart."

"I have to say part of what you do causes something of an issue for me. I actually admire your efforts to stop trafficking. But I hear that's not all you've been destroying."

"I'll stop anything that's a harm to innocents."

"Heroic of you. But you see where this alliance could come to an impasse."

"You don't condone trafficking, so we're aligned there," Ana says. "Anything else . . . well, even you said a little threat keeps you sharp."

Silas reacts with intrigue to the challenge she lays down. "If your little vigilante group managed to intercept just one of the types of deals I make, I'd lose millions."

Ana shrugs. "You'll make more."

"You want me to agree to help a group knowing what it could potentially cost me with their meddling later?"

"You'll gain more in assets taking over Lanshall and Forthson than we'd ever prevent you from making through drugs or organ trade or whatever else you deal in," I say. "Besides, mostly, our efforts go to trafficking, and that certainly doesn't go away with Lanshall and Forthson. There are many smaller networks that need to be eradicated, and call us *little* all you want, but Xoid expands through far more States than just D.C."

"I'm aware," Silas says, but I think I've surprised him somewhat.

He finishes off his drink and crosses his ankle over his knee as he leans back. His shift in demeanor makes me think we've made it past his assessment round. I don't relax.

"So, you wouldn't disappoint me by coming here without a plan," Silas says.

Ana takes a deep breath. "I think Forthson could still believe we're on his side. He knew I wanted to get Rhett out, and that once he was out, Alistair would know I'd betrayed him. His hope was that I'd convince you to ally with us without a marriage, but Jacob would be in on it with us to take down Alistair and get a share of his assets."

Silas chuckles. It's a mocking, dark sound. "Forthson might be the biggest idiot of them all. What does he have that gives him a seat at this table?"

"He's merely a nepotism kid who's never lost in his life," I say bitterly.

I want to rip Jacob Forthson's head from his fucking neck.

He sold my little bird. He sold Allie, and if I find out I'm wrong and Jacob's had her all this time, I'll struggle to choose where to begin with his suffering.

Silas hums, pulling out a cigarette as he fixes his thoughtful gaze on the ceiling. He offers one to me. "If you're not going to accept a drink to take your visibly sharp edge off, this might help," he says.

I glance at Ana. because if she's even remotely put off by it, I won't smoke in her presence. She smiles, and it's all I need to dull my edges really, but this conversation with Silas is far from over. Ana leans over, accepting the cigarette. She puts it between her lips to light it with a Zippo, then she takes it out, reaching out for my mouth with it between her two fingers.

I want to bend her over the pool table to our right so badly with how she's seducing me with those hazel eyes.

"I'm not a stranger to team sports," Silas says casually. "This feels like an invitation."

It might be how Ana leans in, brushing her chest to mine, or how her hand has inched so high on my thigh that stretching her fingers would brush my cock. She shifts away with a devious, coy smile. But my eyes turn firm no matter who the fuck he is. Ana is mine. Only mine.

Before we came, she assured me that despite what Alistair wanted to do—to sell her as a fucking bride—Silas was never interested in her. His sights were fixed on Kenna from the moment he saw her.

I take a deep drag of the cigarette.

Ana says, "If we can set Forthson on Lanshall believing he'll have your alliance at the end of it, we'll get to watch them tear each other apart."

"I'm not convinced Forthson will accept that role so easily. But we can try this your way first, princess."

Ana's face firms, and I turn defensive for her without knowing why.

"Why did you let me leave your club that night?" she asks. It's in her slight tone of hurt that I realize she feels betrayed. Though she expected it and knew how Silas could be, she made the mistake of believing he could come to be considered a *friend*.

"Everyone has to make sacrifices," Silas says. He looks at her with what I think is the best of an apology she'll never see. "Had I let you in, I never would have let you leave, because Lanshall was coming for you anyway. He sent you here that final night in an attempt to get you to sway me one last time before he planned to take you away to punish Kaiser for something *he* failed to do."

I'm slammed by a brick with that insight. It was my fault. The isolation. The assault. Every trauma and torment Ana has been though was because of me, and I had the fucking audacity to think I could chain her to a life of this.

Ana tries to grab my arm as I stand, stubbing out the cigarette and pacing away.

Silas goes on. "Had I kept you in this club, even under the impression I was claiming you like he wanted, there was talk of Kaiser's death, that no punishment without you would work, and after three months they weren't any closer to getting him to do what they wanted. You had his location, and I managed to intercept that. I figured if I got Kaiser out, Lanshall isn't a brash idiot – he'd lose everything in killing the president's daughter one way or another, so you were safe."

"Safe," I huff resentfully. The word is a fucking mockery.

Ana was safe in her life before me. Perhaps Gregory Forbes would have been found out another way, and she would have lived an ordinary and carefree life.

"We should go," Ana says.

"Meet with Forthson and report back to me," Silas says. "This is all a ticking grenade we're passing around now, and I won't be the last man holding it."

No, he won't be. I will. Even if I have to be the one to carry it right to the end and go down in the explosion. If it gets rid of Alistair, I'll do it.

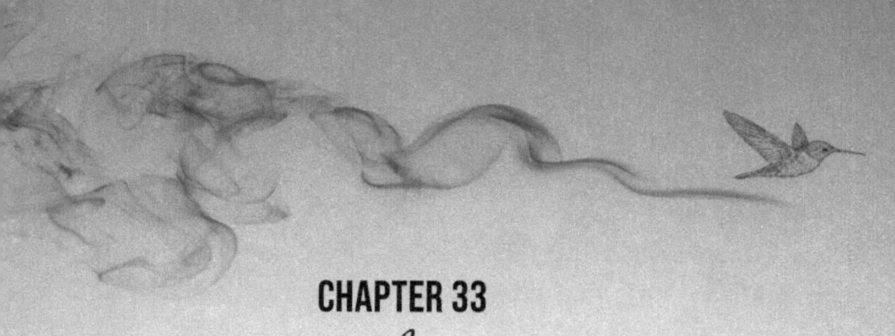

CHAPTER 33
Anastasia

Rhett is speeding. Usually I wouldn't care, but all I can think about is how he can't be seen, and if the police pull us over . . . I'm flashed back to memories of how cold and uncaring the officers were when telling me about Rhett's accident. His death.

"Slow down," I say.

He doesn't listen, and then I realize we're not going the right way to the warehouse apartment.

"Where are we going?"

This could take us to the Den, until . . .

He passes the intersection to head that way too, and I only know one dreaded location this way.

"Rhett, stop."

His knuckles turn white against the wheel.

"You're scaring me—stop!"

My heart is wild against my ribs when he finally eases off the accelerator.

"You're going to your parents for a while. It's the only safe place for you."

"Like hell I am! Pull the fuck over, or so help me, I'm about to make you."

His eyes cut briefly to me, pulsing with dangerous challenge. I don't back down, and maybe I even frighten myself with how sure I am that I'll reach for the steering wheel and take the impact of whatever happens next. I don't know where these impulsive, reckless thoughts are coming from, but I can't stop them.

I reach out, and Rhett catches my wrist before slamming on the breaks. He's pulled down a back alley anyway, but his cool eyes are livid for what I was about to do. I rip my hand out of his and unclip my seat belt. I have to walk off this anxiety-riddled rage.

"What the fuck was that, Ana?" Rhett demands, getting out of the car too.

Night is falling, and I stand in front of the headlights with the car still running.

"You don't get to give me back!" I yell. My eyes prick, but I will not cry. "It took me a long time to find you, and you don't get to give me back like that."

His face tries to soften, but his feelings echo mine. There's so much pain and fear between us it makes our closeness fragile.

"I don't want to give you back," he says, edging closer. "I want you to see that I'm not good for you. I want you to walk away, because I can't."

"I don't just mean since you were taken," I say, my voice falling. "It took me a long time to find you because I haven't felt like this before, and I never will again. I know you lost someone once and it terrifies you to lose again, but the difference is, she didn't know about any of it, and I do. I know it all, and I want to stay until the very end. We're no different to anyone else hoping the end will be very, very far away. We're no different, Rhett. We're owed just as many years as anyone and promised none of them just the same too. So don't give me away in the name of protecting me just because we can see the faces of our monsters. I'm scared too, but I'm more scared of being without you."

Rhett's hand slips over my jaw. His fingers thread through the back of my hair and then tighten. My lips part with a spark of wild desire when he forces my face closer.

"No one has ever driven me as crazy as you do. Every new taste of your blooming wild side is a drug I feel I should be horrified by, like maybe I'm corrupting you. But oh, Anastasia, I didn't think it was possible, but you're corrupting me, mind, body, and soul."

"We're all going to die, and I choose to go by your side whether it's sooner or later. I'm just really hoping for later."

"So much fucking later. I still have the world to give you."

"And I still have hell to give you, remember?"

Rhett slams his lips to mine in a kiss that's as wild as it is searching. He lifts me onto the hood of the car, leaning into me as if he can't get close enough. My skirt rides up to feel his hardening cock against my core, and I crave the wildness of how open we are.

Until I remember Rhett is a secret, and it pains me. Otherwise I wouldn't care who could trespass, likely call the police —I would risk it all for what is blazing my skin right now. But Rhett can't be seen.

I can't pull away when I'm practically lying on the hood of the SUV, grappling his clothing like we're two starved animals.

"We need to go," I pant.

Rhett groans, but he doesn't stop his assault against my mouth, my neck. I want him to take me in the car right now, and I'm close to suggesting it when his phone buzzes.

"It could be important," I say when he tries to ignore it.

"You're the only thing that's important."

I giggle when his teeth nick my serpent earring, and I push at his chest. Rhett sighs in reluctance, pulling me up to him and keeping his arm around me as he fishes out his phone.

"It's Rix. We should head to the Den before we go home tonight," he informs me, frowning and typing back.

I tug at his shirt. "Home," I repeat.

Rhett's expression softens, but I know it'll take longer to erase the guilt when he looks at me.

"Yes, baby. Home."

"It's going to take time for you to stop thinking I would have been better off without you," I say. "I don't know what else I can say to make you believe it isn't true. Maybe I would have been safer. Or maybe Gregory would have achieved exactly what he wanted, and Matthew would have taken me. There would have been no *you* to help stop it. Perhaps we would have still met someday, but it would have been through your work, when you saved me after it was too late."

Rhett's eyes close at that unthinkable alternative fate.

I force him to look at me. "Say that it's you and me. Say that you have no regrets."

Rhett leans his forehead to mine. "It's you and me, little bird. I promise you that."

"You don't get to lock me in another cage and do this yourself. Don't ever think of that again."

"I'm sorry," he mutters, kissing me once and then lifting me off the hood.

"Good. Now let's get back to work, Agent."

It's past midnight when we get to the Den, and I'm buzzing with nerves and excitement over what could be so important it couldn't wait.

The elevator doors open, and Rhett and I head into the

large empty room. It's just Rix and Adam here, but though I spot them, they don't detect us.

"Oh shit," I mutter, stopping my step, which strains our joined hands.

Since everyone else has retired for the night, my quiet words travel across the space, breaking up a very heated-looking kiss between Rix and Adam.

They push away from each other as if a grenade has been thrown between them.

"He's just pretty to look at, and you took a long fucking time, before you get the wrong idea," Rix grumbles, taking up his seat again. He looked about to climb on top of the desk with Adam under him.

My cheeks flush at the intrusion. I look to Adam, who won't meet my eye.

"I should have been home a while ago, just took charity in him being a loner here," Adam says. He grabs his jacket.

"Wait—we'll go with you after this," I try, but Adam looks ready to bolt out of here.

"Thanks, but I've heard it all. See you later, A," he says to me, not looking back at Rix or at Rhett at all.

When I look up, I don't think Adam needs to see Rhett's glare to feel it. The elevator doors shut to take Adam up, and I whack Rhett's arm. His head whips to me, stunned as if I've snapped him out of a reel of a hundred ways to kill Adam Sullevan.

"What?" he complains.

"When are you going to let go of your grudge with him?"

"Never."

"Why?"

"I don't care about his reasons—he hurt you."

"*I* care about *him*. So you need to get the hell over it."

Rhett kisses my head. "No."

He slips around me toward Rix, and I follow him slack-jawed. This conversation isn't over, but as he begins asking Rix what's so urgent, I settle that issue for now.

"You called me here to show me a track on Jeremy," Rhett says.

"You're going to want to see where he went," Rix says, clacking away at the keyboard.

A map appears and then zooms in. Whatever it is makes Rhett lean in, eyes darting around. "That's a Forthson location," he says to himself.

"Think Alistair really has the balls to send spies inside his number-one enemy's territory? It's the worst offense, and if Forthson found out . . ."

"We need to get him the fuck out," Rhett snaps, straightening and running a hand through his hair.

"He's around a whole group of guys at all times, never alone. We're at a loss, man. If he tries to run, they'll shoot him on the spot. We try to close in, and it could end in a bloodbath."

"I'll meet with Jacob," I say.

"Not alone," Rhett counters.

"I should. He's not best fond of you and might not talk. He's not a fool to trust you."

"He won't trust you either in that case. Anything he says to you, you'll relay to me anyway."

I purse my lips. "We would meet every second Sunday at a rooftop restaurant in the city. It's been a couple of weeks, but I imagine he figured out what happened with Alistair and realized why I haven't shown. We should go this week and hope he turns up."

Rix says, "Should we tell him about Lanshall? If we really think he's buying that he's part of our team, he might be able to get Jeremy out next time he's sent to his location. Fake his death as a weeded-out spy or something."

"I don't like this," Rhett mutters.

I watch the wheels turning in his mind as he surveys the screens, but he's not attentive to anything on them. He stands with arms crossed, his chin in one hand. "Something doesn't feel right," is all he says.

It wouldn't seem like much from anyone else, but I trust Rhett's intuition more than anyone's.

"Let's just meet with him. Perhaps you'll get a better sense of whether we can trust him then," I say.

Rhett nods. "We can't give up Jeremy's position as one of us yet. It's too much of a risk."

"Damn it," Rix exasperates. He looks so tired and concerned. I don't know exactly how long Jeremy has been in Alistair's clutches, but Rix is getting desperate.

"I know," Rhett says, and the concern of a brother lingers in him too.

"He seemed well when I saw him a few weeks ago," I say. It's not much, and my chest is tight as I think of his kindness. "He really helped me. Asked about Frodo and Sam. I think he's worried about your wrath when he gets out."

"At least he's keeping confident he'll get out," Rhett mutters.

"That's always him. It's like he believes he's fucking Batman sometimes," Rix grumbles. His mouth slowly upturns, and he chuckles. Even Rhett almost smiles with his breath of humor. "Fuck. I miss that damned kid."

"We'll get him back," Rhett promises, but I hear the note of wariness in him. "It's late—we need to all get some sleep."

The thought of going to bed in the warehouse apartment with Rhett sounds like the best thing in the world right now. I wish we could have a week, just one full week, to spend locked up in there alone before we have to dive into the devil's work. For now, I'll take every moment, however short, that I can get.

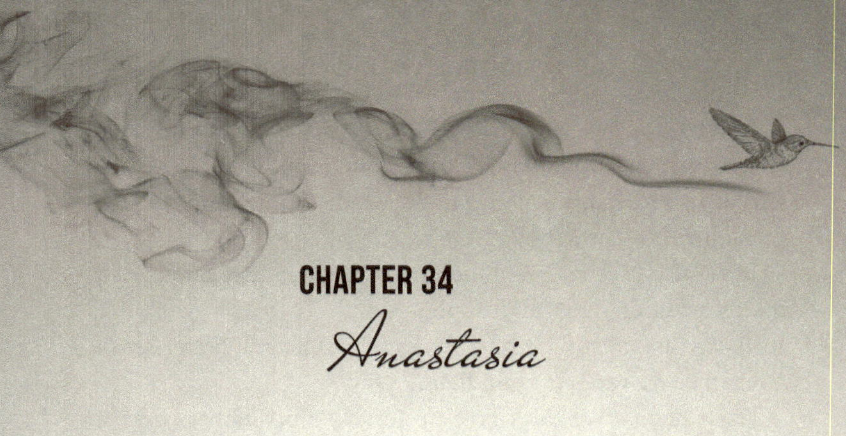

CHAPTER 34

Anastasia

"I'm glad you're here, but I also wish you weren't," I say to Rhett.

I sip my water again as we sit hand in hand at the usual table I meet Jacob at in the rooftop restaurant.

"Would it make you feel better if I dyed my hair as a disguise?" Rhett muses.

My eyes rove over him, trying to imagine brunette, black, or red in place of his silver-blond hair.

"Absolutely not," I decide.

He knows my anxiety is that he'll be seen by the wrong person. I don't know what I'll do if law enforcement gets ahold of him. It would cause far worse friction between my dad and me. I wouldn't care what kind of crazed person it would make me look if I defended someone who, to my parents and everyone else, is a fraudulent criminal they've concluded could have been part of Gregory's setup to assassinate my father.

"We're being careful." Rhett consoles me, slipping a hand over my bouncing knee. "Rix has eyes everywhere, and we're diligent before going in anywhere."

I nod. I know this, yet I can't smother my nerves.

Just then, my already racing heart leaps at the sight of Jacob strolling in wearing a gleam of excitement as he assesses both Rhett and me while making his way over.

"As much as jealousy plagues me, I have to admit, there's something satisfying in seeing two undeniably suited pieces back together."

"I wasn't sure if you would come," I say. Time to pull on my mask of composure.

"We still have an ongoing concern, darling. I would be hunting you instead had you no sense to meet me here."

Rhett's fingers flex on my thigh, and my hand slips over his as if it might calm him. I can practically feel him straining against lunging for Jacob.

Jacob orders a glass of white wine. Then his gaze flicks to Rhett. "I still don't see what Lanshall and Ana see in you personally, but you've caused quite a bit of trouble for all of us, Kaiser."

"Then I'm doing my job," he replies calmly.

"I lost a lot of money because of your interference at my gala last winter. It's brave of you to be here right now."

Jacob leans back arrogantly in his chair when his wine is served. His cool eyes on Rhett simmer with dark intent. "As I hear, you're about to gain far more than you lost in this new alliance with Silas Balenhaizer to take down Lanshall, so I guess we're even."

Jacob's chin tips up slightly. "Not yet," he says, but he drops that topic for now when his attention returns to me. "I want to meet with Silas again for my own peace of mind. You two have done enough, and it's time for the adults to take over."

"You wouldn't have him without me," I say.

"If not your hand in marriage, what did you offer him to keep his interest in this?"

I expected the interrogation, and I keep myself as straight and confident as he is. "He has an interest in someone in Alistair's network. We happen to have a connection to her."

"You expect me to believe the infamous Silas Balenheizer would risk his name and resources on this for a no-name, no-advantage woman?"

My jaw clenches at the amusement lining his tone as he speaks about Kenna though he doesn't know her. His observations have some merit—at least to someone as cold and power-hungry as Jacob.

"He doesn't just get her. He wants Alistair's network. All his assets. She just happens to be a keen motivator for it, and she belongs exclusively to Lanshall himself right now," Rhett says.

I know it disgusts him to speak of Kenna like this too, but it's the only language Jacob will understand. Given Silas's name, he would expect ruthlessness and for Kenna to be nothing more than something to be used like those women Jacob tried to sell.

"I see," Jacob says, taking a sip of his wine.

I'm finding him hard to read right now. He's debating something, harboring a hidden triumph, and I can't figure out what it is as he looks between us with a ghost of a smile.

"Silas has extended an invite to Lumina for you," I say.

That grabs his attention. "I had my doubts about you, Anastasia, but you seem to have gotten everything you wanted."

"Not yet," I say. "I want Alistair Lanshall dead, and he's ours to do away with when that time comes."

Jacob nods. "Agreed. As a celebration of our alliance, I want to extend my own invite to you all, and I hope Silas will accept too. I have a new venue opening, a gentlemen's club, on the south side next month. I'd like you two to be my guests of honor."

A few heartbeats of silence pass. Of course we don't want to attend the opening of something that is no doubt going to be used for nefarious means. It goes against everything Rhett stands for, and I realize that's why Jacob wants us there. It's the equivalent of getting Rhett to kneel for him.

"We'd love to," I say.

On the contrary, Rhett's expression is scarily firm and resistant. Jacob only delights in it.

"Excellent. And I would like to send you a gown to show my utter appreciation."

"You don't have to—"

"I insist."

I smile tightly. He won't take no for an answer. I wonder what would happen if I disregarded his choice of gown, but the mere thought rattles me. I can only think it's another way to sink Rhett lower so he can bask in the sight of me in his chosen clothing.

"Thank you," I force out.

Rhett's breathing is deep and calculated. His eyes pin Jacob with so much loathing I'm afraid he could break and ruin this.

"Why Allie?" he asks, so cold it licks a chill down my spine.

"Alyra DeVerre had a buyer who came to me personally before I knew she was part of your adorable little crime-stopping efforts," Jacob says. "It had nothing to do with you at first. Until she slipped up in her search for the jewelry. I had to wonder how she knew about the earrings that were destined for her. I wondered what you would do if you were forced to choose which woman to save."

Rhett's other fist tightens until his knuckles turn white. "I'm going to fucking kill you," he says, so low and deadly.

"We have to let bygones be bygones, Kaiser. Don't want to

risk the safety of your girl and your network threatening me like that again."

I know a storm has to be crashing in Rhett's mind to keep his words at bay because we're walking on *very* dangerous ground.

It's not a threat; it's a fucking promise.

We have to keep smart and composed. Jacob is the one we're luring into our trap. His words are crafty and maddening, and it's hard to be convinced they mean nothing.

We will win this time.

"Do you know what happened to her?" Rhett asks tightly.

"Unfortunately, no. I got my payment for her before Maddox Cuvier was killed. I have no interest in what follows."

"Doesn't exactly look great for business if your buyers turn up dead," Rhett accuses.

"You're right. But there is nothing linking me to his death. As I hear, it was amateur work, and it's still an open case with the might of the DeVerre law firm breathing down law enforcement's necks, as he was one of their managing partners. I wouldn't risk that kind of press and recklessness."

I get a really bad feeling with this insight. Rhett told me of his suspicions that Liam could have interfered, but I found the idea outlandish.

Liam Forbes . . . capable of killing a man, and how the hell would he have gotten her out himself? I know he still has feelings for her even after many estranged years, but I still can't picture him capable of this.

Yet at the same time, I'm *hopeful* for it.

Even though I'm not sure how to save him from the mess he's in because of his father and what they might condemn him with too, and now, if he could be pinned for murder . . . *Oh god.*

I'm starting to feel lightheaded, and I take a longer drink

of water. Maybe Rhett can sense my rising panic as he shifts forward, preparing to leave.

"Enjoy your time at Lumina. I can't say I'll look forward to seeing you again, but I'll tolerate it." He stands, linking our fingers and pulling me up too.

"Piss me off, Kaiser, and I won't mind earning favor with the president instead by turning you in and saving his damsel of a daughter who fell for a fraud and a criminal."

Anger boils in me at that threat, but our backs are against the wall right now.

We don't look back as we leave.

In the car I can't console Rhett's tangible anger with my head spinning on Liam.

"He has a house," I remember suddenly. "I don't know exactly where it is, only that it's very remote and his parents never knew about it. No one did. He bought it after shuffling money from his trust into another account for years and passing it off as material expenses."

"Liam?" Rhett inquires, and I guess this works to distract him too.

"Yes. He wanted a placed no one else knew about, and I always wondered why." I bite my lip, closing my eyes with the wave of guilt that passes over me. "Now I can't stop wondering how bad it was for him. If Gregory or Matthew were abusing him—if not physically, then emotionally. If he was so lonely or worried that he thought he might need to hide someday, and I didn't see it." I shake my head, turning angry at myself. "That's a lie. I did see it, I just never questioned it deeper."

"Whatever was going on with him and the Forbes is not your fault. You were a great friend to him. That was clear."

"A great friend would have seen past the surface," I mutter.

Rhett doesn't speak, but he takes my hand, and that's enough.

"Do you think it would be in D.C.?" he asks gently.

I try to think back to that long-ago conversation when we'd dreamed about the future. "He spoke of Boston," I recall. "He said he grew up there until he was sixteen. I don't know if that's where he'd want to go back to, but it might be a start."

"He wouldn't have used his own name if he wanted it to be untraceable. Xoid is good, but we have barely anything to go on."

My phone rings, and I dip my hand into my pocket for it. "Shit. It's my dad." I pick up with a forcibly cheerful greeting, but he rambles right over it. His speech is fast and panicked, but also relieved, and I try to focus on the actual words. "I'm fine. What are you talking about?" I try to cut in.

"Your apartment, Ana. Your mother and I stopped by, and it was a wreckage. We've been worried sick."

I blanch, not considering the state Alistair's guys might have left my apartment in, nor that my parents might come by.

"I didn't know," I lie, and it burns my throat like acid. "I-I decided to take a break away. Some spa resort just outside the city. I'm safe. I promise."

Rhett's expression is pulled together in concern and question.

"We're coming to get you," Dad says.

"Don't. I'm okay here and have no idea what happened there. Likely some thieves watching the apartment realized it was empty and decided to see if there was anything of value in there."

I scrunch my eyes, propping my elbow on the car door and holding my head. It hurts to lie to them so badly, but the truth would be catastrophic.

"At least tell me the resort," he says.

"Lakomora," I say. I've been there once. I'm terrified he might go there regardless. "But I check out tomorrow."

"Then I'll arrange you a stay at one of our hotels in the meantime, and I'm assigning you a guard."

"I don't need one," I protest.

I want to scream with how unfair this is. That I have Rhett back and he's the best protection I could have, but my dad would have him arrested and be utterly outraged at his fraudulent death on top of his credentials now.

Rhett rubs my thigh, and while I want the comfort of him, I'm in pain that he's my secret.

"I'm not arguing with you on this," Dad says firmly.

He's changed so much. We both have, and this friction between us cuts deeply. When he assigned Rhett last year he fully sympathized with my resistance to having a guard, and we talked a lot. Now he doesn't negotiate. I get it—his job is more intense than ever. The threat against his life and mine was real once, and there could be far more out there with a vendetta against the president.

I want to disappear again, shrink slowly back into who I was before I met Rhett—one who would have hidden from the world rather than face it.

"I'm texting you with the details, Ana. Go there tonight, and your guards will be there."

I don't answer, just hang up, because I think my voice will crack.

"We'll work through this." Rhett tries to comfort me.

I watch the buildings zip by, and all I want is to go back to the warehouse apartment. "It's not fair," I whisper. My throat becomes too tight for anything more.

"I'll try to find a way to sneak by them," he says.

"I want to go home. To our home. After these past few torturous months, we're owed that." I swipe away a resentful tear.

"We'll have endless months to come."

"Of secrets and lies and sneaking around."

The stretch of silence weighs heavy between us.

"What can I do?" he asks, pained.

"Take me home."

I think he's going to sigh and tell me how my safety is too important and that my father is right. He doesn't. Rhett squeezes my thigh.

"Okay, baby."

CHAPTER 35
Rhett

I shouldn't have brought Ana back to the warehouse apartment, but how was I to fucking deny her and make her pain worse?

Despite the night falling and it only being a matter of hours before her parents realize she's disobeyed, Ana looks so relaxed here, like it's a different world between these four walls, one made just for us. I decide that's worth risking everything for.

After taking off her shoes and coat, she makes her way over to the dresser. We managed to get some new clothes and pajamas while in town today, but she drops the bags and opens the drawer of my T-shirts and hoodies anyway.

It swells in my fucking chest.

I'm hovering, observing her every movement like a stalker. She strips out of her black skirt and top, takes off her bra, and pulls on a black hoodie with a snake embroidered in black down the center.

It reminds me. "You didn't pick out anything with color today."

Ana crawls onto the bed, and she's so fucking sexy my

dick twitches at her enticing smile. "Neither did you," she says.

"We weren't shopping for me."

"I like the darkness." She stretches out with a contented inhale. Her long legs are just begging to be wrapped around my shoulders.

"Did you wear black for me?"

Her head falls to look at me. "Yes. Part of me was mourning when I had no assurance you were alive other than my gut instinct. But it also made me feel like I had a piece of you."

My hand curls around one of the four bed posts. I'm overwhelmed with love for this woman. Absolute devoted and entirely undeserving of her.

"Are you going to stand there looking at me all night or join me, Agent?"

For years I didn't know what being alive truly felt like. Then I met Ana, and I don't remember what feeling completely numb to the world was like. She's a beating heart. *My* beating heart.

"Your parents are going to be looking for you, and it'll only grow more intense the longer you avoid them."

"Then I guess I'm your secret now too."

I slip out of my leather jacket, then I pull my T-shirt over my head. I'm a selfish, deplorable bastard for this. I should agree with her father and take her to that hotel with new guards even if she fights me. But I can't. I fucking *can't.*

"You might want to start picking your new name," I say jokingly.

"Ana Kaiser," she says with a low, seductive edge.

When I ease onto the bed her legs part, knees settling around my hips. I take her hands, interlocking our fingers and sliding them up over her head as I hover over her.

"You don't get to be just another creature of the underworld," I say. "Are you ready to work for what it takes to rule it?"

Her eyes spark with a thrill. "Yes."

"That's my girl."

I kiss her, long and deep. Her knees tighten around me, pulling me closer, and she lifts her hips to grind her pussy over my aching cock, tight behind my jeans.

"Impatient," I mutter against her lips.

"I need you inside me."

Music to my fucking ears when I've thought of being buried in her tight heat again for far too long.

"Will I take you here? The kitchen island? The wall?" I kiss down her neck with each suggestion, and she becomes increasingly breathless. "What will it be?"

"All of them."

"Still not one to choose." I smile against her throat.

I reach my hand down when I can't wait to feel her a second longer. She's soaked through her underwear, and I groan.

"I want to fuck you just like this. In my hoodie."

"Then hurry up and fuck me."

My cock jerks at her demand. I want more of it. Her taking control and commanding exactly what she wants. But for now, I'm the impatient one, slipping her panties to the side and sinking a finger in deeply. The wrapping of her slick heat around my fingers or my cock will never fail to make a deranged man of me. After a few thrusts I add a second finger and watch as her body curves, beautiful as always.

I can't wait any longer, fumbling my belt undone and pulling out my cock. My jeans stay on as I line myself up at her entrance and sink into her slowly, savoring every inch disappearing into her. Fully seated, I take a moment to collect my sanity with the heat of her pussy creeping over my whole damn body.

"I love you," I say, leaning in to kiss her. "And I missed you so goddamn much."

Ana's hands thread into my hair, tightening as she turns more passionate and needy. I'm still, but she tries to fuck me herself, lifting her hips in a way that makes my head spin.

"Fucking hell, little bird," I rasp, pulling out of the kiss and dipping my head down to watch her.

"I want it hard," she says, chasing her pleasure in precious little pants.

"How hard? Because I want to fuck you so deep into this mattress you won't remember where you are."

I begin a slow, teasing pace to savor the feel of her. My hand glides under the hoodie, over her ribs, until I cup her breast. Ana pushes her chest into me. I didn't know how fucking sexy it would be to fuck her in this.

"I'm expecting you to hold true to that as a promise," she purrs.

I groan, pulling out of her suddenly with the snap of my restraint. Hooking her panties, I pull them off and toss them aside before taking her hands. Ana sits up at my silent instruction, and I pull the hoodie off her next.

Nothing competes with Ana's naked body.

"You're a goddess."

She takes my cock in her hand and peers up at me through alluring lashes. If she puts it in her mouth, I won't be able to stop myself from fucking her throat, and I don't trust myself to last long. I want to reclaim every part of her that was taken from me for too long, but I can be patient.

"Turn around. Get on your hands and knees."

Ana stops her tight, maddening strokes of my dick and does as I say. Her perfect bare ass in front of me almost surges me to the edge of release. I've never been this effortlessly and insanely turned on by a woman. Ana drops down on her forearms, back curving, giving me an even more impeccable view as she tilts her head down to meet my gaze.

I realize I've been standing there fisting my cock absentmindedly, in a complete trance over her.

"I'm waiting, Agent Kaiser."

I almost pass the fuck out.

I strip off my jeans. She's right on the edge of the bed, and as soon as I step forward I'm deep inside her again. I don't go slow this time. Ana cries out at the plunge of my cock, and the angle hits so deep my vision pricks with dark spots.

I'm desperate to spill inside her, but I also don't want this to end so quickly. I want to fuck her for hours. Days. She fits my cock like a fucking glove, and I've starved for her after three months of hell away from her.

Leaning over her, my hand wraps around the back of her neck, pushing her into the bed. Her moans get louder, but I worry about hurting her.

"Harder," she says as if she can read my damn mind.

She is fucking *made* for me.

It's undeniable in the way her body moves with mine. How her mind aligns with mine. Her heart beats with mine.

She's all *mine*.

"Tell me how it feels, baby," I say, not slowing my pace.

I don't know if she will when her face is pressed into the mattress, so beautifully pinched in focused pleasure.

"It feels . . ." she says through short breaths. "Deeper than ever before."

"Still not deep enough," I growl. I pause, only to reach for her wrist and guide it back. "You never should have showed me your flexibility. I've thought of endless ways to test it. Legs together and arch your back a little more."

She does so perfectly, and I guide her arms to fold them behind her knees. I have to pull out just to see her positioned and vulnerable to me, so exquisite.

"Such a good girl," I say, and I reward her by kneeling in front of her soaking pussy and licking through her folds and over the curve of her ass.

Ana gives a louder moan as I explore that particular new territory. I do it again, lingering at her other hole.

"Oh my god," she says, burying her face in the covers. "That seems so wrong, but . . ."

"If it feels good, nothing can be wrong with you, little bird."

I haven't forgotten her willingness to let me try to fuck her there. She angles an unsure look back as if she thinks I might suggest it tonight.

"We don't have what I'd need to prep you for that, don't worry." I drag my teeth across her flesh, and she squeals.

"I wasn't worried," she says, still perfectly in position as I stand again.

"Curious?"

"Maybe."

"Did you enjoy my tongue there?"

"Yes."

I lean over and kiss her shoulder. "Good. Nothing is wrong or off-limits to explore between you and me. You can tell me anything you desire."

"Have you done it before . . .?"

"Anal? No, actually. I don't need nor expect it from you if you don't want it. I just find myself going out my mind wanting to claim you in every way you'll allow me to."

Ana contemplates. "I want to try sometime."

I fucking love that about her. Her inquisitiveness and the willingness to push out of her comfort zone in all things. It took her a while to know she could, and now it's my damn life's joy to watch her flourish.

"Ready to finish with me?"

She nods against the mattress, and I grip her hips to

plunge back inside her. I prop a leg on the bed, so lost to her my existence shatters with bliss. Ana cries so sweetly, hugging herself backward to keep her pretty little ass high for me like a good. Fucking. Girl.

My release is right there, but I don't think Ana will be able to finish with my cock inside her alone, and this position won't allow her or me to reach her neglected clit.

It takes all my willpower to pull out, flip her onto her back, and thrust back in. Ana's gasp of surprise is swallowed by a loud moan when I circle her clit with my thumb, giving it my full focus and tuning into the right motion, right pressure, until her pussy begins to tighten around me like a damn vise.

"That's it. Come for me, baby."

We come together, exploding in a tangled mess of ecstasy. I fuck her in deep strokes when she becomes so tight I can barely keep going. I fall over her, trying to reform everything that scattered from me.

Her fingers weave through my hair tenderly while our hearts slam against each other.

"I fucking missed you," I say, breathless.

"You said that already. But it was better to feel it."

I kiss her, slipping out of her, and we both shudder. "You're going to feel it every night. I'm going to have my way with you in places and positions that might scandalize you to hear."

She bites her lip. "Tell me."

I shake my head, kissing her throat. "I like collecting your reactions, your specific moans. I have a feeling I haven't even got to the best of them yet."

As I ease myself off her, Ana props herself up on her elbows.

"I have ways of surprising you too," she says.

If she keeps seducing me, she's going to find herself unable to walk tomorrow as I'm seconds from having at her again.

"You surprise me every day, little bird."

We've quickly found warmth in each other, but I need to at least light the fire. There's heating in the apartment, but I've found spending time by the fire is better.

Stepping in for a quick shower to wash off, Ana joins in behind me.

"Do you want children?" she asks quietly.

The question throws me off-guard.

"You're not trying to tell me your birth control expired?"

She chuckles, circling her arms around me from behind. "No. It might seem crazy to have the thought right now, but thinking of the future helps me believe we'll get to see it."

"Of course we will," I say. I fucking promise that. "I've never given any thought to kids before, to be honest. But with you, I could want that if you did." When she doesn't answer, I turn and reach for the soap behind her to read her face. "Do you want children?" I ask.

"I don't know. I love children. I would adore having yours. But I can't see it yet. There's no certain number of years from now or age when I think I'll be ready. But I'm not ready now —not even close, I don't think."

Hope blooms in my gut, the likes of which I've never quite felt before. Ana would make an amazing mother, and to see her having my kids would be fulfillment like nothing else. But I'm also sure I would be the luckiest, most satisfied bastard alive just to be hers.

"Whatever you want, baby," I say, kissing her head. I lather soap in my hands, wanting to feel her soft skin as I wash her. "If it's just you and me against the world forever, I want that. If you decide fun-size Kaisers should join us, I want that too."

Ana giggles, and it's the most precious sound.

"They won't be fun-size forever."

"To me they will be, and they'll know it too."

Her hazel eyes flick up to me, and I don't know why pride swells in me with the look she gives. Then her sight falls down as her fingers trace the flat line on my chest. I don't like the way sadness clouds her expression. More so, I hate how the tattoo doesn't feel right anymore. I will never forget Sarah, and I don't wish the tattoo gone; it just seems . . . incomplete now.

Then I realize it's missing a beat. The one in my arms that brought a dead heart back to life.

CHAPTER 36

Anastasia

"They can't file me as a missing person when my dad has a text clearly stating I'm fine, and he spoke to me on the phone," I grumble in the passenger seat as Rhett drives.

"He may be your dad, but he's also the President of the United States, little bird."

He's concerned about the police detail that might be set on finding me. I am too. Rix is keeping tabs on law enforcement, but I realize the risk I'm putting Rhett and Xoid in by disobeying my powerful, influential father.

"I wish he wasn't," I mutter. I don't know how much I mean it. I love my dad despite our tension right now, and I'm proud he's living his dream, but I wish I could be a nobody. Nobody but Rhett's.

Rhett sighs. "I know."

I gave him my phone last night, and somehow he's confident they won't be able to trace it. For now. The longer I hide from my dad, the more advanced his search will become. I considered throwing it out, but Rhett was right in saying a few texts could come from anyone, so I kept it to a call at least once a week.

We get to the Den, and seeing Shadow is the first thing to lighten my mood. He's been staying here while our situation is too unsettled. Here he's an asset, everyone loves him, and he gets to be spoiled by so many.

"Hey, boy," I say, kneeling to hug him. "I've missed you."

Shadow was the only thing holding me together most days for months. There's something so unexplainably healing about canine companionship.

"Shit, Ana, do you know how out of his mind your dad is about you right now?"

Adam's voice is the first to bound over to us. We meet him and Rix at his usual station.

Rhett says to him sharply, "You can't keep coming here right now. It's too much of a risk if they decide to try track you thinking it might lead them to Ana."

Adam's brow furrows, and Rix tips a look back at him where Adam stands behind his seat.

"I told you he'd be pissed you're here," Rix says.

"He's always pissed I'm here," Adam grumbles. Then he directs to me, "What are you thinking though? This is getting out of hand."

"Nothing is ever *in* hand about what we do. Get used to it or get out," Rix says.

He's typing away and clicking through various channels I can't keep up with. I cast a look between them, but the tension can be felt. I won't pry about what's causing it.

"That's it then? I got you into the club and now I'm not useful?" Adam bites back.

Rix stops what he's doing, spinning in his chair. "Are you hovering until I give you some task to do? I would have found another way into that club. Get over yourself."

"Me?" Adam says incredulously.

Rhett edges closer to me with a tiring expression. "We shouldn't have come here."

"You said we needed to check on the Liam and Allie search," I say.

His arm curves around me. "I could have called in, and I have my own equipment at home. I'd very much like to take you back." His face inches closer with every word until his lips are hovering over mine.

"I thought they called you in for something?"

"I don't care about whatever it is anymore." He kisses me, bringing our bodies flush, and I wish we'd never left our bed either.

"Rhett," Oma calls over.

Rhett groans, letting me go to glance over at the elderly woman lingering in her doorway as usual. I smile and wave to her.

"I thought you said you needed me?" Rhett asks Rix over his low bickering with Adam.

"I didn't. Oma made me get you in."

"You haven't talked with anyone yet," I say.

I wish he would talk to me about what he went through at the hands of Alistair, but I can't force it out of him. He coaxed me to seek help with Oma, and I can't explain how she has this natural ability to dissolve a person's walls and let the flood drown them, then teach them how to swim.

"It can wait," Rhett says, turning his focus back to the monitors.

"So can sex," I say.

He hooks a brow at me in challenge. "Is that a threat?"

I shrug. "It's motivation."

Rhett's eyes flex on me, debating whether I'll hold true. "One hour," he concedes.

A piece of me flutters with relief. It's a start. Rhett relays some instruction to Rix before he heads over to Oma. She gives me a reassuring warm smile as Rhett slips by her inside.

I hover over to where Adam leans with arms crossed,

pissed off, against the other side of the desk while Rix works. Though the tension in him comes out in his fast clacking against the keyboard and his intense scowl at the screens.

"So how long has this been going on?" I hedge, waggling a finger between them.

"There's nothing going on," Rix says flatly.

"Right." My gaze flicks to Adam, who might have told me more if we were alone, but he merely gives a shallow shake of his head.

Instead he says, "I never would have guessed Liam Forbes to be the kidnapping type."

"He hasn't kidnapped her." I reconsider. Well . . . I suppose you could call it that, if he's taken her to some secluded home god knows where and forced her to stay there. But I know in my heart that he wouldn't hurt her.

"I'm going to hurt him when I get a hold of him," Rix mutters darkly.

"She could have met a far worse fate," I defend.

"Yeah, but to not let her tell anyone she was safe? She'd know how to get us a message, so I'm assuming he's made sure she can't."

Rix is hurting about this. So is Rhett. Allie is like family, and even if Liam has kept her safe, I understand how sick with worry they are.

Something clicks in me unexpectedly at Rix's words. "He'd know how to get me a message," I mutter.

Oh my god.

Rix and Adam's attention turns to me, but my mind explodes with a clue. I grab my phone out of my pocket and read Liam's last text to me.

Meet me at Twilight.

It was the day before my world collapsed with the news of Rhett being gone.

"That sneaky little shit," I say. I don't know if what I think is right. It's both brilliant and laughable, and the fact "Twilight" is capitalized gives my theory further merit.

"Want to share?" Rix drawls.

"One time I forced Liam to watch a *Twilight* marathon with me. He hated most of it, but he loved their home, secluded in the woods with so many glass panels for walls."

"You're not telling me he's in Forks." Rix cocks a brow, leaning back in his seat.

"You've watched *Twilight*?" Adam asks.

"Of course. It's an emo teen classic. Rewatching it at least a dozen times is practically a given no matter how much cringe grows each time. If you haven't, I'm envious of your emotional stability."

That earns a partial smirk from Adam, breaking down some of their tension at least.

"No. He's not in Forks," I say. "But I need to go to my parents' old home. Do you have a car I can borrow?"

"I like my balls, and if I let you leave without him, I won't have any."

My eyes flick to Oma's door. "I'll be back before he's out."

Give or take.

Adam says, "That place is surrounded with surveillance and still housekept. Someone is bound to see you."

"I'll be careful, or if they do see me, I'll be out of there before they can contact anyone. Rhett can't come with me, and you know he will. If I do get caught, he can't be seen, or my little rebellion against my dad will be the least of our problems."

Rix contemplates. He knows I'm right, but he's also right that Rhett will be furious to find me gone.

"I'll go with you," Adam says, pushing off the desk.

I nod and Rix groans, running a hand down his face.

"You'd better be back as close to him coming out as you can. I won't be able to stop him coming after you."

He reaches into a drawer and keys rattle as he pulls them out. Adam reaches for them, but Rix snatches his hand back, cutting him a look.

"Ana drives. I don't trust you in my baby."

"Why the hell not?" Adam snaps.

"You're kind of pissed at me, and your innocent-guy act doesn't work on me."

"I don't have to be driving to damage your car, dick."

Rix's eyes flex in warning, but his mouth is trying not to curve.

I thrust out a hand, and Rix lets the keys go.

"Deep blue Chevrolet Corvette out back. Take care of it."

"Flashier than I expected for you," Adam mutters.

"I won it from Allie. We had a race to hack a highly risky network and find the location of one of Alistair's trafficking leaders last year."

He smiles in somber reflection and lingering triumph.

"I'm an excellent driver," I sing.

Adam scoffs. "If you don't count that one time over the summer I had to take the fall for—"

"Let's go!" I cut him off, smiling sweetly at Rix's widening look.

I'm skipping out before he can change his mind.

In the elevator, I mumble, "It was barely a scratch."

"I had to have the whole fender replaced," Adam counters. "And it wasn't even anything epic. Parking is not your strong suit."

"Which is why I said I'm an excellent *driver*."

He rolls his eyes at me. "I have a bad feeling about this," he says as we cross the lot toward another warehouse.

I don't tell him that I do too.

CHAPTER 37

Anastasia

We don't park too close to my parents' estate. I know every entry and exit to this place, and I've snuck out plenty of times. Still, I'm riddled with anxiety.

"You haven't even told me what we're here for," Adam says.

We watch the driveway past the gates, but I haven't seen any people yet. I know there's a grounds worker and likely frequent house maintenance—I just have to hope luck is on my side and it's not a day they're here.

"A book," I say absentmindedly. I wish I had binoculars. We're lousy spies.

"Why?"

"Because I think Liam took more than just home inspiration from *Twilight*."

I'll be highly amused if I'm right. My gut sinks at the thought of him. I miss him, and I'm so terribly concerned for him and how we'll get him out of the mess his father created when we do find him. The others may have their reservations, thinking he could be hiding a sick, twisted side like Matthew,

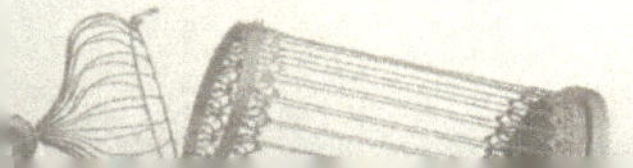

but I don't believe it, even for a second. They don't know him like I do.

Adam says, "I should go in. You wait on standby in the getaway car. I imagine it's on that little bookshelf that floats above your desk."

It's not a bad idea, actually. As much as I hate the thought of sitting idle here.

"Yes, it is."

I give him my keys, and Adam unclips his seat belt and gets out the car. I'm still scrambling to convince him I should go with him.

He takes a route I know will elude the surveillance cameras, but I worry they'll have something new in place at the back door now the property is vacant and more vulnerable to thieves. I bite my thumb and bounce my knee as ten minutes turns to twenty. *He should be back by now.* I try calling his cell, but it rings out.

"Damn it, Adam," I mutter.

My eyes flick up just briefly and catch a flicker of movement trying to creep up on my side in the mirror, and I know it's not Adam. My hand lashes out for the lock button just in time as the man tries my door, and I gasp, heart thundering, as I stare right at the gun in his hand.

"Miss Kinsley, we're armed police," he says, producing a badge as he brings his face to my window. "Is there anyone else in the car with you?"

I'm scrambling with what to do. This was over before we even got a chance. Did my father already anticipate I might come back here?

"We're under order of the president to detain you. If you will please cooperate with us, ma'am."

Like fuck I will.

It's in that second I make the most crazy, reckless, and

dangerous decision. I pull off the hand brake and kick down on the accelerator.

Sirens pursue me in a heartbeat, and I have no idea what I plan to do next.

I've lost my damn mind.

I try Adam's phone again. This time he answers, and I'm about to scramble nonsense words in my panic about what the fuck to do, but it's not his voice I hear.

"Anastasia Kinsley, you will stop that car right now!" my father yells.

I quickly hang up.

"Shit!" I hiss into the car.

Adrenaline is pumping my blood hot and fast as I focus on the road I'm speeding dangerously through. I cut into less busy areas, but I don't know what the fuck I'm doing. *Who* the fuck I think I am. All I know is that as soon as my dad has me, he'll put me under lockdown.

I won't be separated from Rhett again. Though a high-speed police chase is a radical declaration of love, even for us.

Rhett's going to be pissed as hell when he finds out.

I wasn't lying when I said I was great driver. It's as if the stakes make me more focused on the road, the possible hazards, the consideration of others. This car drives like a dream, and I decide it's better than the Porsche I typically favor.

My phone rings again, and I only just catch a glimpse of the caller ID in my focus. I can't tell if I'm awash with dread or relief to see Rhett's name.

I pick up and press the speaker.

"Ana, where the fuck are you?" he growls into the phone.

"Have I ever told you how sexy you sound when you're angry?"

I can't help my smile as I imagine his absolutely seething scowl.

"I'm coming to get you."

"Don't! You can't. I'm, uh, taking the long route, but I'll be back soon."

"I can hear sirens."

"They're just passing."

"Ana," he warns.

I hear Rix in the background next. "Oh, hell no! Gimmie that phone."

There's muffling through the speaker like a struggle before Rix's voice comes through more sharply.

"Please tell me I'm watching some other maniac in the same deep blue baby trying like a damn idiot to outrun a police squad."

Shit. Fuck. Shit. "It's on TV?" I blanch.

"My TV, yes! Not broadcast, as I'm sure your dad has a leash on that, but what the fuck, Ana! Did Adam put you up to this?"

"No, I'm alone. I think he got detained in the house. I don't know how he was onto us so fast."

More muffling, and I wince this time at Rhett's outrage. "You're alone?"

Now my panic is starting to seep through my adrenaline.

"I don't know what to do, Rhett," I admit quietly. "I'm scared he'll find a way to keep me locked up if I stop."

All that keeps my foot pumping the gas and disregarding all logic are thoughts of getting back to him. My vision blurs, but I blink it back, and a delirious laugh escapes me because it's official . . .

My love for Rhett Kaiser has made a crazy, unhinged, thoughtless fool out of me. And I think I'm the happiest woman alive because of it.

"You have to stop, baby. There's no way out of this."

"You're telling me you've never successfully outsmarted the police?"

At that a small note of amusement filters into his voice. "Three times, in fact."

I laugh, but my brow pinches in fear. "Then tell me what to do."

"I'm telling you to stop. For me. It's the safest way, and you're not a criminal with nothing to lose."

"I have you to lose."

"That's impossible, little bird. Stop, please. Your father is only concerned for you—he's not a villain in this."

"He made a villain out of you. That's enough for me."

"Please, baby."

My hands tighten on the wheel and defiance locks my bones.

But I know he's right. I'm a risk to more than just myself right now.

"Don't leave me," I say, finally slowing on the gas when I dip down into a city underpass.

"I'm right here, always."

I wish that were true. That he was right here beside me and would go with me to face my dad. What tears me apart is that he's the reason I keep stretching myself from my parents when I told myself I'd start to mend my relationship with them as soon as I got Rhett back. Now I might be even more bitter and resentful toward my dad for *making* me do this even though he doesn't know it.

When the car stops, it's the first time I realize the one cop car that pursued me has multiplied to four. The officers flood out of them, all pointing guns at the car, and I'm terrified. I know it's not for me—it's a precaution in case there's anyone else in here making me do this.

"I love you, Ana."

"I love you too."

The call cuts out. I know he'll be hacking my phone right now, erasing all trace of him, and my heart cracks more.

I get out, holding my hands up, and a cop beckons me to him cautiously.

"Is there anyone else in the car, Miss Kinsley?" an older man asks.

"No."

Once they're finished checking, they put their weapons away.

"Sergeant, we've to take her to the White House in an unmarked vehicle, and your team needs to be warned about any mention of Anastasia being leaked to the press." A woman in a business suit comes over to us.

Most of the officers look pissed as hell at me. I give no reaction. It's human nature to judge on actions, and rarely will anyone be curious enough to know the reasons before they condemn someone.

I follow the woman into the back of her car, and I stay silent despite them pressing me for answers. *Why did you do it? Is someone threatening you? Whose car is it?*

Shit, Rix is going to be so pissed with me. I hope I can get the car back since I'm confident he's made sure it's untraceable to him.

I'm flanked by three security to enter the White House. It seems ridiculous, but I won't allow this to feel like a cage. They lead me to a large lounge room, where my mom sits on the elegant sofa while my dad paces at the window. When Mom spots me she whimpers, rushing over and pulling me into a hug as if I was presumed dead until now.

I meet eyes with my dad over her shoulder and it's like we're estranged. He's absolutely furious in a way I've never seen before, and right now I don't think I'm his daughter. I'm a law-breaker, a rebellious delinquent, a coldhearted bitch.

"What were you thinking?" he asks in a controlled calm as I step away from Mom.

"That I wouldn't be dragged here to be locked inside a golden cage."

Dad laughs, so far from friendly. "There will be nothing golden about it, I assure you."

My temper begins to flare. "I'm not staying here. Not for one night."

"You're out of control. Ever since the death of that damn *criminal*." He yells the last word, and my jaw locks.

"Rhett was never the danger to me—he's the one who saved me from it."

"You let him brainwash you, darling."

"Victor Ross," I snap. Dad stops pacing. "Did you look into him like you did Rhett? Of course not, because then you might have found out you *did* place a criminal by my side. That he spent his salary from *guarding* me on raping trafficked woman."

Mom covers her mouth with a small gasp.

Dad shakes his head, and inside me everything twists with ugly, agonizing, hatred. Because I can see he doesn't believe me. Doesn't *want* to believe me, he's so set on Rhett being the one who *broke* me. Who took away his perfectly quiet, afraid, and sheltered little girl.

He won't accept that Rhett is the only reason I'm free from an existence that was killing me inside.

"This isn't you," he says, disappointment coating his tone.

"Because you never wanted to *know me!*" I cry. It breaks the seal on a vault I didn't know I was locked in. I love my dad— *god*, I do—but the truth I've buried comes clawing out. "You've always been so focused on work and image that you wanted me to be picture-perfect. School, press, hosting, appealing, campaigning. Sometimes it's like you've only ever seen a prop, and now I'm not putting on *your* show, it's a shock to see what becomes of my independence. I'm not sorry I'm not your innocent little girl anymore. I'm not sorry for wanting to live my life. And most of all, I'm not sorry I fell in love with the only person to *see* me. To say he's proud of me. To steer me toward what *I* want."

Mom is crying, and I hate to see her hurt, wish I could comfort her, but I'm shaking too much with anger as I stare off with Dad.

"My biggest regret will always be allowing that man into your life for the poison he inflicted."

My heart shatters where I stand. "I'm in love with Rhett Kaiser," I say.

"He's *gone*," Dad says coldly.

My smile is made of the broken pieces. "Not to me," I whisper.

I turn to leave.

"Your phone," Dad says at my back.

My jaw flexes in irritation and humiliation. I'm not a child. But he has all the power in the room, and it's like I don't know him anymore. I wouldn't put it past him to order a body search even if I was kicking and screaming.

I pull it out, leaving it on the coffee table. I don't look to either of my parents before I stroll out the room.

There's security all around the foyer. I'd likely be tackled, dragged to my room, if I tried to leave now. So I head up there myself.

In solitude, exhaustion sweeps me out of nothing but pure sadness. I want to crawl up in the bed and cry for hours, but I don't, because I don't think I'll stop. I want Rhett to be curled up with me.

Reaching into the inside pocket of my jacket, I pull out my new phone from Xoid. It doesn't have typical apps and functions like a regular cell. I have to wait for Rhett to somehow contact me through it like Rix did. He'll know how and when I can escape this place.

The first message to come through doesn't contain any

words. It's a little bird animation that flies across the dark screen, and I break into a sob mixed with a laugh. Sinking down against the wall, I wait for what follows.

How are you, baby?

I think I'm officially the world's worst daughter.

That's a high achievement. I'm proud of you.

He pulls more laughter from me, and it's healing until the sharpness in me cuts again. My head tips back for a moment to collect myself. I need him with me right now.

I miss you.

His next text slides onto the screen before dissolving away like the ones before.

What's the plan of breakout?

We're considering our options, but it's looking like I might need to show you how to successfully lose the police after you break yourself out. I'll be waiting.

No fancy tricks?

Fast and dirty, baby.

My heart skips a beat.

Tonight?

Unless you want to stay. As much as I want
you, your parents mean well, even if it doesn't
feel like it right now. You can take some time
with them.

No. Nothing will be fixed even in a week
locked here.

Midnight then.

I clutch the phone to my chest and try not to stare at the
time. All it does is wrack me with guilt. I know I owe my
parents part of me back, and right now, every confrontation
with my father makes me fear I'll never give it to them. He's
trying to get through to me, but the problem is, he won't listen
to hear it's not what I need. When all this is over, with Alistair
and Jacob gone, I'll figure out how the fuck I'm going to make
this divide work. One life for Rhett, my truest and happiest,
and maybe I'll have to accept living a life of pretend for my
parents, who will never understand.

CHAPTER 38
Rhett

I'm antsy as fuck waiting in the car with ten minutes until midnight. Ana was out of my sight for one hour and got herself into a shitload of trouble, so I decide she's not getting five minutes without me once I have her back.

"What if they grab her before she can make it past the gates?" Adam asks, practically pressing his face to the tinted glass in the back seat.

Rix says next to him, "We have a distraction in place. One gunshot, and their security will flock to the threat before they lock down the shit out of that place. It gives her two minutes tops to take that window of initial panic."

"I'm going out," I say.

Rix's protest is cut off with the closing of my door. My hood is up, and a black scarf covers my lower face. I blend into the bushes far enough away from the White House that no one will make out my figure from there. But I dare a fraction closer to the exit Ana indicated she'd take. I don't want to risk her not seeing the car, which is black and blends in with the dozen others on the street we've parked on. This could be the difference between being home or in a cell tonight, because I'm not leaving her, no matter what.

Exactly at midnight the gunshot goes off, and the reaction is immediate. My attention is sharp, watching bodies dart away from the place Ana should emerge from, but soon they'll be stationed around the entire perimeter with laser focus.

I could make out Ana in any light or darkness. Even her silhouette wraps my whole being in contentment. She's so close my body itches for her, but she's careful, waiting for people to pass before she darts right through the gaps in their net. She's running straight, but not in my direct path. I risk leaving the cover to intercept her.

My gloved hand muffles her scream of fright, but a second scanning my eyes is all it takes for her to relax in my arms.

"Hello, little bird."

"Rhett."

Hearing my name in her breathy voice makes my heart soar. I take her hand, jogging across the street.

"Stop!" someone yells out.

Which of course means "get the fuck out of here."

I open the passenger door and Ana slips inside, and I look up to gauge what we're up against. What I don't expect is to see President Kinsley.

He's surrounded by armed security, out here likely against every protocol for a potential gunshot threat. Our eyes lock, and even from this distance and in the dark I can see his terror for his daughter. Yet he doesn't advance, and neither do any of those around him since they can't break their protection for him even if he demanded it.

He can't fully see me, but I'm almost certain he knows who I am despite my face covering and his belief that I'm dead.

I can't waste a moment considering his feelings when Ana is the only thing that matters—and she called for me.

I'm speeding off the moment I'm in the driver's seat.

"Holy shit, we really just kidnapped the president's daughter!" Rix says.

"This is insane," Adam mutters.

Ana twists in her chair at his voice. "Did you get the book?"

"This was all for a *book*?" I ask irritably.

Sirens wail in the distance, and it's only a matter of time before they clock our car since we were seen. I try not to speed to avoid flying our guilt like a flag sooner.

"Yeah I got it," Adam says, passing it to her. "I've never seen your dad so pissed, and mine threatened to cut me off if he found out I was hiding things for you. So I... kind of snuck out and haven't been back. I guess I'm a fugitive now too."

"Shit," Ana mutters. Then she giggles and I snap an incredulous look at her.

She only grins wider. "Look at us, a band of the president's most wanted criminals," she muses. She's so casually composed, as if we didn't just set off a terrorist alarm at the White House, take the president's daughter right in front of him, and we're now risking a hot pursuit. I wonder if I should be concerned or proud.

I have no idea how any of us are going to wrangle our way out of the shitstorm we've created, but I decide all that matters is that Ana seems happy.

I catch a glimpse of the title on her book. "What is *Twilight* about that could be so important for this to be worth it?"

I'm met with the combined gasps of Ana and Rix.

"You've never heard of it?" Ana questions like it's a personal offense.

"I have a feeling I don't want to."

"It's like a drug," Rix says. "Bad, but fucking addictive."

"Thirty seconds," I inform them.

"For what?" Ana asks, but we're here.

Driving down into an underground parking lot, I cut the engine and swing out. Rix and Adam are a heartbeat behind as I open Ana's door.

"The best way to get out of a police chase is to never let one begin," I say close to her ear.

"That's kind of cheating," she says with a devious smile. "I was looking forward to you wreaking havoc on the streets."

"I will wreak havoc on *you* for the little stunt you pulled."

Two of my guys emerge from each of the awaiting two cars. I toss the key to our getaway car to one, and they get to work on changing the plates before they drive out of here.

"I guess you'll be working remotely while the smoke clears," Rix says.

"For a few days. Keep me updated if you find anything."

"Will do, boss."

"Stockbridge," Ana mutters.

I turn and find her with the book open, but she's holding a card she found within it. Her eyes light up, scanning the front before she flips it over.

"He's in Stockbridge, Massachusetts," she says, more hopeful, before holding up what I see is a postcard.

"What does it say?" I ask.

"There's only a number on the back."

Rix crosses the space and plucks the postcard from her. "It has to be coordinates," he says. "I think I like this guy."

"Let's hope it leads us to Allie. Can you take care of it? I want to be in on it, but we have Silas and the upcoming Forthson venue opening party."

It's tearing me apart not to be able to put my full focus on getting Allie back, but we have so many high stakes on the edge of collapse.

"Of course," he says, studying the picture with new hope as he heads to his car.

I walk around with Ana to the passenger side, but before

she gets in I catch her wrist, spinning her to pin her against it with my hips.

"Good work, little bird," I say and kiss her hard.

"No reprimand?"

"So eager for punishment," I muse. "Don't worry, I'm not finished with you yet."

I open her door, and her eyes, sparkling with desire, make my cock twitch as she slips inside.

Half an hour later, we're parked down a deserted dirt road ten minutes from the warehouse apartment. I don't want to take any risks to compromise that place, and so we've switched cars again, and now we're waiting to see if anyone followed.

In the silence I'm left to reflect on the hour under Oma's intense interrogation. She dragged all my demons to the surface. Thing is, once she did, they were mine to fight head-on.

I find myself needing to show them to Ana. After all she's risking for this, for me, I owe her that, in case all of this is for nothing if she decides she wants to leave.

"Alistair kept me in a room. There was a mattress and a TV screen to watch you on almost every day. I think he wanted me to believe you were moving on, that he was succeeding in making you his." It comes out of me before I can seal it all away again, the beginning of a hellish three months.

She says nothing right away, and the weight of my vulnerability crushes slowly.

"He locked me in a room too," she says quietly. "You know that, but I want to tell you myself."

We need this so much. My body locks tense, and I know my anger and resentment will be palpable the more we exchange.

"They would take me out a couple of times a week for

various torture," I say. "Drowning, cutting, electrocution. That part was all a punishment for my desertion."

I have to know what she's thinking, but her face only crumples with sadness.

"You're the resilient one, Rhett. There's not many people who wouldn't break under all that."

I don't respond, but I appreciate her faith in me.

Ana takes a deep breath to give a piece of her story in return. "He didn't demand the cuts on my thighs, but I wanted to know what it felt like for you."

I'm slammed by incredulity and heartbreak. Ana shakes her head, and I understand she doesn't want to be reprimanded for it.

Ana bled for me . . .

My head tips back against the headrest in disbelief. "I kept track of the days, scoring them on the wall. It took 126 little birds to get back to mine."

I let the weight of my head fall toward her. Her lip wobbles, gaze dropping to her lap.

"I trained so hard every day even though I knew he had other plans for me. I wanted to be strong and brave and smart enough to get you back, because I couldn't accept you were gone no matter how much I heard it."

We give each other pieces like the sharp edges of our terror, and trauma sews us back together. Tighter than ever before.

I swallow hard when I reach the worst of what I have to tell her. "They started to test my limits. Not physically, but emotionally and mentally. I was given a gun, which either did or didn't have a single bullet—there was no way to be sure. They made me stand before a teen kid and point the barrel at his head. If I didn't shoot, they had you on a monitor while you were unaware. I don't think they would have killed you, but I didn't doubt they were allowed to follow through and at least hurt you gravely. By the fourth kid . . ."

I have to pause. My fists clench so tightly in my lap until Ana's close over them.

I go on. "I would have killed him had there been a bullet in my gun, but they didn't take the chance. So he was shot by proxy by the one I was always under charge of. One sick, deranged bastard. His name was Micah."

A shuddering breath escapes her, and Ana quickly swipes a tear. I'm torn apart where I sit, desperate to touch her, but I can't tell if she's repulsed by what I've done.

She says, her voice wavering, "He locked me in a room with a camera watching me. I had a table and some paper and pencils. I don't know why. I don't know how long I was in there. I didn't think to track time. It was long enough that I lost it for a moment. I got on the chair and tore down the camera, thinking it was a triumph, but it was my biggest mistake. A man came in and barely said anything, but by the dark look of hunger in his eyes, I knew what I'd done. I fought him as best as I could, but it was like everything I'd pushed my body through, every skill and tactic to defend myself, became as good as child's play. He had me pinned and managed to undo my shorts, and his hand . . . his hand touched me. His fingers were inside me. Then I felt one of my snapped pencils, and the next thing I knew, it was in his neck."

Ana pauses and lets her tears roll down her face, one after the other. Her eyes are terrified when they lift to mine.

"His name was Micah."

It's hard to explain the absolute horror that washes through my entire body and punishes the very core of my being. I stare out the windshield into pure dark nothingness, a calm rage collecting a storm inside of me. I want to kill him a thousand times. I can't ask her, and maybe it's sick of me to wish him alive only because I haven't had my vengeance, but if I get it . . . he's going to regret ever being born.

"Say something," Ana croaks.

I don't know what to say. There aren't enough words or gestures to convey how sorry I am to her, and I'm right back in my turmoil that everything she's suffered is because of me.

She sniffs, and I vaguely hear her shuffling in her seat. Then her hands are on my shoulder, but I'm numb to it. I help her on autopilot as she climbs over, sitting across my lap with her back against the door.

"We both got out," she says, resting her head on my shoulder. "More times than one."

"There should never have been a first time," I say. I don't feel anything right now, and I know she deserves more.

"I would go through it all again to have you."

"Why?"

"Because I love you."

Then I have to look at her. I tip her chin back as her head rests against the window. "Why?" I repeat, more desperate now.

She bites her lip and shrugs. Then her hand reaches up for my jaw.

"I think that's the thing about love—love like what we have. There is no *why*."

How is she even fucking real? I don't know what I did to deserve an angel in hell's depths, but I'm the luckiest damn bastard alive.

"You are my life, Ana."

Her head nestles back between my shoulder and neck where her soft lips press. She's absolute bliss in this dark world.

It's safe to go to the apartment now, but I can't ask her to move with how content I am.

"This is kind of creepy," Ana says, staring out at the trees in front of us as we sit with all the lights cut under the cover of darkness.

"Afraid of the dark?"

"Not the dark, but what could lurk within it." She lifts herself from my chest, and there's an enticing shift in her expression.

"You're thinking bad things," I say.

"Or very *good* things."

Ana adjusts her position, giggling at the awkward maneuver between me, the steering wheel, and the console. She squeezes and manages to straddle me. I don't expect her boldness as she drags the heel of her palm over my dick, but it jerks to life at her touch.

My voice turns to thick gravel. "What are you doing?"

"Do I need to spell it out for you?" she says in a tone of lust, squeezing my cock over and over.

"You want a distraction? Then stop being a tease and bury my cock in your throat before I do."

"Very demanding," she taunts.

She moves so agonizingly slowly, purposely driving me to the brink of my restraint. *Wicked, beautiful thing.* She undoes my belt, slips open my button, and drags down my zip, all while her lips press along my jaw. Then her tongue traces up my neck, and I groan, tensing with the madness growing in me for her.

Ana pulls back, straining to reach down between us and under the seat. She feels for the lever, and when the seat slides back she grins in triumph. It gives her barely enough space to slip her knees down to the footwell.

"I don't want to ask if you've done that before," I growl.

She moves like a pro in this car, and it stirs a dangerous possession in me.

"You just did," she says with a sultry lilt. Her hand takes

my cock, but it's her alluring eyes locking on me that spurs my lust more. "You're my first car thrill, Agent Kaiser."

Her tongue flattens on the base of my cock, licking from my balls to my head in a long, hot stoke. My hand threads through her red hair.

"Suck," I grind out.

Ana's small, sinful smile makes my dick twitch against her lips as she torments me to the brink, pressing her lips along my crown and squeezing her hand at my base.

"Say please."

Oh fuck.

"Please," I say, barely a raspy breath, without missing a beat.

"Please what, Agent?"

So fast I'm delirious, on the brink of exploding against her lips.

"Please suck my cock before I lose the mind to fucking breathe."

She chuckles, and the vibrations of it tighten my damn balls.

As soon as her pretty little lips wrap around my dick and swallow me down, I throw my head back with a groan, and my hand can't help gripping her hair tighter. She sucks me for a moment while I rally composure to watch her. I use both my hands to keep her hair from her face and get the most impeccable sight of her at work with her fist and mouth.

"So beautiful taking my cock in your throat. Deeper, baby. Take all of me."

I know she can, and she doesn't need to be told twice. Watching me disappear down her neck seizes me with an impending release. I want to fuck her so badly, but I can't find the will to get her to stop. I'm too far gone, lost in the heat of her, and I try to match the bobbing of her head, but the tight fit of the car keeps my thrusts shallow.

"Fucking hell, *Ana*." I growl her name as my release crashes through me. I slip a hand around her throat, wanting to feel her swallow everything I give her. "My good fucking girl."

She hums, continuing to suck me dry and stringing out my orgasm as it begins to blacken the edges of my vision. I'm barely holding myself together when she finally lets go, but my abdomen tenses, and I hiss at the aftershocks of oversensitivity when her hand strokes a couple more times.

"Torturous thing," I mutter, chest still heaving.

She braces on my knees, pushing up to bring her lips to the shell of my ear. "Take me home. You owe me one in return."

I tuck myself away far too eagerly because I risk getting hard again that quickly. Ana crawls back to her seat.

"I'm going to give you far more than one, little bird."

CHAPTER 39

Anastasia

I'm pacing the length of Silas's pool table while Rhett sits opposite him on the sofas. I'm reeling over various plans we're trying to string together to cross Forthson and Lanshall and take them both down together.

"Does she always do this?" I hear Silas mutter.

"It's a good sign," Rhett says.

He's asking about my pacing, and I meet Rhett's look with a hint of a smile.

"So you met with Jacob and he invited you to his event," I mull over. "Is anyone else getting a bad feeling about this new *venue?*"

"I've looked into it. Everything checks out. Not quite my taste. *Gentlemen's club* is a rather obnoxious term for a strip club if you ask me," Silas says.

"You declined his invitation." I relay what he told us of his meeting with Jacob.

"Once I heard you two were going, I thought it might work to coordinate our evenings."

"If you're taking out Lanshall, I want to be there," Rhett says darkly.

"I understand, truly. But if you think you're owed his death, then reevaluate, Kaiser."

Silas takes a long drag of his cigarette, his eyes impressing a challenge. Rhett's jaw sets.

"He's my uncle. My fucking problem."

"You escaped him. There's someone who never got that freedom for a day, never mind the many years you had."

"He killed my fiancée and hurt Ana. I've dreamed of his death every one of those damn years," Rhett snaps.

"You lost a person you loved, but Kenna never got the chance to love anyone because of him."

"Then she's fucking lucky."

Even I tense at that. Silas's expression turns lethal as he leans forward, forearms braced on his thighs.

"Lucky?" he repeats in a chilling calm. "Have you ever looked at a beautiful creature in a cage and called it *lucky*? Or a butterfly with broken wings? Or a bird without its song? They're once vibrant things of nature, now broken to believe they're *safe* that way. It's not luck—it's a fucking tragedy."

Rhett shifts a gaze to me, and I can only meet it with understanding. His is weighted with a note of guilt.

"What if she doesn't want to kill him? Or even want him dead at all," Rhett says.

"I think she does," I say, reflecting on the last time I saw her. I whisper, still haunted by the fact. "She was only fifteen."

Silas's dark gaze targets me immediately. "Only fifteen when *what*?"

He knows. Yet he wants me to say it. I can't. I've already said too much that wasn't mine to share, but it's the only way I'm sure Kenna would want to be free of Alistair.

Silas stands, taking one step toward me, and that's when Rhett shoots up, beating him to me with an arm curving around my waist. I can't tear my gaze away from the palpable retribution simmering in those dark brown eyes.

"He raped her as a minor?" Silas asks plainly, but it's wrapped in pure violence.

"I don't know everything. All she told me was what I said." If he wants the certainty, he has to earn that from her himself.

Silas targets Rhett, and my heart begins to speed up knowing he could turn on us at any moment. "And you still think you have the fucking right to his death?" Silas seethes.

My hand slips over Rhett's in concern, but to my relief, his expression relaxes as he thinks. He knows that as much as his rage and vengeance have been the driving force of his life since Sarah was killed, he's not had the time to consider there was someone else he knew still alive who might have suffered more than him.

"No," Rhett concedes.

My body relaxes when some of the tension between them defuses. Rhett runs a hand through his hair as Silas goes back to the table and resumes his cigarette.

"I didn't know she was still alive. I went back for her long ago, but he convinced me she was dead." Rhett debates going on, but I think he sees how serious Silas is about her well-being. "Kenna Radley is not her birth name. The birth one is not mine to give, so don't bother asking. It won't help her escape Lanshall."

"No, it won't, but I fucking will."

I run a hand up Rhett's arm, but his body is locked stiff. "So you'll be infiltrating Alistair's manor the night of Jacob's opening next week?" I ask Silas.

"One night, two bastards down. I'm a firm believer in swift efficiency. We should both walk away with what we want."

"What happens after?" Rhett asks.

Silas breathes in a long drag, tipping his head against the sofa to cast the cloud into the air above. "I respect you, Kaiser. We have a common repulsion to human trafficking. That will stop in the networks I take over in D.C. But that's where my promises to you end. If your guys mess with any other shipments and dealings of mine, I won't call you before my guys put a bullet to their heads."

"If they get caught before we succeed."

Silas yields a hint of a challenging smile. "I'm not Lanshall or Forthson. That's the only warning I'll give you."

Rhett gives a slight nod of his head, acknowledging the alliance will technically end, but I think they've gained a mutual respect for each other. It's all I could have hoped for.

"I guess we'll see you again when this is over," Rhett says as a cue to leave.

"On the other side, my friend," Silas says. His eyes slip to me as I reach Rhett and he takes my hand.

I don't know why unease crawls in me. We have his word, but I can't shake the feeling it could be voided for another price if the bidding is right. At the same time, there's always been a feeling in my gut that inexplicably trusts him.

CHAPTER 40
Rhett

I never thought I'd see myself on TV, and it's weird as fuck.

"My kidnapper," Ana muses, circling her arms around me from behind as I stand with arms crossed, glaring at the news report in the Den.

"You shouldn't say that with pride," I say, but I smile.

We're headlining across news outlets, and it's pretty fucking bad. A problem I can't even focus any effort on right now, when we're close to taking down Alistair.

"You have a fan club online," Rix says. I turn to him, still wrapped in Ana's arms. He's sitting by his desk, and so is Adam, both of them scrolling their phones.

Adam smirks at his. "Lexi_cat92 tweeted, 'He could tie me up and stomp on my back and I'd thank him.'"

Rix reads, "thatintrovertedkate tweeted, 'Rhett Kaiser is the type of psycho boyfriend we all dream of really.'"

"Always the quiet ones," Ana says in amusement. She pushes up on her toes so her lips hover over the hollow spot of my ear. "She's not wrong."

I squeeze her waist, and she giggles. "Enough of that," I tell them.

I didn't expect the president to blast this publicly when he's been trying to keep a cap on Ana's behavior. I'm now the con-artist boyfriend from hell who faked his death just to kidnap Ana later. It's an outlandish stretch, but the world is going crazy for the story.

Despite how much shit we're in, Ana has been in a particularly light and playful mood, as if nothing exists but us. I'm concerned, but I don't want to burst her bubble just yet when she's smiling more than I've seen her do since I got her back.

"Are you okay? *Really* okay?" I ask her, lowering my voice and leaning into her ear.

Her grin up at me stops time. "Yes. Really yes."

"I don't know how we're going to fix this particular mess."

"One mess at a time. I'm happy, Rhett. I won't let it be delusional. I feel surrounded by family right here," she says, glancing around at everyone at work, laughing and chatting together because it's how we survive the pain. "More than I think I have before. And at home with you no matter where we stay, but I hope we can keep the warehouse apartment. It might be my favorite."

She's so resilient and bright, and I don't think I'll ever stop finding her remarkable. I capture her mouth in one long, deep kiss.

"You're always home with me, baby."

"I know."

"I have something," a woman calls from across the Den.

It grabs all our attention and I'm moving on instinct, knowing the station she's at is tracking new trafficking set ups.

Scanning the monitor, dread and rage pools in my stomach.

"Forthson is targeting the summer carnival?" Rix concludes as I do.

The setup is obvious as we've been tracking some of his

men, anticipating they were getting ready for something. With the loss he sustained from those we saved last summer from his gala, he'll been needing to compensate and the carnival is exactly the place for many opportunities to lure women and children away.

"We have to stop him," Ana says. My arm curves around her, so glad she's right with me with the thought of who could be already taken by Forthson and what targets they'll gain tonight. The carnival has been here for two days already.

"You think you're ready for your first mission, Red?" Rix says.

"No way in hell," I growl.

"I want to help," she protests. Her frown is adorable, but everything in me is objecting to her want to put herself in the line of danger for this.

"I only just got you back." I try not to sound pitiful but what can I say, this woman puts me on my knees.

"You'll be close by and the rest of Xoid will have eyes on us. They're looking for vulnerable young women and I'm perfect prey to trap and end their sick trafficking ring at this carnival." She pulls me by my jacket. "I'm in this. I'm with you. And I'm not afraid."

I am. I'm absolutely terrified but at the same time my pride quells some of it.

"We're front-page news, baby. We can't risk being seen out there," I say apprehensively, but she's so excited I know I'll risk anything to keep her like that even for one night.

"That makes it all the more thrilling," she says daringly.

Before I can try to argue how terrible of an idea it is, Rix has the whole room buzzing to go. Though we'll be on a job, he's brought a light to the dark ongoings with chat about what rides and games they'll play to enjoy the night after we succeed.

An hour later, I'm seriously regretting this decision.

It was Ana's brilliant idea to wear face paint in an attempt to disguise ourselves since there'll be plenty of it at the fair. So here we are, with everyone in the Den bringing the most color this place has ever seen.

Ana can hardly stop giggling between her paint strokes, and I'm beginning to concern for what she's drawing on my face. Coraline has painted big, impressive butterfly wings over each of Ana's eyes in pinks and reds. Her hair is half pulled up in twin buns, braided at the fronts, with thick glitter down her part. She looks fucking adorable.

"No dicks on my face," Rix warns Adam from behind us.

"I'm debating it since you won't let me see what you did to my face," Adam grumbles.

"I didn't want to influence your idea of vengeance."

"All done!" Ana exclaims, pulling back with a bright, giddy grin.

"I don't think I want to look," I say.

"Don't be a killjoy." Ana grabs the hand mirror, and I brace for the worst.

It's not bad. I might actually admit it's kind of cool. She's painted a skull-like feature on the lower half of my face.

Ana grabs a black baseball cap and slips it onto my head as she straddles me in the seat. I grip her ass.

"You looked so sexy in the face covering the other night when you rescued me," she purrs.

My cock hardens, and I want to grind her pussy on me with it being right there in her cute little denim shorts.

"I can't kiss you right now, can I?" I groan.

"Absolutely not. We can mix red and black later, on the way home."

"Maybe I don't want to go anymore," I murmur huskily, leaning for her neck.

Ana laughs, cringing away so I don't smudge my black paint against her skin.

"I'm so looking forward to leaving a visible trace every-where my mouth plans to devour you later."

Ana pushes her hips froward subconsciously, and my hands tighten on her perfect round ass.

"Kids in the room," Rix calls over to us. There's no one under the age of twenty here.

I don't even have it in me to scowl when I see the paint job Adam is finishing off, and the light amusement that rises in me feels so forgotten. When Ana tosses a look over her shoulder she bursts into laughter, still in my lap, and I join in too.

"What have you done, fucker?" Rix's face falls in horror. He pushes Adam away and storms over to a mirror hanging on the wall. Ana passes her hand mirror to Adam.

When they realize what they've done, they turn to each other with flat looks.

"A pair of clowns seems fitting," Ana giggles.

"So unoriginal," Rix grumbles to Adam.

"You thought of the same thing," he snipes back.

"Did you catch a look in the monitor reflection before you did mine?" Rix accuses.

"No! I figured it fit considering the circus I've had to endure with you."

Rix fights a smile. I don't know what's between them. I don't plan to.

"All right, let's go. Should be in full swing and busy enough for us to get lost in the crowds," Rix says.

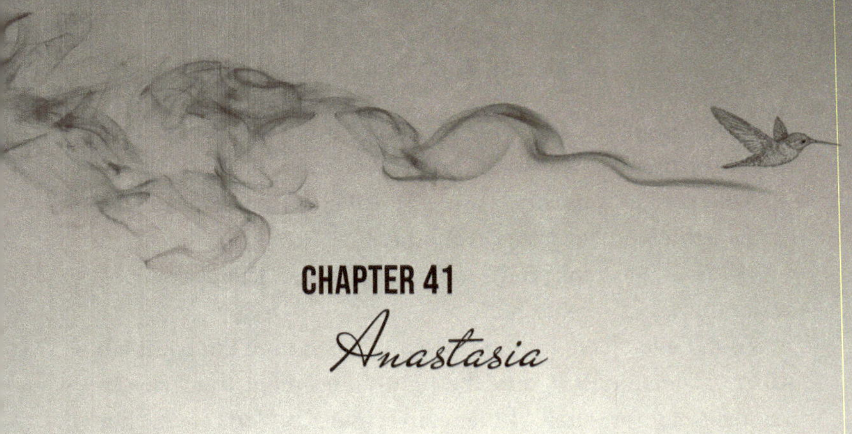

The carnival grounds are packed with bodies, loud with music and game sounds, and bright with all the strobe lights. We have some of our people tracking the guys who are targeting women for Forthson tonight, we're just waiting for their signal and I'm growing antsy.

"Would it be terribly cliché to want to ride the Ferris wheel?" I ask Rhett as a distraction, strolling hand in hand with him while I bite off pieces of my cotton candy.

"Probably."

"Excellent." I pull him along. "We're fulfilling one full night of the most lovesick movie clichés."

Every time I glance at him I grow embarrassingly wetter between my legs. I can't explain how sexy he looks in his half-face skull makeup. I did a pretty great job, if I do say so myself.

"This line is terribly long," Rhett says.

"Does Mr. Grumpy need a snack to pass the time?" I tease, breaking off a piece of candy floss and reaching up to his mouth.

He takes it from my fingers with his instead, and when he directs it back to my mouth, I open for him too eagerly.

"If we get on this thing, I can't promise I won't make a snack out of you."

His thumb presses down on my lips, his head angled enough to partly shield our faces with his baseball cap. My tongue flicks out before I hollow my cheeks around his thumb. Rhett groans softly, daring to slip a hand over my ass.

"You're being highly inappropriate," he growls.

"You started it."

It only takes thirty minutes for our turn, which is fine for me but absolutely torturous for someone like Rhett, apparently. We scoot into the little round carriage before it begins to rise.

He looks out over the grounds with an elbow hooked over the side. "What is the appeal in this thing?"

"It's romantic!" Honestly, I think I'm trying to persuade myself there's something magical in this painstakingly slow carousel.

Rhett shifts closer and lifts my leg over his thigh. "It could be," he mutters huskily before cupping my pussy hard over my denim shorts. I gasp, darting my eyes around, because these carriages are open as fuck. I don't see anyone noticing, and I don't want him to stop.

"Do you think I could make you come before we get off?" he asks, undoing my button.

"It's a very short ride," I breathe.

"That sounds like a challenge."

I'm deplorably turned on by the fact we're in public. Rhett's fingers massage my clit, and I suck my bottom lip under my teeth with the first sparks of pleasure.

"I want to fuck you right here and not care who we disgrace," he says at my throat.

"Rhett, people might see," I whisper. We've passed the top and are heading back down.

"That turns you on, doesn't it? I can feel you growing wetter by the second."

I try to shift, turning toward him in an attempt to look innocently enamored as we reach the bottom and go around again. Rhett's fingers curve inside me as we do, and my nails scratch into his neck, which tenses.

"Come on, little bird. Give it to me." My shorts restrict him being able to fuck me with his fingers the way I'm aching for, but his attention on my clit speeds my breaths, and I come so close . . . so fucking close.

"I think I'm going to—*oh fuck.*" My arms clamp around his, my body tensing at the impending orgasm.

Then he stops.

His hand slips out of my shorts, and I'm delirious and panting, sinking at his refusal to let me finish. By the time I've pulled back, Rhett has buttoned my shorts, pulling his fingers, which were inside of me, out of his mouth with a wicked smile at my look of irritation.

"So inappropriate," he tuts.

I'm speechless. And mad, wanting to get him back for that little stunt that has me riled up and needy.

"By the end of all this, you'll be begging for my cock."

We reach the bottom again and the worker swings open our gate. Rhett takes my hand, which is just as well, because my knees are wobblier than the carriage.

I'm walking around looking for a plan when my eyes light up on the fun house. As I drag him to it, Rhett smirks at me as if he knows what I'm thinking, but he has no idea.

Game on, Kaiser.

This line is only ten minutes—a lot quieter than the Ferris wheel. When we get to our turn, I plant a hand to his chest just past the entrance.

"Twenty-second head start," I say.

His eyes darken in challenge. "Ten."

"Fifteen."

"Nine. Eight."

This motherfucker.

I turn and jog down the hall and around the bend. Eerie clown music plays, and I navigate a spinning wheel, rope stairs, and through a room of wacky mirrors before I decide to hide in here. It only takes seconds for Rhett to catch up.

"If you come out, I'll finish what I started," he says.

My pussy is still hot, and my whole body feels like it's hanging on the edge of a climax. When Rhett gets close enough I lunge out, catching him by surprise when I slam him to the wall. Keeping one hand pressed to his chest, I undo his belt buckle with the other.

"What are you—? *Shit,*" he hisses when I pull out his cock and drop down. My lips wrap around him with no teasing or finesse, just quick sucking that has him cupping the back of my neck to bury himself deeper.

"Dirty fucking girl," he growls, beginning to thrust his hips to meet me.

I pull him out of my mouth and pump him hard and fast in my fist as I stand.

"You're close, aren't you?" I reach up on my toes to say it into his ear.

"If you keep—*yes. Fuck yes.*"

I stop pumping, starving him off at his base, and Rhett's head tips back, his brow pinched in tortured pleasure.

"That's too bad," I say and let him go.

As I walk off, I hear his chuckles at my back. I get out of the fun house before he does.

I squeal when I'm lifted off my feet from behind. Rhett sets me down only to spin me around and lift again, my legs circling his waist.

"Is that how it is?" he says darkly.

He looks so menacing and daring and downright sexy it isn't fair.

"I like to win too, Agent."

His smile through the makeup is so sinister but alluring. "Oh, little bird, it's far from over yet."

Rhett's hold tightens on me but his faraway look tells me someone is talking in his earpiece. He sets me down and suspense bubbles inside me. When his pained, concerned eyes fall down to me I know it's time.

"They're here?" I ask.

Rhett nods. "We don't need you to do this. There are other ways to catch them."

"I'm part of this network now, let me work too."

He's torn between admiration and fear, but I want to show him I can handle myself and prove useful even at the front lines of what he does. There are monsters lurking in the playground, and I'm going to take pleasure in watching them capture the prey that turns to the hunter.

Rhett sighs as he plucks out a second earpiece from his pocket and passes it to me. I focus on keeping my hands from trembling as I fit it in place.

"I'll be with you the whole time," he says, lips coming torturously close to mine I'm regretting painting his now. "You're so fucking brave."

He makes me feel like I can conquer the world so long as he's right by my side.

"Let's get this over with," I murmur, running a hand down his chest. "We still have a game to play."

He tenses when my palm drags over his cock. Then I step back, turning I squeal when he slaps my ass as I walk away.

I weave through the throng of people and decide to stop to buy a lollipop. The sugar keeps me calm and gives me something to fidget with.

"Coming up on your left, little bird," Rhett says in my ear.

My tongue swirls around the lollipop while I casually glance around.

"Did you really need to buy that?" he asks thickly.

Okay, maybe I'm being subtly provocative with it because I know Rhett won't take his eyes off me for a second, and he'd sparked a challenge between us since the carousel I'm determined to win.

I smile coyly, not knowing where he is exactly but he'll see it.

To my left is a dark passage between two tall containers, and I only make out the figure against one because I was expecting him. Wandering over to the carnival game right in front of that ominous slither of darkness, I suck on the lollipop and pretend to engross myself in the spinning wheels some are throwing darts at.

It doesn't take long before I'm approached.

"You don't want to waste your money on rigged games with cheap prizes," he says smoothly. I glance at him, keeping my repulsion down even though he's fairly young and quite handsome.

"Are you saying you have a fairer game with better prizes?" I play along.

He grins with such a gleam in his eye that believes he's won me far too easily.

"You could say I'm known for it."

Known for being a vile piece of shit.

I smile sweetly. "Alright then, show me."

He thinks I'm flirting and that he's caught me easily tonight. What sinks in my gut is how he doesn't seem surprised or like he expected the resistance, which makes me wonder how many he's lured away and kidnapped under the guise of being a harmless young man to enjoy some attention from for a night. The world is cruel and full of nightmares with pretty faces.

When I feel his hand graze mine I refrain from a violent reaction. Instead I grit my teeth, allowing his palm to slip across mine as he leads me down the dark passage.

"Seems we're going the opposite way from all the fun," I remark.

"The most thrilling things are found in the dark. You'll see," he says smugly.

Two more figures appear at the end and my heartbeat picks up. Subconsciously I squeeze the guy's hand and he chuckles.

"Relax, sweetheart. It's not a party without friends."

"Is it just the four of us?" I ask, only to try gain any information.

"You sound like you're hoping for more," he says, and my skin crawls to the suggestion that thickens his voice.

"He has a gun in the back of his jeans," Rhett informs me. "Don't do anything reckless unless you have no choice. We're closing in soon. And that hand of his is getting ripped from his body first for touching you."

I want to snip back playfully at his overprotectiveness, instead I pluck the lollipop from my mouth and smile.

"It's hardly a party with just you three," I say as we get closer to the other men who appear older than this guy.

I realize my complete faith and security in Rhett as I don't feel even the slightest bit nervous anymore. All the unsettles in me is giddiness to watch their grins of triumph fall to frightened children when Xoid came.

"We have more friends for you," one of the new men say, his voice gruff like he's smoked twenty a day for a century.

"How many women?" I ask.

He looks down at me with a hint of confusion.

"Do you bat for both teams, princess?"

Rhett said not to do anything reckless, but I'm feeling pretty justified.

This guy doesn't expect me to know about his gun as I pull it from the back of his jeans, nor does he anticipate my fingers jabbing into his throat when he tries to reach for me. When he chokes I push his chest which crashes him into the wall and point the gun at his face. My head snaps in warning to his friends. Their sly smiles have turned to vicious fury.

"How many women and children have you taken from this fair?" I ask, slower, with all the sinister intent that pours out of me thinking of those frightened victims.

"She won't shoot," the other guy says.

That gives the one under my gun the confidence to try grab me again but he's not that much taller than me and I land a hit with the gun across his temple.

He yelps, clutching the bleeding wound. The other two drew guns, pointing at me.

"I have friends too," I say.

"Baby, I thought I told you to wait for me," Rhett's voice is almost a purr, caressing down my nape.

"You took too long." I shrug.

Rhett takes the gun from my hands, only to slide another in place. This one has a silencer attached.

I see commotion in my peripheral vision, figuring our people from Xoid have detained the other two.

Rhett grabs the guy's hand, pinning it by his head. "You haven't answered her question," he says, low and menacing. "How many women and children?"

"I-I don't know man."

I watch, twistedly high with adrenaline, as Rhett stuffs a cloth into the man's mouth to smother his scream when he snaps his wrist. He keeps twisting past the initial break and I almost wince imagining the agony. My heart pounds thinking he might actually follow through on his threat and tear the man's hand right off. When he looks close to passing out, Rhett stops.

"That's for touching my girl," he says calmly. The man would have fallen to his knees but Rhett pins him up with a choking hold around his neck. "Where have you taken the victims?"

"I don't think you're getting the answer out of him now," I mutter, still aiming my gun but he's no longer a threat of attacking back or making a getaway.

"Dammit," Rhett says half-heartedly.

He lets the man go who falls to a crumpled heap instantly.

"Those who enjoy to inflict malicious pain on others typically do have the worst tolerance themselves," Rix comments. I flick a look over my shoulder to find him standing cross-armed behind Rhett. "I've never been in on the action, this side is kind of fascinating."

"Ana," Adam says my name with quiet horror. He looks between the gun and me as if he doesn't know who he's seeing.

"You knew I wasn't going to confront this with a teddy bear in my hand," I answer.

Rix claps a hand on Adam's shoulder. "Welcome to the violent and ugly side of the underworld, pretty boy."

"Welcome to reality," I mumble.

Meeting Rhett's eye, he contemplates just for a second before giving me a small nod.

I'd told him I wanted to be the one to stop at least one evil soul tonight.

Permanently.

I pull the trigger aimed for the man's chest.

Even though I was prepared, I'd wanted to do it, I don't think the twinge of regret, *fear*, will ever go away. It's the kind that adds a small tarnish within me but I'm glad for it, when it's the thing that separates me from the man I killed. Good from evil. Not the act but the intention and the emotions we bear toward it.

Rhett's touch is gentle over my hands still clamped around the gun. I let him take it from me, then he tilts my chin up from staring at the body.

"Are you okay?" he asks, searching my eyes to know if I lie.

"I think so," I whisper.

I flash a look around Rhett for Adam's reaction. He doesn't give away much; a little disturbed but it's hard to tell if it's toward what I've become or if it's impacting him more to see the monsters behind the trafficking he's only heard about so far.

When our eyes lock, I have my answer in the way he eases a small smile. It's painfully understanding.

"Let's get away from here," Rix says.

"Are you sure nothing can trace this back to us?" Adam asks apprehensively.

Rix slaps a hand to his chest, deeply offended. "Dude, have you not been paying attention at all?"

They walk ahead as Rix continues voicing his dismay about Adam's doubt in Xoid.

"You looked sexy as hell when I found you," Rhett says, creeping closer to me. There's a man I just killed lying a few feet away and yet he has the ability to make that insignificant in the way he speaks and reaches for me. "I almost didn't want to intervene just to watch my violent little creature at work."

My lips part to the rumble of his words cascading down my neck.

"Now you're being inappropriate."

He grabs my ass, pulling me closer until his thigh is between my legs.

"I thought we were still playing?" His hands coax my hips

to move and I can't help myself. I grip fistfuls of his t-shirt when pleasure starts to mount.

"We can't do this here," I pant.

"Why not? I don't think he's going to tell."

This should be all kinds of wrong. There's something fucked up with me not to give a damn about the body behind us. All I care about is *him. Rhett, Rhett, Rhett.* His name chants in my mind like an exhilarator to my impending orgasm.

"Please. I need—" my words are cut off by my own cry of tortured frustration when he grips my hips tight, stopping me from grinding against him anymore.

"I'm not above fucking you next to the blood of our enemies, even over it, but the other's will be back to clean up the mess any minute and no one is getting to hear those sounds from you but me," he says, equally as breathless.

I'm so needy that my underwear is soaked through. Rhett takes my hand, leading me out of the dark passage between the containers and we emerge into the bustling carnival again. My cloud of lust disperses enough to begin relaying what just happened.

"Will they find the women and children that we were too late to save?" I ask.

"Yes. We have the two others he was with. One of them was quick to give it up. These guys are always the easiest to break. They're at the bottom of the chain; unreliable and flakey crooks just looking for a quick payout with the least involvement. The moment they get spooked they usually back out."

It's a relief to hear. Rhett goes on to explain how it's not often they get a trace on the "poachers" as he calls them. Tonight we got lucky.

"There's no redemption for someone like that," I say, though I think I'm trying to convince myself after what I did.

Rhett pauses our walk to face me. His eyes are all serious.

"Make no mistake that piece of shit had every intention to take you. He would have been the first to rape you and then watch as he wouldn't be the last. I've met countless victims, Ana. Their stories are all unique but similar in the most tragic ways. That man you killed… this isn't his first time kidnapping women and children, and he would have done it again until he was stopped."

I nod, grateful for the assurance. Rhett pulls me to him and my tension dissolves in his strong, warm hold.

"You guys win anything yet?" Rix's voice travels over to us.

We release each other and I turn to find Adam carrying a medium-size teddy bear, and Rix holds a single goldfish. He lifts it up when they stop before us.

"Another for the Xoidship. I'm sure Jer will appreciate it," he says.

It twinges in my chest and on Rix's face for a second to think of Jeremy.

"Another game?" I say to Rhett. "Whoever wins the biggest teddy bear gets their job finished by the other?"

His eyes dance, knowing my meaning. I smile innocently at Rix, who hooks a suspicious brow.

"Deal," Rhett says, taking my hand.

Rix and Adam follow us as we scope out the games to choose our competition.

"Oh!" My eyes land on a long shooting range. It's childish, with a cowboy scene of small targets and shotguns with pellets. I pull Rhett toward it.

"You're choosing a losing game," Rhett warns.

"Wow, you really have to shoot down my skills like that." I give an innocent side-smile at the pun, and he rolls his eyes.

There's room for four to play at a time, so Rix and Adam join us.

I lift the shotgun to take my turn, but I notice Rhett hasn't touched his. I slide him a look.

"I'm not missing a moment of how hot you look right now. Go ahead," he says.

"You're distracting me. This is cheating."

"You know you're getting far more than the *job* from the Ferris wheel finished no matter what. I'm just going to string it out in punishment for your attempt at retribution."

My body tightens with a shiver.

I try to focus on my game. This gun isn't real, but the skill of aiming it is. I hit the first, narrowly skim the second, but I miss the third target, and the booth mocks me with a cowboy's *yeehaw*. Rhett doesn't disturb me. I hit the fourth, miss the fifth, and hit the sixth, seventh, and eighth, but barely. The last is my best shot, close to the center.

I beam in triumph when it's finished, winning a small bear.

Rhett's eyes make me erupt with pride for some reason. He doesn't say anything as he turns for his game. It's over far sooner than mine, and I think I turn to a puddle watching him aim and shoot like a pro, hitting dead center of all the targets. But when he finishes, something isn't right.

His jaw locks and his chests rises with deep breaths. The guy behind the counter asks him which of the huge teddies he wants, but Rhett isn't even present. He sets down the gun as I hastily ask for the pink one and struggle with it being the same size as me.

"Hey, you with me?" I say, taking Rhett's hand.

He blinks, and I try to figure out what's wrong. Until he winces at the shots Adam and Rix are firing and his expression shifts to anger.

"Let's go," I say, tugging him. He's rooted like stone.

I push us through the crowds until we reach the back of

some trailers that gives us a moment of privacy. Rhett sits on some steps, and my heart speeds at his distress.

"I killed a kid," he says.

Then it slams into me.

I set the teddy bears down and sit with him.

"No, you didn't—"

"You don't get to take that off my conscience," he grinds out.

"It's never on your conscience," I say firmly. "It's no more on your conscience than if the bullet had been in your chamber and fired by your finger. That kid didn't stand a chance the moment Alistair got ahold of him, and you know it."

"Then I should have fucking stopped him sooner," Rhett snaps, pushing himself up.

"You're just one person," I say sadly. "A victim, just like any of them."

"Don't call me that," he says, almost a plea.

"It's true, and you need to accept it. You're his victim. Not his monster. Not his assassin. His *victim*."

"Stop."

"No. Because you've never fought back for *you*," I say. My nose stings with how much I hurt for him. "You've been wanting to avenge Sarah, stop his crime on others, but you didn't deserve what he did to you. For six years before you got out. For what he made you become to stop him when he ripped apart your life again. Nothing is your fault, and if you won't fight for you, then I will. I'm not going to let you fester in guilt you don't deserve."

Rhett doesn't answer. I swallow past my tight throat, fearing I won't be enough. That he might push me away and not let me save him from drowning.

But he moves suddenly, and my back's pressed against the metal trailer behind when he claims my mouth with a wild, unleashed passion that I don't even care about the face paint anymore. I moan when his tongue sweeps into my mouth, and our kiss turns deep and lustful.

"I guess I owe you for the win," I say breathlessly.

"I don't care about that," he growls, spinning me. I gasp, pressing my palms to the cool metal. "I'm going to fuck you fast and hard right here. You're going to owe me by coming on my cock."

He undoes my shorts, pulling them down just enough to slide his cock between my thighs without entering me. I mewl to each pass of his tip hitting my sensitive clit, thinking if he keeps going I could come just like this.

"Don't stop," I rasp, pushing my hips out more.

It's so deplorable for where we are. The different clashing carnival music and constant murmur of voices makes me hyper aware how public we are.

"Such a bad girl," he says, low and gravely across my ear as his hand slips around my neck and he pulls me upright, back curving to keep his cock teasing along my pussy. "Look at all those passing people. Any one of them could decide to come down here, but that turns you on, doesn't it?"

It would be strange for someone to come down this way, but I can see the movement of bodies down the dark space between the ride trailers he's close to fucking me against.

Rhett pulls back and his cock pushes inside me. I gasp at the sudden fullness.

"Doesn't it, little bird?" he prompts again.

"Yes," I choke out.

"You're so ready for me."

Rhett starts pounding into me and I bite his fingers that slip up my throat. He groans, dragging his teeth over my neck in return and I'm becoming delirious with the wild high of this.

"You're going to feel me dripping out of you for the rest of the night here," he growls.

I need it so badly I start pushing back, meeting his punishing pace. Rhett adjusts his position, gripping my hips ready to spill inside me.

"You first, baby" he says, barely holding onto his release.

"I need more," I pant, lost in pleasure but not quite ready to finish.

"So greedy." Rhett pulls out with a grunt and spins me.

I'm quite lightheaded that when he leans down and pulls off my shorts, I don't register what he plans to do next. He grips around my thighs and stands with me, I'm completely thrown off guard. I don't get a second to protest or register the height with my thighs wrapped around his neck now when his mouth devours me. He sucks my clit hard, flicking his tongue too, and that's what tips me over the edge. The music is loud but I clamp a hand over my mouth with the explosive orgasm that detonates inside me. Rhett is unrelenting and I can't get away, can only trust he won't drop me while my body trembles against the metal trailer and I tighten a painful grip in his hair. Pleasure rocks endlessly through me. I'm a shuddering, helpless mess when he slows his assault. Licking and kissing me more gently but each time jolts through me with bursts of pleasure edged with pain.

"Holy shit." I gasp as he drops me down until my legs are around his waist.

"My turn."

I claw at his nape but he swallows my cry with his mouth over mine when his cock plunges back into me.

He doesn't go slow or teasing. Rhett uses my body for his pleasure now and I let him, squeezing his cock with my pussy. He swears, thrusting a couple more times before his dick twitches, his face buries in my neck and his raspy, choked sounds are my favorite in the world.

Rhett spills every drop inside me with slow, long strokes that I lose all sense of time, wrapped in a hot, sweaty entanglement.

I whimper to the lick of cold in his absence as he lowers my feet to the ground and tucks himself away. My knees are boneless but I'm spared from having to reach down for my shorts when Rhett does, helping me into them before pulling them up and fastening my buttons. He takes my hand but I think if I move his release will trickle down my thighs.

Rhett smiles deviously. He cups my jaw, leaning in to whisper huskily across my ear, "You either keep all of me in or let this whole carnival see who you belong to."

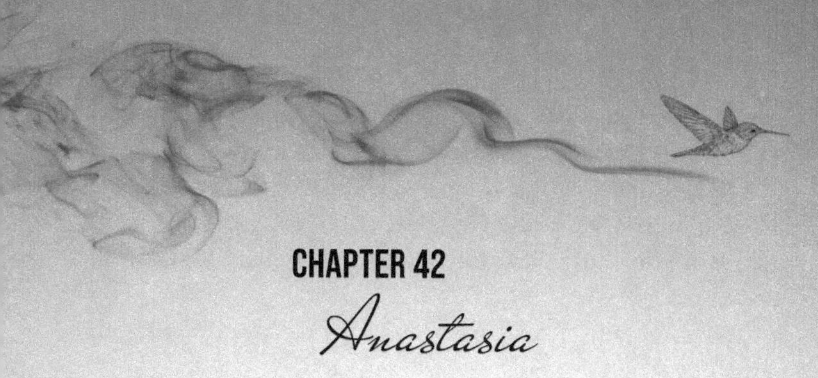

CHAPTER 42

Anastasia

Jacob had my attire sent to the rooftop restaurant for me to collect yesterday. I sit cross-legged on the bed staring at the elaborate white box while Rhett showers after me and my hair air-dries.

"I already opened it to check it won't detonate," Rhett says, approaching me with a towel slung low on his hips while he dries his hair with another.

I forget all about the stupid measure of possession from Jacob in a flash of pure lust at the godly sight of him. His tanned skin glistens with droplets of water over his impeccably toned abdomen. I shift to my knees, crawling across the large bed until I can hook my fingers around the waist of his towel, drawing him closer.

"We could be late," I say enticingly.

Rhett's blue eyes flash with desire as he drops the towel for his hair. His hand curls under my chin.

"We'll miss the whole thing if I start with you now."

He leans down to kiss me, and it's just as well he has more restraint than I do to pry my fingers from his towel. Rhett smirks at my pout, circling around the bed to where his all-

black tux hangs. My makeup is done, my hair won't take long, but I'm dreading having to wear what Jacob wants.

I think Rhett feels it too, the power move of it.

With a sigh, I pry the magnetic clasp open with the bow already undone, throwing the lid open. I'm horrified to see all the white.

"Why white?" I wonder aloud, irritated and trying to figure out what message he's trying to send.

"I'm not sure," Rhett says, detached, like he's trying to pretend it's *just* clothing.

There's a box inside, which I pick up.

"It's a pearl necklace," Rhett informs me before I can open it. "There are also matching bracelets and earrings."

"I don't want to wear any of it," I mutter.

Rhett's expression falls. He's wearing a pair of sweatpants as he comes over.

"I know, baby. You're mine no matter what. After this night, we'll have the peace we're owed."

It feels so close, so hopeful, and that also makes our peace terrifyingly fragile.

"Well, after we figure out how the hell we're getting out of the kidnap fiasco too," I say.

It's completely insane, and I'm surprised my dad let it out when he's always tried so hard to keep our doors closed and any scandals under the radar. I'm partially furious, because I'm certain he *knows* I'm not kidnapped and that I left willingly. He's striking out at me for keeping Rhett a secret and still choosing him.

"Maybe I can get emancipated. Then I'll make a public appearance and give a statement that I'm in love with a criminal and I chose to be with him." I crawl over to where he's sitting with his back to me.

"Then what? Leave everything behind? You may think you can live with never seeing your parents again, but I will not take that from you. Eventually, you'll resent me for it. Maybe not so clearly, but it will always linger under the surface."

He's probably right, but I've lost all sense of reason and judgment in my desperation to keep him. My hands trail up his back, stopping on the scars that are new to me with a growing ache as I discover more. I kiss between his shoulders, then I kiss his nape. Pushing up on my knees, I kiss the side of his neck and drape my arm over his chest.

"We'll figure something out, but if it really becomes a choice, I'll choose you. I won't resent you for it. I'll resent my dad for letting me go because he couldn't put my happiness and wants above his own for once."

Rhett takes my hand, kissing my knuckles. Then he turns, hooking an arm around my back, and I smile as he leans in, climbing over me.

"Changed your mind?" I say, hooking my knees around his hips.

"No, little bird. Only because I'm desperate to get this night over with so we can come back triumphant, and then I'll celebrate every piece of you for endless hours. Then we'll sleep, with our monsters killed and the world ours to claim."

My brow pulls together with emotion. I want it so badly it hurts. Our peace. My fingers trace down his chest, and my face relaxes in surprise. I run my index finger along the horizontal line like I have done countless times, except this time I follow it up then down before it tapers off a little. A single beat.

"You," he says. "You're the reason it beats, Ana."

I'm so choked with love and gratitude that my mouth flounders with what to say.

"When?"

"We had a few hours to kill while waiting for your great escape, and there happened to be a late-night parlor across the street."

"Rhett . . . I—"

He kisses me, stopping a likely incoherent, blubbering mess of all my emotions.

"It's you and me, baby."

I nod, and as he pulls back he takes my hands, so I sit. I'm ready, with more determination than ever to see this through, and I glance at the box holding the white dress with spite and hidden victory. Jacob will get me in white, but I plan to leave in red.

Rhett pulls up on a street that confuses me with its dark abandonment. I glance back, then around, trying to find something that might look like a venue Jacob Forthson would buy. But even if there was one here, I doubt his patrons would show up given the roughness of the rest of the block.

"There's no way I'm getting out of the car if we're here," I say.

When I look at Rhett, I don't expect his slow grin of amusement as he cuts the engine and gets out before I can protest.

"This is a small stop. We're early," he says when he opens my door.

I slip my hand into his awaiting palm apprehensively. "A drug deal? A hit? I don't think Jacob will appreciate me ruining his pristine image of me."

"None of those. And I truly don't care. Ruin the dress if you want. I'd actually like to see his abhorrence."

I realize I'm a complete mindless fool for this man as I'm allowing him to lead me without question or even fear up a set of steps toward a clearly long-abandoned chapel. There's graffiti on the outside, some messages making me particularly uneasy, such as "Hail Satan" in blood red.

We slip inside the pried-open door, and it's cold, dark, and ominous as fuck.

Until we get past the small entryway and moonlight floods in through the stained-glass windows, some of them shattered. The space is hauntingly beautiful, though it's not what slows my steps.

"About time!" Rix says from a bench near the front. "I'm beginning to feel a possession taking hold in this creepy-ass venue. You couldn't have picked somewhere better?"

Adam is beside him, and he casts me a smile over his shoulder, but I'm shocked, trying to figure out what's going on. They're dressed in tuxes for Jacob's event too. There are a few others I recognize from the Den, far more casual.

I'm confused even more when a cloud of smoke catches my attention.

Silas leans with an arm hooked over the back of his bench at the back. Some of his men linger around him.

"What is going on?" I ask.

Then a weight slams into me, and maybe it's the fact I'm dressed entirely in white and that this is a chapel, even though neither of us is religious . . .

No, he wouldn't—

"When I marry you, it most certainly will not be in some drug-den chapel," Rhett says, maybe feeling me turn utterly stiff with a reluctance to go down the aisle any further.

I relax. *Thank fuck.*

"Good. Because I'm still missing that ring," I say.

Rix gets up, heading to the shallow platform, where there's an old stone podium.

Passing Silas, I meet his eyes and say, "I'm surprised you didn't burst into flames past the threshold."

I don't think I've ever heard him genuinely chuckle without any edge of taunting or teasing. It sheds a new light on him, and just for a flicker, I see the human under the wicked devil.

"I did feel the heat, but it seems I'm spared another day considering my charity in being part of this sad audience."

"You can't miss your last ever graduation," Rhett says.

My head snaps up to him, then I look around and it settles, the realization of why everyone came. Even Silas.

"Oh my god," I whisper, stunned and overwhelmed by the thoughtfulness.

"I think this is the only place you've called for him where he might approve."

I whack my purse against Rhett's chest for his deviance.

Rix is holding my diploma, and I shift a look at Adam as we pass, having no doubt he's the reason they got it. Our eyes speak of all the friendship and gratitude between us.

I flush as Rhett helps me to the side of the small platform, and even though everyone here is a friend in some way or another, I'm awash with nerves at the attention. At the fact they all showed up to this ridiculous place for a mock graduation just for me.

"This is too much," I say. It comes out as a croak through the marble in my throat.

"Nothing is too much for you," Rhett says.

A cap is placed on my head from behind, and my hand reaches to steady it in place. I turn to find Adam holding a gown too.

"I'm guessing this is not a rental," I muse, sliding my arms into the sleeves.

"I'm sure they won't miss one gown," he says deviously.

I smile, so full of joy, and wordlessly step into it. Adam's embrace is slightly tense, and I can only imagine Rhett's frightening stare on him from behind me.

"All right, take your places, and let's get this ceremony on the go," Rix calls.

Rhett plants a kiss to my head before stepping down and sitting in the front row. He's so devastatingly handsome, and the most caring, loving, and darkly alluring man I've ever known. Getting to call him mine explodes my chest every time.

"We're gathered here today—"

"Wrong opening line," Adam calls. "Not a wedding."

"Fuck you, asshole. This is my graduation setup," Rix bites back.

I giggle, my eyes blurring with tears of glee that tremble me. Rhett watches me as if I'm the only thing in the world to him. He's utterly lost to me in this moment, and it steals my breath.

"We're gathered here to celebrate the underdog of the class of 2024," Rix goes on. He casts me a prideful smile. "I never thought I'd hold one of these in my life," he says, holding up the blue diploma. "And honestly, it might be making me jealous. Ana, I haven't known you that long, but I plan to know you for a lifetime."

My first tear spills, and I have to bite my lip to keep myself together. Adam comes back up, taking the diploma from Rix, who comes over to hug me tightly.

"I may have a little brother, but I've always wanted a badass little sister," he mumbles into me.

I chuckle through my tears. Rix is the big brother I never had, and he is more than worth the wait.

He steps down and sits next to Rhett, who's still smiling fondly.

Adam is at the podium to speak. "Ana, I've been a huge dick to you, but I'm not sorry, because jealousy is a bitch. I may have one of these diplomas we're delusional to believe will help us figure out our shit, but I think we both know we might be toasting by a bonfire made of them some day. At the end of these six years it took to get it, all I really want to keep is you. As a friend, to be clear, before Kaiser has my balls."

"They're still not safe," Rhett mutters.

I'm chuckling and choking and trying helplessly not to ruin my makeup too much, but they're making it impossible.

To my surprise, Silas saunters up the aisle, taking a last drag of his cigarette before he stubs it out on the front bench. He takes the diploma from Adam, who then crosses the stage, and I hug him tightly.

"Thank you," I whisper.

"Anytime, little A."

"I still hate that name."

He pulls back with a bright grin. "I know."

Silas takes a deep breath, examining the diploma before leaning in with one hand braced on the podium. "I don't know why the fuck I'm here," he says, but when his eyes slip up to me, we both know why. "Except to say, to find a rose that looks like glass but is really made of steel is rare, and this diploma is a key to your unexplored potential. I say we have that bonfire sooner rather than later. I might have had my doubts about you, but I need you to remember you're no fool, Anastasia."

To my parents, to society, even to Riley, who I miss so much, everything they're saying would be an outrage and bad influence. To me, I'm standing in a room full of people who finally *see* me. The way Rhett always has, from the first day he met me.

Rhett stands next, and my eyes fill as he takes the diploma from Silas. He doesn't come to hug me, but his eyes give the same effect anyway.

The silence that falls as Rhett is last to speak cracks my composure. He could just stand there with his eyes of adoration, not saying a word, and I'd be a complete mess.

"I disagree," he says at last. The room starts to tunnel away from me until only the two of us are standing there. "I think this diploma is the first trophy of your resilience. To have endured the years it took to get it without a light at the end of the tunnel. Teach, perhaps. Research, perhaps. What I do know is that you don't fear uncertainty anymore. You don't fear being you. Taking what you want. I met you as Miss Kinsley, a little bird in cage, and I'll go out with you as Mrs. Kaiser, the little bird who broke it."

I walk across the stage, barely holding my tears back. Rhett hands me the diploma, but he doesn't let go; his arm draws me to him instead.

"I don't think this is how the ceremony goes," I say quietly.

He kisses me anyway, as if there isn't an audience of our friends, some of whom start to whoop and holler.

"Sure starting to feel like a wedding," Rix comments.

They clap, and I'm bursting with euphoria, pulling out of the kiss.

"I love you, Rhett Kaiser."

His blue eyes sparkle, and I'm staring at my entire future in them, not the piece of paper between us.

A loud, slow clap echoes out of cadence with everyone else. As soon as my sight finds who the attention-demanding sound comes from, my smile is wiped immediately, and my happiness frozen entirely.

I barely hear Rhett and the others pull out their guns, but I feel it when Rhett's hold tightens, pushing me a fraction behind him.

Then the wicked voice drawls in mock endearment, "What a lovely little ceremony."

Alistair Lanshall.

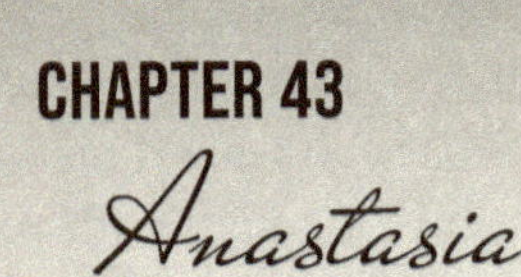

CHAPTER 43

Anastasia

My hand tightens on Rhett's arm with the cold dread that washes over me. I don't believe I'm seeing things right. Alistair is so arrogantly composed, sauntering in knowing he's cornered his prey. Then I try to figure out how he found us here, but my thoughts are a racing, terrified mess at being so blindsided.

"You can put down the gun, nephew. We have you completely surrounded."

Rhett remains defiant, and I'm terrified he could shoot out of blind rage with his whole body as stiff as a rock, straining against it.

"It's okay," I whisper, trying to coax him to lower it with my hand sliding across his.

Rhett's jaw grinds, his eyes turning Alistair to smoke and ash in his mind. But he knows there's no series of shots that could get us all out alive with the chaos it would erupt. He lowers his gun.

"How did you track us?" Rix seethes.

I imagine Rix would have been diligent in all our move-

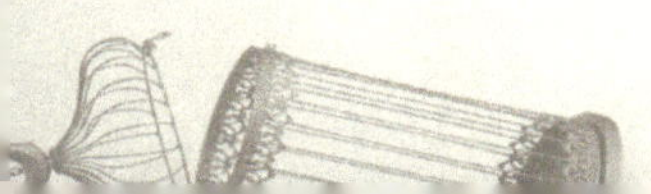

ments, ensuring we weren't followed or caught on surveillance.

I don't expect the answer to come from anyone but Alistair.

"It's nothing personal, princess," Silas says, pushing up from the only lax position in the room I didn't notice until now. "Just business."

My whole body slumps with a betrayal that has no right to be as gut-wrenching as this. I was wrong, so terribly wrong, to trust him. Yet above all, I'm not as angry as I am sad for it despite the notorious name he carries.

"Why?" I breathe, not sure if he even hears it.

He slips a hand into his pocket, and I watch as Alistair gives way to him, *yields* to him. I should have fucking known.

"I don't like mess, and he came to me with an offer that gives me everything I want."

"Kenna is detained in the manor for you," Alistair says.

That surges Rhett forward, and I grip his arm tighter. "You fucking sick bastard," Rhett snarls at Silas.

Silas's eyes darken and his jaw sets.

I say venomously, "You claim to be better than them, yet you bought her just like them."

"I don't expect an heiress and an amateur vigilante to understand, nor will I waste my breath explaining," he says coolly.

"Traitorous bastard," Rhett snaps.

"Only a fool can feel betrayed." Silas's eyes slip to me at that, but there's no emotion in them.

His words repeat in my mind, over and over, as he gives us his back and walks out without a care in the world that he's left us at the mercy of the vipers.

Only a fool.

"I have something each of you want," Alistair says. His gaze shifts from me to Rhett. "All you have to do is bring me the body, or just the head, of Jacob Forthson—whom, as I gather, is awaiting you tonight."

"So Xoid can be the target of his network for his death?" Rix grinds out.

"Be glad I'm not killing your precious sweetheart instead for her collusion with Forthson against me. You thought yourself cunning, Anastasia, but for once, I believe I was wrong about you. You don't belong in this world, and you should have listened to your father."

"You're wrong," I say, boiling with anger.

Rhett's phone vibrates. Then mine rings too in the small purse I'm holding. Rhett and I exchange a look as I retrieve my phone, and only then does he too. When I look at the screen, there's an unknown number, the same as Rhett's.

Rhett picks up, and the moment he does, his eyes close and his head drops in utter defeat. "Allie," he says, strained with agony as his grip tightens on the phone. "I'm coming for you, okay?"

Then it's my turn, and I know who I'm going to hear as I keep my eyes locked on Alistair, who watches me like he's won.

I bring the phone to my ear when I pick up. It's silent, but I can hear his breathing. "Liam?" I whisper.

"I'm sorry, Ana. I'm so fucking sorry—"

My stiff body flinches at the grunt of pain that cuts him off. "It's okay. It's going to be okay, and I'm going to get you out of this."

"Don't come for me. But please, you need to get Allie. Promise me that?"

I want to tell him there's no way I wouldn't fight heaven and hell for him, but it's not what he needs right now.

"I promise."

He gives a labored breath of relief.

"You have until the end of the night," Alistair says, and he turns to leave as the line between Liam and me is cut off.

The phone lowers in my hand, but I don't feel tethered to gravity anymore. "What do we do?" I say vacantly, staring after the ghost of the most wicked man to exist.

"We're going to go to that fucking party," Rhett says.

"Killing Jacob was only an option because we had Silas to take his reins before his network came for blood for the death of their leader," I argue.

"I don't care anymore. This ends tonight if we have to burn the city to take those bastards down and get to Allie."

"And Liam," I say.

Rhett gives a tight nod.

"What are we doing, boss?" Rix asks.

He's more lethal and focused than I've ever seen him before. The rest of the members of Xoid look to him with fear and determination to do whatever he asks.

Rhett checks his all-black watch. "We have an opening to get to." He turns to me with a storm of conflict. "I want you to go back to the Den until all this is over so badly, but I need you. Jacob is expecting you for this ruse, but you have to promise me you'll do as I say when I say it."

I know I can't promise that. I think he knows it too, as his eyes close for a pause, containing his will to shout at me, fight me, perhaps try to push me into the hands of one of his guys to keep me from going with him.

I grip the edges of his tux, tugging him. "It's you and me. Don't go back on that when things get frightening. We're all fragile under the right impact—you told me that. The right impact is you leaving me behind."

Rhett wants to disagree. He wants to push me away. But in the end, I'm glad he defies the terror that he'll lose me just like he did Sarah. When he kisses me fiercely, I believe we can take on the world together.

"You and me, baby."

CHAPTER 44
Anastasia

We walk hand in hand over the red carpet toward Jacob's venue. Rix and Adam follow behind us. I spent the journey reeling in my composure, and Rhett barely lets go of my hand, knowing I'm itching with anxiety and what that does to me.

I have to keep it together. My senses have sharpened, and I'm ready, confident even, to see this through to the other side.

"There's my darling," Jacob gushes upon seeing me. He hardly pays Rhett any attention, and when he reaches for me I reluctantly let Rhett go. His hands take mine as he looks me over. "Absolutely exquisite."

I allow him to hook my hand through his arm and lead me inside. Everything in me wants to look back, but if there's one thing I can contribute more than anyone, it's putting on a show to blend in with this hall of rich, pretentious assholes.

From the bridal-white he dressed me in to the claim he made of me without acknowledging Rhett, compliance to Jacob tonight only consists of allowing him to bask is his subtle, delusional methods of possession.

"How is my ruby diamond?" he purrs in my ear as we walk.

"Bored already. I do hope you have more to show me here than another fancy room containing too much arrogance to breathe."

Jacob shifts a cocky smile down to me. "I understand you're no stranger to a grand party. Trust I plan to make it worth your while."

I accept a champagne flute, sipping lightly while I scan the room he leads me inside. Dark cigar smoke mingles with lighter cigarette clouds in the low light. It's more like a reception space, with many deep burgundy Chesterfield sofas, long and singular, creating social groups. I try to find any women, but to my growing unease, I don't find any. All the men are in tuxes, drinking and smoking. Some cast me looks of intrigue, but their stares hardly linger. It's like they know a gaze over my body could spell their end.

"A nice venue," I comment.

"Not very complimentary to the place I designed wholly with you as my muse."

I start to take in more detail to figure out what he means by that. Perhaps it was the red carpet outside that matches the drapes over a low stage. Focusing on that color, I start to see it more. The napkins at the bar, the straws, the ties the bartenders wear, the rugs, the red-and-gold filigree detailing that climbs the pillars in the room. Then I see the violinists in the corner setting up to start.

"I'm flattered," I say, but I'm the opposite. I don't know what it means, but Jacob does everything with a purpose.

Jacob stops, curving around to face me. "I hoped you would be," he murmurs, low and personal, before bringing my knuckles to his mouth.

I can't stop my eyes, which flick to Rhett this time with my growing discomfort. His jaw is tightly set, and though he's trying to let Rix and Adam distract him, the corners of his eyes are blazing on Jacob.

I gasp when Jacob's fingers grip my chin, tearing my sight from Rhett back to him. His hold isn't enough to bruise, but it's a warning.

"You're mine tonight," he says.

"Then why did you even invite him?" I bite out.

I'm trying to stay on his good side, but he's making it too fucking difficult.

"Because you wouldn't have come otherwise."

We lock stares, and a shiver of realization snakes down my spine. It turns to ice when he smiles slowly as if he can see my thoughts right through my eyes.

I came with Rhett, but Jacob doesn't plan for me to leave with him.

"Why did you want me here?" I ask.

"You'll see, my love."

"I'm not your—"

"Come. I have guests eager to meet America's first daughter."

I'm led over to a table of men, and while they greet each other I risk a quick look, only needing to keep track of exactly where Rhett is. He's by the bar with Adam and Rix.

"A great honor to meet you, Miss Kinsley," an older gentleman says.

I plaster on a smile.

Smile and pretend.

"It's an impressive tale to hear of your dedication to Mr. Forthson," another says, sipping his whiskey.

Jacob's arm curves around my waist. I wasn't anticipating how bold he would be with me. I try not to let my confusion show.

Jacob says, "When you find the right one, it's worth shaking a country for."

"What an admirable engagement gift, an entire venue for your bride," another comments.

Then I think I understand. *No. He can't possibly mean . . .?*

The squeeze of his hand on my waist echoes like a siren. It turns in my stomach, and I blink away my dizzy sweep.

Jacob pulls me away from that group, and as he leads me to another, I take the moment alone to voice my dismay.

"You said you wouldn't want me if I had to be bought," I snap under my breath.

"I haven't paid a cent for you," he replies calmly.

"We had a deal."

"One that you broke, and I don't like to be made a fool of, Anastasia." He turns me into him when we hit a shadowed patch of the room, out of the light. His expression falls, frightening. "As I hear, Silas has allied with Alistair in exchange for a woman and the majority running of his network in private, so long as Alistair remains the head in public. I had hoped to hear it from you. Perhaps we could have worked something else out. Now I'm furious yet still absolutely smitten with you. This is my resolution. To have you. Break you and reshape you. As for Kaiser, he'll get to watch it all. He'll guard you, be close to you, watch as you fall for me and listen behind the wall as I fuck you."

That jerks me back, but his hands tighten on my waist.

"There will be nowhere to fly once I clip those wings, *little bird.*"

"I'll never want you," I hiss.

"You will," he says, and it's chilling how quickly his expression eases back to doting on me for the crowd. He tucks a strand of red hair behind my ear.

I swallow hard. *Keep it together.*

Be brave, little bird.

I breathe consciously. They're just words. He won't win this.

My steps are hollow as I let Jacob resume our walk around the venue. We greet more men, and I don't really hear what they say.

The next time I risk a look over at Rhett I don't know what the fuck is happening. He, Rix, and Adam have their attention on a young server holding a tray of champagne. But something is wrong. Terribly wrong. Rhett meets my eye then, and even across the room I can feel the creeping chill of terror in them. He doesn't give a lot away. Anyone else would look over and think they were just unsatisfied with the waiter's hospitality. He has his back to me and he wears a cap, but something looks familiar.

"We were just heading out now, in fact." Jacob's announcement snaps my attention back to the gathered men.

They look at me enviously, hungrily. I'm used to these looks, yet something is different this time.

"Where are we going?" I dare to ask.

Jacob gives me a convincing smile of adoration. "To marry, of course."

My world is spinning too fast. Of all the things I thought this night could turn into, this wasn't one of them, and yet it's become the worst. We thought of an ambush, gunfire, or just a night of pretty words.

I can't move, but I know Jacob is coaxing me to. Rhett isn't looking this way anymore as he's talking to Rix, and their conversation looks intense.

This can't be happening.

"Come, darling," Jacob says, and I tremble at his threatening tone. He leans his mouth to my ear. "I'm being merciful in allowing Kaiser to remain in our lives, but make no mistake, I'll put him down if you keep resisting me."

That forces me to move. With a break in my heart, I look away from Rhett and follow Jacob out a back door.

"What was the point?" I say. I'm numb and scared, but I get into the back of the car, and he follows me.

The car has facing seats, and Jacob leans back opposite me. He pulls off his bowtie and undoes the first two buttons of his pristine white shirt. I can't predict what he might do, and I'm thinking the worst, which isn't going to do me any favors.

Be brave, little bird. It's all I can chant to keep Rhett close while I'm alone and terrified.

"Kaiser's worm made the mistake of testing his luck too far. Getting into Lanshall's network, then finding a location of mine through it to try to be a double agent. Sound familiar?"

I puzzle over what he's telling me. Then it hits me with dread.

"Jeremy?"

"Little Jeremy," Jacob muses with a shake of his head. "Gotta give it to the kid, he's got arrogance. The waste is a shame, but I don't give second chances to rats."

"What did you do to him?" *Oh god*, all I can think of is the young face with curly brown hair that has so much kindness.

"Tonight I wanted to show you what I can build for you," he says.

"It's nothing more than finery-coated evil," I snap.

"I extended the invite to every man who owes me a debt I'm growing impatient for."

The way he speaks, avoiding my questions and ignoring my responses, it's like he's climbing toward the climax of a song, and my heart begins to race faster.

"Please don't hurt them," I say, because in my gut, something is growing so terrible and frightening.

"Do you remember what I said about debt, Anastasia?" My name rolls off his tongue like a sick lover's caress.

I would never forget what he said when it was followed by the merciless killing of Matthew Forbes.

"With what he owes me for you, I don't think I'll be seeing it in bills . . ."

So blood it is.

"No," I breathe, spinning in my chair to look helplessly out the back window, but we're already far from the venue.

"No!" I yell.

Recklessly I grab the car handle, but it's futile. I'm locked in here, but my fist pounds on the tinted glass as I cry.

Rhett, Rix, Adam . . . I can't lose them all.

"Take me back," I sob.

Take me back. Take me back.

I'm utterly hopeless here. Trapped.

"You'll find a new family in what I have to offer you. I promise." His gentleness is so jarring. In his delusional mind he believes somehow he'll convince me to want him. "You're into blonds after all. Am I really so terrible in comparison?"

I can hardly look at him with the manipulation he's trying. He's blond, but it has nothing on the unique silvery lightness of Rhett's hair. His eyes are green, nothing like the depth of a clear ocean in Rhett's. He's not fucking Rhett.

"I'll never be yours," I say coldly. "I'll never want you. Never love you. I'll fight you every day."

"You're already mine. You have been for some time."

My brow furrows, trying to understand what he's trying to trick me into. "I belong with Rhett."

Jacob pulls out a sheet of paper, extending it to me. I don't think I want to see what's written on it.

"It was a pleasure getting to know you as Miss Kinsely, but you've been Anastasia Forthson since the day you signed this license."

I can't take it. I can't see it.

But I remember the day I signed my name carelessly when all that mattered was getting Rhett, and that was the price.

The car stops. I'm going to be sick. Really. As soon as the

door unlocks, I tumble out and wretch. *Anastasia Forthson* repeats in my head, and my skin flushes too hot as if evil is taking over me. The white dress makes sense now, and as I peer up I see a small chapel.

I'm Anastasia Kaiser. I'm Anastasia Kaiser. I'm Anastasia Kaiser.

He can't take that away from me no matter what a piece of paper says.

A handkerchief floats into my vision, and I take it, wiping my mouth and straightening despite my body feeling like a boulder.

"Nerves are to be expected," Jacob says casually, knowing damn well I'm not sick with *nerves.*

"Burn in hell, you twisted son of a bitch."

"Don't start your vows yet, darling."

"Why are we here if it's already done?" I spit.

"Because I want Kaiser to come for you here only to find out you've been my wife the whole time you were with him. He'll know that he was fucking what's *mine,* and he'll likely believe you knew all along and kept it from him. I win, Anastasia. You thought I wouldn't be aware of your ruse with Silas, that he'd ultimately chosen a deal with Lanshall. I wasn't letting you get away with giving me nothing, so I set up the marriage, because if I didn't have him, I was going to have *you.*"

"It means nothing. That can't possibly be valid, and I will fight you."

"You'll want to reconsider. The explosive strapped around young Jeremy has two triggers, should you keep resisting."

My blood runs cold.

I back away until my back is pressed to the cold metal of the car. "You're a monster."

Jacob takes that as a compliment, and I've never had more

violent thoughts toward someone than right now. My hatred for him might trump what I harbor for Alistair.

"Come, wife," he says, hooking my arm, and when I try to pull free his fingers dig into my forearm. "Keep resisting and I'll give my guy the signal to blow little Jeremy to pieces. I have no doubt Kaiser and his dogs have discovered it too right now and won't leave his side."

I whimper and follow him.

I will never break for him. Never love anyone but Rhett.

I turn hollow when we enter the small hall with three rows of benches on each side. There's a priest waiting at the end, shaking and terrified. I can't blame him when there are four men surrounding us. One has his gun out casually in his clasped hands.

Jacob takes my purse from me, setting it on the bench.

"What are we doing?" I ask, trembling with dread.

"We never got the chance to have our ceremony." He addresses the old, scared man beside us. "Skip the intros, priest. We have a wedding night to enjoy."

Jacob takes my hands. I'm beginning to feel lightheaded, uncertain I'll make it through the quick ceremony now he's planted the news of worse horrors that could be forced upon me tonight.

"Eventually, I'll take you back to your father," Jacob says softly. Maybe he feels my stability wavering, and I can't fight when he pulls me to him with an arm around my waist. "Kaiser gave us the perfect setup. I'll be a hero to the country, returning America's daughter from her crazed ex-boyfriend. Then how we fell for each other. Our love will be legendary."

I swallow back my nausea as the priest begins. Blood roars in my ears so loud I hardly hear it. I speak when I'm told to, but I'm not registering what I'm saying anymore. I think I'm disassociating. I'm trying not to, because that would mean losing my fight.

"You may kiss your bride." I hear that, and it returns everything I've pushed down.

I struggle against Jacob's hold, but it turns painful.

"Warner," Jacob snarls.

My sight flashes to the guy who moves, and he's holding a button. I've watched enough movies to know what it is.

I stop moving.

Jacob's hand slides across my cheek.

"You'd better convince me that you mean this, because if not, I'll be very, very angry, Anastasia. I never wanted to buy you, and that remains true. I can give you everything you've ever dreamed of and more. All you have to do is open yourself to the idea I could make you happy. I notice the way you look at me too—there's a magnetic attraction you can't deny. Just let yourself feel it."

His lips have inched closer to mine, and my entire body is so stiff. Guilt wrecks me completely. I have no choice, but it's a betrayal to Rhett all the same. Jacob kisses me, and I can't feel it. His hands squeeze my waist in warning, and I lean into him, trying to pretend I'm anywhere else just to get past this.

Of course it wouldn't end in a chaste kiss to seal the vows. He turns hungry, and I whimper against his mouth. His tongue sweeps against mine and he clutches me tighter. Tighter. Tighter.

He pulls away abruptly with a wild look in his eyes. He's breathless, and I'm weighted with shame.

"That was far better than I ever imagined," he says. "How I can't wait to have all of you, wife."

Every piece of me breaks at that.

Jacob takes my hand, leading us over to where his guy has left a copy of the license I signed many weeks ago.

Oh god, when Rhett sees it . . .

I stare and stare at the names. How wrong they look together. I try to imagine Rhett Kaiser and Anastasia Kinsley.

And like a tiny reprieve from my misery, it tugs a fraction at my mouth.

Then we leave, and I don't think I'll know who I am anymore if I'm not Rhett's.

He made me see there was more inside of me that I was too afraid to show the world. He's the reason I believe in myself more than I ever have.

Back in the car I begin to tunnel away, knowing what will come next.

"Can you let them go now?" I whisper.

"Would that make you happy?"

"Yes."

"Then I will. But if they get in my way, I won't stop to consider it again."

"Thank you," I say. Only because it'll keep him satisfied to hear the hollow words.

"It'll all be over soon, darling—"

The gunshot comes out of nowhere. The explosion that follows, sending the car in a tailspin, shatters the world around me. It's all I hear. All I am. Something slams into me, and the world is all crashes and pain and spinning, spinning, spinning . . .

I cough violently, then splutter, at the hot liquid that comes up. My ears feel like they're bleeding too with the mixture of ringing and cracking that fills them.

I hear voices, but I can't make out many words. They sound so faraway, as if I'm trapped in a void and no one will find me here.

When I open my eyes it takes a few tries to gain focus. Slowly, I make out the horror of my situation. The car has flipped onto its side and I'm lying in a bed of shattered glass. Tipping my gaze up, I see I'm alone.

Did I fall unconscious while Jacob got out?

I fight tired sweeps, unable to uncurl myself from the

pitiful heap that doesn't want to move. I don't have any fight left to push the pain away and get out of the wreckage. I know it's dangerous to stay here when I can see amber diffusing outside. I'm lying in a ticking time bomb.

I want to live. I want to live. I want to live.

I am Anastasia Kaiser.

I hold on with everything I am.

CHAPTER 45

Rhett

I've gone over at least a dozen ways I want to kill Jacob Forthson in the ten minutes he's flaunted his possession of *my girl* to this venue packed full of rich shits.

Tearing his hands from his body for touching her would be a start. Stabbing my thumbs into his eyes for looking at her would be justified. Cutting off his worthless dick for *thinking* of her would be next.

"Should we follow them?" Rix asks, sounding as pissed as I am.

"No. She agreed to this and wants to keep things tame for as long as possible."

"So by the end of the night she'll leave with him and we'll try take him out in the car she's in?" Adam repeats our reckless plan.

I despise it more than he does, knowing Ana will be caught in the crossfire.

"It's the only time he'll be without guys surrounding him," Rix says. "We have a guy who knows how to stop a car with minimal loss of control—something about the timing and which tire to blow when. We'll take out the driver, then there'll likely be other cars of his following, and we'll be ready for them too. It's the best way to catch them unawares. If all goes to plan, Ana should be completely unharmed."

If all goes to plan.

I'm pacing like a wild beast inside myself.

"Then we take that bastard to Lanshall and get Allie back," Rix says, laying a hand on my shoulder tentatively, as if I'm a bomb that might erupt. It isn't far from fact.

"You really think he'll just hand her and Liam over?" Adam asks skeptically, ordering a drink.

I slip my volatile sight to him, which has him shrinking away from me a fraction and leaning on the bar.

"What? We have some time to kill, and I'm jittery with the nerves," he defends.

"I'll take what you're having," Rix says.

Adam orders another.

I keep track of Ana, and if there's even the slightest note she wants to back the fuck out of this, I'm not hesitating to kill every man in my path to get to her across the room.

"You're practically vibrating, man," Rix comments, taking a drink.

I'm reeling from earlier tonight. Getting blindsided by Lanshall thanks to being double-crossed by Silas. But we never should have given him an ounce of trust. Ana was so certain, and though I never trusted Silas, I trusted her intuition about him. I know she's hurt by the revelation of his true colors, but that's the thing about a chameleon like Silas, who can shift his colors to make people see what he wants them to.

He truly lives up to the Balenheizer name.

"C-can I offer you a drink?" a voice says from behind us.

It's so uncannily familiar, but I hope to be fucking wrong.

"You little *shit*," Rix hisses, but his face is awash with relief, and he moves toward his younger brother.

"S-stop," Jeremy says.

I've never seen this look of panic on him. Pale, sweaty terror. He's seen unimaginable horrors and been on the front lines of some very dangerous shit, but I've never seen him like this, and it spears my chest with ice.

He's trying to keep his composure, dressed in a server's uniform and carrying a tray of three champagne flutes, which trembles. I scan him once, twice.

"What the fuck are you doing here, man?" Rix rambles on. "I've been out my mind worried! How could you do this to me? This is the last time—"

"Rix," I say.

He stops talking. I think I might stop breathing.

I reach as if to take a flute, but instead I shift the platter an inch, then I confirm the worst possible fucking thing.

Jeremy's other thumb is taped over a detonator.

"Oh my god, is that—?"

I squeeze Adam's shoulder to cut him off, and he nearly folds under my unavoidably tight pressure.

"Shit," I mutter. Now *I'm* sweating. There's no telling how powerful the bomb strapped around him is, but it would be enough to kill him, and I've never experienced this type of all-consuming, frozen fear before.

"How fast can Dean get here?" I ask Rix.

He's my best explosives specialist.

"He's on the squad. He should be in the vicinity."

Thank fuck.

"Get him in here somehow. *Now.*"

I only took my sight from Ana for a moment, but now she's gone.

FUCK.

We anticipated Jacob would keep her here for at least a few hours. Yet never could we have predicted this stunt, and now it makes sense he would slip out. It licks a new trail of tension down my spine to wonder if there could be a timer or a second detonator and we're all minutes or seconds away from being blasted to shit.

"Holy fucking shit. What the fuck are we supposed to do?" Adam rambles. He's losing himself, and I don't have a shred of headspace to deal with him.

"Get the fuck out," I order.

"I'm not leaving you guys."

"I mean this with all the offense in the fucking world, Sull-evan. You're not useful to me here, and if I tell you to fucking jump—"

"I jump, yeah, I got that."

My eyes scrunch, trying to calculate more steps ahead, but it's pretty damn hard to when there's an explosive kid right in front of me.

"He took Ana out the back way. If you manage to see them, follow her. The others should still have orders to stop her car when they see her leaving."

To his credit, Adam doesn't hesitate on that command. He heads to the back of the venue, and I return my focus to Jeremy.

"It's going to be all right, you hear me?" I say to him. The kid is lost to terror.

"Can you tell . . . *shit, this is really bad* . . . tell Rix I'm sorry for disobeying this time. That I kinda wish I hadn't now."

"I would say this will teach you, but I'm sure that would be a lie."

Jeremy eases a pained, trembling smile, trying not to laugh even in his delirium. "I know we're not supposed to say this, but . . . but I'm scared, Rhett. You-you always say fear is a choice, but it really fucking feels like it's choosing me real hard right now."

"You're doing great, kid."

This whole venue of overindulgent assholes is completely oblivious to the fact they could be in pieces in any wrong move or minute. I'll admit, the darkest part of me is thinking they probably deserve it. But Jeremy most certainly doesn't.

The relief of Rix returning is only a small reprieve. "There's no security anymore. Dean got in through the back."

The fact security have cleared out is bad fucking news. This was Jacob's plan all along. I don't know what all the bastards in here have done to deserve his wrath in being invited to this setup, but he expects this bomb to go off.

I take a deep, calming breath to keep a level head. "Okay, Rix. Pick the most deserving guy you can and follow us once we make it through the back. Jer, we're going to go real slow. Chat to me, do whatever you have to, but keep calm and most of all steady as fuck, for the love of god."

"I can do that," he says, pep-talking himself. "Sure I can. It's just nice, cushiony padding under this suit. Considerate of them to include crash equipment."

Not quite what I meant, but whatever gets him moving calmly from here to fucking there.

Rix and I exchange a nervous look and start walking. Every step skips my pulse, every sudden laugh, clink of glass, rise of conversation. The hairs over my body are damn pinpricks.

Halfway. I'm resisting the urge to retrieve my pocket square and wipe my brow. It's suddenly fifty degrees hotter in here.

"Young man, we'll have two of those." An older patron stops him.

I take a breath to collect my sanity. I refrain from the violent impulse to take the flute and jam it down his ancient throat.

Jeremy pauses then tries leaning the tray down, but he's losing the control on his tremor, which starts to shake the liquid too noticeably. If he spills them, we're all fucked, and we'll risk their outrage escalating to physical. Wrestling a human bomb would be their last mistake and all of us would pay the price.

I lean in, plucking the stupid flutes and setting them down against all etiquette. It gains the sneering looks I thought it would, but I force a casual smile.

"Kid's first day on the job, probably his last," I say.

They chuckle and agree, luckily losing interest quickly.

"I can't do this, man," Jeremy says, his resolve crumbling.

"You're one of the bravest guys I know. Of course you can."

"I am?"

"Still the stupidest."

He huffs a barely-there laugh. "I'll take it."

We make it out the back exit with our balls on razors.

There are a couple of back rooms, and we head into one. When I close the door and flip on the light, that's when the lid on Jeremy's panic flies right off.

"Oh man, I'm a goner! Ground beef. Just leave me, save yourself." The last champagne flute shatters to the ground when he lets go of the platter.

"Jeremy, listen to me. Get yourself the fuck together."

"Y-yes, boss."

Rix comes in with Dean, dragging a patron through with a bunch of red napkins stuffed in his mouth. "Best I could do with limited resources," Rix pants, struggling with the man. Dean gives one calculated punch to his temple and knocks the guy right out.

"All right, let me see what we're dealing with," Dean says, fixing his attention on Jeremy and pulling out a kit.

"Be careful," Jeremy quivers.

Dean casts him a deadpan look. "We had bets on how you'd get yourself killed. Most said a bullet, some said drowning, Jackson said you'd get yourself blown up."

"Nice to know you've all been thinking of me," Jeremy

says, casting his sight to the sky, but I think God is up there with popcorn, gloating in our hellish situation.

"You two should get out of here. No point in us all going out if this thing blows," Dean says to Rix and me.

"No fucking way," Rix says. "My stupid brother, my stupid problem."

"Love you too, big bro. Hey, how are Frodo and Sam? Do they miss me?"

"I don't think—"

"Just say they miss me, man. I need something."

"They're absolutely beside themselves, ready to face Mordor again to find you."

Jeremy chuckles breathily.

Rix turns to me. "You go. Ana needs you, and we all need her."

Dean has cut away Jeremy's shirt, and seeing the packages strapped around his lean body hits the severity home tenfold. I almost can't think straight.

I'm absolutely torn. These two idiots are my brothers as well. Dean is like family too. But Ana is my life. Nothing means anything without her anymore.

"What's it looking like, Dean?" I ask.

"It's advanced. Can't be certain this is the only trigger." He reaches for his kit, plucking out a small screwdriver and working meticulously on taking off the control plate.

"My thumb is seriously cramping," Jeremy says.

"Rix, there's a blue disk in the kit. I need you to work on getting his thumb off that thing."

Rix swears, scrambling to find it.

I'm impressed by Dean's calm demeanor. He's even helping me feel like he has this thing under control.

He says when Rix finds the disk, "Good. The tape and scissors too. You're going to have to very, very carefully cut one side of the tape securing his thumb, slide the disk under, and wait for my instruction, but don't fucking let go."

"Shit. Fuck. Shit. Balls," Rix rambles, but he's quick to act.

I take off my jacket and roll up my black shirtsleeves. I've never felt tension like this before, and I've been in some huge raids against the city's most cunning and evil crime lords.

"Go, Rhett. We've got this," Rix coaxes.

I despise having to choose. But there's nothing more I can assist with here.

"You three get blasted to shit, I'm coming back to fit you together and kill you myself," I say sharply.

Rix smiles, but it's heavy, and I fight against every fiber of my being straining to stay. Even though I can't help, we're in this mess together no matter what.

All I can repeat in my thoughts as I race to the car is that Rix is right: we *do* need Ana. I don't think she realizes just how important she is—not just to me, but to all of them and all of this. She's brought a new light and joy to us all and has been so strong, smart, and so fucking resilient I ache with awe and pride for her every day.

I'm on autopilot as I drive and fit my earpiece in. I flip through channels until I'm listening in to the communication of the team set up to stop Jacob. At the same time, I tap through my phone until I have Ana's tracker on my car display screen.

"I'm coming, baby," I mutter, gripping the wheel tighter with my rage to ruin the city for her.

I don't like where her location is taking me. My blood boils as I press harder on the accelerator. The white gown gave me a riddling bad feeling from the start. He plans to try to marry *my wife*. I feel it in my gut with the way he took possession of her tonight.

I haven't had the chance to give her the ring, wanting it to be perfect, and though she's agreed to be mine until our bones are dust, I want to keep it as our prize of salvation at the end of all of this.

Getting to the location, I take my gun and an extra loaded magazine before I storm out. Several members of Xoid are nearby, and two of my guys are quick to come out of hiding to flank me.

We bust in there, ready to shoot anything that breathes.

"Whoa, whoa, don't fucking shoot!"

Adam Sullevan.

"Where the fuck is she?"

It's just him and a ghostly-pale old priest who holds up his book as if that will stop a bullet passing right through it and into his skull.

"I think we just missed her," Adam informs me.

Marching down the aisle, I lose my shit, finding Ana's purse with her phone inside it on the damn seat.

"You might want to see this," Adam says.

I don't think I do as I'll risk detonating. When I glimpse what I expect it to be, my rage is gripped by a moment of confusion when I catch the date on the marriage license. It has to be fake. Forged. Ana would have told me if she'd been forced to make this commitment for whatever reason.

She would have told me, wouldn't she?

My doubt is cold and cruel. Maybe she thought I would hate her for it. *Oh, little bird, a piece of fucking paper means nothing to me.*

My foot flies into the desk and it folds. I grip the first chair, slamming it into the wreckage, then the next, until that paper is buried in the fractures of wood. Someone hands me a lighter and a flame catches on the tablecloth, licking along the wood and beginning to devour it. I can't erase their names side by side on the marriage license from my mind even as I stare at it going up in flames.

"The priest said they only left a few minutes ago," Adam says.

I say to one of my guys, "The plan is active. Get our guys to stop their car."

"On it," Vixon says.

"I'm coming with you," Adam calls, jogging up to me as I'm already back outside.

"You're just another body to worry about," I snap.

"You got another one of those?" he asks, tipping his chin to my gun.

I pause and raise a brow. "Can you shoot?"

He shrugs. "I've been to shooting ranges a few times."

I resist the urge to groan, because that's hardly adequate experience for this, but I don't have time to consider. I pass him my handgun and head around to the trunk, pulling out a case of two pistols. I fit one in my waistband and carry the other.

"This is insane," Adam mutters as we take off in the car. "Did they get the bomb off Jer?"

"I don't know yet."

The silence is filled with the accelerating buzz of the engine.

"Listen, I know I said I won't apologize for anything, but we might very well die tonight, and I guess I feel like I should say you're good for her. As backward as that feels to say given the shit you've dragged her into . . . she's *better* with you."

Any other time I might feel something at his words, but truthfully, I wouldn't care if he told me I'm the worst thing for her. Then I consider what Ana would want. She tagged Adam as a close friend despite everything. I love her fucking heart. And I guess for her, I might try to tolerate Adam being in her life.

"Your speech at the graduation . . . she means a lot to you," I say.

"Yeah, she does. Ana understands me in a way no one has, and I was jealous of you two. I wish we could have worked, but we never would have done."

I don't question his sexuality. I'm certain his feelings for Ana were genuine, but not enough for either of them. Now there's something going on between him and Rix that isn't my business, but it sure will become it if Adam hurts him.

"Thinking you were gone really broke her. So you stay the fuck alive, all right?"

That manages to pull a single huffed laugh from me. "I plan to."

"Oh shit," Adam mutters as I slam the car to a stop.

My world tilts as I stare at the wreckage of cars. *Don't be Ana. Don't be Ana.*

I get out, and when I see the heap crawling across the ground, I know nothing but rage and vengeance. My shoes crunch over car debris, and one car tipped on its side is blazing at the hood. We need to get the fuck out of here before it blows, but I can't tear my target from Jacob Forthson.

"Where is my fucking *wife*?" I snarl, kicking his stomach, which throws him onto his back.

"You-you were too late. She's mine," he says, smiling with blood-soaked teeth.

I see white. Though I have bullets, I kneel over him, and my fists slam into his face over and over. Gunshots ring out, but I'm lost to violence.

"Rhett!" Adam shouts. I would ignore him, but then he adds, "It's Ana!"

Her name is the only thing that rears back the monster unleashed within me. I breathe heavily, staring down the bloodied mess of Jacob, who coughs and heaves beneath me.

Snapping my gaze, I find Adam crouched behind the toppled car, gun poised. I'm in the line of fire of my guys against Forthson's. Two guys come running at me, and I pick up my gun. My surge of instinct is halted when I see the serpent tattoo on one's forearm.

"What do you need, boss?" one asks. I don't know the names of everyone in Xoid. The network is expansive, and only a fraction of the members frequent the Den.

"Take him. Tie him up, gag him, do whatever the fuck you want, but don't kill him yet," I order.

They nod, covering me as I race across to the car wreck.

Peering down through the shattered car window, my heart tumbles out my fucking ass. "Ana," I say urgently.

To my immense relief, she's conscious. A little whimper escapes her as she drops her arms covering her head and peers up.

"Rhett," she croaks.

"I'm right here, baby. Can you feel if anything is broken?"

"I-I don't think so," she says, clearly in shock. She uncurls from herself slowly. My adrenaline races dangerously with the gunshots and the hyperawareness she's lying in an impending blast zone.

"I need you to get up so I can reach you, baby. Just enough for me to pull you out. Can you do that for me?"

"I think so."

Every small cry as she slices herself on the pool of glass bleeds through me.

"Good girl, that's it. Slowly."

When she's standing I manage to hook my arms under hers and lift. I know she's suppressing her sounds of how much she's hurting.

There's a moment of reprieve in all this chaos once she's cradled in my arms, and I duck with Adam behind the car.

"I can't tell if we're winning," Adam says, scanning the area.

It might be hard to check for the serpent identifier our

guys have from here. If I were out on the field, I'd know regardless.

"We just have to get Ana back to the car," I say.

Sirens wail in the distance, and now we really need to get the fuck out of here. Ana needs medical care, but they'd take her from me, and I can't bear that right now.

"Drive," I tell Adam, who catches the keys I throw.

I get into the back with Ana, and though it goes against so much of my instinct to leave the field with my guys still on it, I'm America's most-wanted right now with the president's daughter in my possession. Xoid will know to clear out now, and I pray we didn't lose people in this.

"I didn't want to," Ana whispers, tucked up on my lap.

"I know, baby," I say, smoothing her hair.

"I didn't know about the marriage. He-he made me sign something, and it was reckless of me to do it, but he had your location, and I-I didn't know. I should have known—"

"Shh," I say. "You're mine, little bird. Nothing can change that."

She sniffs, giving a weak nod.

"You're safe now. We need to get you checked out. We'll go to the Den."

"No. Please. I'm fine, just cut up and my head aches. I want to go home."

"Are you tired?"

"Not because I'm too concussed."

"How would you know?"

"Please, Rhett."

"Okay, baby." I kiss her head. "We'll go home."

CHAPTER 46
Anastasia

"Ouch. Ouch. *Ow!*" I'm really trying to be brave, but having micro pieces of glass plucked with tweezers out of the side of my face is making it damn difficult.

"I didn't even touch you that second time," Rhett muses.

"Liar."

I watch the bowl fill up after he's already plucked from my arm, leg, and side as I sit here in new clean black underwear. I'm starting to feel like a porcupine.

"Just a couple more," he says. To his credit, he's very gentle and steady-handed.

Aside from the disorientation and shell shock, I feel fine from the crash. Apparently, it wasn't supposed to happen. Xoid tried to stop the car without a crash, but they were ambushed by Forthson's men after the first shot and couldn't carry it out efficiently. Rhett lost two of his men, and I'm burdened with the loss too. Rix and Dean got Jeremy out of the vest and strapped it to one of the patrons.

Though our plan went completely to shit the moment we arrived, we won. They have Jacob somewhere, and we'll take him to Alistair tomorrow.

"I think I deserve ice cream for this," I say, wincing at the next sting. The glass clinks into the bowl.

"Absolutely. Mint or strawberry?"

"Both. In the biggest chocolate-dipped cone with sprinkles and marshmallows."

Rhett chuckles lightly. "Of course."

When he's taken the last piece out, I brace for the more intense sting of alcohol to clean the wounds. My teeth slam together, and I hiss.

"All done," he says, tucking my hair behind my ear.

"Thank god."

"I don't think any will scar. We got lucky."

"Damn, I was hoping for some battle scars."

He doesn't match my amusement. He's reeling in his turmoil over what happened.

"I'm okay, Rhett. I mean it. Physically and mentally. You said the marriage will be void. He just did it to get under your skin and make me feel like he owned me all this time."

I can't deny the thought haunts me still, but I'm trying not to let it tarnish the memories we have and that we found each other again.

"It's not over yet. And it kills me to see you bleed."

"I know," I say, getting up on my knees. I shift until I'm straddling him, and his hands cup my ass.

I kiss him, and he groans into my mouth. Then I break, trailing my lips over his jaw, down his neck. He squeezes my ass and I press tighter into him.

"You're distracting me from the topic."

"What topic? Ice cream?"

I squeal when he moves. It's as if I'm floating. He's so gentle with me considering my cuts and tenderness. He hovers over me.

"It pains me to say this," he murmurs huskily. I gasp when

his teeth pinch my nipple over the lace. "But get dressed. You deserve your sugar rush."

"Maybe I want something different now." My legs loop around his waist.

"After," he says, kissing me once.

I'm glad Rhett insisted on getting ice cream. We came to a small hotel for it in a quiet part of the city and snuck up to the rooftop to watch the sunset.

I've finished the strawberry top scoop and I'm now licking mint chocolate chip and moaning at the new flavor.

"If you don't stop that, I'll be taking you up here for the city to see," Rhett warns.

My stomach flutters. I moan again. I'm kind of high on pain meds someone brought from the Den. Having an ex-army doctor has it's perks, though I highly suspect the more powerful drugs could be stolen pharmaceuticals anyway.

I look at him with a playful grin and then giggle at his baseball cap and sunglasses. I wear the same as we've become America's most-wanted fugitives, but luckily, no one recognizes us.

"See? We can make this work," I say, swinging my legs off the ledge of the eight-story hotel. "We'll start a hat and Ray-Ban collection, switch up our disguise. Oh! You could grow a mustache. I could get a wig. Maybe we could turn it into role-play by the end of date nights."

When I take another lick of ice cream and he doesn't respond, I find him staring over the cityscape with a troubled look.

"You deserve to walk hand in hand with your love down the street. Be shown off with pride. Be completely and only *you.* Not this. Not hiding and sneaking around like a criminal."

Rhett didn't get any ice cream, only a coffee, which he takes a sip of.

"So do you," I say. "This world isn't fair sometimes. We don't always get what we deserve, but what I do know is that we're lucky. We have more than what most people hope to find even in secret."

His arm around me caresses the top of my thigh. "You're right, baby."

I leave a pause of silence before I say, "When we get Liam back . . . he's in the same position as us. There's a warrant out for him, and I don't know what they could have on him that's tied to his dad."

"If he's completely innocent, I wouldn't worry."

Rhett can't be sure if Liam wasn't involved in Matthew and Gregory's conspiracies, but I am. I've been preparing myself to discover what he might have been aware of, but I hope I'm right in believing he was never privy to it.

"Why shouldn't I worry?"

"Well, I should say I wouldn't worry if Allie loves him back. She's a damn good lawyer. If there's anyone who can clear his name, it's her."

I don't know how that didn't come to mind, but it's a beacon of hope.

"If not, we might need more baseball caps," I say.

Rhett chuckles, finishing his coffee as I bite my way down the ice-cream cone.

Night is falling, and the diffusion of orange and pink against the sky is a sight that stops time. When life is usually too busy to stop and check the hour, it's rare to find a place to watch the sun that gave us the day as it promises a new tomorrow with the beauty in its fleeting rays.

"I promise to love you, Rhett Kaiser," I say, staring at the last of the amber glow. "Until our very last tomorrow."

Rhett guides me to look at him by my chin. I can't explain how sometimes I see him and I erupt inside like it's the first time. Then I want to cry in absolute joy, because I found him. This is it. And life has never felt so promising just knowing he'll be with me wherever we go.

"Until our very last tomorrow," he says, then he kisses my deeply. Kisses me until we're both struggling for breath, but neither of us want to let go.

When we do, and the night grows darker, I get to my feet and take off my sunglasses. I'm not usually great with heights, but since needing to hideout on the ledge of the penthouse apartment I guess I'm beginning to conquer that fear. I don't look down as I cast my arms out for balance.

"Stability has never been your strong suit. Please get down," Rhett says.

"Or you could join me."

I'm glowing with euphoria walking the ledge. Maybe it's the thought of facing Alistair tomorrow when we only narrowly escaped Jacob. Maybe it's the fact we survived today that makes me feel a little delirious.

Rhett walks on the floor beside me, looking braced to grab me if I wobble the wrong way. "Ana, get down."

"So bossy."

I hop from one foot to the other, making Rhett jerk, and I giggle at his scowl.

"If you don't get down—"

"You'll spank me? Maybe that's why I'm still up here."

Rhett's blue eyes darken, his mouth almost curving a little.

"Devious little thing."

"Catch me," I call. Spinning, I throw all my trust at him in a backward fall. *"Omph."*

I break into a grin as he cradles me then sets me down.

He's looking at me in a way I can't decipher. Not smiling, not quite concern . . .

"I didn't think I'd meet anyone like you, Ana," he says. My grin falls at the unexpected seriousness of his tone. "Tell me you want me despite all I've done."

I don't miss a beat.

"I want you—everything about you."

"Tell me you'll never regret choosing me."

"I'll never regret it."

"Tell me you'll love me even in the times you hate me."

"Rhett, why are you saying this?"

"Please."

"I love you. I'll always love you."

Rhett dips a hand into his pocket, producing a small black velvet box. My eyes widen on it, and my breath catches.

"Is it the proposal I'm thinking of this time?" I breathe.

He flips the lid open, and I'm stunned by the unique beauty.

"The diamond is from my mother's ring, but I wanted you to have your own design. Something that's ours."

Two snakes give the illusion of twisting over the silver shank, their heads meeting in the center. Two ruby side stones compliment the brilliant square-cut diamond center stone.

"Who knew bodyguards came with taste?" I say, tearing up.

I blink my eyes clear to gawk at the most perfect ring I've ever seen. It's not just me reflected in it; it's both of us.

"I was going to wait until all this was over, but we never know when that last tomorrow might be," he says somberly. Taking the ring from the box, he slips that back in his pocket before taking my hand and sliding the ring on.

"I'm glad you didn't wait," I choke. "But we're going to have so many more tomorrows, Rhett Kaiser."

He kisses me hard. Claiming. It turns desperate and needy,

and before I can feel movement my back is pressed to the wall. I grip his hair, his jacket. My leg hooks around him and he pins it to him.

"Want to go home?" he murmurs breathily over my neck.

"No," I rasp.

"Anyone could come up here."

My lust only surges at that with inspired adrenaline. "Better be quick then," I say.

"Such a bad girl." Rhett's hand slips between us. "Did you wear a skirt on purpose?"

"Maybe."

I'm not wearing tights since the night is warm, and I moan at his fingers teasing me over my underwear. "This isn't being quick," I whine, only desperate to relieve the growing ache for an orgasm.

"I never agreed I would be." He pulls up my skirt, and the cool air wraps around my ass. "We could get a room downstairs," he suggests, but he doesn't stop devouring me.

"After," I say, eyes closing and back arching into his touch when he untucks my tank top and reaches for my breast.

"Good idea."

Rhett kneels, pulling my panties down with him. Then he hooks my leg over his shoulder and his tongue lashes my pussy, drawing out a cry from me with the burst of pleasure. My hand threads through his hair and my hips push into his assault.

His fingers tease my entrance until one pushes inside, so achingly teasing.

"I need more," I beg.

"I know," he says between flicking my clit with his tongue and driving me to madness. "I want you to beg for each finger until you've taken three."

I remember the faint burning stretch of three, and he didn't push all the way in with them that time.

"I don't know if it'll fit."

"You can take it, baby."

He pumps that single finger, hooking it on occasion to add a pressure somewhere between wanting to orgasm and to pee. It's new, and I don't know if I should lean into the pleasure of it.

"Another," I rasp. "Please."

"Good girl."

He fucks me with two fingers, alternating between licking and sucking my clit and around where he sinks into me. I'm becoming a puddle, with my wetness trailing down my thighs, so needy for the release he's pushing me toward but also starving me from with his slow pace.

"I need— *Oh god.*" My voice quivers like my thigh around him. Rhett's teeth bite into my thigh, and I gasp, the contrast of pain and pleasure shooting straight to my clit.

"Look at me," he growls. I do, and it's so sinful to see his hand working me, his mouth over me, how exposed I am on this rooftop. "Who is fucking you?"

"You are."

"So call my name."

"Rhett, please."

"Another?"

"I-I don't know. I need . . . I need . . ." Shit, I don't know words anymore.

"Tell me," he purrs, voice dripping with such allure that his talking surges me toward a climax as much as his fingers do.

"Faster, harder, *please.*"

"Can I add another finger, Ana?"

"Y-yes." I'm such a breathless, needy mess.

When he next pulls out, my chest expands with a deep inhale, and then I'm being stretched to my limits. He doesn't force himself inside, withdrawing in shallow strokes that sink deeper each time as my body adjusts for him.

"So fucking exquisite," Rhett marvels.

"Are they all the way in?"

"Not yet."

Oh fuck.

"I feel full. Too full."

"Do you want me to stop?"

"No."

The burn returns then fades. Soon I'm moving with each coaxing stroke, wanting him so deep inside me that the possibility feels endless.

"That's my girl," he says. "Taking everything I give you. Your pussy looks so good wrapped around my fingers."

Part of me is flushed with shyness at that, but the more dominant part is so close to orgasm I want him to keep praising me, telling me what he sees.

"I need to come," I moan.

"Then come, baby."

Rhett fucks me with three fingers for a little longer before he switches back to two, hooking them as if he knows of a secret button inside me. When his mouth joins, I'm done for. My leg barely supports me anymore as I lose myself to the most earth-shattering orgasm. It gushes out of me—I think literally. I don't know what's happening except that pleasure detonates from my core and seizes my entire body for a measure of time that could be hours for all I'm aware.

When I come back around, Rhett's standing, still pumping his fingers, but slower as I ride out the last waves of my orgasm. His arm circles my waist, and he's just as breathless as I am, resting his forehead on mine.

"That was fucking sexy as hell," he says thickly.

I look down with him, and I'm shocked at the small

puddle at my feet. Heat creeps up my neck and along my cheeks.

"I didn't mean to— I didn't know I could—"

He cuts me off with a kiss. "I was hoping you would. How was it?"

I'm still fucking collecting the shattered pieces of me. "Mind-blowing."

Rhett smiles triumphantly. "Good. Now turn around and brace your hands on the wall. I'm not finished with you yet."

While my body is spent, my pussy clenches on air at the thought, and I turn eagerly.

"Bend lower and arch your back for me, baby," he instructs. When I do, he kicks my feet to widen my stance. "Good girl. You look so fucking beautiful I could come just watching you like this."

I tune in to every sound of his belt coming undone, his button, his zipper being pulled down. It builds on my anticipation to have his cock inside me.

He teases the length over my soaking core, leaning over my back to press a kiss to my shoulder.

"Keep those hands flat and your arms braced. I'm going to fuck you hard and fast here. Only so I can fuck you slow and savor the night in our own bed later."

"Okay," I whisper.

"I love you." He kisses my shoulder again as his hand slips over my throat, locking me to him. Then he plunges inside me, right to the base.

I cry out at the fullness, but he's already moving. He's true to his word, and the obscene sound of our skin slapping and the wetness of my pussy fills the space around us. Rhett's groans never fail to spur my pleasure more. Hearing how much he's enjoying it gives me such power and triumph I want him to fuck me harder, faster, however he needs.

"I need you to come with me," he grunts.

I push back as his fingers slip through the mess between my thighs and he circles my clit. I didn't think I could reach another orgasm after the intensity of the one he gave me before, but I feel it gathering in my lower belly, and now I'm desperate for it.

"I'm so close, baby. Come—now," he growls.

It's like a fucking trigger, and after a few more sparks as he hits the right spot inside me and presses on my clit just right, I come apart. It's not as explosive as the first orgasm, but I still shake, and tiredness sweeps me faster. Rhett comes with a loud groan, pulling me up with a hand around my neck so my back is bent against his front while his cock juts inside me, spending himself.

"How are you even fucking real?" he says, gathering his breath.

"Honestly, I'm not even sure right now," I say in a lust-clouded daze.

Rhett chuckles breathily, slipping out of me, and I moan at the cold awareness without his heat.

While Rhett tucks himself away, I scoop up my underwear that will do little to help the wetness soaking my legs.

"Do you want to get a room here?" he asks, weighing up my predicament.

I shake my head. There's no place I'd rather be than the warehouse apartment.

"The world might end tomorrow, so our bed will give us the best night's rest."

CHAPTER 47

Anastasia

I'm looking at Alistair's elaborate manor in the woods, hand in hand with Rhett with Shadow by my heel, picturing the next time I'll stand here, when we'll feel the heat across our faces as we watch it go up in flames.

We have Xoid in every possible surrounding place, hidden nearby and remotely, though we have no plan and no idea of what we'll face once we go inside.

Jacob is watched by two of our guys beside us. He's been beaten up pretty badly, bound and gagged, and I have to say, it's satisfying to see his face not so pretty and smug anymore.

"We're not here to try to attack Lanshall today," Rhett says.

I think he's trying to convince himself more than anything. It's going to be damned hard to face him and only hand over Forthson for Liam and Allie. He has the alliance of Silas Balenheizer now, and we're severely outmatched against the both of them.

"One day," I say, squeezing his hand.

"Nice ring," Jacob says, barely coherent through the tight fabric tied between his teeth. "I would have done better though."

I let go of Rhett's hand, and he shifts as I step in front of Jacob. I hate him so much my hands tighten painfully to keep from trembling.

"You don't know the first thing about me," I say.

"I think you despise me because I know you *too* well."

His mere presence has been probing at a trigger within me, and now I can't stop my impulse. My arm pulls back, and I put everything I have into the punch I deliver across his jaw. Pain lances over my knuckles and up my arm too, but unaware, Jacob sprawls to the ground, and it's worth it to see the freshly bleeding cut along his cheekbone.

I grit my teeth, flexing my tender fingers as I stare down at him with loathing. Large, gentle hands take my throbbing one, and I'm drawn to watch Rhett examine my injury with a slow-blooming smile.

"You've gotten far better at that," he mutters bittersweetly. "No splits, but it will bruise significantly. You pack a powerful punch, little bird."

"With the right motivation, yeah, I think I can."

Rhett huffs with a shake of his head and then leans in to kiss my forehead.

"I'm hoping you won't be inspired again."

I grip the front of his black T-shirt to coax his lips to mine. The kiss is short but needed.

We head to the entrance, which is eerily open for us. My skin is crawling with a sense of dread, but I measure my breaths. Inside it's too quiet. I'm used to seeing several intimidating men floating around the place, but there's no one. We go to Alistair's office. Shadow remains alert by my side, and the only noises disturbing our tense silence are Jacob's shuffles and groans of pain as he's dragged along behind us.

We don't find Alistair in his office, but my heart goes from leaping at the sight of Kenna, perched cross-legged on his desk, to falling to my stomach at finding Liam gagged and strapped to the chair behind it.

"About time," Kenna drawls, bored.

She looks absolutely lethal in tight black jeans, heeled ankle boots, and a leather jacket. Her long, straight black hair is in a high ponytail that swings when she hops off the table.

"Kenna," Rhett says, as if he's seeing a ghost and the name is uncertain to him. When he last saw her, they were only sixteen and he knew her by another name.

"I don't know you, just as you don't know me," she says coldly. "Who we became under these names. We're strangers and enemies, Kaiser."

"You don't mean that," he says, pain slipping through his mask of indifference.

"Don't make me show you just how much I mean it."

I ask, "Where's Alistair?"

"Leaving the fun to me," she says with a sinister playful edge. Kenna retrieves a knife from her side, and I tense as she circles around to Liam, who locks his terrified green eyes on me.

"Don't hurt him," I snap. Rhett grabs my arm to stop my advance. "We brought him Forthson. That was the deal to let him and Allie go."

"He will stick to his word, but it's no fun to just hand them over."

My blood chills at the way she says that.

"Allie is being watched by Micah."

Rhett arms himself that instant, and it's me who has to stop him from storming out of here in his rage and erupting through his fists and his gun until he finds her. The idea of Micah with Allie turns me nauseous and ice-cold. *He's alive.* I thought the pencil in his neck surely must have killed him, but I guess my mistake was snapping them all as it can't have sunk in deep enough.

"You should go to her while we have our time here," Kenna says to him.

"What happened to you?" Rhett snaps.

I squeeze his arm in warning. He doesn't mean to lash out at Kenna—she's not responsible for any of this.

"I survived," she says, devoid of any emotion.

Rhett vibrates beneath me. "Go find Allie. I'll be okay here," I say.

Conflict wars in his eyes, but he nods tightly, cupping my face for a lingering second before he follows one of Alistair's men waiting to escort him.

"It's not too late to let us help you," I say gently.

Kenna doesn't take well to it. Her smile is cruel and beautiful. "It's not me who needs any help, Ana. Not from you or him or fucking Silas."

"I understand why you didn't come to Lumina. It would have felt like being passed from one possession to another," I say.

"You don't know anything."

"He came for you anyway. Except this way, he betrayed us for it instead."

I shiver at the new voice that interrupts.

"Only seems fair, don't you think?" Alistair circles around like a vulture from behind me. "After all, you betrayed me."

"You had Rhett captured and tortured all this time," I seethe.

"I did. And had you been good, and he cooperative, I would have allowed you to reunite. It's all I wanted. I see how strong you are together."

"We had a deal. Forthson for Allie and Liam."

"We had no such thing. Don't twist my words, dear."

"You said—"

"I know what I said."

Shadow growls at him, and I'm tempted to get him to bite.

"Watch that dog before I put him down without a second thought."

It's the only reason I keep Shadow glued to me. We brought him only to aid us if things went to shit, which is looking pretty fucking likely right now.

"This place will erupt into a war zone if you kill me or Rhett."

"I have no desire to kill either of you."

"Then let us all go."

Alistair walks deeper into the office before he turns back to me. His eyes dip to my hand. "Congratulations," he says. "From the moment you came to me, I knew you would be part of this family one way or another. My niece. I don't wish you harm."

I recoil at the new term, *claim*, he stakes on me. "You locked me away for *weeks*."

"You may find my methods harsh, but you turned out better for them."

There's no getting through to someone as delusional as Alistair. He sits in a chair by the unlit fireplace. I wander closer, shifting a look at Liam, who tracks me, but I give him a nod—the only slight reassurance that I'm okay and he will be too.

"I can get him cleared of the charges, you know," Alistair says. He takes out a cigar but doesn't light it yet. "I can spin a whole new story that will have your father convinced by the police and politicians around him that he was wrong and this was all a big misunderstanding. Rhett will be free. You will be able to be seen together. All you have to do is swear your fealty to me."

I want Rhett more than anything. For our relationship to be open and free.

But not like this.

I come around his chair, standing over him as flame sparks

from his Zippo to catch on his cigar. "He's not like you," I say. "He never has been, and he never will be."

I pull out my gun, aiming for his head. Alistair doesn't flinch.

"We've been over this before. You're no killer, Anastasia."

"You made me one."

"No. I made you smarter, braver, harder. I made you a master of deceptive charm and allurement. I thought it would work on Silas, but it seems I chose the wrong woman for him."

When I look up, I see Kenna poised with a gun aimed at me. The reason Alistair is so calm about my threat. Our stares challenge each other, and my chest pounds.

Her eyes flick behind me for a second, and that's when I throw all sanity away and shoot.

Alistair's yell of agony from the bullet in his thigh cuts the tension in the room. His cigar flies from his hand, catching on the long curtains, which catch fire instantly.

Well, shit.

I'm still free of bullets, and I look up with my heart in my throat at Kenna, who's still pointing hers at me. She approaches slowly, tracking me with the barrel, while Alistair flounders in his chair over what to do with the blood pouring from his leg.

"He's not my kill," I say, trying to keep my voice from wavering as I can't be certain she won't kill *me*. "He's not Rhett's either."

"Get out," Kenna says calmly. She reaches down for the cigar, watching the curtains get engulfed rapidly by flame.

Liam's muffled struggle spikes my adrenaline. We have to get out of here.

"Come with me," I beg her.

She merely takes an inhale of the cigar and wanders over

to the next window. Kenna pulls out another lighter, flips it open, and holds it to the curtains.

"What are you doing?" Alistair hisses. "I made you, Kenna Radley!"

When her eyes flick to him, so does her gun, and I tense at the sudden gunshot. It hits his abdomen, and the room becomes a tango of his wails of pain and the crackling of spreading fire.

"You killed Kenaleigh Aster. *I* made Kenna Radley," she says, so cold and detached. Kenna takes one final drag of the cigar before she flicks it into the growing flames.

I'm stunned, heartbroken for her all over again learning her birth name. Her dead eyes lift to me, and I snap into action, racing over to Liam and undoing his bonds. When he's free, he surges up, grabbing me as if he can protect me, but we both look to Kenna, frozen with what to do. I want to yell at her to come, try to drag her away, but I know it would be futile.

Smoke starts to sting my eyes, and I cough, stuffing my face into my elbow.

"We need to go," Liam says, pushing me toward the door.

"We can't just leave her!"

"She's made her choice!"

Kenna is so cold and chillingly calm in the destruction around her as she climbs onto Alistair's lap, straddling him. I can't begin to understand her mind, what this means to her to slay her monster, and maybe she believes she's truly become part of him too. Her lips angle to his, but there's nothing in the kiss. Like she's a ghost.

"We have to believe she'll get herself out before it's too late," Liam says. This time I yield to his push with the heat climbing dangerously.

It breaks my heart to leave Kenna though I don't know her

well. The image of her in that room is a tragic end to a tale I'll carry forever.

"Rhett should be with Allie," I say, looking around the hall frantically as I don't know which room they could be in.

"Allie!" Liam calls, uncaring of who else it could attract.

"Rhett!" I join in.

No one echoes back.

Both of us flinch at the loud sound of shattering glass.

"This whole place is going to go up in flames soon," Liam says, panic lacing his voice.

Gunshots ring out, and we clutch each other, scanning for the source, but it's not inside.

I rush toward the exit despite Liam's protests, in case it's Rhett in trouble. Or Rix and Adam, who are stationed somewhere around the property along with so many others from Xoid.

It's none of them.

He has his back to me, one hand in his pocket while his other tattooed hand pulls a cigarette away from his mouth. Fear rattles me as Silas begins to turn around.

When we lock eyes, I realize I was right to harbor the small kernel of hope.

"Only a fool can feel betrayed." I echo his words from the chapel.

Silas smiles, pleased. "You're no fool, Anastasia."

It's what he told me in his speech.

My next exhale is a whoosh of relief. "You never allied with him?"

"Why accept a seat when you can take the empire? I just had to buy a little time for backup to do so efficiently."

I regard the two men he indicates with his gaze. One leans smoking against the front pillar of the house. His hair is as dark as Silas's, but a little longer, more rugged. He sports a wicked scar over his left eye, which is dark green.

"Mason Balenheizer." He greets me with a smile as daring as Silas's.

I'm taken aback, and when I slip my sight to the other guy sitting on the steps flipping a dagger, I realize these are his two brothers.

"This is Teirnan, since he won't bother to introduce himself."

Teirnan doesn't even look up at me. "You said there'd be action," he complains to Silas in a grunt.

"Soon, brother."

"Where's Rhett?" I ask Silas.

He shrugs. "Said he had to retrieve something and headed back inside after passing off a woman to one of his guys. Where's Kenna?"

My eyes widen. "Inside. And there's a fire."

That shifts his expression immediately. His brothers swear and straighten before shifting into action, heading away from the property.

"A fire?" he demands darkly. "You should have fucking started with that the moment you came out."

"You caught me off-guard!"

"Damn it, Ana. Get the fuck away from this place. Run, as fast as you can, *now*!" He storms up the steps.

"What is it?"

"We have the basement of this place set up with explosives. If that fire reaches it before we can clear out, we're all fucked."

"Liam!" Allie shouts from across the front lawn.

I spin to him with a new trembling coating of fear, but my adrenaline keeps me sharp.

This is really fucking bad.

"Go! Warn them all and get as far away as you can! Take Shadow with you."

He takes Shadow's collar, but Liam doesn't want to leave

me. Allie is struggling in Rix's arms and will head this way if he doesn't.

"Find him and get the hell out, please," Liam says.

I nod and don't waste another second, running back inside the ticking time bomb of a house.

The fire has spread so quickly I blanch at the inferno. It seems crazy, but I race upstairs.

"Rhett!" I call, heading along the hallways to my room as the first place I know.

I barge in. He's not here, but a flicker outside the full-length window catches my attention. The figure disappears, racing though the trees at the edge of the cut lawn, and I know it's Rhett.

Back downstairs I pass Silas carrying Kenna, who appears unconscious, but I hardly regard them, shooting past. He calls my name, but I'm sprinting to make it out the back door. Raging flames lick up the walls in this part of the manor, but I keep going against the heat sweltering on my skin and the smoke choking the air. Suddenly, the house is too big, too fucking long, but I make it.

The fresh air hits me like a first breath and I inhale it greedily. My vision clouds, and I curse the dizzy sweep from the smoke? Adrenaline? I have to keep going.

I run in the direction I saw Rhett disappear. He didn't get far into the woods, and I stumble toward him, stopping just past the tree line and trying to blink him into focus.

He's kneeling over someone. *Alistair.* I make him out with my next attempt to see straight. My urgency to get us far away from the house pushes me forward as Rhett lands another punch.

When I get close enough, I break at what I see. The tears down his face, the agony that contorts it. The limp form beneath him. His monster finally slain. It pricks my eyes to watch him mourn, because I know it's not for what he had to do to get here; it's for all he lost in himself.

"Rhett—"

I barely get to croak his name before the world around us . . . erupts.

CHAPTER 48
Rhett

I'm hardly containing the rage that wants me to wrap my hands around the guy's throat in front of me. There are two others following, but I'm confident I can take them out too. What stops me is the need to see Allie before I lose my shit completely.

I'm haunted the moment I step inside the small lounge area. Allie is tied up and gagged, her stunning face tearstained and terrified. When she sees me she sobs hard, yet I contain a wrecking ball inside me. Micah is across the room, relishing in her fear. I don't see the months of torture at his hands when I look at him; all I see is what he did to my Ana. I've never wanted to kill a person as much as I do him. Not even Alistair. I can't explain the type of stilling, calm fury that ripples over every inch of me. It's not explosive anymore; it's pure, calculated, murderous.

"We've been waiting for you, haven't we, Alyra?"

"You're a dead man fucking walking," I say, low and promising.

"I take it you heard about the taste I got of Anastasia. She's absolutely delicious. Feisty too. I do love it when they fight back."

I breathe. Focusing on it. *One. Two. Three.* If I don't, I feel like I could become something dark and bloody.

"Where's Alistair?" I ask.

"Watching."

"What game is this?"

"First, hand over your weapons, Kaiser."

When I don't move, Micah produces a gun, aiming it at Allie. Her eyes scrunch shut, and she cries with a new wave of panic.

"Allie, it's going to be okay. I promise you," I say with all the gentleness I can muster.

"You shouldn't lie," Micah sings sinisterly.

My vision sways at those words. I've heard them before, when I held Sarah Carter's lifeless body. I *lied* to her.

I untuck my gun from my waistband and a guy takes it from me. Then I reach under my jacket and pull another from a holder at my ribs.

"Only two? I thought you'd come more prepared than that," Micah says.

I hold my hands up with my lethal stare on Micah as someone pats me down. The two guns are all I had, but I am more prepared than that.

"Fine. Let's get this thing going. I've been looking forward to it all day."

Behind me someone else is brought in. My teeth clench at the sight of the boy. He has to be a preteen. Then more commotion, and I feel nothing at seeing Forthson thrown in front of me like a sack of wheat.

"Jacob!" the young boy cries.

Confusion drags my sight down, and Jacob's head snaps up in horror, but he winces with the pain from all his beatings.

"You son of bitch," Jacob grits out, but he's scared. Terrified.

Then it hits me that this is Jacob's younger brother—the one Alistair discovered.

"He knows nothing about any of this and has nothing to do with it," Jacob spits, getting awkwardly to his knees with his hands bound behind him.

The boy is made to sit in a chair near Allie, behind a desk. Then Micah steps forward, placing a gun on it. Dread sinks me as I'm flashed back to the hell I escaped from. Having to point that gun and not knowing if I would kill an innocent kid or not.

"Remember this game? Except this time, you get to choose where to aim."

"You sick motherfucker," I seethe.

"It's always been Lanshall's brilliant idea. You have ten minutes before I come back and shoot them both, then you," Micah says. He stalks over to me, stopping by my side. "He's always owned you, Everett."

Everyone working for Lanshall leaves, so I don't have the chance to fire at any of them.

"Jacob." The boy whimpers for his brother.

"Hey, Mark. It's all right, buddy," Jacob says.

I despise him. Jacob ranks third on my list of people to kill, but I can't deny I have a stupid fucking heartstring in this situation for his kid brother. This is the most human I've ever seen or heard the bastard.

"Kaiser, man, he's just a kid," Jacob pleads.

"I can fucking see that," I snap.

"He doesn't know anything about this."

"It's your damn fault he's here anyway."

"I know, I know. Just *please*. You don't owe me shit, but you can't kill him."

"Don't tell me what I can't do, Forthson," I warn.

I make my way around to Allie and undo the gag tied at the back of her head.

"Rhett! They came out of nowhere. We were in this small town for months. Liam's house is so remote, I-I don't know how they found us—"

"Shh. It doesn't matter. Fuck, am I glad to see you're all right."

I untie her arms, and the moment I do, they're clamped around my neck, and she sobs. I hold her tight, letting her release what she needs to before I get stern with her.

"Is Liam still alive?" she whispers.

"Yes. He's with Ana."

That breaks new sobs, and I peel her arms from around me.

"I need you to be brave, Allie. Can you do that for me?"

She sniffs and nods. Then she takes a deep breath of composure. "You know, I imagined being part of the action with you someday. I think I'll stick to being intel in your ear though," she says, pulling on a mask of calm.

I smile, smoothing down her hair. "You're best at that."

When I turn, I find Jacob on his feet, twisting awkwardly, trying to reach for the gun on the table with his hands bound behind his back. I snatch it up in a surge of rage.

Grabbing the fucking desk, I whirl around it and my fist flies across his jaw. Jacob hits the ground, coughing blood. I'm surprised he's still conscious.

The soft sniffles of his brother are grating on me. He's an innocent despite his vile brother, and I don't wish him to see this violence. It will scar him.

"Kill me," Jacob wheezes, withering in pain on his back.

I don't expect him to give up so easily. Until I flick my sight up to the boy quivering in the corner, who looks so much like a young version of Jacob—blond hair and green eyes—and I understand why. Jacob has a corrupted mind and a thirst for power and violence, but he loves his brother like anyone else would.

Jacob says, "He said you get to choose where to aim. Aim for me, Kaiser. It seems to be over for me regardless. But I have one request. Make sure he gets home, please. Keep them all safe. They're victims of it all, just like those you swear to protect."

I don't know how much longer I have left to choose, but his offering seems like the perfect solution.

So why am I hesitating?

"You tried to force Ana to marry you," I hiss through my teeth.

"I did."

His consciousness is only half-here. Jacob's eyes flutter, pinned on the ceiling.

"You would have hurt her."

"She would have kept resisting."

My hand tightens on the gun to keep from shaking. "You would have raped her."

"Probably."

My hand rises to aim for his head.

"Don't let him watch," Jacob whispers. His eyes close.

I flick a look to see Allie has the kid, holding his head to muffle his ears between her chest and her hand. She meets my stare with desolate eyes. Then she gives a small nod, accepting what I'm about to do.

"You trafficked many women and children who are living the worst hell, and their families are suffering without them. You would have continued to put a price tag on flesh for many years if you weren't stopped."

With no regret in my chest, I pull the trigger once. *Blank.* Twice. *Blank.* The third . . .

It kills him instantly, through his right temple.

I'm completely numb to the death, only focused on what is

next. And next. And next, until we're out of this nightmare and I have Ana by my side.

I cross to the kid, kneeling down and peeling him from Allie. His face is too young to look so distraught, but I can't explain the desperation in me at seeing him as a second chance for Jacob.

"Listen to me. You're going to grow up with this shit trying to twist and turn you. You're going to feel rage, even guilt, as if there was something you could have done to save your brother. He might not be with you now, but there is a way to save him, you hear me? Be. Fucking. Better. A better man. Be good, *help* people. Vengeance is lonely and maddening. That's not the life you live."

I'm harsh with my tone, tight with my hold, but I think he understands in his timid nod.

"Whatever you do, don't look down," I say.

The door swings open, and Micah whistles low. "Of course I saw that coming. So I'm here to set you up with round two."

I don't immediately stand. Mark's small frame covers me enough as I click out the barrel of the revolver.

"I have to say, it was rather anticlimactic though. I expected more of that rage to come out before you put the bullet through his head," Micah says arrogantly.

They checked me for guns and knives, but they didn't feel the single bullet I have tucked away in my jacket. I slide it into the barrel, set it back, and don't waste a breath as I aim it at Micah's chest.

It fires, and he cries out, slamming into the back wall. Then I'm moving on rage and instinct. Two guys enter, and I grip the first guy's wrist, snapping it back, and his piercing wail only irritates me more. I take his gun, firing into his skull, and then my next two bullets enter the chest of his buddy before he can lift his own gun. With them down, I storm to Micah, who's slumped in a pool of his own blood, but still alive like I hoped.

"You want to see my violence, you piece of shit?" I snarl, then I hit. Again and again and again. He becomes limp meat beneath me, but I can't stop.

"This is for touching my fucking *wife*."

When I slam his head to the stone I think it's over. I can hardly stand to look at the mess of him, but even then, it still doesn't feel like enough for what he did to Ana.

"Rhett . . ." Allie says my name tentatively.

I'm gathering my breath as I push up, blinking myself back to reality with my violent adrenaline dwindling. Allie doesn't look down; she holds Mark, keeping him from looking at any of the bodies either.

"Let's go," I say, reeling myself back and realizing what I did in front of her. I wouldn't blame her for wanting nothing more to do with me. Knowing about what we do is one thing; seeing it is a whole other bloody clarity.

I'm alert as a hawk for any sign of Alistair's men, who could ambush us and take Allie around a back exit. As soon as we're outside I spot Rix and Adam by the trees at the back of the property.

"Stay with them—I'll be right back," I say to Allie.

"Please get Liam out," she croaks.

I nod, and it's a relief to finally be certain he didn't cause her harm. He somehow managed to save her from being taken and kept her away from it all for months. I'm indebted to the guy.

I don't have time to linger with Ana still in there. Taking a new gun from Rix, I run back inside and straight to Alistair's office. Something doesn't feel right. Sound right. It's too hot, and before I can place what it is, an impact slams into me.

My head pounds from the force, but I get up, blinking away the disorientation. To my horror, I'm staring right into

Alistair's office through a blasted hole in the wall. The side of the building has blown through too, opening out to the back lawn.

Through it, I spy Alistair *fucking* Lanshall hobbling toward the trees. I step through the wall despite the blaze and the smoke choking my lungs. I'm about to chase after him when I scan the room for Ana, hoping to god I don't find her.

The form on the ground slams me. My relief is wrapped in crushing guilt because it's not Ana, but I grit my teeth, letting Alistair get further away as I scramble over debris to Kenna.

For a second, fear grips me that she's dead, but her chest moves, and these fluctuating emotions are going to be the death of *me*.

"Shit," a voice hisses.

Looking up, I don't have the capacity to care that Silas is here. I'm livid over what he did, but all that matters is that he came for Kenna.

"Get her out of here," I snarl.

He cuts me a glare as he takes her into his arms. "This place is going to blow in minutes, Kaiser. You'd better run fucking fast."

I don't really register what he means when I'm already jumping through the wall and racing after Lanshall. There's no way in hell he's getting away from this, even if I have to go down with him.

He didn't get far into the woods, shuffling on one leg and clutching his abdomen. The moment I catch up to him I lose myself. Slamming him into a tree, I shake violently with rage, but also . . . so much sadness it unexpectedly drowns me.

"Why me?" I yell in his face. "Why did you have to make me this way?"

He doesn't respond. I don't know if he can, or if he's even fully conscious, as his eyes can barely stay open.

I punch him across the face, and he falls. Barrels of agony

pour over me, and I brace on my thighs to fucking breathe. I can't fucking *breathe*.

"I didn't deserve it," I say, shaking my head. "I didn't want it, but you kept sharpening me. I was a fucking *child*, and you wanted a *weapon*."

When he doesn't speak again I kick him. Once. Twice. Then I lose count, because I can hardly see through the infuriating blurriness.

I kneel over him, gripping his coat and pulling his limp body off the ground. He groans, still holding onto the threads of his life.

"I was just a kid. You thought you saw yourself, but I will never be anything like you. I had a life, and you could have just let me fucking *be*. I loved, and you took that. I was good, and you corrupted that. I'm not your nephew. I'm your fucking *victim*."

I break. In every way a person can be broken. But I've found a person who can mend what's left of me. If I didn't have Ana, I don't think I'd have the strength to keep the pieces of me from shattering to the point of no redemption.

"Rhett—"

Her quiet voice is a reach toward salvation before it's stolen from both of us.

The blast is endless yet short. I can hardly move with my consciousness struggling to hold on, but I remember her voice, my name made of her beautiful voice, and I fight *harder*.

The world is smoke and ash and embers. Then the treetops peek through, and I roll. *I have to find Ana. I have to reach Ana.* I drag myself through forest debris, trying to blink a clear visual. Pushing myself up, I find her. She's hurt, but she's finding the strength to push herself up too.

"I'm coming, baby." I barely get those words out in a breath, but I'm coming to, more and more.

When a gunshot fires I think I must be in hell. Or I wish to be fucking dead, and this a horrific nightmare.

One I've lived before.

I'm on my feet now, knowing nothing but her. No agony. No emotions. Nothing.

Alistair falls back, his hand goes limp, but I rip the gun from him and fire into his chest, then his skull. I drop the gun the moment it's over and crash to my knees next to Ana.

This can't be happening. Not again. She's pale and panicked, and I can't let myself go back there, to when Sarah wore that look.

"Rhett?"

"Yes, baby?"

"I . . . I love you."

"I loved you first, Ana. I promise you that. I'll love you every day of our forever. So you can't sleep, baby, okay?"

"I'm . . . I'm trying not to."

"Good," I say, lifting her into my arms. My teeth grit at the pain roaring through every bone and muscle in my body. Her cries of pain mix with my sounds as I strain to my feet.

"Stay with me, Ana."

Her eyes flutter, trying so hard to stay open.

So brave. So fucking brave.

"It's really c-cold."

I don't have anything else, so I hug her tight. If I could give her the flesh off my back, I would. I'm praying to anything that will listen as I try to walk more than a shuffle, but it feels impossible.

"Rhett!" Rix calls in the distance.

Thank fuck. Thank fuck. Thank fuck.

"You're going to be okay," I say, but I'm tormented with the fear it's a lie.

She doesn't respond, and I look down at her beautiful face, needing to pause.

"Ana," I plead. She's so deceptively peaceful, and I turn hauntingly desperate. *"Ana!"* I shake her, and my heart tumbles from my fucking chest when her eyes flutter open.

"Rhett?" she whispers, not fully conscious.

Her face blurs, but I can't miss a flicker of her. "I've got you. Always."

Rix and the others find us.

"Shit, I hoped you'd made it far enough away," Rix says, examining us.

"She's been shot," I rasp.

Liam comes up to me. "Let me take her. We need to move fast, and you don't look like you can."

I have to concede, but I lean my forehead to Ana's. "You stay awake for me, okay? I still have the world to give you."

"Okay," she says weakly.

I let go, having no choice but to let the buzz of people take her from me. I follow like a ghost as Rix hooks my arm around his shoulders to try to keep up with Liam and Ana. Allie is here too, keeping Ana awake by talking to her and trying to find out where the shot hit.

The journey to the front of the house feels too helplessly long, but a car comes speeding down the wrecked driveway. Adam is in the driver's seat.

I get in the back. Liam passes Ana to me, and though her sounds of pain tear through me, her silence would end me, so I'm grateful she's keeping awake at least. Allie slips in on the other side, scooting into the middle with Ana's legs over her and leaning over to put pressure on Ana's collar. Liam gets in beside her, and Rix gets in the passenger seat. Adam speeds off.

"The best we can hope for is it that it didn't puncture a lung. How's her breathing?" Allie asks.

I try to listen. "A bit fast."

"Shit, I don't know. I don't—"

"You're not a doctor, love," Liam says gently at Allie's helplessness. He comforts her with a hand stroking her thigh. "We'll be at the hospital soon."

There's so much to find out about what happened after my phone call with Allie when she was taken months ago. Later. I'll find out later.

"I'm still awake," Ana says tiredly. "And I still really, really hurt."

I kiss her head. They're good signs, and she's so damn brave.

"Good girl. Keep telling me that, please?"

She nods against me weakly.

"Rhett?"

"Yes, baby?"

"It's over."

I'm overwhelmed by those two words, wanting to believe them so badly, but I can't. Not until Ana is in full health and Alistair is in ashes will I believe it.

I'm numb, ready to follow her wherever she decides to go. This life, another. There's no me without her.

CHAPTER 49
Rhett

At the hospital I'm filled with adrenaline and more aware, so I'm able to lift Ana out of the car and carry her. I need every single second before I'll have to let her go.

"Still with me?" I ask.

"We shouldn't . . . you shouldn't have brought me here. You need to leave," she says.

I can't take the chance she'll need equipment we don't have at the Den if the gunshot hit anything major.

"It's going to be okay, baby."

The others are dealing with the staff, and I do nothing but hold her, watching her beautiful tired face.

"You need to leave," she insists.

"I'm not going anywhere. They're going to take you from me, but I'll be right fucking here, so you stay wake for me."

Ana whimpers when I have no choice but to lay her on the gurney they bring. I'm working on autopilot, following in hot pursuit as they roll her away. The frantic crowding of doctors and nurses around her is a slam of reality at the gravity of it all.

Ana was shot.

Sarah was shot.

No. I can't keep thinking that way. Ana *has* to make it, and *fuck*, I'm never taking a day, a minute, a fucking second for granted with her. She'll find me insufferable eventually for it, but she'll be alive and with me, always.

"You can't come in here, sir," a nurse says, holding a hand up to stop me from following them into the room where they start attaching things to her and cut open her shirt. There's so much blood I nearly collapse to my knees.

"What are they doing?" I ask, hollow.

"Assessing the wound and prepping for surgery. The bullet is still inside."

The nurse leaves me, and Ana isn't in that room for long before they're wheeling her out again. I follow, untethered to gravity as I watch my worst nightmare unfolding. Until I reach another barrier they'll stop me from going past.

Then silence.

Cold, terrible, haunting silence as I'm left staring through the double doors they took Ana through, not knowing if she'll come out.

My back meets the wall and I sink down it. My hands thread into my hair, elbows propped on my knees.

"Sir, there's a waiting room just along the hall," a male nurse says behind a desk.

I'm not fucking moving.

I don't know how much time passes. It feels endless, mocking. Like I'll be in this unknowing circle of nothingness forever.

Footsteps pad up to me. Several of them.

"Oh, Rhett." Allie's hands are on me. I think she's sitting beside me, but I can't feel her warmth. "She'll pull through."

"You can't say that," I say. I'm harsh and icy, but I don't care. "None of you can fucking promise that."

I know she's not the only one here, but I don't look up to check.

"The police are about to arrive, man. You should get the hell out of here," Rix says.

"No."

"You're no use to her locked up." Adam's is the harshest voice addressing me.

I take a deep breath and tip my head back against the wall.

"I'm not going anywhere." I promised her that, and I'll be damned if I break my promise.

Allie slips her arm through mine and leans her head on my shoulder.

"I'm so sorry, Allie," I say.

"Nothing is your fault. So don't waste your time."

Everything is my fault. I don't know what I did to deserve people who will try to cover up that fact just so I can sleep easier.

"You were in trouble. I let them take you . . ." I trail off.

"You were eight hours away. It can't be your fault, because I found out who *bought* me like some slab of meat," she says irritably.

Allie is so fucking incredible, and I hope Liam damn well knows it if there's something going on between them.

"I hear they're grieving his murder, but I'm ready to make it an annual celebration. Birthdays are old-school. It's cheers to the death of sick, twisted assholes from now on."

I want to chuckle, but grimness weighs it down.

Alistair is dead.

The last shot I fired into his skull repeats over and over, as if I'm convinced there's still a chance he could resurrect like he has done all throughout my fucking life.

"Where's Silas?" I ask darkly, glancing up at Rix. "He has Kenna."

"I think he's on our side. Honestly, I'm fucking confused.

The guy just shows up and we're all like, *shit, another mother-fucker,* ready to warn you, but he's like a ninja. Had he been on Alistair's side, we wouldn't have stood a chance. His guys took out all of Alistair's in minutes—guys we'd had pinned for hours. Then he told us about his brothers setting up explosives in the basement. The plan was to get you guys out and then blow the place to shit as Silas's first message that he's in charge now, basically. Then the fire happened, and, well . . ."

I take a moment to gather, repeat, and make sense of it all.

"He sold us out," I say.

"A ruse to buy time. He said he needed the help of his brothers, who were in Miami, to establish his claim on two very high-profile and intricate networks before they scrambled to chaos without a leader."

"So he did it. Silas owns everything of Lanshall and Forthson's?"

"He has control of it all for now, it seems. Which is better than a loose bunch of criminals with a whole load of illegal shit they can run wild with. No one will try to challenge Balenheizer."

"And Kenna?"

"Haven't heard anything. I'm sorry, man. But for what it's worth, he looked really fucking concerned for her and left immediately to get her medical care like we did."

"He's not here?" This is the closest hospital.

"Nope. I doubt he'd risk it, and he probably has private medical connections."

I have to see Kenna. Talk to her for real. I don't know how I'll ever apologize enough for getting it so wrong that she suffered by Alistair's side for more than a decade.

I failed Sarah.

I failed Kenna.

I failed Allie.

And what cuts the deepest is that I keep failing Ana.

I stand, wanting to punish myself so badly, but I don't know where to start.

"Maybe you're right," I say to no one in particular. "I shouldn't be here."

"Rhett Kaiser," Allie snaps at my back. "Get some coffee, go for a walk, do whatever you goddamn need to, but don't you *dare* leave her now because you think it's better for *her*."

My teeth grind. I don't want to lash out at her, but she's prodding a dangerous nerve. "She's in there because of me."

"No. She's in there because of Alistair. We're all here because of him. And he's *dead*. Ana needs you, she wants you, and you're a coward if you turn your back on that out of some selfish guilty conscience."

Liam gravitates closer to her when I turn with a heated stare. It flares me more that he would think for a second I would hurt her—verbally or otherwise. Allie is precious to me, and he'd better fucking get that soon.

"You know how much I hate it when you're right about me," I grumble.

Allie's posture relaxes, and with all the shit right now, I'm so glad to see her real smile showing off her playfulness. "Which is why you need me," she chirps. "Best hacker and motivator."

"Best what?" Rix challenges.

"You know it's true."

"We drew."

"That's just what you say to help you sleep at night." Allie pats Rix on the shoulder. "You're a lot taller than what I imagined, by the way."

"What did you imagine?"

"Some short kid who sees sunlight about twice a year and is too skinny from a sugar diet."

Rix squares his shoulders like he's wondering if that's a

description he lives up to. He doesn't. While lean, he packs good muscle and has deeply tanned skin.

"First of all, I'm older than you by two years. And I thought you'd be a short, too hot for her own good, arrogant — Yeah, you're exactly what I pictured."

She slaps his arm with a blooming smile.

Rix flicks a look at Liam, who's pinning him with a glare. "Best work hard, Forbes. You might have competition," Rix says, giving Allie a wink.

It's only to rile him. Rix has never been interested in women, sexually or romantically. Allie knows that about him, but her deviance sparkles in her eyes as she doesn't relax the tension in Liam by letting him know.

Behind me there's a new burst of commotion and thundering footfall. I knew this moment would come, but it strikes me to come face-to-face with Archibald Kinsley. His expression turns haunted to see me, then absolutely furious. He's flanked by a scary amount of security, but I don't move. I don't see the President of the United States; I see Ana's dad and how I can't possibly be hers, while he sees me as nothing more than a criminal.

"What are you all waiting for? Detain him!" Archibald roars.

Security skip ahead toward me, but to my surprise, Liam and Adam rush forward as a barrier between us.

The president does a double-take at Liam, then they start talking in quick, hushed speech, but two security guards grab my arms. One snaps a cuff around one wrist behind my back.

"Wait," Archibald says before the second can be secured. "Take him to a conference room for now. Nothing about this gets out yet, and keep a close eye on him."

At least I'll still be in the hospital. I'll fight them if I have to, if they try to take me out of here.

"Liam Forbes, we have a warrant out for your arrest," a police officer interrupts.

Allie pushes past me. "On what grounds?" she demands, slipping into her lawyer persona, which I've never seen before. It makes her stern and authoritative in seconds.

"Suspicions about his involvement in the conspiracy against the president with Gregory and Matthew Forbes."

"Suspicions don't mean shit. Show me." She holds out a hand, but the officers clearly don't expect to be challenged. They fumble to find the warrant, which is a scrunched-up piece of paper with lunch stains on it.

Allie only takes a few seconds to read what she needs. "I can't stop them from taking you in, but that's all they have the right to do. Don't say a word until I get there. This is bullshit, and they know they have nothing, okay?"

Liam nods. He's put in handcuffs, and Allie looks at them, distraught. They're both resisting a touch, and ultimately, neither cave as Liam is led away.

"You'll get him cleared," I say.

"Of course I will. I'm the best damned lawyer in the city."

Pride blooms in my chest. She's always doubted herself thanks to her asshole father. But she has to believe in herself for this.

Allie squeezes my arm. "You're getting out of this shit too. I promise."

I force a smile before I'm led away. The searing look the president holds on me wavers that confidence though. I'm certain he could orchestrate my assassination right here.

All that matters is Ana, and every doubt, worry, and fear that isn't about her leaves me as there's nothing I can do now but wait and fucking pray.

CHAPTER 50

Anastasia

When it feels like I'm waking up to the worst hangover of my life, I wish my consciousness would quit for a while longer. I never sleep on my back, and that's not helping matters, but I also don't recall my bed having a forty-five-degree angle.

I peel my eyes open reluctantly to investigate, hoping to find Rhett and that he'll make some quippy remark about how I fell asleep when I don't remember doing so.

My groggy attention starts to sharpen quicker when I don't recognize my surroundings at all. A beeping machine starts to bring my awareness back to the fact I'm in a hospital. Then I'm suffering the flashes of memory of what brought me here.

"Rhett." I can barely get his name out of my bone-dry throat.

"Darling," a voice says gently.

My head falls to find my dad, and that doesn't help—my panic surges more, and the beeping intensifies.

"Where's Rhett?" I demand, trying to sit up, but I wince at the sharp stabbing pain in my shoulder that shoots across my chest and my arm, which I realize now is in a sling.

Right, I was shot. This fucking sucks. Somehow I know it could have been a lot worse. I feel okay, all things considered.

"Please keep calm, Ana. You're okay."

But I'm not worried about myself.

Two nurses enter and check things around me, but I can't take in any of it.

"Where. Is. He?" I demand again.

"In the hospital. Detained for now."

I can't think straight, see straight, but as I'm consistently pressured to calm down by the nurses I fear they might sedate me, so I try to reel myself back in to prove I'm fine. I just need Rhett here.

"I want to see him," I say, unable to look at my dad with the way I know he'll be torn with concern and anger.

"Your mother is on her way."

I close my eyes. He's not fucking listening to me.

"If you let them take him out of here, I'll never forgive you."

He drags his chair closer to my bedside, and neither of us speak for a painfully long moment.

"I've been trying to understand, Ana," he says in defeat, "why you continue to defend someone who is dangerous, and with all the things he's done. He told me who he is, what he does."

My heart picks up again at that, and I pull the stupid pulse monitor off my finger. "You don't know him. You've never once tried to. Never asked *why*."

"I'm asking now. Because Adam and Liam seem to be on his defense too. As much as I'm not sure I can trust Liam either after his father's exposure."

I turn my head, and my look isn't friendly. "It took them saying something for you to finally listen? My word wasn't enough. Telling you I loved him wasn't enough. Because I'm just a silly little girl, too lovesick and emotional to make a valid fucking judgment."

"Ana—"

"I told you he only ever protected me. I didn't deny what you found out about him, but you wouldn't hear his whole story. You don't deserve to, because Rhett is a better man than you'll ever have the privilege of knowing."

Dad shakes his head, and I twist in disappointment. But he surprises me with his next words.

"If you'll let me, I want to know. All of it, every truth, and I promise it'll be held as your dad, not as the president. If you can trust me to tell me, I won't take it as anything legal."

"The truth? The truth is, Rhett Kaiser is exactly who you think he is and nothing like it at all. He kills bad people and saves innocents by sacrificing his own morals. He's a criminal in your eyes, but a savior in far more. And he loves me—more than I can ever explain. There's nothing he wouldn't risk to protect me, no limit to what he'd do for my happiness. If you ask me to choose, I'll choose him."

Dad sits with my words in silence. I don't really care what he does next, because my mind is made up. I'm ready for the next outlandish plan if we have to break Rhett out of custody, and I've come to terms with the fact I might have to sever ties with my parents to do it.

"Tell me why he took the job. Start right at the beginning. I need to hear it all," he says.

I have nothing to lose in telling our story. So it comes pouring out of me. I'm lost in it as if I'm replaying the memories just for me. I laugh, and I cry, and my stomach erupts at all our firsts. I leave out a lot of details about our private life, but everything that brought us to now is so unique and terrifying and wonderful. By the end, I'm reminded of how bonded we are, and how inevitable we've always been.

When Dad stands, I don't know how much time has

passed. He smiles, and I don't flinch away when he leans in to kiss my head. I whimper because I've missed him so much.

"So it was all a misunderstanding," he says. Confusion knits my brow, but Dad merely heads for the door. "I'll make sure the press flips the story as soon as possible. Rhett Kaiser didn't take you. He saved you from a trafficking operation led by Alistair Lanshall, which you got caught up in because of Gregory Forbes. They tried to frame Kaiser to get away with it and faked his death."

Relief slams into me and my eyes pool. "Thank you, Dad."

"I'll get a coffee and meet your mother outside. I think there are some other visitors waiting in line for you."

My tears fall as he leaves. *We're going to be okay.* More than okay. We'll have the life we're owed for the hell we walked through to get here.

I'm not alone for long before Rix, Jeremy, Adam, and Allie all file in.

"Thank god!" Allie gushes, coming around to my side and leaning in for a hug. I wince, trying to return it. "Sorry. I can't help it. I'm so glad you're awake."

"It's okay," I chuckle. "I'm so glad you're safe."

Allie's eyes flood with yearning, and pain furrows her brow. It tells me there's a lot behind what happened.

"Hey, I snuck you in a little pick-me-up," Jeremy says, pushing his brother out the way. He turns, and I burst into laughter though it hurts. I reach a hand up to pat the Chihuahua heads poking out of his backpack.

"Don't make her laugh, dude—she'll rip her stitches," Rix scolds. Then his face softens on me. "You really are a Kaiser to have survived this shit, that's for sure."

Pride bursts in me.

Adam sits on the end of my bed and squeezes my calf with a concerned smile.

"Are they letting Rhett go yet?" I ask.

"We haven't heard anything," Rix says.

"Liam?"

Allie says, "Don't worry about him. He happens to have a damn good lawyer on his case."

That reminder is a flood of relief. "You've really been with him all this time?"

A blush creeps along her tanned cheeks, and my intrigue piques.

"Oh, I am definitely getting that whole story," I say with giddy amusement. "Save it. I think I'll want wine and chocolate to hear it all."

Allie flushes more, but her smile widens. "I guess it's been a very long, *nonexistent* while since I've had a decent girl's night. You'd better recover fast. I'm looking forward to it now." She squeezes my hand, and just then the door opens.

When I see the stunning silver locks and Rhett's worn, dirt-smudged face, I crumble inside.

Allie stands from the chair, and Adam slips off my bed.

"I guess I shouldn't leave Liam suffering at the station any longer. I just know he would have wanted me to stay to see you pull through."

"Thank you," I whisper.

"Can you give me a ride, Rix?"

He nods, and they all bid me farewell. Jeremy coos into the bag like a crazy person when one of the dogs gives a little yap, and I giggle.

When they leave and I meet Rhett's eyes, I don't expect to fall apart so much that I have to cover my face with the one hand I have right now as the emotions rock through me.

"What's wrong?" Rhett asks softly, pulling my hand away and brushing my tearstained cheeks.

"I don't know," I say, smiling now, and maybe I am concussed and someone should be concerned, because my emotions are all shades of fucked.

I scoot over, but Rhett eyes the space warily.

"I'd barely fit on that thing myself," he says.

"Please."

He gives me a look that reprimands me for using the sympathy card. Rhett slips off his shoes and lies beside me. We maneuver carefully and slowly in consideration of my wounded shoulder, until I'm comfortably tucked against him.

Rhett strokes a hand down my hair. "How are you feeling?" he asks in a whisper.

"Happy."

"You might be the first to wake up after an explosion and a bullet wound and say that."

"I mean, physically, I feel like I want a new body, because this sucks big-time."

I can practically feel his smile. "That's more like it."

"But I'm happy to suffer in this one. To heal in it. Because it's yours."

He tips my chin back to press his lips to mine. "Yes, you are."

"How many ice-cream trips do I get for this?"

Rhett breaks into a grin. "Fuck me, Ana. I've been pacing and worried and going out of my mind, but I'm so damn relieved you have your spirit in full swing."

I say nothing, basking in our comfortable silence, which feels different. It feels like true peace.

"We made it," I whisper, lighting up inside with so many hopeful endeavors we'll get to take. No more looking over our shoulders.

"Yes, we did. And somehow your dad decided I'm an okay kind of criminal after all."

"We should get a plaque," I say. "'Xoid: Presidentially approved criminals.'"

The vibration of Rhett's chuckles under me lighten my chest.

"They'd love that, actually."

Rhett takes my hand, and I only notice my ring is gone when he slides it back on. It takes my breath away and turns me inside out like the first time I saw it.

"They had to take it off for surgery."

I wiggle my fingers to watch it sparkle. "You can get the upgrade," I say, pushing up on my good arm. "Husband."

Rhett cups my face, his eyes flaring. "Say that again."

"Well, I mean, we need the vows and the cake, and—*oh!* Can you imagine Shadow in a little doggy tux? Then, of course, choosing wedding bands and guest lists—or should we elope and save the hassle?"

Rhett lets me ramble on, and I find his stare so preciously content, so happy and burdenless, that I hope today is the beginning of seeing far more of it.

"Whatever you want, baby. But even without all that, I want to hear it again now."

I lean back down, hovering my lips over his. "So demanding, husband."

Rhett erases the space to kiss me, hooking an arm around my back and coaxing me to lie back instead. He breaks it first but trails his lips featherlight along my jaw.

"I won't test my luck by asking your father's permission yet."

"Probably for the best."

"But you've been my wife for a while, because if I wasn't going to make it past what we had to face, I had to feel what it was like to call you that, think of you as that. Mine, forever."

My brow pinches tightly. *Fuck*, I don't want to cry, but these are tears of such joy and belonging. "Say that again," I whisper.

Rhett smiles, and it's all the treasure I ever hoped to find in life.

He kisses me once. "My wife."

Epilogue

ANASTASIA

Six months later . . .

My breaths are calculated with the speed of my adrenaline. My focus is razor-sharp and my skin is slicked with sweat. I can't lose. I won't lose, because I have once before.

I straighten, squaring my shoulders, getting ready to take down my target.

Then it's all sand, volleyball, and crushing Adam fucking Sullevan no matter what.

He and Rix have the opening shot, and Adam slams it over the net. Rhett lunges to punt it up as I run and leap, hitting it back to them. After a lot of physiotherapy for my gunshot wound last summer, and being near insufferably fussed over by Rhett, it feels good to put my arm and shoulder back into action.

"Nice hit, little bird."

"Praise me later."

The ball is back to us, and this time I'm the buffer. I get to watch Rhett's impeccable body stretch out and slam a powerful hit. Adam and Rix try to save, but ultimately, they lose momentum, and the ball hits the sand.

I cheer and double high-five with Rhett, but even though this is only our first score, I squeal as he hooks a firm arm around my waist and lifts me so my legs circle around him. We're both wearing sunglasses, and he looks sexy as hell in his.

"How would you like me to praise you, Mrs Kaiser?"

I don't think the sparks in me will ever subside at hearing him call me that. Especially when it's dipped in such suggestion it shoots straight to my core.

"I don't think you need instruction," I say.

"I rather like it when you demand though."

Rix hollers, "Are we settling this before lunch? I'm getting hungry."

The volleyball showdown is the result of a few rounds of cocktails, a lot of power play, and a metaphorical gauntlet thrown between me and Adam when the reminder came up that he beat Rhett and me in California last year and I challenged him to a rematch.

Rhett and I are in Hawaii for our honeymoon. The tagalongs Rix and Adam booked a trip out with us, swearing we'd hardly see them. We've only been here a week and have seen them more than they promised. Neither of us mind though. It's actually been nice to have them with us.

Our wedding was as grand as I could suffer. My mom wouldn't take my request for "small" into consideration. When I said we might just elope, you'd think I'd suggested getting married at a circus. Which might have actually been more appealing.

It was front-page news everywhere, and we couldn't understand why people were so invested, even more so than the bride and groom. We're just two ordinary people. We have a wild story behind us, but the entirety of it will never be known to them. They will never know "America's Darlings" are still creatures of the underworld. Despite my reluctance to all the fuss and flamboyance at first, the wedding was a thing of fairy tales.

Riley, my best friend from six long years of university together, flew in from New York for the wedding as a surprise, and seeing her was such a burst of light. I told her everything that had happened to me, which was her first demand after seeing wild clips and stories of my kidnap then rescue in the press, and plenty of other stuff I'm sure was completely made up. It was one long, heavy, exhausting night. Allie was there for it too, and I was glad she could take over some of the explaining at times. We cried and laughed, and I got to hear about how her internship was going at Keithlington. Which also meant I heard a lot about Nolan Flynn. How their rivalry in the classroom has become even more intense in the work-place. She wants the job at the end of her year-long internship so badly that I'm not above working some shady shit through Xoid if need be to help her get it.

Allie has been working tirelessly to get the charges off Liam, and they might have been with us here too if Liam wasn't under house arrest. It's far better than prison. They think they might have something on him for the murder of the shit-face lawyer who tried to buy Allie. It's all speculation, but they're fighting her hard, and it's her own family's law firm she's up against. It's the last cloud of burden from what we all went through, but we're staying confident Allie will succeed through the painstakingly slow trial.

Silas has been elusive about Kenna despite Rhett's pester-ing. We haven't gotten a chance to really speak to her since she was taken in by him. Rhett wouldn't have stopped trying if she hadn't told us herself she wanted nothing to do with us—in very colorful words. She's safe with Silas for now, but last we saw, she was reluctant to be there, and I imagine all this time she's been crafting her plan to leave him too eventually. To be on her own, since she trusts no one. Xoid is keeping tabs on her as best we can, because if she runs, we won't be able to let her disappear until Rhett gets to say his peace and apologize to her. I know the past with her will always tear him apart.

I glance over the beach as Adam pushes Rix's chest with a disgruntled expression. Rix is grinning at whatever he said, and the contrast between them is a regular thing to witness. What's fairly new is how Rix grabs Adam's wrist as he tries to walk off and pulls him back. They kiss, and I look away then to give them privacy. We all knew something's been hot-and-cold with them for many months. It still is hot-and-cold, but they don't try to hide it anymore.

"How about we ditch this game and head back to our villa?" Rhett suggests, enticing me with a kiss to my jaw, then a bite to my neck when I tighten around him.

"We need to beat him, or we'll never get to live it down," I protest, but he's making a very persuasive case.

"*You'll* never live it down. Your competitive streak is sexy."

"You'll suffer my complaining, so *we*," I say, pecking his cheek and uncrossing my legs.

Except when I turn back to the net, Rix and Adam have turned more heated, and the sun isn't what flushes my skin. They don't even regard us as they break away but remain close. Rix says something in Adam's ear that causes him to playfully punch Rix's chest before they walk off.

"Do we win by forfeit?" Rhett mutters.

I'm still slack-jawed they just left us like that, but I'm also not complaining.

"They did say they'd hardly interfere with our honeymoon," I say, turning back to Rhett. Circling behind him, I reach for his shoulders, and he naturally bends for me to climb his back.

We have three more weeks of getting to sunbathe, relax, and enjoy our time alone away from work.

Xoid is thriving, and I've enjoyed more than anything getting to be a part of what Rhett built. But I've started to make something of my own now, with the school I wanted to open well under construction. I should be able to announce an opening date for the new term this year.

My life is split by two contrasting desires, but I like to think it keeps me balanced.

Rhett walks the whole way back to our private villa carrying me on his back. When we're inside I moan at the cool lick of the air conditioning. In the bedroom, I squeal when Rhett twists and throws me off him and I land on the plush mattress.

He's upon me a second later, and I giggle at the tickling assault of his lips on my neck.

"We're both too sandy, and we'll regret it later if we get it under the covers," I say, but I don't have much more to protest if he disregards that warning.

"Hmm," he says, then he flicks his tongue over my serpent earring. "Then you have three seconds to get this pretty little ass into the bathroom before I'm coming for it."

My pussy flutters at the thought. Rhett doesn't move off me, so I hook a leg around his hip and push his chest, flipping our position.

Before I head for a shower I reach behind myself, pulling at the red string of my bikini top. Then I pull the tie around my neck. Rhett drinks me in with wild eyes as the material falls away.

I wasn't kidding about the sand, and it clearly got into every crevice with how gritty my skin is with it.

I slip off Rhett, and he props himself up on his elbows to watch me. I walk backward toward the open glass doors leading out to our private pool.

"You'll have to catch me first, Agent Kaiser," I say.

When I pull the ties of my bikini bottoms, they fall to the floor. Rhett all but launches off the bed, and I yelp, running out and jumping into the pool. I immediately swim as fast as I can, but I don't get far before the splash of him follows mine. He's too fast, grabbing my ankle before I can even reach the other side of the pool.

Rhett hooks me around the waist and pushes us to the surface. I barely get a breath in before his lips steal my next. Between the heated kiss and clamping myself around him he floats us to the side of the pool, where he presses into me against the pool wall so I feel his hard cock against my core.

This end of the pool is shallow enough for Rhett to stand easily. When he does, his large hands grip my waist, and I gasp, clutching the ledge as he pushes me out of the water.

He doesn't waste a second before hooking my legs over his shoulders and cupping my ass, bringing his mouth to my pussy. I throw my head back with a moan, fingers threading through his hair.

"Fuck, *yes, yes.*" I quickly chase an orgasm, so turned on by the open air and the wildness unleashed between us on this holiday.

"So responsive," Rhett growls, feasting on me like he's been starved all day.

I can't explain the need that turns me more feral for this man every damn day. I lean back on one hand while my hips undulate, trying to take more from his mouth as it sucks and licks right where I need it.

"Greedy fucking girl," Rhett growls, his hands slapping my ass, and I moan louder. "Get inside."

I tense with a pleasurably sharp gasp when his teeth nip my clit before he pushes away, only to hoist himself out of the water. It doesn't matter how many times I get to watch him do that, it steals my fucking soul every time. Especially when he's naked.

Rhett takes my hand, leading me through the house and into the elaborate bathroom. The sunken bath is already filled with bubbles and rose petals, and my heart melts at the beauty of it. Champagne and chocolate-covered strawberries have my mouth watering. Then I notice two other things that almost make me blush as I glance at him.

His eyes merely sparkle, and he steps into the water before helping me in. The tub has a wraparound ledge like a hot tub, so we're able to sit above the depth of the water. Rhett hands me one of the champagne flutes and then lifts the other.

"You're having a drink with me?" I ask.

"Yes, baby."

My brow pinches. I wouldn't have minded if he didn't; if he never had a drink again. But this is so much more than that. He feels safe here. We're both entirely safe here, and that overwhelms me.

"To my fearless, smart, utterly stunning wife. To my absolute world. I might have had to trek through hell to reach you, but you were worth every step," he says, clinking his glass against mine.

My laugh is partially a sob of utter joy.

"To my insane, reckless, sexy as hell husband. Hell, heaven, and every place in between, I'm trekking it with you until the very end."

We drink, and the light in his smile steals my breath.

Rhett takes my champagne and sets it behind me.

"Open," he says, then he takes a long drink of his own before curving a hand over my nape.

I do as he asks, and my head tips back at his touch. The champagne is still cool as it passes from his mouth to mine, and I moan after I swallow, and he kisses me deeply.

"Again," he murmurs huskily.

I open, but this time chocolate hits my tastebuds, and my lips close around the strawberry. We don't break eye contact as I bite, and my body tightens with the hunger in his stare as he leans over me. When he pulls it away, his teeth bite at the rest, plucking the stem.

His hand encircles my throat. "Swallow."

I do, and a low, deep sound of satisfaction leaves his throat with his darkening gaze. Then he kisses me hard. Our tongues, teeth, and mouth clash feverishly, and I'm aching for release.

Rhett pulls out of the kiss with a groan. "Turn around, knees on the ledge, and brace your hands on the side."

I turn giddy as fuck at the dominance overcoming him. He has a plan for right now, and my sight trails again to the small vibrator and lubricant beside the strawberries.

"Do you trust me?" he asks, planting a kiss on my shoulder.

My "yes" turns into a moan with his fingers sliding over my ass and down through my slick pussy. I'm only under-water up to mid-thigh positioned like this. Rhett slips two fingers into me, and I push my ass out to him, trying to meet his slow, torturous strokes for *more*.

"I feel you, baby," he says thickly, pulling out and replacing his fingers with his cock. "Fucking incredible."

He fucks me to the sound of our mixed pleasure for a while, until I feel his fingers again, teasing around my ass. I can't help but tense up with a nervous inhale when one slips inside.

"Relax, little bird."

He thrusts slow as he works his finger at that same pace. I start getting the sense he's restraining himself from unleashing what he wants to unleash on me. I listen to him, easing down onto my forearms.

"Fuuuuck," he growls. "I'm going to add another. You're made for me, baby. Take all of me."

I want to please him, and I want this. It's been on my mind several times, and he's done this before, but we've not been all the way to having his cock in my ass, and I know that's where we're heading.

"Such a good, good girl," he says as my back curves, and I feel so deliriously full with his cock and fingers.

Pleasure starts to build rapidly, and I push back, chasing the orgasm.

"Come on my fingers and my cock," he demands, picking up pace. I'm surprised when my release soars without him needing to touch my clit.

I cry out with the pleasure rocking through me, unlike any other orgasm. So full. So, so full, and I don't want him to stop as I tremble against the cool tile floor.

I vaguely hear the cap of the lubricant again, but I feel it drip over my ass.

"I don't know if I can," I say. The thought starts to creep through me with doubt when it's more than two fingers.

"I think you can," he murmurs over my shoulder.

Buzzing fills my ears, and I barely register the toy until I jolt forward at the sensation of it against my overstimulated clit.

"Rhett," I whimper. God, it's both a torture I need a break from and a bliss I don't want to stop for a second.

He slides over my apex. Back and forth. Until the sensitivity starts to subside form my last orgasm and I'm ready to start chasing another. Then I feel his cock teasing my ass.

"Keep relaxed for me. Let me in, baby."

Shit, I want him to fuck me there so badly it feels both wrong and so right.

His head pushes in, and I breathe out. The sensations of

the vibrator and his breach are dizzying. I want so much more, but my mind is spinning.

"So tight," Rhett says, his voice strained.

I know he wants to drive into me and fuck my ass senseless, but he's being patient for me. I focus on the vibrations and on my next inhale as I push back deeply.

"Fucking hell." Rhett's breath blows down my spine. "Easy, little bird. I don't want to hurt you."

"You won't. Please fuck my ass, Rhett."

His fingers tighten on my hip. "You're going to make me explode with that demand alone."

The burn is lessening, and the stimulation against my clit is already building my next orgasm. Rhett pulls out then back in. The next time he does, he pauses.

"What's wrong?" I ask.

"The sight of my cock buried in your ass is about to make me come. Give me a damn second for sanity."

"I feel so full," I moan, laying my cheek against the tile.

"Good though?"

"Yes, *very.*"

"You never cease to amaze me." He leans over to kiss my neck, then my cheek, then my ear.

"Please," I whisper, needing him to move.

"I'm going to fuck you now, and I'm not stopping until neither of us remember our goddamn names. Keep this on your clit, baby."

I push up again, bracing on the one hand and taking the toy from him between my legs. Rhett gives a few shallow thrusts to allow me to adjust, then he lets go. I become mindless to the pleasure, knowing when he's through with me I'll be boneless too. I didn't expect to enjoy this as much as I do, but with him pounding into my ass, this won't be the last time we do this.

"Harder," I say. I can't explain my feral need for him to ruin me.

"If I fuck you any harder, you won't be able to walk to dinner tonight," he growls.

"We'll order it to us."

"Christ, Ana." Rhett shifts his stance, and his grip shifts to my thighs, making me fuck him back.

I curve my hand more until the vibrator slips inside my pussy. The change of sensation is new, and it immediately pushes me over the edge. Rhett hisses too, then he follows his release with deep, endless growls of pleasure that begin to match his slow, deep thrusts as he spills himself into me.

Pulling the toy out, I can barely turn it off as I'm vibrating more than it.

Rhett is still inside me, panting as much as I am, because that was the most world-rocking orgasm I think either of us have found in each other—which is an impressive bar to reach.

"I love you, Anastasia Kaiser," Rhett says, finally pulling out, and I shudder at the emptiness. "Fuck, I love you more I thought possible."

I let him hook an arm around my waist and help me up. I'm completely spent and sore and gloriously high. When he pulls me, I'm floating, until we're lying in the tub with my back against his front.

"I think I want to do that again," I murmur sleepily.

Rhett runs tender hands up my thighs. "We have all the time in the world, baby."

We do. My soul is found, and my heart is home. With Rhett, life seems too short, but also so long and prosperous. I don't plan to take a moment for granted when we've seen behind the broken parts of ourselves and loved each other through it all. We've glimpsed inside the wicked with each other and survived it hand in hand.

For us there's no hiding behind darkness anymore. Whatever comes next, I have everything I need and all I've ever wanted in Rhett Kaiser.

The end of Rhett and Ana's story, but maybe not fully goodbye…

Acknowledgments

This duet started as a fun idea of: what if Faythe and Reylan from An Heir Comes to Rise series had an AU story? As soon as I sat down to explore the what if, Rhett and Ana's story spiralled into their own unique creation that became surprisingly dear to me. I enjoyed writing this ride or die couple so much and can't explain how Ana as a character resonated with me deeply. I hope you enjoyed my first step into contemporary romance, which turned into more of a romantic suspense with the plot that unfolded, and that you'll look forward to potentially more stories from other couples mentioned in this duet!

To you, my readers. Thank you for following me on this curve ball of a journey into a new genre. As always, there's no me without you and I'm grateful every day that you chose to pick up my stories to escape for a while.

To lyssa, my own ride or die. Thank you as always for being there to bounce my plot ideas, crack theories, and being the biggest cheerleader.

To Bryony, thank you for your incredible editing work on this duet as always. You've been with me since the very start of my author career and I'm so lucky to have you.

To my dogs, Milo, Bonnie, and Minnie, and to my family, you keep me grounded.

To my haters, I wouldn't have wrote this book without you.